STACY M. JONES

Helix Syndicate

First edition

ISBN: 979-8-218-58660-7

This book was professionally typeset on Reedsy.
Find out more at reedsy.com

For Annie

Acknowledgments

Thank you to the detectives, special agents, and forensics teams I've had the pleasure of working with through the years and the knowledge and expertise shared with me.

Special thanks to 17 Studio Book Design for bringing my stories to life with amazing covers. Thank you to Dj Hendrickson for your insightful editing and Liza Wood for proofreading and revisions. Thank you to my early readers for their feedback and my loyal and new readers who have truly made this series a success.

CHAPTER 1

FBI Agent Kate Walsh twisted her fingers over the edge of the armrest as the 747 bumped down on the runway. She held on so tightly her hands started to throb. Still, she didn't release her grip. The familiar screech of landing noises echoed throughout the plane. It had been a turbulence-ridden flight from their layover in Chicago where Kate and her partner-turned-boyfriend, Agent Declan James, had grabbed coffee and snacks and discussed the case that awaited them in Los Angeles.

As the plane came to a halt and started to taxi to the gate, Kate wiggled her fingers and breathed a sigh of relief. She craned her neck to look up the aisle while Declan looked out the window.

Kate didn't like admitting it to herself, but after years of flying around the globe, she had started to develop a weird flight anxiety that came over her about forty-eight hours before she'd have to put her life in someone else's hands. While she wasn't claustrophobic, the interior of the planes lately seemed smaller than usual. Heights had never bothered her either, but recently she'd been keenly aware of them. While she fully admitted she could be a control-freak, Kate had never minded putting her life in the hands of a capable pilot. The last few flights it seemed all those minor niggles had woven a ball of anxiety that clouded her mind.

Kate had not told Declan or her boss, Spade. She had tried to ignore it and power through. If it kept up, Kate knew she'd have to address it. There was no way around flying in her line of work. Occasionally, the FBI gave them a plane but more times than not, they flew commercial. So far, it didn't matter the destination, the anxiety persisted.

"Are you okay, Katie?" Declan asked, leaning his shoulder into her, so close she could feel his breath on her neck. "You seem far too tense."

Kate intentionally relaxed back in the seat. "I'm tired, I think. It's been a long morning."

Declan cocked an eyebrow. "You snored like a lumberjack for most of the flight. You should be well-rested." While he didn't crack a smile, he was teasing her.

Kate faked one for him. "We both know I don't snore. Maybe it's the case." Spade had tossed around the idea of going undercover. It wasn't something Kate enjoyed but was a plausible enough cover for how she was feeling.

Declan took the bait. "After reading the case file, I don't think undercover will be necessary. He seems to target older women, fifties and up. You're not his demographic."

Kate nodded but didn't offer up any commentary. She wanted off the plane as quickly as possible. "Let's get the rental car and then you can drive while I look over some of the files again. I'm not feeling quite grounded in the case yet."

"It's fairly straightforward," Declan said, agreeing to the plan. "He meets a rich woman, usually divorced or widowed, dates her for a while using her money, and then she ends up dead. It's only after the murder that the families realize the victims were seeing anyone. Once they start going through the bank records after the deaths, the unusual transactions and large sums of missing money become apparent."

"Is there anyone unusual in the wills?"

"No. He's been careful not to leave any evidence like that. That would give him away. Until now, he's flown completely under the radar."

The details Declan explained were the same Kate had read. The anxiety clouding her brain hadn't allowed her to absorb the information like usual. She'd have to go through it again to better understand. The one thing Kate had gleaned from the files and she found the most odd was that no one in the victims' families had met this mysterious man.

They were walking into the case essentially blind. They had no identified suspect. No description of him. The victims, eight in all, were all women in their fifties. All were killed the same way. Strangled in their beds. The method of the murders also left little evidence behind. The only reason the cases were connected was because a savvy solicitor in London had identified two of the cases as similar more than a year apart. He had alerted Sam Harris with the National Crime Agency, the FBI counterpoint in London.

As an experienced homicide investigator, Sam saw the similarities right away and surmised that if there were two cases there might be more. He worked with other investigators and identified five cases in London going back seven years. He reached out to the FBI who searched the database and found a cold case from ten years ago in Los Angeles and then an open homicide case from just three months ago. One other case was identified in Paris.

Kate was leaving room for something Declan had said early on – there could be more victims around the globe that hadn't been connected yet. That wasn't their goal though.

Spade had sent them to start with the Los Angeles cases, especially the most recent. Then they were to head to London to provide Sam Harris support and review his cases.

Kate and Declan exited the plane with the rest of the passengers and headed straight to the car rental desk. Kate stood back while he talked to the agent. They had keys in hand within twenty minutes and settled into the car soon after.

Expecting the usual L.A. traffic, Kate pulled out the most recent case file and started going through it while Declan drove. At the time of her death, fifty-five-year-old Andrea Ivy was worth close to twenty million. The money was an inheritance from her family and her husband, Dimitri Ivy, who had been a Hollywood producer until his untimely death three years ago from cancer. They had no children but a close group of friends and associates.

Andrea sat on several nonprofit boards, attended regular Pilates and yoga classes, and had a strong group of involved local friends. This was not a woman who was isolated, unsavvy with money, or impaired in any way. Kate could only imagine that she'd been taken in by a con man, thought she was in love, exploited for money, and was murdered.

The age of the victims had struck Kate the most when reading the files the first time. The women were strong and capable and had strong family or social circles, sometimes both. They were not isolated or impaired in some way.

Andrea Ivy had lived in a six-thousand-square-foot newer home in the Bird Streets in West Hollywood Hills. Blue Jay Way to be exact. The file indicated that the Ivys had bought the property in 2017 and had torn down the original home to build. The five-bedroom, seven-bath home had stunning views of downtown Los Angeles, a lap pool and hot tub, and had been an oasis for the family before tragedy struck. First by Dimitri's death in 2021 and now Andrea's murder.

Kate raised her head from the file long enough to give Declan directions. "It says here Det. Kurt Longmuir has the case. There is a note in the file that after three months, he still doesn't have a suspect and not one of Andrea's friends knew she was seeing someone. The only thing her friends noticed was that she was a bit more reclusive starting about six months before her death. They saw her less as she seemed to retreat from her normal social circles. A couple of her girlfriends had asked if she was seeing someone. While Andrea didn't confirm, she didn't deny it either."

Declan glanced over at her. "I wonder why she didn't tell anyone."

Kate didn't know. It was a long enough time after her husband's death that she should have been able to date without any question. "I imagine the guy asked her to keep it secret. He probably made up some excuse that he wasn't ready to go public yet. Depending on his con, he might have also manipulated her to think it was her idea."

"They had dinner together out in public," Declan reminded her. "Did you see the report from the waiter at her favorite restaurant?"

Kate hadn't gotten that far. She had skipped over it on the first read earlier that morning. Kate flipped through the pages until she found it. The statement was brief and to the point. Andrea had a favorite waiter at Norah's on Santa Monica Boulevard. Andrea and Dimitri were regulars at the place, according to a statement from one of her friends, and it was a place she continued to frequent a few times a week. The staff knew her well.

About six months ago, right around the time her friends had started noticing her becoming more reclusive, Andrea had met with a man for dinner. She had come to the restaurant four more times with the same man over six months. The staff also indicated Andrea's visits, which had always been twice a week like clockwork, had dropped down to once a month and always with the same man. It was an unusual change after frequenting the restaurant at a regularity for years.

The staff took notice. No one had asked about her absence, they weren't that bold, but one of her favorite waiters had given the police a statement about her change in demeanor and a description of the man.

The dark-haired man stood about five-foot-ten, had a medium build and complexion, wore glasses, had a handsome face, and had been dressed in an Armani suit each time. The waiter did notice something strange – his credit card declined on the first visit. It had been a potentially embarrassing situation that Andrea had smoothed over with ease. Without saying a word, she pulled out a credit card and handed it over. The waiter noticed each time they came after that Andrea paid.

On those last few visits, Andrea had seemed quiet, sullen even. The change though had happened at the first dinner. The waiter indicated Andrea had seemed stiff and unfriendly. The staff had greeted her with their usual friendliness but noticed right away she pretended as if she'd only been to the restaurant once before. The staff, ever accommodating, had played along.

It made Kate wonder if Andrea might have suspected something was off with the man. She had gone to a familiar place, a safety spot, but had played it off as though she'd been there only once.

Did she want someone to see her with the man if something went wrong?

Kate noticed the last visit to Norah's was three weeks before Andrea's murder. "She wanted someone to see her with him," she said after a moment's contemplation. "Of all the restaurants they could have chosen, Andrea picked somewhere she was known. She knew them well enough to know her behavior would be seen as strange. I think she knew something was off with the guy. Maybe she was already in too deep and couldn't find a way out."

"You got all that from the statement?" Declan asked with a little laugh. "I was just happy we had a description. We aren't even sure he's the guy."

"He's the guy," Kate responded with a knowing deep in her gut. It was a huge mental leap and Kate couldn't explain more than that. *She just knew.* As Declan drove up into the hills, Kate explained her rationale. "Andrea goes to Norah's all the time. She's comfortable there. The staff all know her, but she purposefully acts as if she doesn't go there often. The staff, sensing something is off, play along. She changes how often she goes there and each time pretends she doesn't know the staff as well as she does. Andrea is doing this on purpose. If she was truly trying to hide, she wouldn't go somewhere she's so well known. There's a reason she's choosing this place where she feels safe, yet is downplaying her connection to the people there. The only thing missing from the file is a photo of the man and a name from that initial credit card transaction."

Kate was disappointed neither had been included in the file. She wasn't surprised. None of the staff would have been so bold as to snap a photo. Their video surveillance probably played on a twenty-four or forty-eight-hour loop. There would have been no reason to keep it. They didn't know Andrea would end up murdered.

"We're here, Kate," Declan said as he put the SUV in park at the curb. He sat back and took in his surroundings. "It's quiet up here at this end of the street. I guess that's partly why there is such a premium on real estate. I heard there are a lot of celebrities in the Bird Streets. I wonder who's up here."

Declan wasn't a fanboy of anyone other than sports figures that Kate knew. "Is there someone you're hoping to run into?" she asked, suppressing a smile as she closed the file and put it in her bag.

"No. Just found it an interesting place for a murder." He cut the engine and stared at the sliver of house they could see from the road. From the documents, Kate knew most of the house was built into the hill not visible from the street. "I don't like the architecture. It's not like in Boston."

"You mean hundreds of years old with drafty windows and cold floors," Kate said, thinking about her brownstone where they were living in Boston. There were always so many repairs that needed to be done on a house that old. She'd never trade it in for something modern like this, but she saw the appeal.

While Kate wasn't focused on the architecture, she did note the isolation of the neighborhood. Not many people were around to hear her scream on the night of the murder. That is if she even got that chance.

CHAPTER 2

As Kate got out of the SUV, a black Chevy Tahoe pulled alongside them. The guy behind the wheel offered a head nod as he passed by. He parked then exited the vehicle.

"Agents James and Walsh?" When they confirmed, he said, "I'm Det. Kurt Longmuir. Call me Kurt." The tall muscular man with thick forearms covered in wispy blond hair took a few steps toward them with his hand extended. He shook Declan's hand and then Kate's. He had movie star good looks but a pained look on his face. "I'm happy the FBI is involved. I heard you're specialists in this sort of thing."

"We're part of a specialized unit in the FBI based out of Washington, D.C.," Kate explained. "We are based in Boston and have agents with a range of specialties scattered across the United States. I have a background in forensic profiling and Declan's focus is the scene. We have an excellent crime scene investigator, but we don't have a fresh crime scene so we didn't bring her out with us. Sharon Esposito is her name. She said she'd be happy to look at any evidence you have collected. We can send her anything we need along the way."

"Seems like exactly what we need." Kurt looked toward the house. "It was only recently I learned this case is connected to others. I was contacted by Sam Harris in London." Kurt turned toward the house. "It's an awful thing that happened here. I've not been able to get a handle on the case from the start. I have one of the best homicide solve rates in the city. It's why I was assigned the case, but I don't have a suspect."

Kate felt for him. It wasn't easy to have a case like this grow cold with no new leads and no suspect after a few months. "Sam is an excellent investigator and he's in the same situation. We worked with him on a serial killer case in Edinburgh. He's the one who recommended us. I don't know if we'll be able to do much more than you have. Looking at the cases in totality might be the key to solving them. That's why we are here – to look at all of them as one."

Kurt gestured toward the stone walkway and the real estate sign posted near the front door. "The house is still available. It was put on the market a month ago by the Ivy estate. Andrea's niece is the sole beneficiary. She was living in Chicago when her aunt was murdered. As you can imagine, the house isn't selling."

"It will eventually," Declan said. "After some time passes, people have a way of forgetting."

Kate knew he was right. "I'm sure solving the case will help too. It's good it's still available so we can get the lay of the land."

"The house has been staged. All of the Ivys' things were removed." Kurt handed Declan a file. "I sent the FBI some crime scene photos. These are the rest."

Declan didn't open the folder. Kate knew he'd wait until they were in the house. "Who found her?" he asked as they started the walk toward the front door flanked by two swaying palm trees.

Kurt punched in the code on the lockbox and got the key. As he unlocked the door, he turned back to them. "Andrea had a housekeeper who came once a week. As you might have read, in the six months leading up to her death, Andrea changed drastically. She stopped texting and calling her friends. She rarely answered calls or texts. She skipped her Pilates and yoga classes. She had pulled back from her nonprofit work and stopped being seen in her normal social circles.

Andrea also cut her housekeeper's hours from a few times a week to once a week."

Kate didn't remember seeing the housekeeper's statement in the file. "Did you get a statement from her? I don't think I read it."

Kurt opened the door and stepped back so they could walk in first. "Annie Carter was the housekeeper. She's a young woman in her twenties, trying to make it as an actress. She has been cleaning homes and working as an assistant for the past few years. She was hysterical when she found Andrea's body. She gave me a brief statement about what she saw, which didn't amount to much. Annie noticed the smell almost immediately. She didn't recognize it as human and thought an animal might have died on the back patio. Sometimes the coyotes get cats and rabbits. She called out for Andrea and quickly found her in the bedroom. Annie went running out to the street and called 911 from her cellphone."

As Kate moved through the front door, she expected to be in a foyer. Instead, they were in an open courtyard that ran the length of the home. The courtyard had chairs and a long couch along with native cacti and a firepit. To the right was a wall of glass that looked into an open dining area and kitchen that flowed out to a living room in the back of the home. Off to the left was another wall of glass that overlooked two bedrooms. Neither of them looked big enough to be the primary bedroom.

"Those walls open up to the outside," Kurt explained as he slid the kitchen wall open. "It's an oasis here. The home was designed not only for living but for entertaining, which Andrea's husband did a lot when he was alive. Andrea didn't entertain much after he died."

There wasn't a finish in the home that hadn't been thought through. The kitchen had a sophisticated Italian design with high-end appliances.

"Is this the way Annie entered into the home that morning?" Declan asked as he looked around the kitchen. When Kurt nodded, he followed up. "Does this side connect to the other side with the bedrooms?"

"It does," Kurt confirmed. "Andrea's bedroom is on this side of the home. Everything on the other side is guest suites, a gym, and an office." Kurt showed them the steps Annie took when she discovered Andrea's body. Declan had stopped at a kitchen counter long enough to pull the photos from the file. He glanced down at them and surveyed the kitchen as it had been that day and then followed behind Kurt to the bedroom.

Kurt gestured to the far wall of the bedroom. "The room is set up in the same way it was when we found the body. That wall of glass opens to the back of the home and the pool. There's a hot tub too." He went to the wall and unlocked it, sliding back the glass. "Just about every room in this house opens to the outside in this way. All of it was locked up tight when we found Andrea. You can imagine my first thought was that it had been a stranger. Not that this backyard is easy to access, but it's not impossible. If Andrea had slept with this wall open to the outside, she would have been easy prey."

"Was she known to sleep like that?" Kate couldn't believe a single woman living alone would open herself up to the elements like that. Not only to possible criminals but also animals.

"Her friends said she had done it a few times. Not always intentionally but after a few glasses of wine."

"Was she known to drink?"

"Yeah," Kurt said with a sudden stiffness in his voice. He turned to Kate with raised eyebrows. "She had developed quite a habit after her husband's death. Friends had been concerned. She had never been much of a drinker before. An occasional glass of wine with dinner or mimosa with brunch. Her doctor had prescribed her sleeping pills and she wasn't supposed to be taking those with any alcohol. But

Andrea admitted to friends she had mixed the two on particularly bad nights."

The woman was grieving and self-medicating. It made her even more vulnerable to a conman. Declan turned to Kate to hand her three photos. She glanced down – one was of an empty wine bottle on the kitchen counter. Another was the bathroom sink where a prescription pill bottle sat uncapped.

The final series of photos were from the doorway of the bedroom. Andrea's body lay covered with her hair fanned over the pillow. She did not look deceased but rather asleep. From that vantage point, it was impossible to see what the close-up photos had shown – her unusual skin color from decomposition and the angry marks from strangulation across her neck.

"I don't understand," Kate said, handing the photo to Kurt. "Did Annie come into the room and up to the bed or did she only see her from the doorway?"

"Up to the bed." Kurt pointed to the photo in question. "As you can see, Andrea was left in such a way that it looked like she was sleeping. We believe the killer covered her up and arranged her hair on the pillow. He was making it look like she was asleep. He took some time with her after she was dead."

While Kate was focused on the photo, Declan asked, "What about prints?"

"We have a few sets of unidentified prints. The bathroom and the bedside tables were wiped down. We ruled out Andrea's prints and Annie's. We also took prints from some of her friends and ruled those out too. We have three unknowns. While Andrea didn't entertain a lot, there were still people in and out of the house. The prints could be from anyone."

Kate left Declan and Kurt to talk about the case. She went into the attached bathroom and looked around. She had to remind herself the home was staged now and none of the effects belonged to Andrea. The bathroom was connected to a large walk-in closet with floor-to-ceiling shelves, an area for about fifty pairs of shoes, and racks for clothes. There was also a vanity area where Kate was sure Andrea sat to put on her makeup and fix her hair. Kate didn't know what she was looking for specifically, if anything.

What she needed was to get a sense of the woman, more so than what the file had told her.

Kate moved from the closet and bathroom, across the bedroom, which was now empty, to the far side with the open wall of glass and stepped outside onto the grass. Declan and Kurt stood on the edge of the property deep in conversation. Kate couldn't hear them from where she stood. The backyard was a long rectangular strip, mostly taken up by the pool and the area around the pool. The grassy area could be cut in probably less than fifteen minutes.

Kate took in the scene. The outdoor chairs, couches, and tables would be perfect for hosting. The view of downtown Los Angeles was magnificent. What didn't escape Kate was the quiet, which was nearly too much to bear. While there were neighbors to the right, it was impossible to see the yard through the thick palms that marked the edge of the property.

The canyon created a steep slope at the back. There was nowhere to run.

While Kate understood why Kurt might have immediately assumed the murder had been committed by a stranger, it would have been nearly impossible to breach the back of the home. She understood now why Andrea might have slept with her doors open. Given everything Kate had witnessed in her work, she'd never have done it, but someone not as jaded to the violence in the world might have been free to experience the cool evening breeze as they slept. Sometimes Kate envied people who didn't have to bear all the knowledge she had and the imagery from cases that would never leave her mind.

Kate let the feeling of despair Andrea might have felt that night wash over her and leave just as quickly. She called from where she stood, "Did Annie ever meet the man?"

Kurt turned to her. "She said she never saw Andrea with any man at all. She had seen men's clothing in the closet and toiletries in the bathroom but she never met him. When Annie was here, the only other person here was Andrea. She asked Andrea once about the clothes and toiletries. Annie said Andrea offered a sad smile and shrugged. She didn't say anything about it and Annie didn't press the issue. I asked Annie about it and she said she didn't want to make Andrea feel like she couldn't move on. She wasn't working for the family when Dimitri was alive. She came to work for Andrea after his death. It was clear to Annie how much Andrea still missed her husband."

Kate walked toward them. "Where is Annie now?"

"Back in New York. She got a theatre gig and moved back home. I have her statement back at the office. Other than what she initially saw when she discovered the body, she didn't know anything relevant. I tried to send you the most important information first. That's what I was instructed to do."

Kate held her hand up to stop him. "I'm not angry. Just curious. It sounds like Annie was cleared right away. Was there anything that struck you as odd about the case at the start?"

Kurt pursed his lips and shook his head. "It was a run-of-the-mill homicide, except for not being able to come up with a viable suspect. As time went on and the leads dried up quickly, I realized there might be more to it than meets the eye."

"What about the money?"

"I didn't know about the missing money until a couple of weeks into the case," Kurt admitted but didn't offer more than that. He gestured toward the house. "If you're done here, I scheduled an appointment with Andrea's financial manager. He has a lot to say about her financial situation. I think it's probably better for you to hear it directly from him."

CHAPTER 3

Kurt had offered to drive Kate and Declan to Chris Senter's office not far from Andrea's West Hollywood home. Declan had declined before Kate could respond. It wasn't until they were alone in the car and Declan had pulled up directions to the office on his phone that Kate asked why he hadn't wanted to share a ride with the Los Angeles detective.

"I don't get the best vibe from him," Declan said with ease. "I don't think he's a bad detective, his closure rate alone says he's not. But there's something about him I don't vibe with, and there's something off about this case."

"Is it the fact that we only got half a case file with pertinent information missing?" That had bothered Kate even though she hadn't mentioned it to Kurt. They should have received the full case file. It begged the question of why he was giving them information in a dribble instead of coming right out with all of it.

Declan agreed that was part of it. "He also said a few things about Andrea that didn't sit right with me." Declan focused on the road and Kate waited until he was ready to tell her. She wasn't going to push him for the information. They had been partners long enough to know he'd come out with it when he was ready.

Declan took one left then a right following the directions. When they stopped at a red light, he turned to her. "He insinuated Andrea couldn't have been that smart to fall for a conman. He said most people would have known right off that he was after her money. If she wasn't desperate, she might have protected herself sooner." Declan thumbed his palm against the steering wheel. "You know when a detective has those kinds of feelings for a victim, he's not going to do his best."

Kate couldn't argue the point with him or defend Kurt. "Do you think it's a general misogyny or is it specific to this case?"

"I don't know," Declan admitted with a shrug. "All I know is it made me uncomfortable and made me question some of the decisions he made on the case. I suggest we go to his office, get the full file, and strike out on our own. I also get the sense that Annie, the housekeeper, might know more. That statement should have been included in what was sent to us. She found Andrea's body. Everything she witnessed when she walked into that house is critical. Do you believe him that Annie never saw the guy?"

Kate wasn't sure if she believed it or not. "It's reasonable to think Andrea cut Annie's time if she didn't want her to meet him. I have a hard time believing in all the time Annie spent in that house, she doesn't know more than Kurt told us. I understand that it was traumatic, but she's a key witness."

"Exactly," Declan said with a defiance Kate knew he was feeling. They worked hard to build good working relationships with local law enforcement when they could. Sometimes local detectives resented the FBI getting involved in their case and did everything they could to derail the process.

Declan focused back on driving as they fell into silence. They arrived on Melrose Avenue without too much delay. The traffic in Hollywood wasn't as heavy as Kate would have thought. It was mid-morning and she assumed most people were in their offices.

Declan found a parking spot on the street and pointed out Kurt who had parked a block down. The detective left his flashers on and got out in search of them. "I wonder what that's about." Declan stepped out before Kate and flagged down Kurt. The detective jogged over to him, said a few words, and then headed back to his SUV.

Declan returned with a broad smile. "He got another call and has to head to a scene. He said we can meet with the financial advisor alone."

Kate's muscles tightened. "It's not one of these cases, is it?"

Declan assured her it wasn't. "Guy murdered across town from here. It frees us up without having an awkward conversation. Let's take the win. He said we could go by his office later and sign out the files or use their conference room."

Kate got out of the SUV and followed Declan down the sidewalk dotted with high-end boutiques. Declan noticed her staring into the Chanel store as she passed by.

"Doesn't seem like your style," he said, pulling her into him.

"It's not. I was thinking about what would ever compel me to spend that much money on a purse. No judgment on those who do. It's just never been my thing."

"I don't know that I could date you if it was."

Kate laughed, knowing that was probably true. She gestured toward the glass building wedged between the boutiques. "I don't know why but I was expecting this to be in a high-rise. It's a simple two-story office that looks like it was once a shop."

"He's got a good location."

Kate couldn't argue with that. She was expecting a business like her financial management team in Boston. Her parents had left her a healthy estate, so much so that she never had to work a day in her life if she chose. She had kept the same financial company that had managed her parents' money, changing managers as time went on and people retired. This didn't have the same feeling, then again not much in L.A. felt like Boston.

Declan pulled the glass door open and held it for Kate. A young woman sat behind a desk near the door. Kate flashed her badge and introduced them. "We are here to see Chris Senter. We had a meeting set up with him. Det. Kurt Longmuir made the appointment. He's been called to another case."

"Of course," the young woman said as she stood. Her eyes shifted to Declan and her lips turned up in a smile. It was the usual reaction Declan got from women. She didn't fawn over him the way some women did though. She led them directly to a plush office with comfortable chairs around a square table. She offered them something to drink, which they both declined.

A moment later, a younger man that Kate guessed was no more than thirty-five walked into the room and extended his hand. "I'm Chris. I can't tell you how relieved I am to know the FBI is involved. I've been hoping something would come of this case."

"Det. Longmuir has been involved since the start," Declan said, a question left hanging in his tone.

"You're right." Chris pulled out a chair and sat. "I don't want to speak ill of him. I don't think he and I saw eye to eye. He didn't take what I was seeing seriously."

"What is it that you saw?" Kate asked, already feeling comfortable with him. He might have been younger than she had anticipated, but he seemed on the ball.

Chris looked between them. "I was concerned about Andrea for months before her death. About four months roughly, give or take a few weeks, she came in here and wanted to liquidate close to three-hundred thousand. She wanted the cash."

"Cash?" Declan asked, interrupting.

"That's the concern. It's her money and she could do whatever she wanted with it. I'm not here to police her, but it did raise an eyebrow. Andrea told me she was investing in a friend's business. I offered to have someone on my team research the business and we could make a formal investment of capital. It's something we do all the time. Andrea refused to give us any information. I asked if she was in some kind of trouble and she assured me she wasn't. She didn't seem like herself."

"In what way was Andrea different?" Kate asked then paused, reconsidering. "Give me an idea of who she was before her husband died."

"I was a junior associate and worked with the Ivys' previous financial advisor, Edward, who has since retired. I took over their finances after Dimitri was diagnosed with cancer. I only met him a handful of times when he came into the office to make sure his estate was in order and his wife would be taken care of after his death. He seemed resigned to his fate. Back then, I only met Andrea a couple of times. I don't have a clear picture of who she was before he got sick. Edward used to tell me she was the kindest, friendliest person he knew. He said a few times he didn't know how Andrea lived out here because she was so real. She wasn't able to do that fake L.A. Hollywood thing we see so frequently."

"After Dimitri's death then? Did Andrea change?"

Chris nodded. "The grief hit her hard. She knew it was coming, but they had a real love. I don't think anyone can be prepared for that. Andrea didn't work, so she came in and set herself up on a monthly allowance that would cover the bills and her expenses. She was never wild with money. She didn't take risks. Not once in all that time did Andrea call to say she needed more. She wasn't a spendthrift. Neither of them was, so their financial portfolio was sound. That's why it was so strange to me that all of a sudden Andrea was asking for a large sum of money without relevant information. She had invested before, but we thoroughly vetted it for her."

Declan shifted in the chair, leaning forward on the table. "Were there any personality changes around the same time?"

"Definitely," Chris said definitively. "Andrea had always been open and friendly, even at the height of her grief. Around this time, she became sullen. Depressed, even. The day she came in to sign for the money she requested, I thought I smelled alcohol on her. She didn't seem impaired or I wouldn't have allowed her to sign the papers or get the cheque she deposited into her account. We didn't give her cash here, but we provided a cheque she cashed at her bank. After that, we have no idea what she did with the money."

"No other investments or property purchases to account for it?" Kate asked, trying to come up with something that could account for it.

"Not that we ever found. There is nothing Andrea bought or owned at the time of her death that would account for that sum of money. Even if Andrea had been drinking there was no sign she was gambling or had developed a drug habit either. We looked into everything. I didn't trust Det. Longmuir, so between you and me, we hired an investigator to look into the financial end of things for us. We've done that with other clients. I can give you her name if you'd like. She uncovered some spending starting about six months back that was unusual. It's not something we would have seen here as we weren't monitoring her checking account or credit card statements. Andrea preferred to handle that on her own and we were fine with that. That was how Dimitri always did it. As I said, she was paid each month. What she did with the money was her business. She didn't run up debt until those last few months."

There had been nothing in the files about any debt. Kate was starting to suspect Declan was right about Kurt. "I wasn't aware of any debt. Are you talking about credit card debt?"

"That's exactly it. Andrea normally paid off her credit cards in full at the end of every month. As I said, she spent very little compared to other women with her social standing. After Andrea was murdered and I connected with her niece, Rosalie, she gave me access to Andrea's full financial record. We went through the credit card statements because Andrea was spending so much more on trips, restaurants, and such. More so than she had ever spent. The dinners looked like they were for two people and Rosalie had no idea her aunt was seeing anyone. None of us did. Even with taking the three-hundred thousand, I didn't assume she was being conned or there was a man in her life. I simply didn't know what she was doing with the money other than what she told me – investing in a friend's business. For all I knew one of her female friends needed start-up capital."

"I assume someone checked that out with her friends," Declan said.

"We did," Chris concurred. "None of them had any idea about the money. There was no accounting for it. None of her friends knew anything about a business. If you speak to them, they will also explain Andrea became withdrawn and didn't engage with them much."

That brought Kate back to the one question that hadn't been answered yet. "If Andrea didn't tell you about a new man in her life, didn't tell her niece or any of her friends, how did anyone discover there was a guy?" There was the waiter's statement, but that didn't mean much to Kate if they couldn't corroborate that anywhere else.

"My investigator is the one who discovered it. She turned everything over to Det. Longmuir."

Kate would need the name and address of the investigator. "Did your investigator get the name of this guy?"

"Not his real name." Chris gave Kate the investigator's name, address, and phone number. "Det. Longmuir has all of this information. I'm surprised he didn't hand it over to you. She reported all of her findings directly to him."

Declan raised his eyes to Kate. "Information has been sparse," was all he said. His tone covered the rest. He turned back to Chris. "Is there anything else we need to know?"

Chris folded his arms across his chest. "I'll tell you the same thing I told Det. Longmuir. Andrea was not a stupid woman. She might have been going through a hard time, but she wasn't stupid. If she was being conned, either he was that good or she got in too deep too quickly and was afraid to get out."

Kate was starting to suspect the same thing. They thanked Chris and, armed with the investigator's information, they headed to her office.

CHAPTER 4

Jessica Davis had an office at 445 S. Figueroa Street in downtown Los Angeles. It was in a building known as Union Bank Plaza. Declan found a place to park in the adjacent garage and they made their way through the lobby up to the seventh floor.

It was prime real estate for a private investigator. The building was full of attorneys. Kate had scanned the directory near the elevator and had stopped counting the firms when she hit twelve. There were many more but the open elevator had stopped her counting.

"She must be doing well for herself," Declan said as they stepped out onto the floor.

"I'd assume so." Kate took in the plush carpeting and standard artwork found in similar buildings. "She must be paying hefty rent for a space like this."

They made their way through the maze of halls until they found number 707 on the door and a placard next to it with Jessica's name. She had no signage indicating she was a private investigator. It had been the same on the directory too. Kate assumed it was for Jessica's protection. Most private investigators tried to stay as inconspicuous as possible.

"I assume we just go in." Declan turned the knob on the door and pushed it open, neither of them quite sure what to expect. Declan stopped cold and turned to Kate at the scene before them – people rushing around, an administrative assistant on the phone, and the noisy hum of a busy office. The office must have had some good soundproofing because they hadn't heard a peep in the hallway.

Declan's mouth fell open. "I don't know what I was expecting but this isn't it."

"I was expecting a woman alone in an office," Kate admitted, taking in the bustle of activity. She counted six people moving from office to office, two people standing in the middle of the room deep in conversation, and the woman behind the desk who ended one call and started another.

"Can we help you?" a woman said through the haze of activity. She took a few steps toward them as Kate and Declan flashed their badges. "We don't get the FBI here often. I assume you're here to see Jessica."

Kate confirmed. "We apologize for not having an appointment. We are here working on a case and only now just discovered Jessica had been hired by the financial management company." Kate gave the brief details and the woman nodded along in understanding. She never identified herself but ushered them down a short hallway to the last door. She knocked once then pushed it open.

"Take a seat and Jessica will be right with you. She's probably in another investigator's office. I'll find her for you."

Declan thanked her. "How many people work here?"

"Twenty-seven including four admin staff and two staff in billing and human resources. I know it's probably not what you were expecting. Jessica built this business from the ground up ten years ago. We handle everything from personal injury to criminal defense and family court. Most of the law firms in this building are our clients."

"Impressive," Kate said and meant it. They'd interacted with a handful of private investigators over the years. Most were retired law enforcement working out of a home office or in some shady part of town. There were only a couple they'd seen like Jessica's.

Kate had to keep her expression neutral when the young woman with thick, dark, shoulder-length hair, big bright blue eyes, and a welcoming smile walked into the room. She was a little shorter than Kate's five-foot-eight and had a trim build. Kate thought Jessica was about her age, in her mid-thirties.

Jessica extended her hand to Kate and introduced herself. "I got a text from Chris a few minutes ago telling me you'd be by. I'm glad you're looking into this case. I could only do so much."

"It wasn't a case you should have ever had to take," Declan said, not seeming to care that in one comment alone he was solidifying this opinion of Det. Longmuir. He knew what he was doing because he followed that up. "I understand you handed all your evidence over to the detective assigned to the case. We only arrived in LA this morning, but we were not informed of your involvement until Chris told us."

"That doesn't surprise me." She gestured to a table and chairs in the corner of the room. "Take a seat while I pull the case file. I'm happy to turn over everything I have." She walked out of the room with the other woman who still hadn't identified herself.

Kate sat down, feeling the relief she hadn't felt when talking to Kurt. "At least we have someone else to rely on."

Declan looked over at her. "You're not going to admonish me for making that comment?"

Kate shook her head. "I get the sense no one thinks Kurt handled the case appropriately. We'll see what information Jessica shares and what we can dig up on our own. I'm not going to worry about a tiny pebble on the path."

Declan chuckled lightly. "That's one way to look at it."

"It's the only way that's going to keep us pushing forward." Kate grew quiet for a moment. "We don't know what's going on for Kurt. He might have a caseload that's too much for one detective. He might have been getting pressure from higher-ups in the department to move on to other, more pressing cases. We don't know the politics of his office or even his perspective. I have to give him the benefit of the doubt as we sidestep him and work around him. If he gets in our way, then we can squish him like a bug."

Declan's chuckle had turned into a full belly laugh. "Hopefully, we aren't going to have to squish anyone."

"Who are we squishing?" Jessica asked as she walked into the room, joining them at the table.

"No one," Kate said, her cheeks tinged with pink. She hoped she hadn't been overheard. Kate redirected. "When did you first get involved in the case?"

"Chris called me and said he was going through a deceased client's file with the executor of the estate and found some irregularities. He mentioned it was a homicide case, but that he wasn't getting much help from the detective. He asked me to quietly look into the financials." Jessica handed Kate the case file. "All of the information is in there. I can go over everything if that's helpful."

"We prefer that," Declan said and Kate agreed.

Jessica sat back in the chair and pushed it out from the table slightly so she could look between them as she spoke. She started with the information Chris had provided them about the change in Andrea's spending as well as the changes in her social life. "There was a drastic shift about six months ago. When I first got involved, I didn't assume there was a man. The evidence points to that though – the clothing in the house the housekeeper saw, the waiter at the restaurant who served them dinner a few times, the trips Andrea took with a companion. Not to mention her dinners at Norah's and other restaurants suddenly doubled in price. We know Andrea wasn't eating alone. She had also not routinely taken money out of ATMs or directly at the bank. If she did it was a hundred here or there. Suddenly, that turned into her taking the max at an ATM and in greater frequency. She was also withdrawing money at the bank in thousand-dollar increments. She was doing something unaccounted for with all that cash. No one was able to figure it out. We can only assume it was going to the man she was seeing. That's not even accounting for the three-hundred thousand. We have no idea what Andrea did with that money."

It was clear to Kate that Jessica had done a thorough investigation. "Can you tell me about the trips? Were you able to garner any information about that?"

"Andrea used her credit cards for those trips as most hotels require that. It was the one piece of evidence that gave me a few leads. I went down to Monterey to the Hyatt Regency Monterey Hotel and Spa where she and another person stayed on three separate weekends. It was the most frequented travel. They always checked in on a Thursday night and checked out on Sunday mornings. The hotel unfortunately didn't have any video surveillance for me. They don't keep it that long, but I was able to get a good description of the guy and a few photos."

Kate lurched forward. "You have photos of him?"

"A name?" Declan asked.

"I have both," Jessica said, giving them a knowing look. "I can't say for sure the name I have is the man's real name. I assume it's not because what I have doesn't come back to anything other than someone who died in 1985. We have to assume that it's a case of identity theft. As for the photos, mostly he offered to take photos rather than be in them. There were a few on the golf course that people took when he wasn't paying attention. They aren't great but better than nothing."

Kate was holding her breath waiting for the information. She didn't want to hurry Jessica along with it though. "People remembered them at the hotel?"

"Yeah," Jessica said with her eyes wide. "Not only remembered them but interacted with them frequently. The guy was a big spender, walking around with a thick wad of cash, showing it off. When they were in the hotel bar, he'd buy rounds for everyone. I got good statements from the guys who played golf with him. They were key witnesses because most of them surmised quickly that he wasn't who he was portraying himself to be. Andrea was quieter and more reserved but friendly. At times, she almost seemed taken aback by the man's outgoing nature."

Jessica reached for the file in front of Kate and flipped it open. "The man's name is Julian Marlowe. The only problem is there's no record of him. The only Julian Marlowe around the same age as this man appears to have died in 1985 at the age of eighteen in Birmingham, England. This Julian claims he is fifty-eight. He appears to be around that age in the photos. He does present with a British accent, although a few people said that there was something underlying they couldn't detect."

"You mean like he was faking a British accent?" Declan asked.

"Possibly. Then again, there are many variations of accents in the United Kingdom. Americans aren't exactly great at telling them apart. For all we know, it was just how the man spoke and he wasn't necessarily trying to cover up anything."

"There are five of these cases in the London area, so it's plausible he is from there or knows the area well," Kate countered. She could tell by the surprised look on Jessica's face this wasn't information anyone had told her. "The FBI is involved because we believe there is a serial conman at work here. He's done this to several women. They are all murdered. Given the financial crimes, we aren't dealing with a garden-variety serial killer. The suspicion is that the murders happen as a way to cover up this man's other crimes."

Jessica recovered from the surprise quickly, pulling her shoulders back. "That puts a new spin on the case for sure. It also brings into question another case I had. I'll get into that after. What else can I tell you about what I found with Andrea?"

"You mentioned the housekeeper, Annie," Kate started. "Did you interview her yourself?"

"I did." Jessica pulled a statement from the case file and handed it to Kate. "You might not be surprised to hear that Det. Longmuir was dismissive of Annie's information, possibly because she was young. She was working as a housekeeper while she was trying to make it as an actress. Annie told me she didn't feel like the detective took her seriously."

Kate lowered her gaze to the statement. Annie entered the home on the morning she found Andrea's body and indicated she knew right away that something was wrong. There was a smell, but beyond that, the kitchen had been left a mess. There were broken dishes in a pile on the floor behind the center island. It looked to Annie like the dishes had been smashed. There was an empty wine bottle left out and a plate of cheese and crackers. She said Andrea would never have left her kitchen that way.

"Could there have been a party the night before?" Declan suggested.

"I asked the same question. Annie said Andrea didn't entertain much but would always notify her because she'd have to buy extra groceries. Annie hadn't been informed of any party. Andrea had texted Annie around eight that evening and asked if Annie would be by in the morning. She didn't mention anything about a party going on."

In the crime scene photos of the kitchen, Kate had noticed the wine bottle and three wine glasses. She hadn't been shown any photos of the floor with the broken dishes or the plate of crackers and cheese. "Was Annie the last person to speak to Andrea before her death?"

"I believe so," Jessica said with a nod. "Det. Longmuir didn't share information with me and barely would look at the information I provided him. At the time I gathered this and gave it to him, he was working under the presumption Andrea had gotten drunk that night, left her glass sliding door open, and was killed by a stranger. Annie said Andrea had been meticulous about safety since her husband's death. In the last few months of her life, Andrea had twice forgotten to lock up when she said she drank too much. Annie also suspected it was when a man had been there."

It sounded to Kate like the two women had a closer relationship than she'd been led to believe. "Did Andrea confide in Annie? We were under the impression Andrea had cut Annie's hours after she got involved with this man."

"Andrea did cut Annie's hours back but she didn't cut her pay. She continued to pay Annie for the full-time work. She refused to let her meet the man. She didn't want Annie around when he was there. The only explanation she gave was that she didn't want Annie subjected to him. Of course, that made Annie question why Andrea would be with someone like him. She was the boss though, she didn't feel comfortable asking too many questions."

Kate knew she had to speak to Annie directly. "Do you think she'd be willing to speak to us?"

"Absolutely. Annie wants Andrea's murderer caught as much as I do. Her information is in the statement."

"What's the other case you had similar to this?" Declan asked, reminding Kate that they had let that slide.

"Lottie Blyth from ten years ago. It was one of my first cases. Let me go get that case file."

When Jessica got up and left the room, Kate leaned into the table. "That's the other victim."

Declan expelled a breath. "Thank God for Jessica."

CHAPTER 5

After spending another two hours with Jessica going over the other victim's file, Kate and Declan went directly to their hotel to check-in. Kate had gotten them an upgrade because she wanted more space to work. She did that often because she knew the government wasn't going to foot the bill for anything other than the basics.

They still needed to get the rest of the files from Kurt. Neither Kate nor Declan had bothered to connect with him again and he hadn't reached out to them. With what Jessica provided, Kate felt they had more than enough to handle for the evening.

After a quick dinner in the hotel restaurant, they retreated to the room. Declan turned on the television to check the evening news while Kate changed her clothes into something more comfortable. As she wiped the makeup from her face, her cellphone chimed. She grabbed the phone from the counter and read the message from Leo Lamiere, the newest edition to their team. Leo had once been known as the Phantom, the most notorious and impossible-to-catch art thief wanted in just about every country. His crimes were not what they appeared on the surface and the FBI had convinced him to join forces with them.

"Leo has his chateau ready for us if we end up needing it," Kate called from the bathroom. She hoped Declan could hear her above the din of the television. When he didn't appear a few moments later, she assumed he hadn't. She finished her nighttime routine and made her way into the living room area of the suite. Declan was standing, rocking on the balls of his feet as he watched the news. Neither of them had hit the gym that morning. Kate knew he needed to burn off excess energy.

Kate put her hand on his back. He wrapped his arm around her and pulled her close. "Leo texted me that his chateau is ready if we need it," she repeated, finally getting his attention. "He's going to work with the agents we sent with him to start going through the art he has. The goal is to get most of it cataloged and for the agents with the FBI's Art Crime Team to work with Leo to find and return it to its rightful owners."

"Did he give you any estimate about how long he thinks that will take?" Declan said, half-focused on her while his focus was still on the television.

"He doesn't know and the supervisor of the FBI's team didn't know either." Kate left him to finish watching the news. The art Leo was working to return was not the art he had stolen. It was art he had recovered from the estate of his stepfather Lucien Lamiere. The estate had been turned over to Leo almost by default when no other heirs were alive. It was after moving into the chateau that Leo had found the underground bunker. Kate had seen it firsthand. Bunker is what Leo had called it, but what she saw was miles and miles of underground temperature-controlled art storage that had more art than most museums. It was Lucien's lifelong collection of Nazi-looted art that Leo was determined to give back to the families who were the rightful owners.

Leo would be working with Kate and Declan when he was needed. In between cases, he'd be working with the FBI Art Crime Team to catalog, research, and return the art. It was the one caveat to getting

Leo to join their team. He retired from art theft – stealing back Nazi-looted art – to focus on returning those his stepfather had purchased and housed in the bunker.

Leo loved living in Cassis in the south of France. He had also purchased and restored a brownstone a few houses down and across the street from Kate in Boston. While she was still getting a sense of the man, she knew he didn't fit in Boston. Having been raised and educated in Europe, there was something distinctly French about the man.

Kate had only been to the chateau once when she had surprised him there and convinced him to join the FBI. She had never seen a place that fit someone's personality so well. It was built in the 15th Century and updated over the years. The chateau had two medieval round towers, a south-facing façade that looked like it had been designed in the Renaissance period, and mullioned windows. There was an entrance pavilion, outbuildings, and an Italian-style garden. There was also an entire orchard of walnut trees and a staff who took care of all of it.

The interior had the same magnificent simplicity. There were wood beams throughout the home and the ceilings were much lower than her brownstone giving the entire home a cozy warmth even though the structure itself was probably twice the size. Kate could see herself retiring there and living in the countryside away from the violence and strife she faced every day.

It wasn't just the chateau that had garnered her attraction – it had been Leo too. He was forty-nine, had seen the world, and there was a steady calmness and introspection about him that pulled her in. She admired him, having given his life for a cause greater than himself – even though it was illegal. Kate had to remind herself of that often. Their first meeting was in Paris when he had taken her hostage. It turned out, it was to save her life.

That was Leo – *a riddle wrapped in a mystery inside an enigma.* The words weren't Kate's. Winston Churchill used them to describe the beginning of the Second World War in a radio address in 1939. Still, it was an apt description of Leo. He had an attraction for her too. Neither of them would cross the line because Kate was with Declan. She was happy with her choice. But every once in a while her mind drifted to Leo and the chateau and a life that would never be lived.

Kate pushed those thoughts aside, glad to have received an update from Leo. They didn't know if they would need the chateau or not. It was still up in the air whether Kate would need to go undercover.

The people who facilitated cons like this were similar to cult leaders – they could sniff out those who'd be vulnerable and easily preyed upon. Kate wasn't sure what it was they saw that others didn't. A certain kind of quiet vulnerability, a questioning, that indicated they'd make good prey. Kate had seen it before with cons and cults and she'd see it again, unfortunately.

She relaxed back on the bed and flipped open the case file Jessica had provided about Lottie Blyth. At the time of her death, she had been fifty-eight, single never married, no children, and worth close to one hundred million dollars. She had been a famous Los Angeles real estate agent, taking the business over from her father. Half her money had been inherited and the rest she had earned through hard work and grit, keeping the family business thriving in a crowded marketplace where new companies had started and grown over the years. At one time, the Blyths were the big name for every Hollywood type looking to buy or sell a house. In the later years, they were still a go-to but competition had cut into their market share.

Jessica had given them the whole history of the Blyth family. She'd been hired by cousins of Lottie who had concerns about the case turning cold when the detective hadn't found any leads. Like Andrea, Lottie had been found strangled in her bed the morning after the murder. Her business manager found her. The leads had dried up quickly and the detective moved on to other murders.

After Lottie's death, the family went through the financials and turned to Jessica to investigate the case. By all accounts the woman was a workaholic. She was fully dedicated to her job. Kate wondered if the conman had been one of her clients who formed a bond with her that way. Reading the statements, she assumed it would have been an easy connection. Lottie went to charity events and mingled within her Brentwood circle, but she didn't seem to do much else. Unlike Andrea, she didn't go to a yoga class, wasn't known to drink, and rarely traveled. It would have meant missing time from work. For Lottie work was money. She had the *work hard* of the slogan down but not the *play harder*.

The first big sign that something was amiss was the men's Gucci loafers found in the far reaches of Lottie's closet. They had been wrapped in fancy wrapping paper. The second big indication something was amiss was the large withdrawals of cash from her banking account that didn't add up. They had started eight months before her death and happened about once every two weeks. There were also purchases on her credit cards at men's boutiques in Hollywood and luxury trips that they realized Lottie never took. Her card had been used in San Diego, Monterrey, Catalina Island, Napa, and then several trips to New York City. There were also purchases in London and Paris.

Lottie's family initially believed there had been fraud on the accounts. It was only after calling the credit card company that they realized Lottie had an authorized user on the account. The man's name was Julian Marlowe. The only problem was no one in Lottie's life knew she had been dating. He'd flown completely under the radar. Of course, with the amount Lottie worked, no one suspected. She rarely spoke of her private life, mostly because she didn't have one.

Except that she had.

"Find anything interesting?" Declan asked, leaning against the doorway, looking in on Kate.

She raised her eyes to him. If Leo had a quiet sexiness about him, Declan's was boisterous and on full display. He had the swagger, confidence, and boldness that turned heads. His dark wavy hair had a perpetual messiness that didn't tame itself no matter how much gel or time he put into it. His chiseled jaw was the envy of most. His seafoam green eyes captured most people's attention.

Declan's jeans rode low on narrow hips and the sleeves of his button-down shirt had been rolled up to show the thick muscle of his forearms. The shirt tails hung loose untucked. He moved about the world with an air of not caring about his appearance.

Declan cocked an eyebrow. "Why are you looking at me like that?"

Kate laughed softly. "I was thinking about how good you look. I've looked at you a million times over the years. Sometimes it still catches me off guard."

"Why are you buttering me up?" he asked with a boyish grin.

"I'm not. I swear." Kate didn't spend enough time being overly sweet to Declan. She wasn't even sure why. She waved him over to the bed, and he came and sat on the edge. Kate leaned into him, wrapping her arms around him. She dropped a quick kiss on his lips. "I'm feeling incredibly grateful we are together."

"I don't know what brought this on, but I'm not going to complain." Declan looked down at the file then back up at her. "I'd like to throw this on the floor and have my way with you. But something tells me that's not going to serve us tomorrow. I don't know about you, but I'd like to get out of Los Angeles as quickly as possible."

Kate agreed with him. She released him and flipped the file back open, detailing for him everything she had read about Lottie. She also pulled the photos of the man attached to Andrea's case. Kate had looked at them a few times, but they weren't great photos. None of them captured the man's face. It was side profiles and from the back, action shots of him golfing.

"These photos don't give us too much of anything. Maybe down the road when we have something for comparison." Kate pointed down at Lottie's file. "Lottie Blyth wasn't a vulnerable woman. She hadn't lost a spouse and she ran a profitable business. Lottie had family, a strong group of friends, and a whole team of people who reported to her. Given she was a real estate agent, she must have had sharp instincts and a good business head. She doesn't seem on paper at least to be the kind of woman easily conned."

While Declan seemed to agree with her, the way he winced up his facial features told Kate he had more on his mind. "It sounds like Lottie might have been lonely. She might have had a moment when her defenses were down and the conman slipped in. He might have been offering her everything she didn't realize she needed. It seems to me Lottie liked her privacy too. If he wanted the same anonymity he required of Andrea, it might have worked for Lottie."

Kate hadn't considered that. "I still find it hard to believe someone as business savvy as Lottie would give this guy so much money. She paid him cash every two weeks and even gave him a credit card. I don't understand it."

Declan cocked his head to the side. "You let me live in your brownstone for free."

"Declan," Kate said in a rush of breath. "That's not the same and you know it. You were broke after your divorce and we were friends. I was giving you a chance to get back on your feet. We fell in love in the process. You pay bills at home and you do more than half the cooking when we are there."

"Half?" Declan said with a laugh.

"Okay. Most of the cooking." Kate had been wondering if their financial arrangement, him living in her brownstone, had been dinging his pride. Declan didn't speak of it often. She wasn't sure if she should take his comment as seriously as it sounded. She didn't want to go down that path tonight. "I can see what you mean. He might have found a vulnerable spot. Let's speak to her best friend tomorrow and see if we can get a clearer picture from someone who knew Lottie when she was alive."

They talked about the cases for a few more minutes until Declan closed the file and gathered up the rest of the papers strewn on the bed. He carried them to the living room. When he returned, he was unbuttoning his shirt and undoing the button on his jeans.

"I decided we can catch up with work tomorrow. We've done enough for one day." He raised his eyebrows in a question. Kate was already pulling her shirt over her head.

CHAPTER 6

Heidi Pearson was a five-foot-two powerhouse with heels that made her three inches taller. Her thick hips swayed as she marched toward Kate and Declan. Her eyes remained focused on them, never looking away. She flipped her hand dismissively to people saying hello.

Kate liked her instantly.

Heidi exuded a kind of confidence that told the world she was going to take up space and not apologize for it. She had chosen a bistro in Brentwood for the meeting and had told Kate and Declan what time to be there. Kate wasn't sure she had ever had anyone speak to her so forcefully or directly, definitely not any other witness they had ever interviewed.

"Heidi," Declan said and extended his hand as she dropped her canary yellow Birkin bag on the table. She eyed Declan up and down but did not shake his hand.

He retracted it and introduced them.

"I remember what she said on the call. I don't forget so easily, Agent James." She flicked her eyes up and down his body again. "You're better looking than I would have assumed for an FBI agent. You don't have that blue-collar look of most Boston men. You have cleaned yourself up respectably." She turned her gaze to Kate. "Your reputation proceeds you. Although, you're younger than I assumed.

It's about time you took this case."

She was rightfully angry no one had solved her best friend's murder. There was nothing Kate could say to take away the pain that was underneath that anger, so she didn't try. "The FBI was only made aware of the case last week. We came to Los Angeles as soon as we were notified."

"LAPD dropped the ball on it," Heidi said matter-of-factly. She paused for a moment assessing them. "You're not going to try to defend them?"

"I'm not looking to defend anyone," Declan said before Kate could answer. "Everyone is accountable for themselves as far as I'm concerned. I've already seen a few things in the cases that have given me pause. The FBI was asked to investigate and here we are. You either believe we can bring a fresh perspective to the case or you can assume we won't. It's up to you how you'd like to participate in the investigation. I suggest you drop the attitude and have a conversation with us." He looked at his watch and then back up at her. "We don't have a lot of time before we have to leave for London to investigate the rest of the cases."

Heidi pulled back as her eyes darted between them. No one may have ever spoken to her like that. Kate wasn't about to run interference. "What do you mean London? Other cases?"

Before Declan could say anything else, Kate explained, "We were brought into the case by Sam Harris in London. He has five similar cases and there is another in Paris. Then there are two here in Los Angeles. We believe the cases are connected and there is a conman exploiting women for money and killing them when he's done. I'm not sure yet if the murders are happening because the women find out what he's doing or he gets to a point where he wants to move on and doesn't want to leave the women alive to come after him."

Heidi squinted her eyes to narrow slits. "Are you telling me my best friend was murdered by a serial killer?"

Kate shook her head. "Not in the traditional sense, no. Typically murder is what motivates a serial killer. That's what they are seeking, the thrill of the kill or sexual gratification from a sexual assault and murder. We believe money is the main driving force. The murders are to cover up the other crimes or prevent the women from going after this man legally."

"Okay," she said softly. "I think I understand. Why didn't the LAPD identify this sooner?"

"It's a valid question," Kate started. "Your friend, Lottie, was murdered ten years ago. She seems to have been the first. The other cases that happened in London and Paris are out of the jurisdiction of the LAPD. They'd have no idea they might be connected to something else. Then another case happened here in Los Angeles a few months ago. There was too much time between the two cases and two different detectives were assigned. They weren't connected."

Heidi shook her head in confusion. "Then who connected the cases?"

"Sam Harris," Declan explained. "He went in search of similar cases and came upon these two in Los Angeles. To be honest with you, we can't rule out that there are more cases across the United States or the globe that are connected. We only know the eight that have been connected so far. We have not spoken to the detective in Lottie's case."

"You can't. He's dead," Heidi said, cutting Declan off. "He died a few years ago. The case wasn't reassigned."

That was good information to know. Kate said, "We have connected with a knowledgeable private investigator who worked with the family."

Heidi pursed her lips. "Jessica Davis," she said with her tone curt. "I met her a handful of times. She's smart and knowledgeable and a good investigator. That doesn't get us justice in the legal system. I know she's tried to figure out what happened to Lottie. The financial records show us Lottie was involved with someone. I knew the woman for nearly thirty years. I never knew her to keep secrets. Finding out she'd been involved with someone was a huge shock. Unlike her."

Kate needed a full picture of their friendship. "Is it okay if we step back? I'd like to learn how you knew Lottie and some of your interactions with her. Then we can focus on the months leading up to her death." When Heidi didn't seem convinced, Kate pressed her. "It's part of our process. Because you're so close to it, you might not realize how the smallest detail can help us better understand her life and what might have led to her relationship with this man."

While Heidi agreed, she added, "Lottie wasn't someone who could be easily conned."

"I realized that when I read the file last night. It's the first thing I said to Agent James. Lottie was a strong, powerful woman like yourself and would not have been easily taken in."

"I'm glad you can see that, Agent Walsh." Heidi stared at Kate before gesturing for her to go on.

Kate wasn't sure what to tell her exactly. "We don't know much yet about the victims in London. The other victim here in L.A. was recently widowed. She was in a vulnerable state and could have fallen prey to such a conman. He must have been convincing for Lottie to have developed a relationship with him. What we don't doubt is she fully believed she was in a relationship with him. This wasn't a garden variety scam she would have seen from a mile away. This was someone who formed a bond with her close enough that Lottie put her faith and trust in him." Kate needed to be careful not to indicate that Lottie was weak or vulnerable. She knew by Heidi's words and demeanor she'd get push-back. She needed to show Heidi she understood.

Declan seemed to understand as well. "Could you give us some background of your friendship? This is where the other detective should have started. We need to start with the basics to build a strong investigation on top of it."

"Fine," she said, her voice stiff. "Lottie and I knew each other from real estate. As you know, she worked in her family business. I got my license after college and worked a few years before I met my husband. He wanted to have children right away and saw no reason for me to work. I quit and had my children two years apart. While Lottie continued to build her brand in real estate, I raised a family. When I found out my husband was cheating on me with his twenty-year-old tennis pro, it was Lottie who helped me get an attorney and take him for just about everything he was worth. My kids were in high school then. The friendship was one of those strong and everlasting ones. We had no jealousy between us. We weren't rivals. We built each other up and were there for each other. Until her death, I had no idea she was keeping the relationship from me. I still don't understand why she did that."

"How often did the two of you interact?" Kate asked.

"Every day. One of us would call. We'd meet for lunch or dinner when Lottie's schedule would allow. She was also involved with my children from the time they were little right up through their college years. Both are off in the world with lives of their own. They are flourishing, but Lottie asked about them all the time and both my kids adored her."

Kate assured her that it was good to have a friend like that. "Did you notice any change in Lottie in the last year of her life? Any dissatisfaction or yearning for a relationship?"

Heidi took a breath and held it for a moment. "Lottie tried to date over the years. She didn't live a completely celibate life. That said, no man or relationship was going to come before her work. Many of her clients were women getting divorced. She saw the way they had been treated by their husbands. Similar to my story. I had quit my job, built a life and home for my husband, bore his children, took care of them, and raised them while he was off in the world making money. Then when he got bored of what was at home, he traded me in for a younger model. If he thought he was going to get off without paying for that privilege, he was wrong. Lottie heard the stories over and over again and she didn't want any part of it. Money doesn't have a mistress."

Kate heard all of that but also heard Lottie wanted control of the relationship. She heard it maybe because she saw herself a little bit in Lottie. Not for the same reasons, but since her parents' deaths, Kate knew she had trouble allowing herself to be close to people. "Is it fair to say Lottie was looking for a relationship that would fit into her world – something on her terms."

"Only on her terms," Heidi stressed. "You know there aren't many men who are going to go along with a woman like that. There were a few over the years, mostly men who weren't as successful as Lottie. They were successful, just not on her level, if that makes any sense."

It made a lot of sense to Kate. If Lottie was financially taking care of him, she was the one in control of the relationship or so she thought. Heidi hadn't seemed to pick that up yet. "Had there been changes in her personality or frequency in which you talked or saw each other?"

Heidi tipped her head to the side as if considering. "She was happier than usual. I had teased her about having a new man in her life. I teased her about that often and normally she'd tell me. She'd met a guy at a networking event or a guy at a bar or restaurant. They'd have a fling and it would be over. Lottie would go back to focusing on work until the next chance encounter. In the months leading up to her death, she seemed a little more preoccupied than usual. When I asked her about it, she said she had some big clients she was handling. That wasn't unusual. Lottie often took on big clients, Hollywood types, and even from the tech industry. She'd get mired down in business for weeks at a time then pop her head back up. I wasn't even suspicious."

"Was there any point she aroused your suspicion or you became suspicious something was going on with her?" Declan asked, using her word.

"No," Heidi said with a trace of sadness. "I know that makes me sound like a bad friend. But, honestly, I wasn't tipped off. The few times we met at her house there was no one else there. She wasn't secretly texting any more than usual, which she said was business. She didn't disappear out of town on trips she didn't explain."

Kate stopped her. "Was she out of town in the months leading up?"

"I didn't mean it like that," Heidi said, correcting herself. "Lottie would travel to other areas of California. She rarely took vacation time. I don't recall her being gone for work at all during the time leading up to her death."

"What about family?" Kate asked. "Did she have siblings or anyone else around her?"

"Lottie had a big family. She was one of six children but the only one to go into the family business. She had nieces and nephews. Many still living in Los Angeles. I'm telling you she did nothing to arouse the suspicions of anyone. It wasn't until her brother, who was the executor of her will, started going through her financials that he grew concerned. It was the sudden change. She had started taking out large sums of money from her bank account. Then there was an authorized user on her credit card and expenditures for travel when we all knew Lottie was in Los Angeles. He called me right away. We had a meeting about it and no one had any idea she'd been involved with someone. We had the name on the authorized user credit card. We turned all the information over to the detective. No one ever found him as far as I can tell. Even the private investigator wasn't able to find much. There were no leads."

"No one in her life knew she was seeing someone?" Kate asked again.

"Not one of us. Lottie was a happy woman, motivated by work. There's nothing wrong with that. She occasionally wanted male companionship. This time it was the wrong man."

Kate glanced over at Declan to see if he had anything else he wanted to ask. She had one last question. When he gestured for her to continue, she did. "You said Lottie dated men who weren't as successful as her. Was it common practice for her to spend this much money on a man? She was paying for everything – his travel, an allowance of sorts. Jessica said it totaled in the millions."

Heidi locked her gaze on Kate. "That was incredibly unusual and what sparked our immediate concern. As I said, Lottie enjoyed her lifestyle. She didn't mind paying for things, but she wasn't someone you could take advantage of. She spotted it a mile away. Whatever this man offered or promised her, he made it worth it. If he's a conman, then he's the best out there because Lottie wasn't someone who suffered fools. It makes more sense now that her murder is part of a bigger case. I can only hope the two of you are the ones who bring him to justice."

Kate had the sinking feeling the man might be harder to catch and stop than she had initially assumed. She asked Heidi a few more questions. When she was satisfied, Kate promised Heidi they'd do everything they could to find Lottie's killer.

"You better," she said as she stood at the end of the table. "If not, I'm going to have your jobs. I'm tired of good-for-nothing cops not getting things done. It's time for justice one way or the other." Heidi turned on her heels and sashayed her way out of the bistro.

Kate believed every word she said.

CHAPTER 7

"We're spinning our wheels here, Spade," Kate said as they sat in the car outside of the bistro talking to their boss Martin Spade. Declan had the car running and they spoke through the Bluetooth while Kate's phone rested on her knee. Spade ran the specialized FBI unit and was an enigma at the FBI. He could open doors no one else could.

"What's happening there? I was assured the FBI would have full cooperation."

"Det. Longmuir isn't sharing much with us," Kate explained, not even worried that she might be burning a bridge. "He doesn't even seem all that interested in the case, even though he said initially he was glad we were called in. The detective on the first case is dead, and no one else was assigned. Our only saving grace is both families hired a stellar private investigator named Jessica Davis, who provided us the majority of the information we have right now."

"Give me a summary of what you know so far."

Kate looked over at Declan to see if he wanted to respond. When he gestured for her to go on, she leaned forward. "It's basically what we knew before we arrived. A man, who has mostly stayed out of photos and video and is flying under the radar with the victims' friends and family, is engaging in some kind of relationship with these women, exploiting them for money under some pretense and then kills them."

Even though Kate said the women had been exploited, after speaking with Heidi, she wasn't so sure Lottie had been exploited. It sounded to Kate as if Lottie was more than happy to share her wealth for whatever she got out of the deal.

"What about the murders? Are we sure it's the same killer?"

"Scenes look the same," Declan explained. "Lottie's family must have received some of the crime scene photos and given them to Jessica because they were included in the file she provided to us. We still need to go to the LAPD and look through all of their official files because Det. Longmuir admitted he didn't provide us with everything. We still have a handful of people we can interview. From what we saw and heard, the murders are nearly the same. Both women were found tucked into bed, their hair fanned out over the pillow and strangled to death. We need to connect with the medical examiner to see if any kind of ligature was used. It's hard to tell from the photos."

Spade absorbed the information, giving his usual consideration to it before asking another question. "Do you have any leads on a suspect?"

"We have a name – Julian Marlowe," Kate responded. "He was captured in some golfing photos and that's the name on the authorized user credit card. The photos aren't great and don't show his face well. A handful of people in Monterrey saw him as did a waiter. We have the basics but we believe this is a fake name, Spade. We don't believe he's using his real name. Julian Marlowe is also suspected to have a British accent. Although, some speculated the accent might be fake as well."

"Let me see if I can run a passport on Julian Marlowe. If he's British, he had to clear customs when he came into the country. Let me at least see if we can find anything on him."

Kate agreed that was a good idea. "Jessica mentioned she found a man named Julian Marlowe who died when he was eighteen. This might be a case of identity theft."

Spade didn't respond to that and it didn't surprise Kate. In most conman cases the perpetrator isn't using their real name. Too easily identified and caught. "Go to LAPD and see what more information you can gather, meet with the medical examiner and any other witnesses you need to speak with, then get on a flight to London. Use the time in the air to come up with a plan. There will be a plane waiting for you at LAX when you're ready."

It was a rare occasion Spade gave them access to one of the FBI's private planes. Kate's heart started to race at the thought of being back on a flight. She put a hand to her chest, pushing the rising anxiety aside and promising to call him when they learned more.

"Off to the LAPD." Declan looked to his side and then pulled into traffic when it was clear. He hadn't noticed Kate's shift and she was thankful for that. She'd need to get it under control.

The process for getting into the LAPD went more smoothly than they anticipated. The officer at the front desk assured them Det. Kurt Longmuir would be at his desk and that's where Kate found him.

"Kurt," she said as she approached him from the side. He turned his head to see who was calling his name and plastered on a fake smile when he saw it was Kate. She knew he wasn't happy to see her.

Kate walked up to his desk. "I know it's a surprise to see me. I need the Andrea Ivy file. All of it. We had a long talk with Jessica Davis and saw what she was able to uncover. We need the full support of the LAPD. If we catch this killer, your testimony and initial investigation are going to be critical."

"Sure, sure," he said with a catch in his voice. "I can get that for you."

"We also need to see any physical evidence that was gathered at the scene. I'm sure that's in storage. Maybe you can walk me down and introduce me. That way you can go back to what you were doing."

Kurt looked beyond Kate. "Where's your partner?"

"He's taking care of the Lottie Blyth investigation. Splitting up will save us time. We are also hoping you might have a conference room or somewhere we can sit to go through the evidence."

"Ahh," Kurt said, finally standing. "I think…"

"What's the deal, Kurt?" Kate asked with a tone that left no room for misinterpretation. "You said you were happy the FBI is helping on this case but you've stonewalled us since we arrived." He started to speak but Kate cut him off. "Don't give me some song and dance either. I know when you're going to lie before it even comes out of your mouth. If you have an issue with the FBI being involved in this case, just say it. Otherwise, give us what we need, tell us what we need to know to do our jobs, and we'll be out of your hair. I was disappointed that a private investigator seems to have investigated this case more than you did and was far more willing to share information. I don't like having to get information from a private source when law enforcement should have been on top of it." Kate didn't even care other detectives were watching her from behind their laptops. She was dressing him down on his home turf and she didn't feel the slightest bit bad about it.

Kurt's chin dropped and his eyes shifted. "You're right," he admitted after a moment, letting some of the anger deflate from Kate's body. "I dropped the ball on this case. I got behind on it and wasn't able to catch up. When Sam Harris contacted me and told me the FBI would be involved, I was glad for the support. I'm embarrassed by how poorly I investigated the case."

Kate stepped back and tipped her head back to look at him more clearly. She'd never heard a detective take responsibility in this way. It was disarming and she wondered if that's exactly why he did it. "Is there a reason you didn't take the case as seriously as you should have?"

Kurt raised his hands in a gesture of uncertainty. "I was overwhelmed with several other murder cases. There were few leads to follow. It seemed as if it might have been a stranger, then when we uncovered the financial records it seemed as if the victim…" he trailed off not finishing his thought.

"As if the victim was responsible for her own murder…is that what you were going to say?" Kate finished the thought for him. It was similar to what he had said to Declan. "I know you don't feel much sympathy for the victim. A rich woman got herself scammed by a con artist. This is why those who are scammed don't come forward. They are embarrassed, but honestly, it could happen to anyone. I want the files then I'll be out of your way for you to get back to your other cases. You can consider the Andrea Ivy murder officially off your plate."

Kurt nodded and led Kate through the detective bullpen and down a set of stairs to the evidence room. He introduced Kate to the officers behind the desk, instructed them to give Kate access to anything she wanted then signed off on releasing the file. Before leaving he turned to Kate and extended his hand. "I am sorry about this. You're not seeing me at my best."

Kate took his cold, callused hand in hers. While she wanted to tell him she understood, she didn't. Instead, she offered him support. "I know you're overworked and you have too many cases on your plate. Try to remember that no matter what a victim said or did, they all deserve justice."

Kurt's large hand enveloped Kate's for longer than necessary. It was as if he didn't want to let go of the physical connection. He apologized again for not doing his best work on the case then finally released her. He left without saying anything more.

The officer behind the desk ushered Kate back into the evidence room and found her three boxes of evidence. He gave her directions to a small room down the hall where she could sit and go through it all.

Kate thanked him and went to retrieve the two other boxes before closing the door behind her. The first thing she did was text Declan her location. He responded he was making some progress and would meet her as soon as he could.

Kate put her phone down on the table, snapped on her gloves, and opened the first box. A large case file sat on top of the rest of the bagged evidence. She moved it to the table and went through each of the items. The bags had notations on each to explain what was inside, the date, and who gathered the evidence. There were the victim's clothes she had been wearing when she was found along with other items from the bedroom. The second box had kitchen items including the wine bottle and three glasses. The third box contained another file with a collection of photographs as well as a thick file of financial documents and witness statements.

Kate wished the majority of this had been sent to them sooner. Seeing the evidence and witness statements firsthand gave her a clearer view of the murder scene. As Jessica had explained, it had been a mess in the house.

Kate could understand now why, if the house was always tidy, Annie would have been immediately suspicious when she entered the home that morning. The kitchen photographs showed the dirty dishes on the countertop, food still in pans on the stovetop, and the broken glass and ceramic from the plates swept into a corner behind the center island.

The plates and glasses didn't simply look broken as if they'd been dropped on the floor, but rather they appeared smashed into tiny shards of glass and ceramic. It looked like a fight.

Kate scanned the photographs for anything else in the kitchen out of place. She focused on even the most minute detail. In the upper right-hand corner of the photo, she found it – a square photo of sunflowers hung askew as if someone or something had knocked against it, shifting it on the hook. In the next photograph, three kitchen chairs were moved from beneath the table.

There was no question now – there had been a physical confrontation in the home that night. And it appeared three people were present – Julian, Andrea, and an unknown.

Kate put the photos down and pulled the thick file from the medical examiner closer. She was looking for something specific and found it on the fourth page. There in black and white the medical examiner noted bruising on the victim's right cheek from being struck. She had additional bruising in different states of healing on her thighs and upper arms – the kind that could be covered by clothing.

Kate read the medical examiner's findings until she found the section she assumed would be there – the victim had suffered from what appeared to be punching, slapping, and pinching before her death. Many of the injuries dated back days and weeks before the murder.

The medical examiner, Dr. Larry Coldwell, had questioned if Andrea Ivy had been the victim of domestic violence. It appeared to Kate that not only was the conman manipulative, but he was also violent.

Kate's head snapped up from the file when the door creaked open. Declan stood there with two large boxes stacked on each other. "I think I found something," she said in a rush of breath.

"What is it?" he asked as he set down the boxes.

"Andrea Ivy had signs of domestic violence on her body from well before she was murdered. This isn't the run-of-the-mill conman, Declan. He's much more dangerous and unstable than I first believed."

"What does that mean for the case?"

Kate knew exactly what it meant as the knot in her stomach tightened. "He's out there hunting for his next victim right now. He's probably already found her."

"Can we stop him in time?"

"I have no idea." Kate's heart started racing again, this time not because of the flight anxiety.

She knew this man was out there – somewhere – engaging with the next victim.

56

CHAPTER 8

The Los Angeles Department of Medical Examiner-Coroner was located in Boyle Heights on Mission Road. The building was not what Kate had been expecting. She had anticipated a brand new state-of-the-art building in glass and metal. She was met with a stunning red brick and concrete building that dated back to its construction in 1909. Originally designed as hospital offices, the building was a mix of styles described as transitional neoclassical, Beaux Art, and Austrian/German Secessionist. It looked to Kate like something out of a 1950s film noir set.

Declan also seemed to be taken in by the building as they climbed the front steps. Kate stopped counting at twenty and entered the building to find an affable man with a broad smile sitting behind the desk in the front lobby. The smile jarred her given the purpose of the building and those who worked inside.

Kate was sure that he dealt with death and grieving families all day and a warm welcome at the front might appease some initial fear. They flashed their badges and mentioned their upcoming meeting with Dr. Coldwell. "He'll be expecting us. We didn't have a set time, but he said he'd be here all day and to stop by."

The man behind the desk gave them directions to find Dr. Coldwell's office rather than one of the autopsy bays. Kate was glad about that. She didn't enjoy having to visit the autopsy bays when it was victims on her cases, let alone having to stare at the naked corpse of someone she didn't know. The medical examiners were always discreet and respectful, but it was a profession that was overworked and never had enough time in the day.

"It's nice to meet you," Dr. Coldwell said as he stood behind his massive wooden desk with four neat piles of files across the front. There was an open laptop, a large glass of water, and two coffee cups.

He stepped around to shake their hands. "I've been keeping watch of the news and even checked in with the detective a handful of times. Good to know the FBI is taking over."

Kate had found out after calling the medical examiner's office that Dr. Coldwell had done both autopsies – Lottie Blyth and Andrea Ivy. She was glad that the doctor who had seen them both would be able to compare them more easily. "There are a few other cases in London that are similar as well. After we are done here, we'll be heading there."

"You think there is some kind of serial killer?" Dr. Coldwell didn't seem surprised.

"I don't know quite what to call him," Kate said honestly. Now that there was domestic violence involved in the cases, they were looking at a different kind of predator, far more dangerous than she had initially believed. Kate had assumed the murders were to cover up the rest of the crimes. Murder might be part of the motive now. Everything was on the table. Kate explained some of her thinking and Dr. Coldwell didn't disagree.

He gestured for them to sit as he walked back behind his desk. "It was the level of violence I saw on the bodies, different stages of abuse, leading up to the murders. It wasn't all inflicted at the time of death. I told Det. Longmuir and Det. Kevin Brown. I know. Det. Brown passed a few years ago and the Lottie Blyth case went cold. Det. Longmuir was aware though."

Kate didn't want to speak badly about any of the detectives with a medical examiner who worked with them all the time. "I think given the length of time between the cases and separate detectives assigned, it wasn't easy to connect them. Sam Harris in London connected them because he had five similar cases. He hasn't said anything to us about violence inflicted on the women before the murders. It doesn't mean it hadn't happened. Do you have a theory about what went on?"

Dr. Coldwell pulled two file folders off the stack closest to him. He flipped one open and read a few lines from his report. It was information Kate and Declan had already read. He looked up at them. "I believe there was domestic violence. Lottie Blyth was a little different than Andrea Ivy. I don't believe Andrea fought back much at all. She didn't have the defensive wounds we sometimes see. Not only did Lottie have defensive wounds but she had broken knuckles on her right hand. I found bruising on Lottie in two different stages. I'd say some of them occurred roughly a week before the murder then the night of the murder. I don't believe she was abused quite as long as Andrea Ivy."

"That makes sense." Declan detailed the information they had discovered about Lottie. "If her friend Heidi is telling us the truth, and we believe she is, Lottie wasn't the kind of woman who was going to put up with crap from anyone. This was a relationship of convenience for her. She wasn't in it for love. We don't believe she was exploited for money in the way Andrea was. It seemed Lottie didn't mind paying in relationships. She had done it before. That's not to say she wasn't a victim. It does make sense to us that physical abuse might not have been going on as long."

"Andrea was in a more vulnerable state after the loss of her husband," Kate added for context. "We read in the report from Det. Longmuir a neighbor indicated he had heard fighting from her house on several occasions but didn't call the police. It makes sense that she had injuries over different times."

"Yes," Dr. Coldwell agreed. "Andrea's injuries were much more extensive."

The physical evidence was finally starting to make sense to Kate. "You indicated you thought there might have been something used to strangle them. We didn't see anything noted in the file. Did you have any idea about that?"

"A cord of some sort – something thin but strong." Dr. Coldwell reached for the file and pulled out a few of the photos. He turned them around so they were facing Kate and Declan. He pointed to the thin red line across Lottie Blyth's neck. "You can see the line and the way it cut into her skin. It's something that leaves abrasions without piercing the skin. A lamp cord or something similar to that. Nothing was found at the scene that I'm aware of. That doesn't mean the killer couldn't have put it back and it looked to the crime scene techs like a normal part of the home. Nothing stood out is what I'm saying. This killer is strong enough to have done the damage he did inside of her neck like that. Her hyoid bone was broken and there was significant damage to the windpipe with both women. There was more pressure applied than needed."

"Overkill?" Declan asked.

"It certainly appears that way. The killer wouldn't have needed to apply pressure as hard or for as long to get the desired result. Yet, in both cases, that's what I see – a prolonged strangulation with much force."

Kate knew the answer to this but she thought she'd ask it anyway. "Is there anything about the murders that might give you an idea about this man's size?"

Dr. Coldwell shook his head. "No. I can't tell that from the injuries I'm seeing. The fact is even a smaller person might be incredibly strong. There isn't a correlation. From the injuries, I believe he was on top of them when he was strangling them. They were face-to-face when it was happening. He didn't strangle them from behind. Lottie had two broken ribs from being crushed. That indicated to me he was kneeling on her or had her between his knees and she was fighting. She suffered far more injuries during the murder than Andrea because she was fighting him off. He didn't overpower her as easily. Both Andrea and Lottie were similar in height and weight. Neither of them were particularly big women at five-foot-five and less than one-hundred and fifty pounds. Lottie had far more muscle. I assume she had done some strength training. It wasn't enough to fight off her attacker." Dr. Coldwell went over more medical findings from the two autopsies but nothing that was relevant to the case.

When he was finished, he asked, "Did you say you haven't reviewed the medical findings from the autopsies in London?"

"That's correct. We were focused on the cases in Los Angeles first," Kate explained. Sam had provided them with an overview and knew the victims were strangled, but the type of details they were getting now from Dr. Coldwell remained unknown. "Would you like to know more about those cases? Do you think it would help?"

Dr. Coldwell sat back in his chair. "We only have two that I'm aware of. I didn't even realize right away the two had been connected. Det. Longmuir contacted me when he got the call from London and told me the FBI was getting involved. I don't know that I can be of much help. I'm happy to speak with Sam Harris or the medical examiner there if you see value in that."

Kate appreciated his willingness to get involved and do more than hand-off reports. "We are grateful for that. If we need anything, we will get in touch."

Before they got up to leave, Declan asked one more question. "Was there anything you saw in either case that seemed unusual? This is the same killer and we are trying to understand his motivation and pattern. We have little information to go on to find a suspect."

Dr. Coldwell thought for a moment as he stared down at the files. He flipped through a few pages and then opened the other file and read something else. He raised his eyes to Declan. "I said a moment ago the murder weapon could have been a cord or something in the home. The injuries to Andrea and Lottie are the same. It wouldn't surprise me if he brought the murder weapon with him in both cases. Given they are ten years apart and the injuries are nearly identical, I don't think he necessarily grabbed what was available to him at the time. This seems more planned out. I'd say even with signs of violence before the murders, it was premeditated. He knew he was going to kill them and came prepared."

That's what Kate suspected after hearing him go over the autopsies. "All of that is helpful information to have. It shows me the murders weren't spur of the moment or the result of a violent outburst. He planned to kill them and most likely planned to kill them all along."

The murders were starting to make a lot more sense to Kate. Most conmen didn't murder. They usually took precautions early on to not be discovered. This killer seemed to have a ritual with his victims from start to finish.

"You have your work cut out for you. As I said, anything you need from me to help you catch him, let me know. This is a dangerous man who doesn't appear to be stopping anytime soon."

Kate and Declan thanked him for his time and left the office with the weight of the case on their shoulders. "What do you want to do now?" Declan asked once they were back out to the car.

"Let's go interview Andrea's neighbor then I want to call Annie, the housekeeper."

Declan drove them across the city back to Andrea's former home. While there was a notation in the file that a neighbor had been witness to some fighting between Andrea and an unknown man, no one had bothered to put the address of the neighbor. They had a name – Mitch

Newburg. As Declan drove, Kate searched for property records and finally came up with an address for the man. It turned out he wasn't a side neighbor as Kate had initially assumed, but it was the home directly across the street.

Declan pulled into Andrea's driveway, leaving the narrow road clear of the obstacle of his car. "Do you want to take the lead?" he asked as he cut the engine.

Kate had taken the lead enough in this case. "It might be helpful if you could speak to him man to man. I don't want to judge him for not calling the police when he saw the altercation. We need to understand why he didn't and what exactly he saw and heard."

There were no cars in Mitch Newburg's driveway. That didn't mean much in this neighborhood when every house had two and three-car garages. Declan and Kate walked down the driveway facing the garage then down a flight of stairs to the door. It was then Kate realized that Mitch wouldn't have been able to see the street from the living room windows of his home. She assumed he had to have been in the garage when he witnessed the altercation.

Declan rang the bell and they were immediately greeted by a young woman with dark hair and eyes. She smiled up at them as Declan flashed his badge. "We're here to see Mitch Newburg. Is there any chance he's in?" They were expecting her to say he was at work. Both were surprised when she stepped back and allowed them to enter the foyer.

"He was on a call. Let me see if he's done," she said as she disappeared farther into the home. A child, probably toddler-aged, yelled something in the background.

"She might be the nanny," Declan said then corrected himself. "Or the wife? She looked kind of young."

Kate wasn't going to say it aloud but she had made the same snap judgment. Before she could respond, a barefoot man with blue

Dockers and a red graphic tee with a band Kate didn't recognize came to the door. He introduced himself and asked how he could help.

As discussed, Declan led the conversation. "We are investigating the death of Andrea Ivy. We understand you saw Andrea fighting with a man. We wanted to find out more about what you saw and heard."

Mitch didn't seem taken aback by the request. "I can do more than tell you about what happened. Let me show you the video."

Declan lurched forward. "You have video of the incident? Did you share that with the LAPD?"

"No, I didn't even know I had the video until a few days ago. I've been meaning to give them a call." Mitch turned and talked over his shoulder as they followed him. "I have cameras outside facing the street. Normally, it records over every morning. One of the cameras broke without me realizing it. When I went back to look at the footage, I realized it never recorded over the last twenty-four hours of footage."

Kate expelled a breath she didn't realize she was holding. Finally, a break in the case.

CHAPTER 9

"It was the strangest thing," Mitch said as they stood in his home office. He aimed the remote control at the television mounted on the wall, clicked through a few buttons, and brought up grainy black and white surveillance video from the front of his home. He hit the pause button so they could talk first. "We get so little crime up here that I don't check this footage often. I happened to notice when I was cleaning up in front of the house that the motion detection light on the camera didn't turn on. I got fiddling around with it and realized it had broken. That's when I went to look to see if there was any footage saved from right before it broke. I couldn't believe what I was seeing."

Declan thanked him for holding onto it. "After you witnessed the incident, did you consider that you had it on video?"

"I didn't," Mitch admitted with a frustrated sigh. "You'd have thought it would have occurred to me right away. I was so stunned by what I saw that day and I was also in a rush, thinking about video surveillance was the last thing on my mind. By the time Andrea was murdered and the detective came around asking if I'd seen or heard anything, I assumed the footage, if there had been any, had been taped over."

Kate could understand that. "This isn't a judgment," she said, watching her tone, "but is there a reason you didn't call the police when it happened?"

Mitch turned to her and nodded. "I wanted to. I have guilt for not doing it. The only answer I can give you is Andrea saw me and told me she was fine and asked me not to call the police. I should have but I was respecting her wishes."

Declan shifted his weight from one foot to the other. "Before we see the footage, could you give us your observation of what you saw and heard? I also believe from the police report this incident wasn't the first."

"It was the first I saw anything happen," Mitch corrected. "I had heard yelling coming from her house before. A few of the neighbors had. It was unusual for Andrea, who had always been such a quiet neighbor. At first, we didn't understand what was happening. She and her husband had been such a loving couple, so sweet and well-liked in the neighborhood. Andrea never had other men at the home after his death."

Declan asked, "Did you or any of the other neighbors speak to her about it?"

"Not at first."

Declan asked what was on the tip of Kate's tongue. "What did you hear specifically? Tell us everything you remember."

Mitch leaned back on his desk. "He was cruel to her, calling her names, telling her she was stupid and useless. He was arguing with her about money. He was telling her she owed him. If she cared about him, she'd help him." He narrowed his eyes and focused his attention on Kate. "Years ago my sister got involved with a man. He came on strong, telling her she was special and he loved her within weeks of them dating. The relationship went fast and they ended up moving in together shortly after. It was then he kind of flipped his personality. He was cold and verbally abusive. She left before it got physical. She kept waiting for it to get good again. The odd part was that he wasn't that way around other people. To me, he'd come across as the greatest boyfriend she ever had. My sister and I have a strong enough relationship that she was telling me what was happening when it was happening and I believed her. Of course, I encouraged her to leave. I've come to learn today that someone like that could be considered a narcissist and he was love bombing her in the beginning. I don't know what Andrea's guy was like in the beginning, but knowing her, I can't imagine she got involved with someone so hateful to her from the start."

Creators on social media had done a good job of showcasing narcissistic abuse. Kate was glad that more information was available. The flip side though was that anything negative someone did was now classified colloquially as narcissism. That simply wasn't the case. What Mitch described though was on point.

Kate asked, "Do you have any idea how far into the relationship the yelling started?"

"No. As I said, I didn't even know Andrea was involved with anyone. I never saw cars in the driveway other than a few female friends of hers. About six months before she died, fewer of those friends started to come around. It got quiet over there until it didn't. I can tell you the yelling started about two months before her death."

Declan asked a few more questions about what he had overheard then asked him about the final day. "Was the last time you saw Andrea the day of the physical confrontation?"

"I saw her two other times after that. I was pulling out of my garage and she was bringing in the mail. We waved but that was it. She was alone and didn't look well. She had lost considerable weight and appeared paler than normal. I wondered if she wasn't feeling well. Maybe had the flu or something. I also wondered if she was still with the guy. I never saw him again after the incident."

"Walk us through what happened on the day in question. Then we can watch the footage."

Mitch stood upright, pushing himself off the desk where he'd been leaning. "I was doing some work in my garage, cleaning things up. I heard Andrea shout and I thought they were in for another shouting match like I'd heard before. All of a sudden glass shatters. I stopped what I was doing and went to the road to see what was going on. At that point, Andrea was running from the house. I called to her but she didn't hear me. She got halfway down the driveway when a man appeared behind her. He grabbed her by the arm and whipped her around to face him. He got right in her face screaming and yelling at her that he needed the money and that if he didn't get it he was going to leave her. I thought good, go. He called her all kinds of vile names. Things I won't repeat here but you can hear in the video. Then he smacked her hard across the face – not a punch but a slap. It knocked her back. That's when I not only called out to her again, I rushed over there."

"What happened when you got there?" Declan asked, urging him to go on.

"The man immediately turned and ran back down the stairs. I didn't even have the chance to confront him. I was going to do so with force if I had to. My only goal was to protect Andrea. I started to push past her to go after him and she stopped me, saying over and over again she was okay. That it was just a fight that got out of hand. I told her she couldn't stay with him. That she was in danger." Mitch pinched the bridge of his nose. "Do you know she took responsibility for it? She said she shouldn't have gotten him so angry. Andrea said she knew better. I told her no it didn't matter what she did, no man should scream at her like that or put his hands on her. She begged me to go back home because I was going to make it worse for her."

"Is that what you did?"

"Yeah," Mitch said with a trace of regret. "Against my better judgment that's what I did. I didn't want to make things worse for her. I told her she had to leave him. I offered my house if she wanted to come over. She could have hidden out with me. I told her to call me if she needed anything. I was friends with Dimitri, her husband. I was walking a fine line between being a good friend and neighbor and getting involved with things that were none of my business."

It made more sense to Kate now why he hadn't called the police. "I assume that's why you didn't call the cops?"

Mitch nodded. "As I said, she begged me not to. I didn't want to make it worse for her. Besides if the cops showed up and she said nothing happened and she felt safe, they weren't going to do anything. I didn't want to alienate her. Andrea seemed like she was at a point where she needed some safe people around her." He looked down at the ground, sighing. "I wish I had done something different."

Declan patted the man's arm. "I think you did about all you could have. Andrea got herself into something that no one could have protected her from. You did what you could."

Mitch raised his eyes to Declan. "I appreciate you saying that. It was frustrating talking to the other detective. I described the man I saw. I got a decent look at him. Not as good as I would have liked. It was enough though. He didn't do much with it. That's why when I found this footage, I got excited."

Declan gestured toward the television. "Play it for us now that we have some context."

Mitch aimed the remote at the television. He clicked play and the grainy screen jumped to life. Kate and Declan stepped toward the screen so they were a few feet from it to get a better look. As Mitch had described, Andrea came rushing up the steps, she looked twice behind her and then across the street at Mitch's house. Her hair was wild and she had mascara running down one cheek. Her lipstick was smeared and her shirt was half-untucked.

Distress. Fear. Those were the two emotions that jumped out the most.

Seconds later, a man about five-foot-ten came rushing after her. He grabbed her by the arm, pulling her close to him. He leaned down and shouted vile hateful words in her face. Andrea stepped back, telling him to stop. He smacked her hard across the face.

That's when Mitch came into the frame rushing toward the pair of them. The man looked up, his eyes wide then he retreated toward the steps, leaving Andrea alone. She stepped in front of Mitch, putting her hands up to his chest to stop him. She pleaded with him not to go after him, saying she'd handle it. That they were arguing and it got out of hand.

Mitch was insistent and she pleaded with him to stop. She promised Mitch she'd handle it and urged him to go back home. Her final parting words were that he'd only make it worse for her.

When the recording stopped, Declan asked him to play it again and this time pause it when it was the clearest picture of the man.

"I know it doesn't show him that well," Mitch said as he did what Declan asked. "He wasn't quite six foot, looked like he lifted weights. There was a bit of muscle on him but he was lean. Given they were fighting about money, I wondered if he was using her for money. Turns out he was."

Kate processed everything Mitch explained. She was more focused on getting a better look at the man. Mitch had made some astute observations – everything he said was true.

Andrea's tormentor had a chiseled jaw, a slight bump in his aquiline nose, lips on the thinner side, and round dark eyes.

She turned back around to Mitch. "It's hard to hear exactly what he's saying in the video. Did you hear any accent?"

"I did. Couldn't quite make it out."

"Any guess?"

Mitch shook his head. "I'm not good with accents. It almost sounded

British."

Declan asked Mitch to play the video one more time.

When it was done, Declan said, "I need you to send me the video file."

Mitch went back to his desk and grabbed a thumb drive. He handed it to Declan. "I had this already for law enforcement. As I said, I was going to contact Det. Longmuir about finding the video. As soon as I realized I had this, I made a copy. I didn't want to risk something happening to it. If you don't mind me asking, why is the FBI involved in a local murder?"

Kate realized then they hadn't told Mitch the full scope of the investigation. "We believe the man you caught on video is a conman and killer. He's conned and murdered several women. Most of the identified cases so far are in London. There's another here and one in Paris. We don't know if there's more."

Mitch sucked in a breath. "I had no idea. I just thought he was some creep who was being violent with Andrea."

"You couldn't have known, Mitch," Kate said, hoping to appease any of the man's guilt. "You are giving us our first solid lead. None of us, not even our counterpart in London, has an image of the man. This is going to help us not only find him but make the case when we do. We appreciate all you've done."

"Anything else, let me know." Mitch walked them out of the house and thanked them again. He assured them if they needed anything else, all they had to do was call.

Kate and Declan had a little spring in their steps as they walked out to the SUV.

"Where to next, boss?" Declan asked as he started the car.

"Nowhere. I want to sit here and call Annie. Then I want to visit Heidi and show her this video and see if she recognizes this man."

CHAPTER 10

The phone call with Annie went better than expected. Kate found the young woman more than willing to describe what she had witnessed in Andrea's house and the interactions with her boss in the lead-up to her death.

Annie described a woman who had descended into a deep depression and sought out male companionship to replace her husband. Andrea had used a range of dating apps to look for a mate. Annie knew because Andrea had asked her to help set up her profiles. It was Annie who showed Andrea how to use them.

There had been Tinder, Bumble, Hinge, and a few others. Andrea cycled through many of them. She'd set up a profile, go on a few dates, get frustrated by the quality of men available, and delete the app. She went through the cycle several times and even went to Annie looking for suggestions on how to date. Annie didn't know what to tell her – they had a significant age difference and wealth gap. Annie had cautioned Andrea when she started that she wasn't going to find a man like Dimitri on the dating apps. Andrea was so desperate for companionship she'd been willing to try. She had also confided in Annie that she'd been too embarrassed to tell her friends.

Annie had jokingly told Andrea she should try to find a matchmaker. There were a few of them in Los Angeles who catered to women like her. Andrea took to the idea.

Annie didn't know the name of the matchmaker Andrea had used. After meeting the secret man, which is what Annie had called him, Andrea admitted she had gone to one. She quickly regretted that decision. It was why she didn't want Annie around him. Andrea was having trouble getting rid of him after he started fleecing her for money.

Annie said clearly, "Andrea got in over her head, was embarrassed by what was happening, and didn't know how to get out. She refused to turn to friends or family because she felt like her poor decisions and desperation for a relationship had led her to where she found herself. She thought she could get herself out."

By the time Kate was done with the interview, she felt for the first time as if she had a clear picture of Andrea and her decision-making. None of what Annie told her had been in the police report. Det. Longmuir had spent about thirty minutes interviewing the young woman and no more.

When Kate asked Annie why she hadn't mentioned a lot of this to Jessica, the private investigator, she explained she felt protective of Andrea's reputation. Annie felt like the FBI would use the information appropriately. Kate couldn't argue with the young woman's reasoning.

They spent the rest of the afternoon driving around Los Angeles showing the video clip to the waiter at Norah's where Andrea and the man had gone to dinner. He confirmed it was the same person. They went to Heidi and showed her the man. She had never seen him but confirmed he would have been exactly Lottie's type. Kate asked if Lottie would have used a matchmaker to find a man and again, Heidi confirmed her friend had used a matchmaker in the past too. To Kate's surprise, Heidi provided them with the contact information.

After getting some lunch and circling the blocks around Wilshire Boulevard in Beverly Hills, they found a spot to park. Kate didn't have a warrant for information and had no idea if the matchmaker, a woman by the name of Nina Laurent, would be willing to speak to them. She hoped the threat of legal action would be enough to compel her to talk.

"Do people pay for matchmaking services?" Declan asked again as he locked the SUV and joined Kate on the sidewalk.

Kate didn't want to admit there was a time she had considered it for herself. She didn't have time to date or go through the screening process for potential suitors. There was something comforting about the idea of someone else doing all the legwork for her and presenting her with potential screened matches of the caliber of men she'd consider dating. She looked over at Declan with a smile. He probably wouldn't have made the cut if a matchmaker were choosing for her and Kate was glad she hadn't gone that route.

"I'm sure many people would consider a matchmaker," she told him as they walked toward the glass and concrete building. "Remember in a lot of countries, families are still involved in finding people their spouse. Even if the marriages aren't arranged, they help set people up. It's not the worst way to meet people."

Declan turned his nose up at it. "I don't want someone setting me up. I know what I like when I see it." He reached for her hand. "Besides, if you had a matchmaker, there is no way they'd let me anywhere near you – a divorced, broke FBI agent."

Kate bit her lip. "I didn't say a matchmaker would make better decisions for someone. I'm just saying I can understand why a millionaire, highly successful businessperson, or celebrity might choose to go that route. Time, effort, and screening process."

"Well, this lady couldn't have been screening her clients that well if she hooked them up with a conman."

"True enough." They got to the building and Kate stood back and looked up at the structure. The sign out front had several businesses listed, from attorneys and real estate to Nina Laurent. It was only her name on the sign and nothing about her being a matchmaker. Her company had a website that detailed her services starting at twenty-five thousand dollars for a year-long membership. She claimed to have close to fifty thousand people in her database. There were qualifications for those looking to employ her services and be listed for free in the database. She also claimed to have an algorithm for matching her clients that no one else in the world had. It was a proprietary service she exclusively offered in addition to her unique brand of matchmaking skills. Nina claimed she was a third-generation matchmaker.

They entered the building, rode the elevator to the fifth floor, and stepped out into the hallway. They took a left and found Nina's office in no time. Declan opened the door and they stepped into a quiet office with plush carpeting, photos of happy couples adorning the walls, and comfortable-looking couches and chairs.

A young woman in a tight red dress sat behind the desk. She raised her eyes as they entered. "I'm sorry," she said as she cocked her head to the side. "We aren't in the business of finding a couple a boyfriend or girlfriend. I can refer you to another service. Poly isn't our thing."

Declan started to speak but looked down at Kate. It was clear he didn't quite know how to respond. Kate pulled her badge out from her shirt and introduced them. "We aren't looking for a third. We need to speak with Nina Laurent related to an investigation."

The young woman's mouth fell open and her eyes got wide. "Oh, my. Umm…" She scurried off without saying anything more.

Once they were alone, Declan asked, "Do people use matchmakers to find someone to cheat with?"

Kate stifled a laugh. "She didn't mean cheating. Some people have poly relationships these days. Just because you aren't into it, doesn't mean others aren't."

He pulled back from her then. "You're not trying to tell me…"

Kate rolled her eyes. "I have enough trouble managing you."

"That's what I thought," Declan said, throwing his shoulders back. "You can't believe someone would go to a matchmaker at all."

Before any more discussion could be had, a woman who matched the photo Kate had seen online – mid-forties, long black hair, bright red lips, and perfect eye makeup – marched toward them with her hips popping with each step. What the photo on the website hadn't shown was her perfect hourglass frame.

She extended a perfectly manicured hand to Declan. "I'm Nina Laurent. I heard the FBI was here to see me." Nina barely glanced at Kate and when she finally did, she eyed her up and down. "You'd be much more attractive if you played up your best features. You're a beautiful woman hiding behind a plain face, ponytail, and men's clothing. I can tell under those pants and shirt you have an incredible figure. Too bad you're hiding it. You'd attract the right kind of attention. I could find you a husband, and a rich husband at that, in weeks. You'd never have to work this dreary government job another day in your life. Leisurely lunches and shopping are how you could be spending your days."

Nothing sounded worse.

Kate's anger bubbled over in an abrasive tone. "It's our understanding you might have introduced your clients to a conman. We are here to discuss that."

Declan recovered for her. "What my partner is trying to say is that we have reason to believe that one or possibly both of the victims in the case we are investigating *may* have met someone through your agency who *might* be a person of interest."

Nina didn't budge. She held her icy position firm, unwavering. Kate stepped forward to say something, but Declan's hand darted back and stopped her.

Declan stepped toward Nina, smiling down. "We are here doing you a favor, Nina. Neither of the victims' families are interested in suing you. They don't even know we are here. We have five more cases in London and another one in Paris. If this guy is using matchmakers to meet his victims, that's something we need to know. If you're willing to help us, we can work to keep your name out of this. If not, we are going to have to get warrants and shut this whole place down. That will give us access to go through all of your files. All of your client files," he stressed. "If that has to happen, then I'm sure it's going to get leaked to the news that you're matching up women with con artists. You don't want that, do you?"

Declan said all of this with a sweet tone and a smile on his face, as if he were doing her a favor. It wasn't the approach Kate wanted to take. She was willing to give him leeway up until a point.

Nina considered Declan's words for only a few moments. Then she called her assistant to cancel her next three appointments. To Declan, she said, "Follow me to my office." She looked over at Kate, grimacing. "I guess your little friend can come along too."

Declan turned sharply to Kate with his eyes as wide as she'd ever seen them. "Behave yourself," he mouthed. He begged, "Please."

"Fine," she said through gritted teeth. Her throat felt like a fist wrapped around it, the anger bubbling up with nowhere to go. Kate bit her lower lip until she tasted blood. She wanted to knock Nina off her heels. Still, she followed them dutifully down the hall to Nina's office.

"What are the names of the victims?" she asked as she moved back behind her desk. She sat and her hands hovered over her laptop keys. Declan gave her the names and she clicked them into the keyboard. After a moment, she looked back up at them. "Yes, Andrea Ivy and Lottie Blyth were both my clients. What's the name of their matches?"

"Don't your files show you that?" Kate asked, tired of hanging back. She marched herself right up to the edge of Nina's desk. "I'm sure you know their matches."

Nina didn't say anything. She clicked a few more keys then stopped. "I'm not prepared to give you all the information in my database. That would be unethical. I need the name of the man you believe is a suspect."

Before Kate could argue, Declan stepped to her side. "One man and we don't know his name," he lied. He pulled out his phone and showed her the snippet of video of just the man's face. He didn't show Nina the man striking Andrea. It was clear there was some kind of confrontation happening. Her face paled and her eyes darted to the right.

"You know him," Kate said with force. "I can tell by the look on your face. There's no point in denying it. Who is he?"

Nina eyed Kate with the kind of dismissive glance of a woman with a lot of power and money who wasn't used to taking orders from anyone. She sat back in her chair and crossed her legs. "He told me his name was Julian Marlowe. He's from London. At least, that's what he told me."

Kate picked up all the hesitancy in her speech. "You're not so sure now?"

"This is all a bit…complex," Nina said, averting her eyes. "You should sit and I'll tell you."

CHAPTER 11

Once Kate and Declan were seated, Nina explained, "My database is filled with both men and women looking for love. I screen these potential matches because my clients are particular. I'm always on the lookout for potential matches, particularly if I have new clients that indicate particular desires. I met Julian at one of the mixers I hold to screen new matches for my database. He was perfect for a few newer clients I had. As you can see, he certainly has the looks. He was also well-spoken, well-traveled, highly-educated, and came from a good family. He was healthy, answered the personality tests I gave with ease, and had no criminal history. He said he was a former model who was living off the money he had made. He also had family money. When I asked what he was doing in Los Angeles, he said he was looking for a change of pace and open to love."

Kate was stuck on the personality tests he had taken. She let it go for now. "Was Julian matched with Andrea and Lottie? Their murders are ten years apart. Was this man in your database for that long?"

"No," Nina said with a shake of her head. "He left after matching with Lottie. We remove people from the database after they match with someone. If they don't come back and tell me the relationship is over then I assume it was successful. Of course, I saw on the news Lottie had been murdered. I didn't connect it with her match because no one came to speak to me about it. They said they never caught her killer. I assumed it was a home robbery or something like that. Julian didn't resurface until several years later. He said he was still single. We commiserated over Lottie's death and I added him back into the database. He matched with one woman and it didn't work out. He came back to me a third time and that's when I introduced him to Andrea."

"What did Julian say about Lottie's death?"

"Just that they had broken up by then. He hadn't been in contact with her, but he was sad for her."

Kate tried to not have judgment seep through her tone when she asked, "When Andrea was murdered, did it occur to you that a common denominator might be Julian?"

"No," she said without a trace of doubt in her voice. "Again, no one came to see me, so it didn't occur to me to connect it to Julian."

Kate was having trouble believing that. She pushed harder. "How many clients of yours have been murdered? A lot?" When Nina stared at her with her mouth closed tightly, Kate went on. "That's what I thought. If I were running a matchmaking business for wealthy clients and I have two murdered clients and I know both of them were introduced to the same man, I'd have connected the dots."

Nina offered a dismissive wave. "I don't know what else to tell you. I didn't connect it. I meet and interact with a lot of people. I don't mean to sound callous, but it wasn't top of my mind. I match a lot of people as you can see on my walls. I've made a lot of happy couples. Some don't match as well for a myriad of reasons. If clients don't come back and provide me the feedback, I have no idea what's happening."

"Do you have client follow-up?" Declan asked. He didn't give her a chance to answer before going on. "Your website said clients pay a membership fee for a year. If you match them with someone right away, are they still paying you for the rest of the time?"

"Yes, it's paid up front. We do some follow-up. However, we cannot force our clients to tell us anything." Nina gestured toward her laptop and shrugged. "We called Andrea and she didn't return the call. I assumed she was happy. Julian hasn't come back to us. I don't have him active in the database right now."

Kate cautioned, "If he comes back to you, do not tell him the FBI is asking about him, notify us right away."

"I can do that." Nina remained reclined in her chair. "I'm not sure what more information I can provide you."

Declan wasn't going to let her off that easy. "We are going to need every bit of information you have collected on Julian – including any background check you did and his personality tests. You're going to provide it willingly or as soon as I step out of here I'm calling to get a warrant. It's entirely up to you. Agent Walsh will remain here with you until that warrant comes through to make sure nothing happens to those files."

Nina held her hands up in defense. "You can have the files. There's no need to strong-arm me, Agent James. I'll provide whatever the FBI needs. If this man is a conman then certainly I want him caught. He didn't show any signs of that to me. I have an instinct about people. It's how I'm so successful. I think you might be barking up the wrong tree here."

Declan stood and leaned over her desk. He aimed his phone so she could see the screen and he played the video clip from start to finish. Kate kept her gaze focused on Nina, gauging her reaction. She had none. Nina stared at Andrea being slapped without showing any emotion on her face. "Did you have an instinct that he was violent with women when you met him? Because this clearly shows he slapped Andrea across the face. According to the neighbor, this wasn't the only incident. There had been several fights about money. He called her names and degraded her."

Nina barely registered what he said. She raised her shoulders in a shrug. "He didn't come across that way when we met or during any interaction I had with him."

Kate had so many questions it was hard for her to know where to start. She sat back down because she wasn't going anywhere. "I want to know when Lottie and Andrea came to you what kind of match were they hoping to find?"

Nina leaned over to look at Kate around Declan. "It's in their files that I can provide to you. I see so many people I don't remember."

"Yes, you do," Kate urged. She knew there was no way this woman had only two murdered clients and she didn't remember every detail about them. "We aren't leaving until we discuss this."

Nina clicked her tongue. "Lottie was looking for something more casual. Not a fling but someone that wouldn't get in the way of her work schedule. She was fine with having a kept man, so to speak."

"Are you saying she was willing to pay for sex?" Declan asked. He looked to Kate for explanation, but she wasn't sure exactly what Nina was saying.

She encouraged Nina to answer his question.

"Don't be so surprised, Agent James. Men have been doing it for centuries. They have women available to them when needed and in return, they pay a woman's bills. Is it prostitution? Not in any technical or legal sense. Lottie had no problem paying bills and giving an allowance to the right man who fit into her schedule and lifestyle. Julian was that man."

"Was Julian the only man matched with Lottie?"

"The only one," Nina confirmed.

"When did you match Lottie with Julian in relation to her murder?"

Nina leaned forward and clicked more keys on her laptop. "About eight months before her death."

"What about Andrea?" Kate asked. "What was she looking for when she came to you?"

"Love. It's what most women come to me to find. Lottie was different. I don't get too many women clients like her. Andrea was far more typical. She had lost her husband and missed the companionship. She seemed lonely and maybe even a little desperate. We had conversations about that because she had turned off a couple of her earlier matches."

Kate didn't hide her surprise. "There were others before Julian?"

"Three. They went on initial dates with Andrea. None of them wanted to continue seeing her. She was…" Nina trailed off and looked away from them. "Too sad, I guess you could say. The dates were depressing. I asked Andrea if she was truly ready to date again. I offered to put her account on hold until she was ready to come back. I even suggested therapy. She insisted she was ready. She and Julian matched well in the database. I use a proprietary algorithm based on their responses to questions and background information. I also had an instinct they'd be good together. I guess I was wrong about that."

She was more than *wrong*. Her decisions had been deadly. Kate didn't press the point. "You said that Julian had been matched with someone before Andrea. Do you know why that didn't work out?"

"No. I wasn't provided that information. Sometimes it just doesn't work between people."

There was something she wasn't saying. Even Declan picked that up. "We are going to need her name and contact information," he said, his tone unwavering.

Nina hesitated for a moment and Kate thought she might force them to get a warrant. She didn't though. She leaned forward and clicked the keyboard to pull up her client database. She read off the woman's name and phone number. "I don't know if this is still her number. She married the man I matched her with after Julian. I'm sure she's only going to have glowing things to say about my business."

Kate knew then that's why she was willing to hand over the contact information so easily. "What were your impressions of Julian?"

"Smart. Articulate on a range of subjects including art, music, and the theatre. He had traveled the world when he was working as a model."

Declan stopped her right there. "Did you see a portfolio or speak to his agent? Anything to confirm that's the work he did?"

Nina's mouth fell open slightly as if she couldn't comprehend the question. "Just look at him, Agent James. He's gorgeous. He wasn't modeling by the time he came to me. It was work he did in the past. I had no reason to go digging around. He wasn't a grifter and he wasn't a slouch. That much I can tell you. He had on Gucci loafers and a Rolex watch. He was dressed impeccably, more so even than most of the people in the database. I suspected he could have been one of our members."

"Did you offer him a membership?" Declan asked.

"He didn't express interest, so I didn't." Nina plastered on a smug smile. "I don't have to sell my services. I have a waitlist. If Julian wanted to be in my database I was happy to have him. He was the kind of man many of my members were interested in. He was a good catch."

"Right up to the point of conning women out of money and murdering them," Kate said wryly, not holding back any longer.

"I don't think—" Nina started to say but Declan cut her off.

He stood and thanked her for the information.

As Nina stood and tried to address Kate again, Declan warned her, "You insulted her at the start. Dismissed your role in these women's deaths and you're not going to win going after Agent Walsh again. Trust me. She's about five seconds from tearing off your head. If I were you, I'd be glad she's a professional at all times. Get me the file on Julian."

Nina blinked rapidly several times but did as Declan told her. She handed over the file without saying another word.

With that, Declan turned to Kate and nudged her out of the office and down the hall toward the front door. "Keep it together for a few more minutes until we get to the street." Declan had his hand on Kate's back guiding her out.

Kate's jaw clamped. Her fists tightly balled at her sides. Declan was right, she was on the verge of losing her temper. She didn't meet too many people that set off this side of her. Nina hit every raw nerve she had.

Once at the front door, Declan shoved it open and ushered them both out into the sunlight. "You can scream or curse or do whatever you want now."

Kate marched down the block away from him and the building, trying to calm down. "She doesn't even care, Declan," she said but he was too far behind her to hear him. "She doesn't even care that she introduced these women to a man who conned them, beat them, and murdered them." Kate seethed as she walked to the corner and turned back, realizing then that Declan hadn't followed her at all. He was waiting in front of the building looking at his phone.

Kate didn't like women like Nina, rich and entitled. She had a cold callous demeanor that allowed her to remain hands-off if something went south. She only introduced them, the rest was on them. That was what Kate had picked up most from the conversation. Of course, Nina wasn't legally culpable. There was no way she could make that case.

Kate stood there on the corner until her fists and jaw unclenched and her back muscles relaxed. Until all the curse words left her brain and were replaced by a desire to continue with the case and forget all about meeting Nina.

Declan waved at her with his phone in the air, calling her back.

As Kate approached him, Declan gestured with his phone again. "I called Sybil Merchan. We can speak to her now. She seemed eager to discuss Julian."

"Let's do this," Kate said with an exaggerated sigh.

CHAPTER 12

Sybil Merchan lived in Hancock Park, a residential enclave dating back to the 1920s. It featured well-preserved mansions in Tudor and Italian Revival styles. The homes were on large lots with broad lawns and porticos. It reminded Kate a little of what Hollywood must have been like in its heyday. She liked the vibe of Hancock Park more than any other area she had seen so far.

Sybil lived in a white with black trim Tudor Revival home with a carriage house in the back, at least that's what the listing indicated. It was built in 1924, and if the real estate records were correct, it was sold once and hadn't been in the market since.

"I wonder if this is her family home," Kate said absently as they pulled to the curb.

"Should I go up the driveway?" Declan asked then decided that was better than the street where they might get towed. He inched up the driveway and stopped short of the carport overhang. Beyond that, the backyard was gated off.

They got out and walked up the walkway, up two steps to the porch. Declan raised his fist to knock but it was pulled open before he could. A small woman with a perfect coif of gray hair stood there in her socked feet and wide-leg linen pants.

"FBI agents, right?" Sybil said as she introduced herself and Kate and Declan did the same. "Come on in. My husband isn't here right now and we are probably the better for it. He'd talk your ear off and doesn't like to hear about my dating history before him." She turned and led them through a tiled foyer then down three steps into a sunken living room with wide windows that overlooked the side of the home and a fireplace. Kate wondered if it ever got cold enough in L.A. to light it.

Sybil eased herself down on the couch and patted the other cushion for Kate. She gestured across the way to the chair for Declan. "What's it like being an FBI agent? I always wanted to go into law enforcement. When I was young that sort of thing was discouraged. I had a real obsession with the private eyes of the forties. I fancied myself becoming one eventually. Of course that never happened. I wasn't encouraged for much other than to become a wife and a mother. Different times."

Kate liked the woman immediately. She had a warmth to her brown eyes and a calm demeanor. "It's still a boys' club, but I make it work," she said with a hint of a smile.

"Hollywood is a boys' club too. Always has been and still is. Women are making inroads, but it's not fast enough in my opinion." Sybil clasped her hands together in her lap. "Well, you didn't come to see me to listen to me go on. You said this was about Julian."

"It is," Kate confirmed with a nod. "It's my understanding you were set up with him. When was this?"

"About a year ago now, maybe more. It was right before I met Tony, my husband." Sybil looked around her living room. "This is a big old house and there wasn't a lot of warmth in it. I had all the money I needed but not the love." She turned and looked right at Kate. "I was married young, in my early twenties and had three children. All the kids are off with families of their own. I see them from time to time and visit with my grandchildren. I have a few girlfriends. It wasn't the same as having a partner. My husband passed away fifteen years ago. I got lonely. I heard good things about Nina. I told her what I was looking for and she sent me Julian. I knew right away he wasn't for me. He was much too young for me, much too controlling and after my money. I'm about to turn seventy. I've been around the block a few times. Julian wasn't what I was after."

Kate's eyes got wide. "You knew that right away?"

"Well, the age thing for sure. Tony is two years older than me. I know it must seem silly to you to go to a matchmaker at my age."

"It's never silly to want love and companionship," Declan said from across the room, drawing their attention.

"I like this one," Sybil said with a head nod in his direction. "You're right, it's not silly. I felt a bit silly going to a matchmaker though. I didn't know how to meet anyone at my age. I'm active and still in shape. I needed to find a partner who could keep up with me. Julian is in his late forties. I didn't know what Nina was thinking. I nearly asked for my money back."

"Did you spend much time with Julian?"

"More than I wanted to."

"How so?"

Sybil moved around getting more comfortable on the couch. "We met at a restaurant even though he wanted to meet at my home. I didn't know him. I wasn't going to have a man I didn't know over here. We met and I knew right off it wasn't going to work. He was a charmer and kept trying. He laid it on thick. So thick there were a few times at that dinner I nearly laughed at him."

Sybil had an instinct Kate admired. "What kinds of things was he saying?"

Sybil chuckled lightly. "We were nearly thirty minutes into lunch when he told me he thought he could fall in love with me. He wanted to take care of me and spend the rest of his life doting on me. He gave me all sorts of compliments. He was saying the sorts of things that women should run from – it's too much too soon. I told him to slow down and he pushed harder. That wasn't even the first time I saw his controlling nature. The man wouldn't even let me order for myself. He said he knew the restaurant better and he'd choose my lunch."

Declan leaned toward her. "What do you mean he ordered your lunch? Like he spoke to the waiter for you?"

"No. He chose what I was going to eat." Sybil pulled back with her eyes wide and an incredulous look on her face. "Can you imagine that? Telling a grown woman of my age what she was going to eat for lunch. He didn't even ask me what I wanted. He told me he was ordering me some fish thing that I most certainly was not going to be eating. When the waiter came over, I spoke right up and ordered for myself. When Julian tried to argue, I told him that I could sit at another table and have a quiet lunch instead. I think that waiter knew right away I wasn't going to be someone who he should mess with, so he put in what I ordered."

"I'll say you have…" Declan trailed off seemingly lost for words.

"Moxie is what they called it in my mother's day. I'm not sure what it was called in mine. I never had it until my husband passed and I was forced to do everything on my own for a few years. It makes you strong and I got addicted to the feeling of it." Sybil reached her hand out to Kate. "You young ladies have it in spades. Keep it because you need it with how people are today. Someone is always looking to take advantage."

Kate could have listened to Sybil all day. "You said you ended up seeing Julian more than once. Is that correct?"

Sybil sighed. "He showed up here at the house even though I didn't give him the address. I called Nina and asked if she provided it and she assured me she didn't. When he showed up here, he had flowers and was trying to sweet-talk me. He apologized for being pushy at the restaurant and trying to come home with me afterward." Sybil took a little breath and shook her head. "That's the part I left out. Even after I talked over him when I ordered, he went back to sweet-talking me. That's when I knew it was all a game for him. After lunch, which I ended up paying for because he conveniently left his wallet at home, he had the audacity to ask to come back to my house with me. He was trying, poorly, to seduce me. Can you imagine?"

"I'm so sorry that happened to you," Declan said with meaning in his voice. "I don't understand men like that. It's not how I was raised. I've had my share of fun, but I never had to try to force someone into anything, and I'd pay for lunch."

"You don't seem like the kind of man who'd have to talk a woman into much," she responded with a wink.

There was more to her statement than flirting with Declan. Kate asked, "Was Julian the kind of man who'd need to talk a woman into sex?"

"I found him creepy," Sybil said in response. "I didn't want to let him into my home. We sat here in the living room talking as I tried to figure out how to get rid of him. I pretended I had to take a call, from one of my children and if I didn't answer, they'd come over kind of thing. I called my handyman who works in the area. He showed up about fifteen minutes later and got Julian to leave. It was quite the confrontation."

"What made him creepy?"

"As soon as I let him in, he started asking about my money and family money. It seemed he had done some research on the Merchant name. My name is technically hyphenated with my husband's last name, but most people know me as Merchant. My father didn't have any sons, and I know it was important to him the family name continued. This is my family home too. My husband was a wonderful man and humored my family's quirkiness in so many ways. We lived here. I grew up in this home. I've never lived anywhere else. Julian knew this and knew I must have considerable wealth. He started telling me he should manage my money. When that didn't work, he asked me if I wanted to invest in his business, which he never detailed. The only answer for him I had was no. After my handyman tossed him out, he dared to show up here three more times. He never got past the front walkway. I thought I was going to have a real issue on my hands. He gave up eventually."

Other than Nina, this was the only person Kate knew who had considerable contact with him. She had specific questions but also didn't want to lead her. "What can you tell me about Julian? We have a photo of him, but what about him otherwise."

Sybil caught on quickly. "He had an accent if that's what you mean. He told me he grew up in London. He told me he was a boarding student at Dulwich College in London. Funnily enough, I know alumni at Dulwich, but when I asked him questions about his time there he changed the subject."

"Did you think he was lying?" Declan asked.

"That's the odd thing. I think he was lying about Dulwich, but I don't think he was lying about boarding school. There was a persnickety quality about him that I've only seen in other wealthy men from London."

That was helpful information for Kate. She raised her eyes to Declan to see what else he might want to know. He asked a few more questions that Sybil answered with ease. The thing that came across the most to Kate was she had recognized the red flags early on and cut him off. That was one of the things that made her different from the other victims.

When Declan was done asking his questions, Kate continued the conversation. "After this bad experience, you were still willing to let Nina set you up. I haven't known you long, Sybil, but that's surprising."

"I already paid her and she refused to refund my money." Sybil gave Kate a half-hearted shrug. "I was still in the market to find a companion. I figured since I already paid and was still looking for someone, I'd give it another go. I was specific with her that I didn't want anyone under the age of seventy and someone nice who had their own money. A kind man, that was the most important thing to me. The next date I went on was with Tony and we were married within three months." She smiled broadly. "Tony is an exceptional man."

Kate was happy she was able to find someone.

"If you don't mind me asking, what has Julian done to warrant an FBI investigation?"

Kate explained his connections to the other victims. "We can't say for certain Julian is our suspect. We don't have enough information to confirm that. We have enough to consider him a person of interest. You were right to stay away from him. We believe he's exploiting these women for money and then killing them."

"I believe that," Sybil said a little too casually. When she saw the surprised looks on their faces, she added, "I can't explain it to you other than to say he had a vibe about him. It was like being around someone wearing a mask. Every so often the mask would slip and I'd see another person. It was a look in his eyes. The way he carried himself. There'd be an abrupt change, usually when I was pushing back on something he was trying to control. It was distinct if you pay attention to it. A shift in his energy, in the air around us. I know it all sounds a bit woo-woo. That's what happened, and I can't explain it better than that. If Julian has done what you said, and I can't help but believe you're on the right track, I feel fortunate I walked away."

Kate asked a few more questions about where Julian lived in Los Angeles and what he did for work. Sybil didn't know. He had shared little about his life in Los Angeles or London other than where he said he was from and went to school. Sybil explained Julian had told her he used to work as a model, the same thing he had told Nina, and that he had family money. Something Sybil didn't believe to be true.

"I thought he was broke," she said as the interview was winding down.

"Did you consider Nina had set you up with him intentionally?" Declan asked and Kate knew immediately his train of thought. Nina was in on the scam.

Sybil nodded. "I considered it when he showed up at my house. Either she was the worst matchmaker in the history of matchmaking or she intentionally wanted me to meet Julian. Given everything you said, she must have considered me vulnerable somehow and thought I'd fall prey to his praise." She held her hands out. "As you can tell, I'm not won over as easily as that."

Kate and Declan got up from their respective seats and thanked her for the information. At the door, Kate said, "I can't tell you how much I appreciate what you shared. I'm glad you had the instinct to see Julian as he was instead of what he was presenting. Two women here and potentially six in Europe weren't so fortunate."

Kate walked to the SUV feeling like she was getting a clearer picture of the man. Catching him would be harder than she had initially thought.

CHAPTER 13

"We are leaving in the morning, Sam," Kate said during the video chat. Sam had been texting her asking how the case was going in Los Angeles while almost all of his leads had dried up. She had suggested once they had retreated to the hotel she could video chat with him. Declan had wanted to go for a run and while he was gone, Kate took the time to call Sam. It was late in the evening in London and she had caught him at home.

Sam relaxed at his desk which was positioned in front of large bookshelves. The man was far more of a prolific reader than Kate could have guessed. He had everything on his shelf from politics, history, and science to the latest thriller paperbacks. Sam held a glass of whiskey in his hand as he spoke. He had explained to her it had been a long day, followed by a long evening and he was over the whole case already.

"You have made far more progress than I ever considered," he said. "I don't have the leads here that you seem to have been able to dig up there. I knew getting you involved would be a good idea. Tell me more about this matchmaker. That's an angle I never considered."

Kate admitted that if it hadn't been for Annie telling them about the matchmaker, they would have never considered it either. Sam was not Det. Longmuir. He was doing everything to solve the case. He was as dogged in his approach as them.

"I don't like Nina Laurent or trust her," Kate admitted. "It didn't cross my mind she could be involved until Declan asked Sybil Merchant the question. It was such an odd pairing connecting Julian with Sybil. Not only the significant age gap, but anyone spending a few minutes with Sybil could figure out she wasn't someone who'd be scammed, at least not easily. Then again the same might be said for Lottie Blyth. I don't know, Sam. Something about Lottie's murder feels much different to me than Andrea's. I don't understand exactly what happened with Lottie. No one in her life knew what was going on."

"That's what I have in my cases." Sam took a long sip of whiskey. He rolled the brown liquid around in the glass. "I don't know, Kate. At least we have a name and an image of the man. What's the plan?"

Kate had been considering their options. If the killer was going through a matchmaker, going undercover wouldn't do much for them. Kate would need to connect with a matchmaker and be a client. The other option would be to tell the matchmaking company and if they were working with Julian, the whole case would be blown before it barely got started. They weren't looking at a lot of good options. She explained all of that to Sam. "Declan and I have a lot to discuss on the plane." Just at the mention of the plane ride, Kate's stomach cramped.

Sam spotted the change in her facial features and called it out. "What's that about, Kate? I don't think I've ever seen you make that face. Is everything okay with you and Declan?"

Kate averted her eyes, knowing she had been caught. She couldn't think on her feet fast enough to come up with something. If she didn't explain, then Sam, who knew about her relationship with Declan, might think there was trouble. She slowly turned back to him. "I seem to have developed a fear of flying."

"Oh is that all?" Sam said with a laugh. "It's common, Kate. I'm the same way. I knock back a few whiskeys." He held up his glass and swished around the liquid. "I'm right as rain after that."

Kate didn't think getting drunk was going to be the answer for her.

Sam peered into the screen and caught her eye. "Did you consider you developed this fear of flying because you suddenly have something to live for?"

Kate cocked her head. "What do you mean?"

Sam turned up his lips in a slow knowing smile. "Kate, I'm talking about you and Declan. You finally have a good relationship. You have more in your life than work. I bet you're seeing a future for yourself that you never thought possible."

Kate stared at Sam, a mix of confusion and surprise. It wasn't anything she had considered for herself. He wasn't wrong. It was the first time in her life that work wasn't the only thing she had. It was still a priority for them both and their relationship in many ways revolved around the FBI. Yet, she worked not because she needed the money but because she enjoyed it. Even if Kate was fired tomorrow, it wouldn't be a big loss. With Declan, for the first time in her life, she had something to lose – something she couldn't imagine losing. The flip side of that was she had something real to live for as Sam had said. Kate didn't have to question if it was the right answer. The truth settled into her body and she felt it in her bones.

A small laugh escaped her lips. "I hadn't even considered that."

"I went through it when I met my wife," Sam said then gestured dismissively. "I know we are divorced and I never talk about her. I don't even know if I ever mentioned I'd been married."

He hadn't. It was new information to Kate. She saw the pain in his eyes and that was enough for her to not ask a question but instead to sit back and wait for him to go on.

"Things fall apart sometimes when you're not tending to them in the way you should. I fell madly in love with her and suddenly I had something to lose. Everything became heightened for me, especially in this line of work. Crime scenes I'd walk into before and not think twice, suddenly I was thinking about her face if she received the news I wasn't coming home ever again." Sam tapped on his chest then his temple. "I don't know if I felt it in my heart or my head more. The love for sure was all heart. My brain played funny tricks on me. I'm sure that's what's happening now."

Kate caught the way Sam wouldn't speak his ex-wife's name and how he didn't refer to her as his ex. She didn't know if the divorce was fresh or years ago. She wasn't going to push for information. That wasn't the point of what he was telling her. "How did you get past it?"

"I had to talk myself out of it. If I held only the fear of losing, the anxiety would have made my life small. I had to let it go to live." Sam paused for a moment and then added, "Hold onto it a little bit to remind you of what you have. If not, you can end up taking it for granted and that's the kiss of death."

Kate said she understood and she did. "I appreciate the advice. I assume it's going to take some time. Our flight is in the morning."

Sam held up the whiskey again. "Then have a couple of these," he said with a laugh. He sighed and leaned back in the chair. "What are we going to do about this case, Kate?"

"What do we know about France's involvement?" It didn't matter how many times Kate had gone to France to work a case, she never had the best experience with law enforcement there. There were territorial issues and the French police didn't like the Americans stepping in. She'd never had the kind of reciprocal back and forth that she had with Sam. It's why what Sam said next surprised her.

"They are hands-off," he said dismissively. "The inspector involved in the case has given me everything he has and they are stepping back from it. They have run out of leads and have other cases to handle. I think there's some frustration around it and the victim's family is breathing down their necks. He didn't want anything to do with it.

When I called and started asking questions and suggested that it was part of a broader international investigation, he said I could have whatever I needed."

It reminded her of Det. Longmuir's response to it. It seemed not too many people cared about these kinds of murders. She wasn't sure if it was the age of the victim or if there had been some prejudice because they had been scammed. "Do you have all the files?"

"I should have everything by the time you arrive."

Kate went over the math of the investigations to try to piece together who was the first victim. That seemed to be Lottie. "Was Andrea here in Los Angeles the last victim? You haven't had a more recent one in London, have you?"

Sam shook his head. "Not that I've been able to find. I can't account for what this guy might be doing across Europe. I've called my counterparts in every country, especially in the big cities. I don't have anything so far."

Kate breathed a sigh of relief. She knew he was out there hunting for the next victim. "He's not going to stop."

"A few of the murders here are only months apart," Sam explained, giving her the dates of the murders. "Do you have any idea why he kills them?"

"I don't have a proper working theory yet. At first, I thought the murders might be a way to cover up the financial crimes. I thought it was a way for him to cover his tracks. The more I learn, the less I'm sure about that. There's definite domestic violence in the relationship."

"I don't have that confirmed in any of my cases here. Of course, I also don't have any witnesses who saw the guy with any of the victims. Everyone was surprised to find out money was missing and the women were involved with anyone. I'll double-check with the medical examiner about the violence."

That had been the hallmark of the cases – the secrecy. Kate informed

Sam about their interaction with Sybil. "She's the best insight we have so far in understanding how this man operates. He seems agile. If one thing doesn't work, he'll change up his game. I think the most consistent thing is his focus on money and control. Do you know much about narcissistic abuse?"

"I know it's become quite the overplayed term on social media."

Kate agreed with that. "Julian has all the indicators of a real diagnosis. The love bombing at the start most specifically. He came on real strong with Sybil but didn't read her right. I believe he assumed because she was older than the other victims he might be more easily able to sway her. She's one tough cookie though and wasn't going to put up with anyone's crap. Her tenacity surprised me. She saw him for what he was right up front and stayed away from him."

"She was lucky," Sam said then saw the look on Kate's face. He cocked an eyebrow. "Not luck?"

"I don't think in this case I can consider it luck. She was uncomfortable almost immediately," Kate explained with a bit of force in her voice. "Let's start with the significant age gap. She wasn't interested right from the start. Then Julian tried being controlling, even went to her home and tried again. Once his façade as love bombing suitor didn't work, he dropped the façade and tried to get controlling with her. That didn't work either. It did raise an interesting point about the matchmaker's involvement. Declan asked Sybil if she thought the matchmaker might have been involved. She didn't deny the possibility."

"That's an interesting take," Sam said wide-eyed. "Do you think intentionally?"

Kate wasn't sure about that. "We know he's charming and good-looking. He has a credible backstory about being a model. He said that's where his money came from. But he doesn't fool everyone. There are people here who interacted with him who suspected he might be a fraud."

Sam went back to what he had asked about the murder. "Do you think the murders are domestic violence related then? Anger spills over to rage?"

Kate didn't think that either. She recounted what the medical examiner told her about the murder weapon. "I think they are planned. There's a practiced methodology to them. He's taking his time."

"What about the file on him that the matchmaker gave you?"

"Nothing," Kate said with disappointment. "There are junk personality tests that are easy enough to fake. There is his name and some information. No photo. I assume Nina has a photo of him, but she didn't share it with us. We'd have to get a warrant and I don't think we'd get that."

The door to the hotel room opened and Declan called her name.

Kate leaned into the screen. "We can talk more about this tomorrow. Declan's back from his run. Thanks for the advice about flying."

"Anytime, Kate. See you soon."

Sam disappeared from the screen as Kate closed down her laptop. She heard the shower start and the urge to be in Declan's arms was too much to resist. She got out of bed and stripped off her clothes, leaving them in a heap on the floor. She made her way to the bathroom to surprise him.

CHAPTER 14

Kate didn't take Sam's advice. She couldn't drink whiskey before the flight that early in the morning. She figured the alcohol would make her queasy. Instead, Kate settled into her seat, across the table from Declan, and shut her eyes. As the plane started its takeoff, one of the worst times for her anxiety, Kate shut out the images of catastrophe and replaced them with images from the night before after surprising Declan in the shower.

Sitting across from her on the flight, Declan seemed oblivious to the thoughts running through her mind. She finally opened her eyes when they hit cruising altitude and found him staring out the window.

She recalled part of their conversation from the previous evening as they lay in bed before going to sleep. Declan was concerned about Leo. He was meeting them in London and it would be the first time that Sam would be face-to-face with him in his new role. Leo had played a significant role in the case in Scotland, but Kate had been the one who had primary contact with him. Sam had conceded that arresting Leo, as he would have otherwise been tasked with doing, wouldn't have been in the best interest in catching the serial killer that had been terrorizing Edinburgh and all of Europe.

When the decision had been made that Leo would leave his role as the international art thief known as the Phantom and work for the FBI, Sam had to be informed. He was only one of two people outside of the FBI, other than the investigator who'd been involved in the case in Edinburgh, who'd been informed.

Given Leo had saved Kate's life twice, Sam had been all the more willing to get on board with the decision. The rest of the world believed the FBI had killed the Phantom and never released his real identity to the public. It was a plausible story that had not even garnered more than a few days of news then passed with no more questions. It went exactly how Spade said it would go.

Leo remained in the D.C. area for training while Kate and Declan went about their cases. Still, Declan had concerns about Sam. Knowing Leo was across the pond working for the FBI and having to work with him in any official capacity were two different things.

Kate understood where Declan's concern came from but she didn't think it would be an issue. She'd never known Sam to be anything other than professional.

Leo had a way of sneaking up on people and charming them.

The flight landed safely and they had a car waiting for them at the terminal. Declan had turned to her, commenting that Spade was rolling out the red carpet for them. Kate agreed, wondering why and what the catch might be. Normally, they flew commercial and had to rent a car on their own. She hoped Spade wasn't giving with one hand only to take something away with the other.

Night had already fallen over London and the rain was relentless. It was coming down so heavy, Kate was glad they had a skilled driver behind the wheel who both knew the roads and how to navigate the rain. It started a few minutes after they landed and had only grown in intensity on the drive from Heathrow to Greenwich where Sam had a home.

Kate yawned. "I hope I'm able to stay awake for this meeting." She checked her watch and it was close to nine. She regretted pushing for the meeting this late and probably should have settled for one first thing in the morning.

Declan leaned into her. "I'm sure it will be quick. What time was Leo getting in?"

"He was taking the train. I'm not sure what time."

"I hope we get there before he does."

Kate had been hoping the same. She should have asked Leo what time his train arrived. She assumed he would have texted her. Kate leaned back and closed her eyes, resting until the car pulled to a stop and the driver alerted them they had arrived.

The rain had not let up. The driver was kind enough to get out with an umbrella and open Kate's door. She slipped out of the back and directly into a deep puddle that soaked her shoes and pant leg past her ankle. The wind whipped her hair and rain soaked her face. Declan shouted over the rain for her to run to the house and he'd get her workbag from the trunk. Their luggage would remain in the car because the same driver would bring them to the hotel when the meeting ended.

Kate thanked the driver as he walked with her to the porch. Once she was under the cover of the overhang, she shook some of the rain from her and rang the bell.

A few moments later the door pulled open and Kate stood face to face with Leo. Her eyes flew open and she tilted her head back. "What are you doing here?"

"Come in out of the rain," Leo said, reaching down and pulling her inside. He stepped out of the way, tugging Kate with him so Declan would have room to enter. "I got here about two hours ago. I tried calling you but it went directly to voicemail. I left you a text too. Then I called Sam and he told me to come right over. We've been here playing chess. I helped Sam with some dinner for you both."

"I guess you're right. My fear wasn't warranted," Declan said as he shook the water free from his body, dripping water on Sam's floor.

He lowered his head and grimaced. "Sorry, Sam," he called. "Do you have some towels?"

Sam finally made an appearance. He walked to the foyer with a broad smile and a tea towel slung over his shoulder. He saw how wet they were and turned around, reappearing a few minutes later with towels for them. "Don't worry about the floors. Least of my worries. Leo was just giving me instructions on how to fix a leak in my kitchen." He slapped Leo on the back. "I'd say he's a brilliant addition to your team. He makes a mean sourdough too."

Kate caught the glint in Leo's eyes. She knew then he had arrived early on purpose to bond with Sam. He was doing his part to make sure everything went smoothly for them. As he smiled over at her, she nodded once, acknowledging that he did well. "What smells so good?"

"I made some beef stew," Sam said, gesturing over his shoulder. "I hope all of you eat meat. I don't remember either of you being vegetarian."

Declan confirmed neither was. "You're here making stew and homemade bread for us. I'd say this is about the best welcome to London I've ever had. Your weather on the other hand…" He chuckled slightly to himself.

As they filed into the kitchen, Leo pulled Kate aside. "My house is ready if you need to go undercover. I'm not so sure that's a good idea, Kate. Sam was telling me about this case and it seems to me that it's more than conning these women. I've known conmen in my day. I've had to use a few ruses. It's not out of the scope of my ability. This guy is something else."

It warmed Kate to know he cared that much. She leaned into him, allowing her shoulder to rest on his chest. "We made some significant progress in Los Angeles. I don't have a clear picture of this killer yet. I'm hoping going undercover won't be necessary."

"I know it's your job," Leo said, pausing trying to find the right word it seemed. "I just don't like the idea of you being in danger."

"I don't think you, Sam, or Declan would let anything happen to me. Don't worry." Even though Kate said the words, the worry line remained creased across his forehead. She changed the subject. "How's the art cataloging going? Making progress?"

"Some. The FBI team is still there. I know Spade didn't tell them my real identity, so they were skeptical about the story at first."

Leo had inherited the art after his stepfather's death. He had only recently discovered its real lineage. Spade had come up with a story as close to the truth as possible. Those were always the best lies, the ones rooted in logic and seemed plausible enough. They were always the hardest to catch.

Kate said, "If anyone is questioning you too much, tell Spade and he'll handle it. I'd call them but I don't know those guys well. I don't think they'd listen to me."

Leo smiled and shook his head. "Kate," he said slowly drawing out her name. "Everyone at the FBI knows you, and all of those guys are completely smitten with you. They talk about you all the time. Spade told them I was working with you and all they talk about is you when they aren't talking about art. I have to try not to laugh when they act like schoolboys crushing on the popular girl."

Kate felt the rush of warmth in her cheeks and she knew they must be pink. "Well if that's the case and you need me to show up and plead your case, let me know. I'd be happy to do it."

"I'll let you know if I need you. The last time you were there, I didn't want you to leave. You look good in my chateau." Leo put his hand on her back and guided her toward the kitchen. "Let's go eat. I'm starving."

Declan was helping Sam deliver the warm bowls of stew to the table. Everything looked so good. It was the perfect setting to start the case. As tired as she was, Kate was glad she had asked for the evening meeting. It was a more comfortable setting than if they had met at Sam's office the next morning. She was glad they were meeting casually and easing into the case.

As they sat down to eat, Sam asked, "What can I tell you about my cases?"

"When did you first discover they were connected?" Leo asked, then looked at Kate and Declan to make sure it was okay that he jumped in.

"Excellent question," Kate said, encouraging him. The more comfortable Leo felt working with them, the bigger asset he'd be. She had wanted to explore more about what he had told her in the hallway, about him using cons sometimes. She knew he had but his knowledge about what worked might be beneficial to know. He could more easily get into the mindset.

Sam tore off a piece of bread and popped it in his mouth. "It was the fifth case that was assigned to me. I didn't know about the others when I first started investigating. There was something about the way the crime scene seemed staged that struck me right away that something was off."

"Staged?" Declan asked.

Sam explained how the home had been cleaned, nothing was out of place. The victim, Georgina Baker, was found in bed on her back with the covers neatly pulled up to her chin. "When the housekeeper walked in the house that morning, she knew something was off. She said Georgina was never that clean. Then she went to the bedroom and thought Georgina was just sleeping. But she never slept that late. The housekeeper arrived every morning at nine and usually found Georgina out in the garden having her morning tea. Not that morning, she was asleep. Only once the housekeeper called her name and went to the side of the bed, she realized something was wrong. As she went to check Georgina's wrist, she pulled back the duvet and saw the dark red line across the woman's neck. The housekeeper knew then Georgina was dead. She told me she screamed, ran out of the home, and called for help."

Sam paused while he took a few spoonfuls of stew. "I knew right away that a scene staged like that might be an indication it wasn't the killer's first time. Once we dug into her financial records and I spoke with Georgina's family, I learned how secretive she had become in the last few months of her life and the millions missing from her accounts. Three million in all was completely unaccounted for. I knew then, this wasn't a typical murder investigation. I went searching for others, speaking to my colleagues, and I discovered other similar cases going back a few years. I broadened my search in Europe and came back with the case in Paris. That's when I contacted the FBI and asked for a search in your database with similar crime markers. They got back with the two in Los Angeles. It came together slowly over time, but we have the eight in all."

Leo tsked. "Over what amount of time were all the cases?"

"The first one seems to be Lottie Blyth in Los Angeles ten years ago," Kate explained and raised her eyes to Sam. "Your five cases followed, correct?"

"They did. At some point, he went to Paris then back to London," Sam explained. "I think he might have been conning two women at the same time, probably going back and forth from London to Paris because there were only two months between two of the murders. Then the last case back in Los Angeles."

Leo looked between Sam and Kate. "All of the cases similar?"

Sam nodded as he finished chewing. "From what I know of the Los Angeles cases they are. He gets involved with these women, takes them for millions, and kills them. There's a lot in the middle that we don't know." He hitched his chin toward Kate. "They did a fantastic job of finding out the victims met him through a matchmaker. What you don't know is that I connected with a matchmaker earlier this morning who believes she might know the man in question."

That sparked Kate's interest. "Has he used her services?"

"A few times."

"How long ago was this?"

"The most recent was a few months ago," Sam said evenly. They all knew what it meant – he was on the prowl for the next victim. "Eat up. The appointment with her is tomorrow morning at eleven. I scheduled it later to give you time to sleep off some of the jetlag. No point burning yourselves out when you just arrived. We have time."

Kate appreciated the scheduling, but they all knew time wasn't on their side.

CHAPTER 15

The next morning Kate opened her eyes to a flash of sunlight peeking through the drapes directly across from the bed. The smell of freshly brewed coffee coming from the living room told her Declan had been awake for a while. She reached for her phone on the bedside table. 8:23 a.m. She hadn't slept this late in a long time.

Kate pushed herself to a sitting position and wiped the sleep from her eyes. "Do I smell coffee?" she yelled as she swung her bare legs out of bed.

Declan stuck his hand through the open door of the bedroom. He was holding a large white cup of coffee with the logo and lettering of a coffee shop from the lobby of the hotel. "I figured I'd tempt you awake," he said as the rest of his body followed the cup. He walked over to the side of the bed and handed it to her. Declan was dressed in jeans and a tee-shirt. His dark hair was in messy waves. The stubble on his cheeks told Kate he hadn't done much that morning other than throw on clothes to get the coffee. "You slept like the dead. I woke up around four and leaned over to see if you were still breathing."

Kate swatted him away. "At least I wasn't snoring like you."

"You didn't hear me snoring. I'm telling you the whole hotel could have exploded and you wouldn't have known the difference."

Kate couldn't argue the point because he was correct. She was asleep before her head even hit the pillow. "Have you heard from anyone this morning?"

"Who would have called?" Declan sat on the edge of the bed.

"Sam, Leo, or Spade? I texted Spade when we checked into the hotel to let him know we had arrived and got some preliminary information. I didn't hear back."

Declan got up from the bed and walked out of the room, returning a moment later with his phone. His head was lowered to the screen as he read off the text. "Spade texted me in the wee hours of the morning. He had to rush to New York City. He didn't say why. He said good luck, but he's going to be unavailable." Declan looked up at her. "It seems we are on our own with this one."

Spade had disappeared like that before. He'd be gone from the office for a few days with no explanation. Not that Kate and Declan would be owed any explanation. Kate knew her place within the FBI unit that she had called home for most of her career.

They knew little about Spade's background. He had started in the military in Vietnam, he spent some time in the CIA and later the FBI. He'd been heading up the unit that took up the basement of the FBI building for as long as Kate knew him. He seemed to know everyone worth knowing in politics, government, law, and business. He held considerable power and sway over people. Kate had long ago stopped asking questions about him because she never received an answer. He'd return when he returned. At least this time one of them heard from him alerting them he'd be away. The last time Spade had gone with no explanation and no response to messages.

"I don't think we'll need him much on this case anyway." Kate sipped her coffee then set the cup down on the bedside table. She stretched her arms overhead. "Leo did well last night. Asked the right questions and did a good job of getting to know Sam. He told me he wanted a chance to do that before we arrived. When you and Sam were alone in the kitchen did he say anything?"

Declan sat back down on the bed next to her. "Sam said he liked Leo and that the FBI did a good thing bringing him on. I honestly thought we'd have some issues."

Kate hadn't thought so. She knew Sam better than Declan did and Leo could charm anyone. "Leo is concerned about this case. He said based on what Sam told him the guy isn't your average conman. I know we were starting to sense that in Los Angeles. I think we ought to sit down with Leo and get more information from him when we can. He might have a better understanding of the man than I do."

Declan didn't disagree with that. "We have more than when we started if it's the same man. How confident are you about that?"

That's what Kate had been thinking about most. They needed to go public with the information and photo if they could. "What do you think about reaching out to Ditch to see if he can clean up the video and get us a better photo for the media?"

Ditch – Kevin Detrick – was a member of their team. Much like Leo, Ditch had been plucked from a life of crime, hacking everyone and everything including the Russian government, and was brought onto the team by Spade. He worked off what would have been a lengthy prison sentence under Spade's watchful eye. They all knew he still freelanced. Spade kept an eye on it and gave him just enough leash to make it seem like Ditch was doing things under the radar.

No one got away with anything with Spade.

Kate watched Declan carefully – the two men hated each other. Declan would much rather do just about anything else other than deal with Ditch. "I'll call him and request his help. You won't even have to speak to him," she promised.

Declan didn't need that much convincing. It seems he had some thoughts of his own on Ditch's involvement. "I've been thinking about reaching out to him, too. Det. Longmuir has Andrea's laptop still in evidence. He never gave it back to her family."

Kate didn't understand. "It wasn't among the information he provided us. How do you know?"

"I texted him last night after you fell asleep," Declan admitted to Kate's surprise. "When Sam and I were alone in the kitchen, he mentioned he had someone go through the victims' phones and laptops for any information. There was communication but the numbers all went back to burners. Andrea's case file only mentioned her phone. I got curious about a computer and texted him. He never had it searched."

Kate had missed that in the file while focused on all the other evidence. "Did you request he send it to us?"

Declan shook his head. "Not yet. I told him to hold it and not do anything with it. I explained we had the best computer forensics available to us. Longmuir promised he'd send it to wherever we needed."

"Let's get Ditch involved then," Kate said, deciding for them. "I'll still call so you won't have to deal with him. I know he's your least favorite person."

Declan was about to say something but was interrupted by his cellphone ringing. It was Sam. He engaged the call and put it on speaker. "Kate and I are both here," Declan said after an initial greeting.

"There's been another body found," Sam said with a weariness in his voice. "I think we all knew this was going to happen. I was hoping we'd be much further along."

Kate sank back on the bed, her body deflating with the news. She had known it was coming. "Here in London?" she asked, fighting the desire to crawl back under the covers and hide.

Sam provided them with the basic details – a woman, aged fifty-three, widowed two years, found like the others strangled in her bed. Unlike the others, this woman had a daughter in her late twenties who found her mother this morning. She knew her mother was involved with someone and it had been a source of ongoing conflict for the past few months.

He added, "I think we might have finally hit on a case that could lend us a good deal of information. I'd like you to join me at the scene."

"Without question," Declan said not even needing to ask Kate. She was rushing from the bedroom to the bathroom. Declan heard the shower turn on and he focused back on Sam. "We'll be there. Give us about an hour and we'll meet you there."

"I'll text you the address so you have it. I'll call Leo, too."

When Kate and Declan arrived the entire street swarmed with police. Neighbors craned their necks to look as they stood in doorways and appeared in windows of the surrounding homes.

Fiona Payne lived in a three-story wide brick home on a corner lot on Cheyne Place. The windows were trimmed in white as was the arch around the black door. The property had a low brick wall around the perimeter with iron fencing atop and then a line of shrubbery. There was a small walkway, cut into a patch of grass on either side, leading to the front door.

Kate and Declan pushed open the iron gate that separated the property from the sidewalk and walked toward the home. They could hear Sam's voice before they even made it to the door. He was telling his team to hold off until the FBI arrived.

"We're here," Kate called as she stopped and pulled on gloves and booties. They entered the wide foyer that featured natural wood floors and a staircase that went to the upper floors. Kate shifted her focus from the right to the left. The ground floor, or what they'd call in the United States the first floor, was a reception room off to the right and a dining room off to the left. The kitchen was straight ahead.

Sam appeared in her line of sight and Kate moved past the staircase toward the kitchen. "Sam, what have you found so far?"

"Not a dish or item out of place."

Kate had noticed the home had a sterile feeling to it. The natural floors were light in color and all the walls were white. Long white wispy curtains hung from each rod covering the windows. There was strategically hung art but even that was mostly black and white photos. If she wasn't showing up at a crime scene, Kate might have assumed the house had been staged.

"Is the home always in this pristine condition?" Declan asked from behind Kate. He too had noticed that there wasn't a thing out of place. "I noticed in the front room off the foyer all the pillows were lined up perfectly as if someone had measured them."

"I asked Ophelia, who has been taken back to my office. She said her mother was always like this. It's one of the reasons she went away to college. She's been living in a flat with her friend ever since. She only came by this morning because her mother called her last night to tell her to get a box of her things from her old bedroom. If she didn't pick them up this morning by ten, they'd be thrown away." Sam gestured around the kitchen, which didn't have any dishes in the sink or glasses on the counter. "The rest of the home is similarly spotless."

The kitchen didn't look like it had ever been used. Even with Kate's recent renovation, her home looked lived in and she considered herself tidy. Kate took in her surroundings. There was a cutting board in the middle of the center island and a row of neatly arranged cookbooks next to an unplugged electric kettle. Other than that there was nothing on the countertops. On the far wall were cabinets with glass front doors which showed everything contained within. There were stacks of plates, cups, and other items. Nothing was out of place. Kate would never have glass cabinet doors. She'd never be able to maintain that level of precision in her stacking.

Declan pointed up. "Is she upstairs?"

"Second floor," Sam said and rephrased. "It would be the third floor for you. Let's just call it the top floor to avoid further confusion. The floor above us has three guest bedrooms, a large family room, and a reading room. Ophelia's suite is also on the next floor. Her bedroom and bath take up the back half of the home. Fiona's suite takes up the entire top floor."

Sam guided them back to the front of the house and up the staircase. They passed the middle floor and went straight to the top. There was a sitting area at the top of the landing with white cloth chairs with a wood table positioned between them. Kate assumed no one ever sat in them and they were only for show.

They went straight to the only door on the floor and Sam nudged it open. "My crime scene team hasn't started yet. That's who you heard me speaking to in the kitchen when you arrived. I've sent them out back to the garden to give us time to have a walkthrough."

"Leo arrive yet?" Kate asked, realizing then she hadn't seen him.

"I told him not to bother coming but to head to the matchmaker at the appointment time in case none of us can get there. I figured if we didn't keep the appointment she might not be willing to meet with us. It wasn't easy getting an appointment with her."

Kate didn't know if Leo was ready for a meeting on his own. Trial by fire would have to do today if she couldn't get there.

Sam guided them into the main sitting area of the suite and back to the bedroom. "Everything is white, even her bed sheets. There doesn't appear to be any signs of a struggle. Like the others she was found in bed with the sheets pulled up to her chin. Ophelia called and called for her mother and then found her up here deceased."

Kate winced at the thought of the young woman finding her mother that way. She let Sam and Declan lead the way into the bedroom part of the suite. She stood back at the doorway and surveyed the room. Fiona was on her back in the middle of the bed with her arms perfectly at her sides. Her hair was perfectly arranged in a halo around her head, her dark strands of hair making a sharp contrast to the white pillowcase.

"It's possible he's drugging them before he kills them," Sam started to say but Declan held his hand up for him to stop.

He took a few steps toward the body. Kate wasn't sure what he was seeing. He leaned over her, appraised the red angry line across her neck and then moved down to her arm and hand. He glanced back at Sam and Kate, lifting her arm slightly. "She fought him. Look at the breaks in her nails. There is no way a woman who lives in a house this pristine would allow her fingernails to look like this."

Kate had to take a few steps toward him to see. Fiona's fingernails were painted a deep red. The nails on the three middle fingers on her left were shredded, the polish pulled in jagged stripes and the nails torn and damaged. Not only had Fiona fought, but there had been some ferocity to it. It was only speculation on her part, but Kate wouldn't be surprised if there was bruising on her body from the struggle.

Fiona didn't go down without a fight.

CHAPTER 16

The young woman with bright pink hair, a gold hoop nose ring, and a tattoo sleeve of brightly colored wildflowers up her right arm sat at the table staring forward. She held a point on the wall opposite the table and didn't move her eyes from it. Her face registered the expressionless stare of someone in shock.

"Do you think she needs medical attention?" Sam asked.

Kate stood on the other side of the mirror watching the young woman in what normally would be the interrogation room. It was the only space available to interview her. Kate wanted the interview recorded and observed by Sam and Declan. They did not consider Ophelia a suspect by any means. She was the first witness who had interacted with the man. Kate needed to be able to extract every detail from her. The shock wouldn't help her memory or the interview process.

Kate had been standing there for at least fifteen minutes observing her. Sam's words cut the silence of the room. She turned back to him and repeated what he said. "I don't want her medicated or a psychiatrist digging around in her brain before we find out what we need to know. If we sedate her, she might come out of it foggy."

Some might say Kate was being cruel to a young woman who had only hours earlier found her mother murdered. Kate had to weigh overall public safety with the comfort of this young woman. In the long run, she'd be better served helping the FBI catch her mother's killer. Some might disagree with her. It was one of those times Kate knew she had to be tough and go against every one of her instincts to provide as much support and care for this young woman as possible. Ophelia had lost her father two years ago and now her mother. It was too much for anyone.

Kate threw her shoulders back. "Make sure we are recording. I might miss some details in the middle of the interview. We can't afford to miss anything."

Declan put a hand on her arm as she headed for the door. He leaned in as if he was going to say something, then thought better of it. His gaze connected with hers and every word of encouragement he might have said passed between them with a look.

Before leaving the room, Kate grabbed the small wicker basket filled with snacks and drinks. Sam had filled it to the brim with things Ophelia might like. She wasn't a suspect and there was no reason to treat her as such, even if they were reduced to the cold sterile interrogation room.

Kate knocked once on the door out of respect for the young woman and then pushed it open. "Hi, Ophelia," she said her tone soft. "I'm FBI Agent Kate Walsh and I need to ask you a few questions. I have some drinks and snacks if you want them. We thought you might be hungry or at the very least thirsty."

Ophelia barely moved other than raising her eyes to Kate. "You're American."

Kate put the basket down on the end of the table and nudged it across. She pulled out the chair and sat. "I am. We believe the man who killed your mom has done this to other women here in London and in Los Angeles. There is also a case connected in Paris. That's why it's so important that we talk."

The young woman blinked rapidly. "You think he's done this

before?"

"If it's the same man," Kate said and put her phone next to her on the table. She didn't want to show her the photo yet because she didn't want to do anything that could be construed as leading the witness. "I know this might seem like an idiotic question, but how are you feeling?"

Before she let Ophelia answer, she confided, "I know a lot of people might say they understand how you're feeling. They try but it's hard unless you lived through it. When I was your age, just twenty-two and about to graduate from college, both my parents were killed in Kenya during a terrorist bombing. My father worked at the embassy in Nairobi. The FBI showed up at my door one morning and told me. I'm an only child too, like you, so suddenly I went from having parents to being on my own. It took me a long time to feel like myself again. Losing them didn't feel real for a long time. I'd wake up in the morning and something would remind me and I'd feel the grief all over again."

"That's exactly how it feels," Ophelia said, finally fixing her gaze on Kate. "Did you really lose your parents or is that one of those things you say to connect with me?"

"I honestly lost my parents. I don't have any other family. My FBI partner has become the only real family I have." Kate paused knowing Declan and Sam were listening in and others might hear this recording. "Family doesn't have to be blood-related. You need to lean on your friends and other family now as much as you can. Do you feel strong enough to talk to me right now?"

Ophelia swallowed hard. "I'm not ready to talk about finding her."

"That's okay. That's not what I need to know. I know you spoke to someone about that already. I need to know about the lead-up to today. Tell me about your mother. What was she like?"

Ophelia closed her eyes. "We didn't get along all that well. We argued a lot, especially after my father died. Then even more when she started dating *that man*." Ophelia opened her eyes, tapped long pink fingernails on the table, and jutted her jaw to the side. "I hated him and it's why I moved out. My relationship with my mother only got worse when he was around. She couldn't see what I saw."

"What did you see?" Kate asked leaning into the young woman's anger. If she was angry, she was shaking off the shock and feeling real emotion. Kate could work with that.

Ophelia tipped her head back, looking right at Kate. "He was abusive and using her for money. He wasn't interested in my mother."

"How do you know that?"

"It was obvious in the way he treated her."

Kate needed her to back up a little bit and be specific. She didn't want Ophelia to lose the anger. But Kate needed real details. "What was his name and how long ago did they meet?"

"Julian Marlowe and they met about six months ago." As Kate started to ask where, Ophelia held up her hand to stop her. "After my father died, my mother said she'd never date again. She didn't for like a year, maybe a little longer. She got lonely, which I understand. I told her to date. I encouraged her to find someone. I was older and had friends and my own life. I felt guilty going out and doing things while she was always home. We might not have always gotten along, but I wanted her to be happy. She was sad all the time. My anger isn't that she was dating. I'm not one of those people who want their parents alone and unhappy. She was never going to replace my father. We both knew that. It didn't mean she couldn't be happy with someone else."

It showed a lot of maturity for such a young woman. It didn't answer Kate's question. "Do you know where she was meeting men?"

"Her friends. Out. Society lunches and her charity work."

"Do you know if she used a matchmaker? We saw that with other women."

Ophelia cracked a smile then. "My mother would never use a matchmaker. She was vibrant and outgoing. She met people easily. My father used to tease her that if anything ever happened to him there'd be a line at our front door of men who could take his place." Ophelia sighed, recalling the memory. "He wasn't wrong. In the days and weeks after, there were so many men milling about trying to help us. My mother sent them all away. She loved my father very much. That's why it was so hard when she met Julian, who was so different than my father that I didn't understand what was happening."

Kate asked her question again. "Do you know specifically where they met?"

"Oh," she said, realizing she never fully answered. "At Annabel's one evening about six months ago. She was there with her friends and there was Julian. I guess he waited until she was alone and then made his move. My mother said he was respectful and kind and immediately won her over."

Kate wasn't surprised to hear of Julian's charm. Six months ago would have also been right after Andrea was murdered in Los Angeles. "What is Annabel's?"

"It's one of the most exclusive social clubs in London," Ophelia explained. "It's located in Mayfair and my parents were members for a long time. I have no idea how they let in someone like Julian or how he paid the membership fee. You also have to be recommended to be a member and there is a waitlist. There's also a dress code. I heard Prince Andrew wasn't allowed to enter once because he had an open-neck shirt. It's that kind of place."

Kate hoped Sam heard that and would be working on getting them a contact there. "After your mother met Julian, how long before you met him?"

"That's the thing. He didn't want to meet me. He wanted my mother all to himself," Ophelia said with a wry smile. She cursed. "I was still living at home then. When he first came over, she asked me to go stay at a friend's house. I was angry, of course. I was being kicked out of my house, so she could have some random man over. She told me he didn't want to meet me."

Ophelia paused and Kate didn't push her. "That's probably not fair. My mother told me Julian said he wasn't *ready* to meet me. That went on though for about two months. It wasn't fair. Every time he came over, I had to leave the house. Eventually, I argued with her enough and one night refused to leave. That's when I met him. After that, I refused to go anywhere when he came over. I stayed home just to annoy him."

A slew of questions ran through Kate's head. "When they first met, do you know if she mentioned having a daughter?"

Ophelia shrugged. "I don't know what they talked about. Everyone at Annabel's knows me. I've been there with my mother. I don't ever remember seeing Julian there. If she didn't tell him, I'm sure someone did."

Kate wasn't sure why that was important. This was the first time Julian had targeted someone with a child at home. "How was he when you met him?"

"Dreadful," Ophelia scoffed. "He was a handsome man. No one could deny that, so I saw what my mother was attracted to. He told her he was in his early forties, forty-three to be exact. He was much older than that. Closer to my mother's age or he didn't take care of himself. But he seemed older to me, older than my mother even."

"What makes you think that?"

"I don't know. The vibe I got from him. The way he dressed. He seemed a bit out of touch with things the way my mother could be sometimes."

"Do you think it was an act? A way to connect with her?"

Ophelia's eyes got wide. "I hadn't thought of that. He did seem to shift his personality. When he was talking to me, he took a strict tone as if he'd replaced my father. He told me more than once, always out of earshot from my mother, that it was time for me to move out. That I needed to give her space and not be involved so much in her life. It's *my mother*. Not involved in her life? He was awful. Then when he was around her, he'd be sweet and kind. He'd speak to me differently too. He was two different people. It was unnerving."

Ophelia described several more instances of him trying to drive a wedge between them and succeeding. The relationship between Ophelia and Fiona had grown so tense that the young woman decided it would be best for everyone if she moved out. She knew it was giving Julian exactly what he wanted.

Kate assured her she did the right thing. "Do you know if she was giving him money?"

Ophelia nodded. "All the time. I have a trust she can't touch that my father left me. Once when I was back getting some clothes, I was upstairs and they didn't realize I was in the house. I heard him asking her for more than two-hundred thousand pounds. I was taken back by the request. He said it was the last time he'd ask her for money, so I knew right then she had already given him some. I didn't know how much then. My mother hesitated and he practically begged her for it. When she still didn't relent, that's when he turned into someone else. He started yelling at her, calling her names, and threatening her."

"Threatening?" Kate asked, interrupting. "Threatening how?"

"He told her he'd make up rumors about her and trash her reputation to everyone around London. She begged him not to. I had never heard my mother's voice sound so desperate. He had turned this fun, outgoing woman into a sniveling mess. I couldn't stand it. I shot down the stairs and confronted him. I lost my temper, screaming at him and telling him to get out." Her shoulders shook with rage. "I hate that I did it now. When I was done yelling at him and he left, I yelled at my mother. She had been begging me to stop screaming at him. I couldn't help it. I wasn't going to allow him to speak to her that way. She assured me she wouldn't give him the money and that he didn't speak to her like that all the time. She was defending him and it made me sick."

Kate could see the worry on her face even if her tone was pure anger. "What did you do after that?" she prompted.

"I know this might seem crazy, but I went to the bank. My mother put my name on her account after my father died in case something happened to her I'd be able to access the account. I couldn't make any decisions on the account, it was primarily hers. I had access if I needed it. I went to the bank manager, who knew my father well, and I told him I thought my mother was being exploited. He confided in me she had withdrawn more than a million pounds over the last few months and he was worried about her too. There was nothing he could do though. It was her money and she was in her right mind. It was her choice."

Her choice to a point, Kate wanted to say. "That was a brave decision. It sounds like you helped her as much as you could. Did you ever see any physical violence between them?"

"No. After that incident, I tried to stay away as much as possible. I'd like to say my mother would have never put up with that. Since she became involved with Julian, she was like a whole different person to me."

Kate reached for her phone to show her the photo and realized she had never asked Ophelia to describe Julian to her. The names might match but she needed to be sure the faces did too. "Can you tell me physically what Julian was like?"

"I can show you. I have photos and a video I took secretly," Ophelia said with pride.

Kate's mouth fell open slightly. This young woman was among the bravest she'd ever met. She hoped it was the answer to all of their prayers.

CHAPTER 17

"This is without question the best footage we have of him," Declan said with excitement after they had one of Sam's tech colleagues transfer Ophelia's photos and video from her phone to a laptop and then back it up on a drive and in the cloud. Kate wasn't taking any chances with it.

They were huddled around the laptop in a conference room. Kate sat right in front of the screen while Declan stood over her right shoulder and Sam her left. They both leaned down close enough that she could feel their breath on her neck. Declan wasn't wrong. Where the footage of the man in Los Angeles had been at a distance, grainy, and they could only see a few seconds of the man's face, this was entirely different.

The video that jumped to life was clear and crisp. Julian had no idea he was being recorded. As Ophelia had witnessed firsthand, Julian changed the tone and inflection in his voice in a matter of seconds. Even his body language shifted and contorted. There were moments it was like watching a few different people in one – like a one-man play where the actor took on various roles while never leaving the stage. It was incredible footage to watch. Terrifying but enlightening.

The photos were even clearer. Ophelia had bought a spy cam online and installed it in her mother's house without her ever being the wiser. The camera was inside a simple silver frame. Ophelia had slipped in a photo of Fiona and her on a trip to Berlin. She had given it to her mother as kind of a peace offering, even suggesting where to put it – a decorative stand with the perfect shot of the living room. Ophelia knew it was Fiona's favorite room in the home and the one where she'd seen Julian and Fiona interacting the most.

The camera battery could hold a charge for up to five days. It had been enough to get the footage. The camera sent the images to an app on Ophelia's phone. She had intended on going into the house and getting the frame to recharge the battery, but Ophelia explained she had never found the right opportunity.

When Kate asked why Ophelia felt the need to take such a drastic step, the young woman said she didn't know how or when the video would ever be needed, but she felt compelled to do it. She had been tech-savvy enough to take some still photos from the video shots and then enlarge them for better images of Julian.

Declan nudged Kate over then leaned over the laptop. He dropped three of the best images into a reverse photo search on the internet but it didn't come back with much. There was a slew of images of men who were similar looking but searching them all and trying to match them would take far too long.

"We have to go public with this," Kate finally said after it seemed they were at an impasse. "We both know he's moved on to another woman or is looking for a woman. I'm sure if we go public it might drive him underground. That's better than letting him kill someone again." Kate could feel Sam remove his hovering presence from her shoulder and stand up straight. She turned her head to look up at him, waiting for him to disagree with her. She knew Declan was already on board.

To her surprise, Sam said, "I'll call our public affairs department to set up a press conference. Do you have any media connections in the states we could use? I want to make sure if we are going public with this we get international exposure. We have no idea where he might have gone. My crime scene techs are still processing the evidence. I'm hoping we get some prints. We can run with the name Julian Marlowe and indicate we know it's an alias."

"Will you handle the press conference with Sam?" Kate asked Declan. "I don't want to go public in case I still end up needing to do something undercover."

"Of course." Declan had become the team's de facto public face. He rarely went undercover and had a strong commanding presence in front of the cameras.

Kate checked her watch. She had about thirty minutes to get to the matchmaker. Sam was still working on inroads to Annabel's. He was going to head over there and discuss it in person. He was hoping to get further than he had on the phone.

Kate pushed back from the table and stood. "If you both work on the press conference and work with the team to get the physical evidence, I'll meet Leo and the matchmaker. There's no point in all of us heading over there." She nudged Declan. "I know we said we weren't going to need Sharon on this case. If you feel like she might be able to help with the physical evidence, we can call her in."

Declan held up his phone. "Already talked to her. Spade has her on another case. She can consult with Sam's team though anytime we need."

Sharon Esposito from the FBI's Boston field office had been a recent addition to the team. They had been relying on local forensic teams. Declan had suggested bringing Sharon on to have the inside track and expert eyes on the evidence. Spade had approved it and Kate had been happy with the decision. It rounded the team out nicely.

Declan glanced over at Sam. "I think Kate's plan works if it's fine for you."

"Fine with me." Sam texted Kate the information about the

matchmaker. He left her with only one warning, with a hint of a smile. "Declan told me you had some tension with the matchmaker in Los Angeles. The woman I'm connecting you with might be even worse. She is the premiere matchmaker in London for the rich and famous. If he's seeking out wealth, that's who he'd see. She goes by Madame Rue and she's particular about who she sees and the clients she takes on."

Kate didn't relish meeting another one of them. "Madame Rue sounds like an actual madam's name or a high-end dominatrix. Have you met her?"

Declan stifled a laugh.

"No," Sam said, trying not to smile. "It's her name. That's all I can tell you. People swear by her, but she's difficult. Try to be on your best behavior."

Kate rolled her eyes. "I'll do my best." She wasn't sure why she was so cranky at the idea of women like Madame Rue and Nina Laurent in Los Angeles. Whenever she was around women like that, the few insecurities Kate had bubbled up. She felt distinctly dowdy in their presence and as if she were constantly being judged for it. Nina's interaction with her had only confirmed Kate's worst fear about women like that.

Kate reminded herself that she'd have Leo with her for the meeting. She texted him that she was on her way. He responded almost immediately that he was relieved.

Kate's driver delivered her to the matchmaker's office twenty minutes later. London traffic had been a little heavier than she had anticipated. She stopped at the entrance to the three-story brick structure in Notting Hill. It had been a long time since she'd been to this part of London. She had gone shopping with her mother in Portobello Market on a family trip when she was in high school. Kate couldn't recall if she'd been back since then. Her job didn't afford her much time to travel outside of work trips. Then it was usually seeing the worst of humanity. It left a weird stain on certain locations for her. Kate often wished she could see the world without the lens of crime over it.

The matchmaker's office sat above a small coffee shop on the ground floor with another office in the middle. When Kate reached the top floor, she had expected a doorway into the office but the space had been left wide open. A young woman sat at a desk amid couches and chairs and a coffee table with a neat stack of magazines. The office was quiet except for Leo's voice which echoed through the hall.

Kate informed the young woman she had a meeting with Madame Rue. "From the sounds of it, my colleague is already with her."

The young woman's neutral expression turned into a wide smile, making her blue eyes twinkle. "Yes, Leo is already back there with her. He's a charming one," she said with a wink.

Leo. Kate didn't realize he was on a first name basis with them. As she followed the young woman down a short hall, Kate wished she had taken the time to look at the website and learn a little more about Madame Rue, at least get a photo of her. She was walking into the meeting blind.

At the doorway, Kate paused for a moment as she assessed the scene in front of her. Leo sat casually with his legs crossed, leaning back in a chair. The woman across the table didn't take her gaze off him. She seemed entranced by Leo's presence. He was regaling her with stories of his art dealing. Kate hoped he was sharing his legitimate work.

She knocked once on the open door. "Madame Rue," Kate said as she entered with her hand extended.

The woman, who appeared to be in her fifties, had a face full of heavy makeup, rings on her fingers, and her dark hair twisted up in a stylish topknot with a red and gold scarf tied around it and knotted at the nape of her neck. The remaining silk flowed over her shoulder and provided a contrast to her gold blouse.

Madame Rue didn't stand but offered her slender hand to Kate and shook it. "Your colleague has been keeping me entertained until you arrived. He's lovely and so charming. I can see how a criminal might confess all of their crimes to him in a matter of moments, especially if you have a woman suspect."

Kate didn't correct her that Leo had never interrogated anyone in his capacity with the FBI. She sat down next to him. "Leo is quite skilled at what he does." She meant that wholeheartedly. He had warmed up Madame Rue for her. "As Leo might have told you, we want to discuss someone who might be in your database."

"Yes that was the message that was left for me about scheduling this meeting," Madame Rue said as she clasped her hands together on the table. "I must say this isn't something I normally do. I told Leo that when he arrived." She smiled at him and batted her long dark eyelashes at him. "He convinced me that it might save someone's life."

Kate had seen women have this reaction to Declan. Now with Leo, too. She tried to suppress her smile at how easily this woman had been won over. Kate got right to the point. "A man named Julian Marlowe is suspected of killing a woman by the name of Fiona Payne. This is only the most recent murder. There were eight before it. I know that Julian did not meet Fiona through your agency, but he used a matchmaker in Los Angeles. We thought he might be doing the same in London." Kate pulled out her phone and scrolled to one of the newer photos of Julian. She turned it around for Madame Rue to see.

As soon as the woman leaned down to look at the photo, she gasped and her hand went to her throat. Madame Rue raised her eyes, filled with fear, to Kate. "You think this man killed someone?"

"Not just one woman. We believe he's responsible for several deaths here in London, Paris, and Los Angeles. We have confirmation that he's had relationships with the women, took copious amounts of money from them, and they ended up dead."

"Oh my," she said with her eyes wide. "Yes. Yes, I have him in my database. I've had him in the database for a long time. I had no idea." She got up from the table scurrying to her desk. She yanked out the chair and plopped down giving Kate and Leo information about how long she'd known the man, eight years, and how she had met him at a social club in London, different from the one where Fiona met him. "He weaves an excellent story about his pedigree."

"What is that?" Kate asked, eager to hear anything this woman was willing to share.

Madame Rue held her finger up to ask Kate to wait. She clicked the keys on her computer. Her face grew visibly pale as if all the heavy makeup had suddenly been wiped clean. "He's going on a date tonight." She raised her head again to look at Kate. "I saw him about a week ago at a mixer I held. He was there meeting people, charming and affable as I'd known him to be. He said he'd only just arrived back in London after a trip to South America and he was eager to find a relationship. He expressed a real desire to settle down and meet a quality woman."

Kate's stomach lurched and her throat tightened. He was about to meet his next victim. "I need all the details of that date."

Madame Rue rushed from behind her desk to the door. "Natalie! Natalie! Get in here please."

A moment later, a woman with shoulder length dark hair, pouty red lips, and heavy dark eye makeup presented herself in the doorway. Kate would have put her age in her late forties.

"Yes, can I help you with something?" she asked in a clipped British accent.

Madame Rue made quick introductions and watched as Natalie's eyes grew wide at the mention of the FBI. "We need to know where

Julian is going on his date tonight."

"Julian?" Natalie asked, his name coming out in a question. "Why would that matter?"

"I don't have time to discuss it," Madame Rue said with force. "Where is he going?"

"I don't know. He didn't tell me and neither did the client. You know we don't always track that."

"Go. You're useless to me," Madame Rue said with a dismissive hand gesture. She turned to Kate and Leo. "What do we do?"

"Call your client and find out where they are going," Leo commanded and then turned to Kate, apologizing for possibly overstepping.

"It's fine," Kate assured him. To Madame Rue, she added, "Leo is right. Are you able to call your client and find out where they are going without alerting her to why? If she cancels on him, we might never catch him. If we can get her name and the name of the restaurant, we can keep her safe." As the words left her mouth, Kate sucked in a sharp breath.

The press conference.

If his photo and name were put out to the media now, surely he wouldn't show.

Kate jumped from the table, punching buttons on her phone as she headed into the hall. "Don't go to the press!" she shouted into her phone when Declan answered. "We need to stop the press conference!"

"It's already in motion, Kate," Declan said, trying to slow her down. "What's going on?"

"We have a lead. He's going out with a woman tonight." Kate's breath came out in short choppy bursts. "Please, cancel it. Do whatever you have to do. We cannot go public with his information yet."

"Consider it done," Declan assured her and ended the call.

Kate slumped against the wall, catching her breath and collecting herself before continuing the interview with Madame Rue. Out of the corner of her eye, she noticed Natalie watching her.

"Are you okay?" she asked Kate.

Kate held her hand up. "I'm fine. Thank you. We have it handled."

Natalie offered her a curt nod and headed down the hall out of view.

CHAPTER 18

At eight that evening, Kate, draped in a long dress made of soft silk in the perfect shade of emerald with gathered bows and high neckline, walked on gold stilettos on Leo's arm into Café Mélodie. The two Michelin-starred opened 1967, and at the time, was the only French restaurant of its kind in London. One of its claims to fame, other than the excellent Haute-French cuisine, was having trained some of the world's finest chefs.

After Kate confirmed with Madame Rue's client, Elise Brauning, where she was meeting Julian and assuring her no harm would come to her, they formulated a plan. It would require Elise to go through with the dinner as planned. She had resisted at first, asking Kate to send someone as a proxy. That was impossible given she had met Julian at an event and they had been communicating since. Kate knew it was a big ask for the woman.

It was Sam who did the hard work of convincing her that she didn't have to do anything more than sit at the table and have a conversation with him like she'd been planning to do anyway. She didn't have to leave the restaurant with him. The goal was to get eyes on him and Sam planned an arrest right in the middle of their dinner.

All Elise had to do was keep her date.

Kate knew no matter how many times they said it to Elise, it wasn't that simple. They were asking her to communicate and come face to face with a conman and a killer. Elise worried about implications about setting him up. Kate assured her he'd never know. Once they had a plan in place, figuring out the rest of the plan for law enforcement had been another task.

Madame Rue would not hear of Kate running to a shop and trying to find an appropriate dress. She insisted on calling her clothing and hair stylists and makeup artist to prepare Kate for the evening. The result of all the help was nothing short of miraculous.

It had been a long time since Kate had worn such a dress and heels. Her hair had been blown out in soft waves around her face, rather than the ponytail she preferred most days. Her face had gone from pale and minimal to a work of art – that's what Leo had called her right after Declan checked her inner thigh to make sure her gun strap was secured. He did lean in to kiss her quickly and whisper to her how beautiful she looked. Kate didn't necessarily care about the compliments.

She allowed herself a few minutes of feeling feminine and lovely before leaving for the restaurant, knowing she had a gun strapped to her thigh and another in her clutch. She hoped she wouldn't have to use either. It was bad enough firing at a suspect in the United States. It was entirely another in the United Kingdom where they had to get a special waiver to even carry their weapon. Most law enforcement didn't.

Sam had asked Kate before leaving what she thought of Julian – would he fight in the restaurant, take Elise hostage, or maybe flee. Kate thought that if Julian suspected law enforcement was onto him, he'd flee. She couldn't imagine him fighting it out in the restaurant or taking Elise hostage, even though clearly he'd shown such a propensity for violence. Kate worried he might not show at all.

She had helped Elise craft the text to Julian to confirm their meeting. He had responded quickly, even asking her if she was sure he couldn't pick her up for the evening instead of meeting her there. Elise had already told him she needed to meet him. She didn't want any man on a first date knowing where she lived. It was smart and made their plan easier.

While Kate was working with Madame Rue to get ready for the evening, Leo had shown up in a navy suit that looked like it had been custom fitted. He had a crisp white shirt under the jacket and a lighter blue checkered pocket square. Kate shouldn't have been surprised that Leo had a suit on hand, something he said he always traveled with should the need arise.

He told Kate later, out of earshot of Madame Rue, that old habits die hard. Sometimes before an art heist he'd need to rub elbows with the wealthy art owner. He was no stranger to high-end exclusive clubs, restaurants, and parties. Kate knew much like the conman they were after, Leo could be a bit of a chameleon himself. He had even shaved his beard and put on a woodsy-smelling cologne. He strode in like a man with money accustomed to fine dining and having a woman like Kate on his arm. No one would have ever guessed his background or that he was working for the FBI. He looked so far from law enforcement most days. Tonight was no exception.

Declan and Sam would be outside with the rest of the law enforcement waiting to make the arrest or chase Julian down if he fled. No one notified the restaurant. Sam was sure any hint that law enforcement was going to disturb their guests and the whole lot of them would be banned from the place. Sam had joked that even in arresting criminals, the British had a bit more refinement than the Americans.

With Kate's arm slipped into Leo's as they navigated through the evenly spaced tables, she noticed a few heads turning to look at them. Kate held her head high, chin up, and her eyes focused on the room, looking for Elise. Because they didn't alert the restaurant, they didn't have a choice of table, so they'd have to make do with wherever they were seated. If it was too far off or they couldn't get a good look, Leo would ask for another table. They had to find Elise first.

"I don't see her," Leo said quietly as he leaned into her. He tightened his grip on Kate's arm.

She barely registered what he said as she scanned the room for Elise. Her heart rate went up a few beats when she didn't immediately spot the woman. Kate's eyes darted back and forth taking in the couples sitting at tables, a party of four sitting in a green velvet booth, one of the few in the dining room. Kate desperately searched for her while trying not to draw attention to her rising panic. Elise couldn't stand them up.

Kate was about to ask the man walking them to their table if he had seated a single woman when out of the corner of her eye she spotted Elise at a far table at the other side of the room. The woman sat at the two-seater table with her back rigid as her hands were folded on the edge of the table. She was squeezing her fingers so tightly all the blood had drained from them. They were a shade paler than the rest of her hands and wrists.

"Calm down," Kate said in a hushed whisper barely audible to herself.

Kate leaned into Leo and turned her head in Elise's direction. "Sweetie, don't we know that woman over there in the table against the wall?"

Leo finally saw what Kate had seen. "I believe we do. She was at that art showing last week."

They were seated at the table, Leo pulling Kate's chair out for her and pushing it in as she sat. They were handed menus and as the man who had walked them to their table disappeared, a sommelier replaced him to tell them about the wine. Leo and the man had a quick conversation, the particulars going over Kate's head. She wasn't much of a drinker and she'd never been schooled the way some had about wine. She had also never taken an interest in the subject. It seemed what Declan knew about whiskey, Leo knew about wine.

Leo ordered for them and the sommelier seemed pleased with his choice. "I hope that was okay for you," he said as the man walked away, leaving them alone for the first time since entering the restaurant.

Kate smiled above her menu. "There are few subjects I know less about than wine. I'm sure whatever you ordered us will be perfect, not that we can do more than sip."

"Of course." Leo read a few of the menu items aloud and then leaned into the table. "Can you read the French or do you need translation?"

Kate knew he was teasing her. "I think I can manage." She couldn't manage. She didn't know what half of the things said, but she could guess based on the few words she knew. Kate zeroed in on the menu items she thought she knew and made a wild guess. When she selected what she wanted she lowered her menu and told Leo her selection. "I'm going to let you order. I refuse to butcher the language."

There was a glint in Leo's eyes as he spoke. "It's so American of you that you only know English. Did you ever take another language in school? I thought that was required."

"It is and I did," Kate said. "I took French from sixth grade through high school and then never used it conversationally. It never stuck with me. I might have a concentration in forensic linguistics but only in English. I have about as much of a head for languages as I do for wine. Normally, I can detect the accent and identify the country, sometimes even the region of the country. Yours stumped me."

"On the rooftop in Paris." Leo relaxed back in the chair. "I do apologize for taking you hostage that day."

"No need to apologize," Kate said absently as she fixed her gaze over Leo's shoulder to Elise. Kate had assured her she and Leo would be there far before Julian arrived. Elise didn't seem any more relaxed than she had been when Kate first spotted her. She wished she could text and reassure her.

Kate refocused back on Leo. "You've apologized a lot for that. You also explained you took me hostage to save my life. It's water under the bridge. I was stumped for a long time about your accent though. Knowing you grew up in Bulgaria then France and came to London while you were still young explains so much."

They talked about their first meeting in Paris while they waited. Leo didn't have any line of sight. "Is he here yet?"

"No," Kate said, starting to worry that something had spooked him and he wouldn't show. She expressed that to Declan. "He might also be intentionally making her wait, upping the anticipation and getting her emotionally on edge. Narcissists like to purposefully toy with people's emotions. Letting them feel high and then crashing them down again. They make it a real rollercoaster. It's too early for him to be doing that to her. He should still be in the love bombing stage where he's acting like he's falling madly in love with her."

"Do women fall for that, Kate?"

Kate smiled over at him. "Do women fall for a charming man who comes on strong, consistent communication, and tells her how she's the best thing that ever happened to him? Do they swoon for a man who says he's been waiting his whole life to find someone like her? That he's falling head over heels and can't believe his luck?"

"When you put it like that," he said with a chuckle. "Would you fall for someone like that?"

"No," Kate responded. "I don't trust anyone who likes me too much. I never have. I'm immediately suspicious."

"Why?" Leo didn't hide the surprise on his face or in his voice. "You must know how rare and wonderful a woman you are, Kate."

"I'm suspicious." Kate thought he had been kidding. Then she noted the worry in his eyes. "I don't have low self-esteem if that's what you're thinking. I've been studying crime since college. I was an early reader of true crime books. I put up a healthy wall until I know it's safe. If someone comes on too strong, I get worried."

Leo watched her carefully then conceded. "I can understand that. Women have to be careful of the men they bring into their lives."

Kate was about to tell him that men needed to be careful too. She never got out the words because a man approached Elise's table and rested his hands on the back of the second chair without pulling it out. He bent at the waist and leaned forward to speak to her. Kate couldn't hear what he was saying and she wasn't able to read his lips. She had no idea what he was telling her. She assessed his height and body composition and quickly surmised this was not the conman they were after. He was shorter and pudgier than the man in question. He wasn't wearing a uniform from the restaurant so Kate didn't believe he was staff.

After a moment of discussion, Elise turned her head to Kate. She had the look of a deer caught in headlights. She raised a thin finger and pointed toward her and Leo. The man turned his head and locked his gaze on Kate.

She inched toward the edge of her seat, anticipating what might follow. The man didn't do anything other than stand back up to his full height and walk slowly over to them.

"A man is coming," Kate said to Leo as she reached for her handbag. "It's not the man we are after." She fixed a look on him as he crossed the room. Kate willed her heartbeat to slow as she took longer breaths to calm her nerves.

They had not been anticipating a confrontation right in the middle of the restaurant.

Leo had his hands on the tabletop ready to push himself up and confront him. Kate would let him if it came to that. "What do you want me to do?" he asked, the tension in his body reflected in his voice.

"Nothing yet."

Kate raised her eyebrows in a question as the man approached. "Can I help you?" she asked the man, forcing herself to sound casual – a betrayal of how she was feeling.

"You're FBI Agent Kate Walsh," the man said in a crisp British accent. It was a statement, not a question. "I have a note for you."

"Who are you?"

"I'm sorry," he said with a smile. "I own a jewelry shop down the road. A man came into my store as I was closing up for the evening and told me it was imperative I give this note to Agent Kate Walsh and that she'd be here having dinner." He pointed across the restaurant at Elise. "He showed me a photo of that woman over there. I was rather confused when she told me she was not Kate Walsh."

"Do you have the note?" Kate asked, her anxiety not subsiding. People in the restaurant were slowly starting to look in their direction. "I'm going to need to speak to you outside."

"The man told me you'd need to. I don't want any trouble. I don't even know his name. I tried to ask why he wasn't delivering the note himself but he left my shop before I could ask."

Kate didn't want to do this at the table. She also didn't want to leave Elise alone in the restaurant. She was watching them carefully. "Leo, sit here and watch Elise for me while I go outside."

"Are you sure, Kate?"

Slowly she nodded. "It's okay," she assured him as she stood. To the man, she said, "Let's take a walk. You can give me the note outside."

All eyes were on them as they weaved their way through the tables as they headed for the door. Kate could only hope once on the street, Sam and Declan would see her and provide backup if needed.

CHAPTER 19

Once they got to the street, Kate shivered as the cool evening air danced across the bare flesh of her arms. "Do you have the note?" she asked with her hand extended.

He handed it over and noted the concern on her face. "I'm not here to hurt you. I swear to you I don't know what's going on. When I heard this was an important message for the FBI, I didn't know what to think. I could stand in my shop and call the police, but that might take too much time. I figured it was best to find you." He pointed up the road. "My shop is right up there. The lights are still on."

Kate wasn't going to turn to look. She held her clutch tightly with the gun inside as she grew acutely aware of the one strapped to her leg. It didn't matter what this man said, she didn't trust him. "There are law enforcement all around. You can't see them but they are there. Tell me about the man."

The jewelry store owner described a man fitting Julian. "He had a cap pulled low on his head. It was hard to get a good look at his face. He was British but it almost sounded like he was trying to pretend to be French."

She unfolded the paper on one side then the other until it was a full sheet. Scrawled across the center of the page, slightly crooked and in cursive it read:

You can search far and wide and you'll still never find us. We are watching you.

Kate's head snapped up as she scanned the area around them. She couldn't help but wonder if Julian was lurking in the shadows watching the scene that he had set up play out.

But it was more than Julian. He had said *us* and *we.*

Kate didn't have time to process it before the man asked, "Are you okay?" His face twisted in concern.

Kate refocused her attention. "Do you have surveillance video in your shop?"

"Of course."

"We'll need to see that. Did the man say anything else to you?"

"He came into my shop and I told him I was closing up. He approached the counter and handed me the note, telling me that I needed to give this to FBI Agent Kate Walsh. That she'd be sitting alone in Café Mélodie. He said I must hurry because the message was important and that you needed to receive it. Before I could ask him anything, he darted out of the shop. I didn't know what to do, so I delivered the note and here we are." It was clear he had more questions but had the sense not to ask them.

Kate reached for her phone and sent a quick text to Declan. She waited there on the street with the man until he and Sam showed up. Sam left with the jewelry store owner back to the shop.

Once they were gone, Kate surveyed the street and told Declan about the message. "He knew what we were doing, Declan. He knew we were here and that the dinner with Elise was a setup. I don't know how he could know. We spent most of the day with Madame Rue and she seemed genuinely horrified that she might have been setting her clients up with a killer. I don't think she told him. I don't know how he could have known."

Kate knew she was spiraling as the words came spilling out of her. She was trying to piece together how it could be possible that Julian would know what they were doing.

Declan didn't have any answer for her. "We need to regroup," was all that he could manage to say. "It sounds like he's not working alone. We need to figure that out."

Kate looked back at the restaurant. They didn't have time to figure that out. "We need to go public right now with Julian's photo and information." When she noted the look of concern on Declan's face, she pushed harder. "He's out there right now. I don't know what the note means. Maybe he's trying to trick us. He could be talking about his different personalities or he might be working with people. We don't know. But we do know what he looks like. The London police have his photo. I know they are watching out for him. Somehow he managed to walk through the streets into a jewelry shop and hand the owner a note that was then delivered to me. He also managed to slip away without anyone seeing him." Kate stepped off the sidewalk into the road, careful of the traffic. She looked down the street. She counted seven buildings between where she stood and the shop. "How did all of you miss him?"

"We were focused on the restaurant, Kate. We were expecting him to come through the front door. We have cops stationed around the neighborhood in case he ran. They are in unmarked cars. When Sam gets the video surveillance and sees what he's wearing, we can notify everyone. One of the cops might have seen him on the street but not recognized him."

Kate nodded as she scanned the street. She was listening to Declan but couldn't shake the feeling he was out there watching them right now. She glanced up to the upper floors of the buildings wondering if he lived in one of them. She imagined him standing in the dark, peering between curtains at the street below. "He's close. I can feel it."

Declan put his hand on her arm. "What do you want to do? Do you want me to call all the officers and canvass this entire area? We can go through the buildings one by one."

Kate knew he was being genuine with the suggestion. If she thought it would do any good and wouldn't be a complete waste of resources, she'd take him up on the offer. "I don't think that's going to help. We have no reason to search inside any of these buildings. All he has to do is just not answer the door."

"Why don't you go back inside with Leo and let Elise know he isn't coming? Then we can meet back at Sam's office to regroup." Declan gestured down the road. "I can work with Sam and get the media out for a news conference. I agree the sooner we get the information out the better. I just don't know if this late hour is the best time to do it."

Kate didn't know if it was either. "I don't want to delay any longer. He knows the FBI is on to him. Make sure the news goes international. I don't think he's going to stay in London for long. Elise was probably his next mark and he knows we will catch him if he stays."

"It's progress," Declan said before making sure she got back into the restaurant safely. Kate waited at the door and watched him walk off down the street.

Kate pushed through the restaurant, her heart racing. Leo sat at a table, two untouched meals in front of him. Her mind raced as she headed straight for Elise. "Has he texted you?" she demanded, taking a seat with a sharpness that caught the woman off guard.

"He called a few minutes ago. I didn't answer," Elise replied, her hands trembling as she fished her phone from her lap. "Then he texted." She thrust the device toward Kate, her voice dropping to a whisper. "Like I said I was concerned about him knowing I helped the police. He said he forgives me… and that he's going to eliminate the threat."

Kate's stomach churned as she read the message. Each word felt like a countdown. "Leo!" she barked, her voice slicing through the restaurant's murmur. Heads turned and a few patrons shot her disapproving glares. Ignoring them, she pressed the phone back into Elise's shaking hands. "I'll have someone escort you home. I'll follow up with you tomorrow."

The dress that had felt so empowering earlier now clung to her like a vice. She wanted to rip it off. Adrenaline surged as Kate dashed back to Leo, who was working to convince the waiter to bring the check. "This is a criminal investigation," she snapped, flashing her badge from her purse at the bewildered waiter. "We'll settle up later."

Without waiting for a response, she pulled Leo to his feet, urgency propelling her forward. As they burst onto the street, she collided with Declan. "He's going after Madame Rue," Kate gasped, the words spilling out in a rush. "We need to get there now!"

Declan's eyes widened, the gravity of the situation sinking in. He didn't hesitate.

Standing at the front of Madame Rue's shop, Kate felt a knot of anxiety twist in her stomach. The street was silent, but a single light glowed in the woman's office, hinting she might still be working. The door stood locked and unyielding.

They had alerted Sam, who was frantically trying to track down Madame Rue's home address, to dispatch another team there. Kate, Declan, and Leo were committed to checking the office first.

Declan stepped back, squinting at the office window. "What's the plan? She didn't answer the phone. We don't know that she's really here."

"We're going in," Kate said, stepping back and squaring her shoulder to the door. Before she could act, Leo grabbed her arm and Declan's voice rang out.

"Stop, Kate!"

"I'll handle it," Declan said, but Leo interrupted.

"Let me," he said, sliding past them, pulling lock-picking tools from his pocket. "Old habits die hard," he muttered as he hunched over the door.

Declan opened his mouth to protest, but Kate raised a hand, silencing him. "Later," she mouthed, unwilling to waste time questioning Leo when he could be their literal key to success.

In mere seconds, Leo had the door unlocked. He stepped back with a triumphant smirk. "Well, go on," he said, gesturing for them to enter.

Declan bolted ahead, and Leo took up the rear, each step echoing ominously in the silence. With every step, Kate's pulse quickened. As they reached the landing, Declan surged forward without hesitation.

Kate chased after him, her breath loud in the stillness of the office. She scanned the room, but everything appeared unnervingly intact – cleaned desk, emptied wastebasket, chairs neatly pushed in, magazines stacked with precision. No signs of struggle.

"She's in here!" Declan shouted from inside Madame Rue's office. "She's alive – barely. Call for help!"

Kate sprinted down the hall, dread pooling in her stomach. She skidded to a halt as she entered the office, where Declan knelt over a badly injured Madame Rue. Blood seeped from a deep stab wound in her abdomen, soaking through her blouse and pooling on the floor.

Kate dialed emergency services, her voice steady but urgent as she relayed the situation. "Is she still breathing?" she barked at Declan.

"Shallow breaths," he replied, panic creeping into his tone. "She's been stabbed. No weapon in sight." He applied pressure to the wound, his hands slick with blood, whispering reassurances to Madame Rue, who lay pale and unresponsive.

"You have to hurry!" Kate urged the emergency services operator, her heart racing.

Minutes ticked by slowly as they waited. Leo stood in the doorway watching Declan try to keep Madame Rue alive and Kate relayed the information on the phone. She caught Leo's eye. "Search around the office to see if anything seems out of place." She needed to give him a job to stop him from hovering. The impatience grew inside of her. Kate knew exactly what he was feeling – a powerlessness she knew too well from previous similar situations.

Finally, the wail of the ambulance echoed around the quiet neighborhood. Leo rushed past the office door again, letting Kate know he'd let them in. She ended the call and stood above Declan, reaching down and touching the top of his head. "How's she doing?"

"Still alive. I don't know how. She's lost a lot of blood."

Madame Rue was a fighter. It's why she would have expected the office to be in more disarray. Now that she was off the phone and could focus on her surroundings, Kate realized nothing in there was out of place either. The woman's laptop remained open on her desk, files stacked neatly on the side, a purple pen laid on top of a tablet of paper.

Kate stepped around Declan and went straight to the desk. The first page was blank but the lines of writing had bled through from the previous page. Madame Rue had a heavy hand in her penmanship or she'd been writing with an emotion that lent itself to force.

Kate peered down at it, trying to decipher the words. She looked for a pencil to try the old trick of shading it in. There was nothing but pens on the desktop.

Kate pulled the chair out, knocking a wastebin to the side as the chair slid toward her. She reached down for it and set it on top of the desk. On top of the rest of the garbage lay a crumpled sheet of paper. Kate took it from the bin, straightening it out on top of the desk.

She leaned over, noting Madame Rue had been mid-word when she stopped writing. Kate couldn't make sense of the words on the page. Three countries were listed at the top – Germany, France, and Scotland. Two men's names after that – Nolan Cook and Rohan Bakshi. The final list was a list of what appeared to be dating websites and apps.

At the bottom was a word or more correctly the start of a word. *Syn.* She had written the start of the word but it diverted to a sharp line down the rest of the page as if she'd been startled.

Kate's eyes were transfixed as the paramedics rushed in. She heard them, a din of shouts and rushing voices, but she couldn't take her eyes off the page. None of it made sense to her. She went through a carousel of words starting with *Syn.* There were too many to consider.

Kate remained behind the desk as the paramedics went to work on Madame Rue. Even with the flurry of activity, Kate's focus remained on the page.

As Declan helped get Madame Rue on the stretcher and the paramedics led her away, Kate stepped back from the desk, the paper still in hand. "I think she knew something, Declan. More than she'd let on to us."

Through sharp breaths, Declan turned to her. "You think this was about more than Elise?"

The sinking feeling in Kate's gut grew. When she coupled what Rue was writing on the notepad with the note from Julian, there was only one conclusion she could draw. "A lot more."

As if waking back up from the haze she'd been in for the last few minutes, Kate saw Declan's red-stained hands and clothing. Madame Rue was in the hands of the only people who could help her. Kate focused on Declan. "Let's get you back to the hotel to regroup."

CHAPTER 20

Hours later Kate, Declan, Leo, and Sam sat in the living room area of the hotel room. It was closer than Sam's house and no one felt like going back to the police station after the night they'd had. Leo had changed his clothes in his nearby hotel room before coming over. Kate was finally comfortable in jeans and a sweatshirt. It had taken Declan more than a half-hour of intense scrubbing to remove most of the blood from his hands and body from where it had seeped through his clothing – which had been promptly discarded as a biohazard.

Sam had checked in with the hospital. Madame Rue needed immediate surgery and transfusions. Sam had notified her family. If she made it through the night, she'd most likely be in the clear. It would take considerable time to heal, the doctor had told him. There were officers with her at the hospital standing guard. No one was letting Rue out of their sight. Not only could she explain to them what she'd been writing, but she could identify the person who had attacked her. She was not a suspect. Yet. Kate didn't consider her in the clear either.

"What do we think this means?" Kate asked, sitting cross-legged on the floor. Everyone had offered her a seat but she refused them. She had taken the note from Rue's garbage and had brought it back to the hotel with her. She had bagged it as evidence and passed it around for all of them to read. Once Sam had it, Kate wanted to know his thoughts. "Sam, does *syn* mean anything to you?"

A faint smile appeared on his lips. "It's what higher calorie foods are called with one of the diet programs around here."

"They call it a sin?" Declan asked with a shake of his head. "That seems..."

"A little too on the nose," Sam finished for him. "It's supposed to be short for synergy."

Kate didn't think Rue was worried about nutrition or diet advice. "That's not what she meant. Look there are names and countries. She was making a list of some sort. I can only assume that word relates to the list."

"It could be another person's name," Sam suggested. "I can't think of anything specific to London that it might relate to. Nothing in the United Kingdom either."

Leo had been silently staring off across the room for some time. Kate worried that the reality of their work was finally setting in. "Syndicate," he said softly, surprising them all. When Declan asked him to repeat what he said, he turned to look at him. "Syndicate."

"Like network?" Declan asked.

"Exactly that." Leo turned his body so he was looking at them more directly. He leaned forward a little as he spoke. "Think about it – if Julian's note to Kate was real, he said *we* and *us*. Rue has a list of names and countries. Maybe Rue was starting to put some things together after we told her about her client. I think she needs to explain herself more. She might know more and not be telling us or she might have encountered some situations after we brought to light Julian's activities that got her thinking."

A syndicate of men like Julian. The idea of a syndicate of scammers wasn't out of the norm. It happened in a lot of various ways. It's what most of the identity theft rings and other financial scams were globally. It was rarely one person.

"They call them romance scams, Kate," Leo said looking right at her. He cleared his throat and then glanced over at Sam before he continued. When no one interrupted him and the floor was his, Leo continued. "When I was in my former life, we encountered a woman who'd been taken for close to four-hundred thousand dollars. Not only was she financially divested, but she was also emotionally destroyed. They are insidious, some of the worst scams I've ever seen."

Kate resisted the urge to ask him how he met this woman. She focused on the crime. "These aren't cases we handle. It's always the financial crimes unit. I don't even know how many they handle, to be honest with you. How pervasive are these scams?"

"Close to four billion in losses last year. The *Nasdaq 2024 Global Financial Crime Report* had the latest numbers. The thing is," Leo paused sighing heavily, "no report can account for the mental anguish and emotional consequences felt by its victims. There's no neat statistic that can give you a clear picture of that."

Declan raised his head to Sam. "Do you know much about these cases?"

Sam shook his head. "Like you, I handle mostly homicide. If the victims in these cases hadn't been murdered, I wouldn't have been involved. I don't handle scams or financial fraud. Looks like Leo might know more than all of us."

Kate could see the hesitancy on his face. "Tell us what you know."

Leo hesitated as his mouth dropped open slightly. "I," he said and stopped.

"What's wrong?" Declan asked, urging him to continue.

"I'm worried about getting it wrong and sending us down the wrong path. What if we waste time? I don't want to be the cause of that."

Declan reassured him, "I send us down the wrong path all the time and so does Kate. It's part of the investigative process. There's no investigator out there who gets everything on the first try. It's not like the movies. It's all trial and error until we stumble on something that sends us in the right direction."

"Okay," Leo said nervously licking his lips. "This happened to a sister of a friend."

The way he said *friend* made Kate realize he was talking about one of the men who worked with him when he was running The Curators, the name his syndicate of art thieves had been called.

Leo gestured with his hands as he spoke. "Adelaide met someone online on a dating website. They started emailing back and forth. Then they exchanged phone numbers but never spoke on the phone. Everything was through written communication. He was texting her all day every day. He had a way of learning early on what she needed. The emotional void she had been looking to fill, he filled it."

"It's what narcissists do easily," Kate said, encouraging him to go on.

"I don't know about the technical psychological terminology," Leo said with a dismissive wave of his hand. "I know this man was destructive on every level. The relationship continued over text and email for months. He constantly made her promises about the future."

Leo stopped himself and then added, "I should have mentioned, she was here in London and he was in the United States or so he said. They were long-distance. That was part of the reason why he said he couldn't meet her right away. They exchanged photos, so she had photos of him. Adelaide formed a real bond with him, a real emotional connection and investment. He told her early on he was falling in love with her and wanted to spend the rest of his life with her."

Sam's face contorted in confusion. "They never spoke on the phone?"

"Never. Not once. She never heard his voice. She also never saw his face. Every time it got down to video chatting, he'd back out and make some excuse. The camera on his laptop wasn't working. The app was giving him a hard time. He wasn't in a place where he could do it. It was excuse after excuse."

"Did she get suspicious?"

"Of course," Leo said. "He had an excuse but would reel her back in with promises of the future. He sweet-talked her right back into complacency. It was about two months in when the requests for money started. First, it was simple things – like he could video chat with her but his laptop broke. If he could get the money for a new one, he'd be able to talk to her. He didn't ask her outright but she offered. She sent him the money."

Kate stopped him. "How? Did he give her an address?"

"No, it was an online money transfer. These new apps for money transfers have made it all too easy. You don't even need someone's real name or bank account information."

Kate knew that had been an issue in other fraud cases. Spade had mentioned that to her whole unit during a meeting a few months back. She had trouble understanding how a woman would send money to a man she'd never seen or spoken to. She had no way of knowing who she was communicating with through text and email. "I assume the requests for money increased?"

"A little over time. Once he got her on the hook, his problems increased. There was an eviction and he was going to be homeless. Things were broken that needed to be replaced. Car trouble. You name it and this guy had it. Every time Adelaide sent money, he would be more loving and complimentary. He was reinforcing it at every step."

"I don't understand," Sam said, asking him to wait before he went on. "She kept sending money to someone she never met. She didn't start to get suspicious?"

"Adelaide had her doubts, but he was always right there with some plausible excuse. What became insidious was how he was able to undermine her relationship with her friends and family. The more they pushed back on this relationship, the more isolated she became. She didn't tell her brother, my friend, or her other friends she was sending money."

Kate felt for the woman. It was hard to imagine herself in the same situation. The one thing Kate never did was rule out her or anyone's ability to become a victim. Once a person thought they were above such things, that became a vulnerability all on its own. "How did the relationship come to an end?"

"Adelaide had run out of money. She burned through all her savings and her inheritance from their parents. She had become isolated and withdrawn and her siblings were not sure how to handle it. Nothing they said worked. Everything they did seemed to push her further toward this man." Leo shook his head in disgust. "Finally, my friend confronted her after this man promised Adelaide he was coming to visit. She waited at that airport for three hours and he never showed up. He had some excuse or another. A few days later, he tried to ask her for more money, and something in her snapped. She started to see through the façade he had created. He was never going to see her. It was never going to be the relationship he had promised. My friend had also been doing some digging and found the man's photos on a modeling website. The photos belong to some other man completely. It wasn't him. It had been a dupe, a catfish, all along."

A solemn mood fell over the room. Kate saw the dismay on each of their faces. It reflected her own feeling. "How is she doing now?"

"She's better. She'll never recoup the financial loss, but it was the emotional toll that was even worse for her."

Declan echoed the same sentiment. "I can't even imagine how difficult that was for her and her family. It must have taken a toll on all of them."

Leo nodded. "She has a lot of support, thankfully. I spent some time trying to help my friend figure out what was going on. What I found was that it was all too common. These scammers cultivate fictitious relationships on online dating sites or social media. They form these fast emotional connections with their victims, often saying all the things the victim wants to hear and has longed to hear. Once they have them hooked, that's when the financial requests start. The scams often undermine a victim's entire support system. She was convinced the relationship was genuine and no one was going to tell her different. He kept reinforcing it by telling her people just didn't understand their love. In some cases I read about, scammers will often use the victim as unwitting money mules, moving money for the scammers without realizing they are laundering the profits of other crimes."

Kate cursed softly at the depths some people would go to hurt others. "Is law enforcement around the globe doing much about these cases?"

"Not really. For a lot of victims, it's too embarrassing to go to law enforcement. They feel grief of losing a relationship that never existed and of being hurt financially. They isolate further and self-blame. It's psychologically devastating for them. For those who call the police, there often isn't enough information for them to do much. Fake name, stolen photos, and an untraceable IP address. The scammer is also normally in another country and is mostly untraceable. There isn't much for them to do. A case with a lot of dead ends."

Everything Leo said got Kate wondering if Rue had experienced something similar or had known clients who had experienced it. She was sure a matchmaker heard a lot of intimate details of women's love lives. If she had started putting things together, it would have made her a threat.

There was just one problem – what Leo described sounded like it was fully online. Julian had taken it offline.

"What's on your mind, Kate?" Declan asked from across the

room. He was good at reading her, not just because they were in a relationship but after years of working together.

She explained her hesitancy due to Julian's methods being far different from the romance scammers Leo had described. "It's possible the thrill wasn't satisfying him anymore."

Leo seemed to understand. "For most of these scammers, the goal is the money. The whole relationship for them is fake. It's about the con and financial gain. What if Julian has a different kind of pathology than that? Maybe he did that for a while and then wanted to take it in person. It certainly ups the thrill. He's tricking people in person, fooling matchmakers. It's like the next level of the same kind of con."

"It certainly sounds plausible," Sam started, zeroing in on Kate. "It would widen the net for us. We could put a call out through the media for anyone who has experienced this to call us."

Kate agreed that was a good decision. "I need to sleep on it. I'll do a little research to see what I can find. It would change how we investigate. Not that what we are doing now is working." She thanked Leo for the information he shared.

After they called it quits for the night, Kate walked Leo to the door. She leaned against the doorjamb. "I'm sorry about your friend's sister. It must have been hard for your friend to live with what happened."

Leo put his hand under her chin and leaned down.

Kate pulled back wondering for a moment if he was going to kiss her.

He got close to her ear, whispering, "Don't feel too bad for him. He found the guy a year later and killed him. He can't hurt anyone anymore."

A shudder went through Kate, a reminder that Leo lived in a whole different world than her with a distinct set of rules. They might have taken him out of that life, but it was still a part of him.

Kate remained still as he left, not sure what to think as she closed the door.

CHAPTER 21

Kate was in the bathroom getting ready the next morning when Declan entered. "Rue is awake. The hospital called and she is eager to talk. Only to you though. She doesn't want anyone else to be there." There was a question in Declan's tone Kate couldn't answer.

She finished brushing her hair. "I don't know why she only wants to speak to me. She might want to speak woman to woman."

"I saved her life."

Kate turned to him realizing then there was a hint of hurt in his voice. "Are you feeling left out?"

Declan shrugged it off. "I just don't understand why we can't interview her together."

"I don't know," Kate said again as she leaned against the bathroom counter. They had gone to bed after everyone left last night and hadn't had a chance to process it together. "What do you think about what Leo told us last night? Do you think this could be a syndicate? Maybe Julian went rogue."

"It makes a certain kind of sense. There's been nothing from the news conference last night. No phone calls to the police station reporting anyone who looks like Julian. The surveillance video of the jewelry shop showed a man who kind of looked like the same guy on the video from Andrea's house. The man last night had a cap pulled low on his head blocking most of his face. If it's not Julian, then we have other factors at play here."

Kate was also considering the timing. "Do you think Julian would have had time to get from the jewelry shop back to Rue's office, stab her, and get out of there?"

Declan leaned against the doorjamb and crossed his arms. "I've been thinking about that too. I've also been thinking about how a lot wasn't disturbed at her office. That downstairs door was locked when we got there. There is a back door we didn't check. He could have come in the back way or she could have let him in. If it was Julian, knowing we were searching for him, would she have done that?"

"I don't think she would have unless she's involved somehow. She must have trusted Julian to let him in after everything yesterday." These were all questions that only Rue could answer. "She's going to be the only one who knows. Hopefully, we'll know far more later today."

While Kate finished getting ready, Declan remained. After a few moments, he said, "While you're interviewing Rue, I'm going to go through that Paris file we haven't reviewed yet."

Kate knew that had been one of the things outstanding they hadn't been able to tackle yet. She finished what she was doing, smoothed down her hair, and leaned into him. She stood on her tiptoes and kissed him sweetly. "I appreciate all you do on these cases. It's a lot of work that goes unnoticed, but at the end of the day, it's what solves cases."

Declan tucked an errant strand of hair behind her ear. "Why are you being so sweet?" he asked with a teasing smile.

"No reason. I don't say it enough. I gave you a hard time last night about Julian getting past the cops when I wasn't even sure it was him. Then today Rue is asking for just me. I did nothing last night to help her. You were fully in command. I kind of zoned out taking in the scene. There was something that was off to me and I fixated on it." Kate kissed him again. "I'm just saying you don't always get the credit you deserve."

Declan grimaced. "Plus I had to watch you go to dinner with Leo. You never dress up for me like that."

Kate didn't tell him that by the end of the night, it had felt like a vise. "When we get back to Boston, we should dress up and go out now and then."

"No complaints from me." Declan stepped back from her and sent a text. He raised his eyes when he was done. "The car will be here in a few minutes. You take it today and I'll hitch a ride with Sam or take a cab." He leaned down and kissed her again, letting the kiss linger before she left.

Kate arrived at the hospital with one mission in mind – find out exactly what Rue knew and what had happened to her. She asked her driver to wait in the hospital parking lot. Kate found the floor and Rue's room with ease. She stood at the door and observed the IV running in Rue's arm, the bandages around her arm, an injury Kate hadn't noticed before, and the bruising around her face. The back of the bed was raised slightly allowing Rue to sit up probably as much as she could with the stab wound. The woman had her eyes closed and her breath remained shallow, the rise and fall of her chest made Kate think she was asleep.

"I can feel you staring at me," Rue said, turning her head slightly and opening her eyes to small slits. "Are you going to stand there and watch me or come in?"

Kate took a few steps into the room. "I thought you might be sleeping."

"I was earlier," Rue said as she tried and failed to push herself more upright in the bed.

"Don't," Kate cautioned. "You might rip your stitches. That was a bad gut wound. It was Declan who kept you alive last night."

Rue settled back into the bed. "I didn't know that. I didn't know who saved me. They didn't tell me much when I woke up. Just that I had a slash wound on my arm, some bruising on my face, and a stab wound. I don't have much of a memory after the attack started."

Kate eased herself into a chair next to the bed and pulled it closer so Rue didn't have to strain to see her. "What's the last thing you remember?"

"I was working at my desk and there was a noise out in the hallway. No one should have been there. I wondered at first if it was one of my staff coming back. The downstairs door had been locked and there were only a few people with a key." Rue pinched the bridge of her nose and closed her eyes. "I got up from my desk and came around to the side of it. A man was standing there at the door. I remember asking what he wanted. That was before I saw the knife. I backed up and asked him what he wanted again. The last thing I remember is him coming toward me. I don't know what happened after that."

It didn't surprise Kate that Rue had little memory of the attack. That was something all too common with trauma victims, especially this early on. Memories might come back later in a patchwork of images or all at once. There was no telling. Kate wasn't focused on the actual assault though. They knew from the injuries what happened.

"You reference a man. You've met Julian. Was it him?"

"No," Rue said with some surprise in her voice. "When he first came into the office his head was down and he had a tweed cap on, pulled low over his forehead. I might have even said the name Julian at first. He didn't respond. I never clearly saw his face." Rue closed her eyes for a moment. When she opened them, she turned toward Kate. "I keep saying it was a man but to be honest with you, I'm not sure. I assumed it was a man. They were taller than me but thin build. How could a woman do something like this?"

Kate kept her expression neutral, not showing the worry inside that ramped up at that admission. "Have you seen this person before?"

Rue rolled her eyes so she was staring up at the ceiling. "I don't think so. It's all so blurry in my mind. Do you think he meant to kill me? Is he going to come back and finish the job?"

"We have police outside in the hallway near your door. You're being protected, Rue." Kate considered her next words carefully. "Is there a reason you think someone wanted to hurt you like this?"

"I think someone is afraid of what I might know." Rue sighed deeply, nearly a groan. Kate wasn't sure if it was from pain or fear or possibly both. "There are things I haven't told you."

"About Julian?"

"I don't know if it connects to him. That's why I didn't mention it." Rue paused, taking a few deep breaths as much as she could. She rolled her head to the side, so she could focus on Kate. "I was scammed and so were two of my clients."

If Kate hadn't had the conversation with Leo she might not have understood. His information allowed her to be immediately compassionate. "By a man you were involved with?"

"It's going to sound so stupid to you. I'm embarrassed by my behavior. I should have known better." She closed her eyes tight as a tear rolled down her cheek. She raised the hand without the IV to brush it away.

"Don't do that to yourself," Kate soothed, inching toward the end of the chair. She moved closer to Rue, nearly close enough to reach out her hand. "This has happened to more women than you know. I found a slip of paper in your bin. Does it have anything to do with that?"

Rue nodded slowly. "I threw that away when I heard someone come into the office last night. I didn't want them to know. Do you think the man last night saw it?"

Kate assured her he didn't. "It was crumpled in the bin where you threw it. Do you think that's why he was there? Is he the man who scammed you?"

"I don't know," Rue said with her eyes wide. "I never saw a photo of the actual man who scammed me. I saw the photo of the man he wanted me to think he was. It wasn't him though. I found the photos he sent on social media linked to another man. That man was married with a wife and children. I reached out and he said he'd heard from more than a few women that someone had stolen his photos and were using them to scam women. He assured me he had nothing to do with it and I believed him."

Kate knew it was going to be hard for her, but she needed the whole story. "Can you tell me what happened and how you found out it was a scam?"

It took Rue a moment to gather her thoughts as Kate remained patient. "I was on a dating website. I'd had a profile up there for a while. The man I was dealing with said his name was Nolan and he lived in Scotland. Later, when I pressed about seeing him as it was only a short train ride away, he said he was in Germany." She smiled ruefully. "I know it seems silly. I'm a matchmaker. You'd think I could find someone for myself. I don't like to date those in my database. It's unprofessional. After all the couples I've brought together, I had a silly notion I might find love too."

"It's not silly," Kate reassured. "Everyone deserves love if that's what they are seeking."

"Kind of you to say." Rue shifted in the bed to look more at Kate. "I had suspicions from the start. He said all the right things and I got a niggling of hope that it might be real. That was my first mistake. By the time he asked me for money, I was hooked. The first time it didn't seem like a big deal. It was for his phone bill. He said he was a little short. We texted so it was beneficial for me that he was able to keep his phone on. Then the requests got bigger, his promises more grand, but there was no follow through. I was growing tired of it all. That's when one of my clients confided in me about her situation."

Kate raised an eyebrow. "Similar to yours?"

"Too similar. Right around the time I was growing weary of dealing with Nolan, my client said she needed some advice. She said she had met someone named Rohan Bakshi who was in France. She showed me a photo of an attractive man of Indian descent. She told me a story that very much reflected my own – the refusal to speak on the phone or video chat, wouldn't meet in public, constant requests for money. She was far more isolated than I was. No matter how much Nolan pressed me not to see friends and family, I didn't isolate myself. I also didn't tell anyone about the relationship. In a sense, I was isolated of my own making. I saw the same story reflected to me. For some reason, hearing her story, I could see right away she was being scammed."

Kate understood the reasoning. "Sometimes we can do for others what we can't do for ourselves."

"That's exactly right," Rue agreed. "After that, it was like the fog over me had dissipated and I could see clearly. I was angry then and that's when I started trying to get information out of Nolan. He slipped up a few times and I kept catching him in lies. During one conversation he mentioned a friend named Rohan. I asked the last name and he refused to give it. Could it be a coincidence, sure. What wasn't a coincidence was the end of my interaction with him."

Kate sat on the edge of her seat, waiting. "What happened?"

"He told me he wasn't the only one doing this. That if I kept trying to track him down, they would come for me. That they have people all over the globe and even if I found one of them, I'd never stop all of them. He told me for my safety to stop pursuing them."

"Did you?"

Rue shook her head. "I used a forensic expert to trace IP addresses for me. It took them a long time as they were routed all over the place. He finally nailed down an address for me in East London, in a warehouse. I went by there a couple of days ago but couldn't get in. I think someone saw me and followed me back here. Maybe they saw the police around and thought I was disclosing what I had found."

"The *syn* on the page you had written but stopped short of finishing. What did that stand for?"

"Syndicate. I thought if there were two there might be a lot more like he said."

It was exactly as Leo had suspected.

Kate assured, "We are going to keep the police outside with you until this case is over. Once you get out is there somewhere safe you can stay?"

"I have a sister up in the Highlands. It's pretty desolate up there this time of year. It might be nice to be out in the country far away from London."

Kate asked her for the address and where she could find the rest of the research. Rue gave her the combination to the safe in the office and where it was hidden. "We are going to do everything we can to stop them."

Rue nodded and closed her eyes. She fell back to sleep as Kate stood there watching her.

CHAPTER 22

Kate had called Leo when she left the hospital room and asked if he'd meet her at Rue's office. It had been officially closed until further notice. Her small staff were all working from home and had been told explicitly not to come in. The FBI still needed access to the site and Rue would schedule a time they could all go in and grab the files and things they needed. Most of the client information was held on their database, which could be accessed remotely.

Kate got out of the car to find Leo standing at the front door. He had his hands shoved into his jacket as he surveyed the street. He looked bigger than usual to Kate, as if he'd been lifting weights and had grown considerable muscle overnight. She realized once she got up close that it was only his wide legged, shoulder-squared posturing. Leo looked ready for a fight.

"Are you planning on someone attacking us?" she teased as she reached him on the sidewalk.

"I'm learning I need to be ready for anything and it's better to look scary. I always wondered why Declan carried himself the way he did. I realize now he's trying to look bigger to avoid the fight. He showed me a few tricks with his body language."

Kate had no idea Declan had done that. It wasn't something they had ever discussed. She wondered then if it was something all men did – squaring themselves in public to appear bigger and tougher than they were. A preventative posturing so to speak.

Kate pulled keys out of her pocket and jiggled them. "We don't have to break in this time. I want to check the back door of the place too. I know the crime scene techs have come through here already and Sam said the back door was unlocked. It wasn't supposed to be. Declan told me he called the building's owner who told him the back door is rarely used. Even the cleaning crew who carries trash out comes and goes through the front door. He had no idea why it was unlocked."

Leo stepped behind Kate as she went to the door and unlocked it. "Whoever attacked Rue probably got in the same way as I did last night. I should be able to tell if the lock was disturbed in some way."

Kate had the key in the lock as she angled her head to look back at him. "You can tell if someone picked a lock? I didn't think that was something that could be done unless the lock was broken in the process."

Leo shrugged it off. "In my line of work, you learn to pick up subtle clues."

He said no more than that and Kate didn't press the issue. She refocused her attention on the door, clicked open the lock, and pushed it open.

Once inside Rue's office, she went to the third office on the right side of the hall. The one Rue had specifically mentioned. Leo waited in the hall while she went behind the desk to the photo of the seascape that hung behind it. She tugged the corner of the gold frame and pulled it out from the wall. Behind, there was a simple silver safe with a black dial. She turned it one way and then the other getting the combination Rue had given her. When the door sprang open, the safe revealed a single thick manilla folder. Kate fished it out from its home and then closed the safe back up.

"It's bigger than I thought it would be," Kate said as she turned to face Leo, who was watching her with his eyes soft. It was the look of a man who liked what he saw. The corners of her mouth turned up in a smile before she could even stop herself. Kate lowered her eyes back to the file and ignored the tension that created a charge in the room around them.

She kept her thoughts focused on the investigation. As Kate moved back toward the door, she said, "I can't tell you how grateful we are for the information you shared last night. I know you don't like to share personal information with everyone. It's given us a good understanding of how these romance scams work. It probably saved me several hours of research."

"I'm glad I could be of help." As Kate passed through the doorway, Leo put his hand out and stopped her, his palm warm against her shoulder. The subtle scent of his cologne filled her senses as he leaned in closer. He lowered his head and locked his gaze first on her lips then raised them to her eyes. "I should apologize for what I said last night. I shouldn't have confided in you that my friend took care of the problem. It's hard for me to remember that you're the FBI."

Kate didn't know how that would be hard to remember given that was the only capacity he knew her in. But she understood what he meant. "I forget about your past sometimes too. Like last night. I admit it startled me and made me question a few things."

Leo's eyes narrowed. "Like what?"

Kate's heart thumped in her chest and a shiver ran down her spine, a mixture of apprehension and something else she didn't want to name. Kate tipped her head back and steadied herself. "I wondered if the story you told us was about a woman you knew and there was no friend. That it was you who eliminated the threat."

Leo scanned her face as Kate held firm. "I can see why you'd think that. I would have eliminated the threat if I had been asked or if someone had done that to someone close to me. It wasn't me though,

Kate. I told you the truth." Leo pulled back from her, removing his hand so she could pass. Kate remained right where she stood. "I told you from the start I'd never lie to you and I meant that. I'm not a violent man. I hoped you'd know that about me by now. I've only killed once and you were there."

Kate expelled a breath she didn't know she had been holding. "When you told me you had taken care of the men who had wanted to kill me. I assumed you meant you had killed them."

"It wasn't me and I didn't call for it. Some of the men I worked with did not take disloyalty well. One of the men, the instigator was killed. The other two were arrested and a fourth was paid off." Leo reached for her, resting the tip of his finger under her chin. He turned her head gently so they were looking directly at each other. "It doesn't matter what's happened in my past, Kate. I will never hurt you. I will never lie to you. I will do everything I can to protect you. You can trust me completely...with anything."

Kate's shallow breathing echoed in her ear. She was sure he noticed the rise and fall of her chest. The air between them crackled with electricity. Kate found herself unconsciously leaning towards him, her eyes flicking to his lips. If he tried to kiss her, Kate knew it would be hard to stop him.

"Declan," Leo said, breaking the spell she was under. "He's probably wondering what's taking so long."

"Right." Kate stepped back from him and started to walk away. Leo reached for her arm and spun her back to him. He pulled her close wrapping her in a hug. Kate's body tensed for a moment before melting into his embrace. She could feel his chest, the steady beat of his heart against hers.

"I wanted to kiss you too," Leo said softly. "I wish we had met before you and Declan got together."

Kate went to speak but found herself unable to make a sound. She stepped back from the hug, offering him a smile. "We'll always have that rooftop in Paris."

Leo chuckled softly. "That rooftop."

Kate stood in the hallway by the front door while Leo checked the back door. He didn't believe it had been tampered with. The question about how someone got to Rue remained. He had his hand on her back as they left through the front.

Even as they reached the street and the cold wind whipped by, Kate felt the ghost of Leo's touch, the warmth of his body against hers. She took a deep breath, trying to steady herself and push away thoughts of what might have been. *Declan.* She said his name into the wind, reminding herself of everything that waited for her and everything they had built together.

Back at the police station, Sam updated them about his progress. He got a message through the cops that the raid in East London, the warehouse that Rue's tech person had identified, had been scheduled for later that night. The warehouse in question was off the A12 near the Olympic Stadium and grounds. Sam said he knew the area well. There were several warehouses in the area and it might be a perfect place for the scammers to blend in.

Kate had no idea what, if anything, they'd find there. The man who had attacked Rue might assume he had killed her before she could share the information she gathered. Then again, they might have gotten spooked and closed up shop. Either way, the case was taking a new direction and Kate hoped Rue's research might prove useful.

Sam also told her that they were stonewalling him at Annabel's. He'd gone and interviewed the manager. Sam was sure the man knew Julian but refused to give him any information. "Kate, he looked at me like he couldn't believe I was asking the question. Almost as if I should know who Julian is."

That was odd indeed. "Is there any way to compel him to tell you?

Speak to other staff?"

"He kicked me out and told me to come back with a warrant or not at all."

Kate couldn't believe that they still had no lead on the man. The media was still playing clips of Julian's photo and every law enforcement officer in the United Kingdom had a photo. He'd not be able to access a train or leave the country without being spotted. Kate assumed he was lying low somewhere until the heat passed. She hoped the pressure they were putting on him would drive him underground long enough that it would give them a reprieve between victims.

Once in the conference room, Leo left to get them coffee and snacks while she started to go through the contents of Rue's file. With him gone, Kate relaxed into the chair. She had to do a better job of managing him – whatever that meant.

She felt like her connection to Leo was growing and her resolve slipping. The last thing she'd ever do was disrespect Declan. She had to get it under control. The best way she knew to do that was to focus on the task at hand.

Kate flipped open the file and stared down at one of the photos she assumed Nolan had sent to Rue. Smiling back at her was a handsome sandy-haired man who appeared to be in his forties. He had brown eyes and a boyish smile. He wasn't classically model-looking handsome.

He appeared to be an everyday guy. A man that, if Kate met him in a bar and he flirted with her, she might have responded positively to. He had a harmless look about him. Kate understood how Rue might be easily taken in with his disarming smile.

She moved the photo to the right and scanned through the next page. It was an email communication between the two. Kate flipped through page after page. Rue had the foresight to save her communication. There was everything from texts to long email communication. It would be the first time Kate would have a front row seat to how the scam started. She set those documents aside to look at what else was in the file.

There, under the thick communication pages, was a document from the tech person Rue had employed. It showed the path of the IP routing that Nolan's communication had taken. He had also been able to get cellphone data from the text messages. There was no identifying information about the tech person and Kate wondered if what he had done was legal. Kate wasn't sure and the only person on their team who would be was Ditch. She knew Declan had called him and asked for his support on the case. He should have gotten his hands on Andrea's laptop by now and started his process.

Kate didn't understand half of what he did. She didn't have to though. She reached for her cellphone and punched in the familiar number. "It's Kate," she said as he groaned a hello. She checked the time. "It's nine in the morning there. You should be awake."

Ditch groaned again, cursing at her for waking him. "I'm in Los Angeles, babe. This stupid detective made me come out here to get the laptop. I just went to bed about an hour ago. What do you want?"

Kate didn't have any word for Ditch other than diva. He was particular and high-maintenance. If someone other than him could do a job, she'd want someone else. There was no one on the planet more highly skilled than Ditch though and he knew it. She explained the information that Rue's tech person had gathered. "We have the address for the warehouse and have a raid planned for tonight."

"They'll be gone by then," Ditch said with a yawn.

"We have some cops watching the place. It's hard because it's in a row of warehouses and we aren't even sure how often the place is used. We also don't have photos of anyone connected other than possibly Julian, but that's not confirmed. It's not like we are going to be able to tell much until we get in there. We planned it for tonight.

These scammers are working around the clock. I think Sam wants to have the cover of darkness on our side."

"Either way, they already left. I'm telling you it's a waste of time." Ditch yawned again. "You can send me the reports you have and I'll take a look. I knew some guys who were romance scammers. It's a good racket for making a buck. Too emotional for me."

It didn't escape Kate's attention that he saw no issue with scamming women out of money. It was the emotion he'd have to pretend that got him. "Were they part of large syndicates? That's what we think we are looking at here."

"That's exactly what they are," Ditch said, the boredom evident in his voice. "What they don't normally do is meet someone in person, have a relationship with them, and then murder them. Are you sure you're not looking at two different things?"

Kate didn't know what they were looking at – some kind of weird hybrid scam or maybe just a scammer gone rogue. "I'll get you this information. In the meantime, let me know everything you find on Andrea's laptop and cellphone." Kate read him off the IP address that had been connected to the warehouse. "If you see that anywhere, let me know immediately. It would be the one definitive thing that connects Julian to the syndicate Rue thinks she found."

Ditch assured her he would. He ended the call with a word of caution. "If you're going after a syndicate, this is a billion-dollar industry. If you threaten their livelihood, they will destroy you."

Kate didn't doubt they'd try.

CHAPTER 23

The cops watching the warehouse had little to report. Sam, Declan, and Kate convened at the set location at nine. They chose to leave Leo out. He'd not gone on any raids before and Kate didn't want to chance it with him in another country. If there were any mistakes to be made, she wanted it on U.S. soil. The last thing they needed on their hands was an international incident.

"There's been almost no movement in or out of the warehouse," Sam told them when they got to the site at the scheduled time. "It has a main entrance that connects to three other warehouses and people have come and gone throughout the day. There were about six people in total. There's not a lot of action in this part of the warehouse complex."

Sam also informed them the tech company that owned the warehouse was Helix Enterprises operated by Benjamin Fuller from London. They specialized in security technology for shipping companies. Kate didn't know if the business was legit or just a front.

The hum of the city faded as she tightened the grip on her weapon, her eyes scanning the perimeter of the dimly lit warehouse. The structure loomed ahead, shrouded in a blanket of fog that hung over East London. Flickering streetlights cast erratic shadows, and the acrid scent of rain-soaked asphalt mixed with the tang of rusting metal churned her stomach.

Declan steadied himself beside her. "We're clear on the entry plan, right?"

"Right," Kate replied, her heart thumping in time with the steady rhythm of their footsteps as they approached.

Sam stood slightly apart, his brow furrowed.

"Something wrong?" Kate asked, stopping to make sure he was with them.

Sam shook his head. "A feeling I can't quite place."

Kate felt it too, a sinking feeling in her gut that suggested something was off. She didn't know what. Then again, they weren't operating with a lot of credibly verified information. They were probably right to feel the way they did.

Declan approached a massive metal door. It had a peeling paint job and the Helix Enterprises sign above it barely readable. Kate felt a chill run down her spine, not just from the cold creeping in, but from the weight of what might lie behind the door. These weren't just any criminals. They were preying on vulnerable women, stealing from them financially and crushing them emotionally. And in Julian's case – murdering them when he was done.

Declan kicked the door open. It swung inward with a groan. The warehouse interior was vast, a cavernous expanse littered with old crates and discarded materials. Dust motes danced in the beams of their flashlights as they swept the room. A strange stillness permeated the air, and Kate's instincts tingled.

Something really didn't feel right.

"Clear right," Declan called, moving deeper into the space, his weapon raised.

"Clear left," Kate replied too softly. It wasn't clear at all. She didn't know what she was looking at other than an empty warehouse that appeared to have been empty for years.

Sam moved toward the far end, scanning the shadows for any sign of life. The only sounds were their footsteps echoing and the distant drip of water from the leaky roof.

As they moved further inside, the emptiness felt oppressive. The initial thrill of the raid began to dissipate, replaced by an unsettling realization. Kate had hoped this was their big break. Yet, it felt like they were stepping into a ghost town. Something about it didn't feel real.

"Over here!" Sam called out, his voice cutting through the silence.

Kate hurried to where he stood, peering at a table in the center of the room. A few laptops sat there with their screens dark. "They left their tech?" she said incredulously.

Declan frowned, glancing around the room. "This doesn't make sense."

"Maybe they left in a hurry," Sam suggested, kneeling to inspect the nearest laptop.

Kate's gaze roamed the walls, noting the lack of personal effects or signs of recent activity. No photos, no belongings – just an empty shell. They should take the laptops and bring them to Ditch. He should be the one to start them. But she couldn't shake the feeling that they had been left for their benefit. "Let's check the laptops," she said finally going against her better judgment.

With a quick motion, Declan powered up one of the devices. The screen blinked to life, illuminating his face with a pale glow. "Password protected," he said as he tapped the keys.

Kate tried to shake the feeling of unease that had settled in her gut. "There's something not right about all of this." She was trying to put her finger on it but the words wouldn't come.

"Almost like it was staged," Declan said, capturing exactly what she had been thinking.

Kate glanced around, her flashlight capturing the empty space. "If they left in such a hurry, surely the laptops would have been the most valuable. Go through the rest of them."

The atmosphere grew heavier as they tried to access the remaining laptops. Each click of the keys echoed ominously in the silence. Minutes dragged on, and the tension escalated. With every passing moment, nagging thoughts weighed on Kate's mind.

Sam, with his voice barely above a whisper, said, "This feels too easy."

While Declan and Sam focused on the laptops, Kate's attention was drawn elsewhere – to faint marks that traced a path leading to what appeared to be an old door at the back, half-hidden by an array of forgotten crates. "There's a door back there."

Declan's head snapped to attention as he straightened, eyes narrowing. "Let's check it out."

They approached the door cautiously, hearts racing as they prepared for whatever lay behind it. Sam and Declan made quick work of removing the crates. The door had a rusted broken handle that came off in Kate's hands as she touched it.

Declan felt along the side for a seam, something to dig his fingers behind to pry it open. After several tries, he wiggled it loose. He pried it open revealing a narrow corridor that disappeared into darkness. The air was stale, thick with the scent of mildew. The tension coiled tighter as they stepped inside, flashlights piercing the void.

A faint sound echoed down the hall – voices. Kate's pulse quickened. "Did you hear that?"

Declan nodded, his brow furrowed in concentration. "It's coming from the end of the corridor."

They crept forward, the sounds growing clearer. Muffled laughter. It was surreal, a stark contrast to the desolation of the warehouse. As they neared the end, Kate's instincts screamed for caution as her eyes locked on the faint light spilling from a doorway at the end.

Sam reached for the doorknob to the metal door, an object that stood in stark contrast to the rest of the building. Not only did it look brand new but it was solid while the rest of the warehouse seemed ready to fall down around them.

They entered into another hallway and down a short corridor to where the laughter and din of voices grew louder. They rounded a corner and stopped short at the scene that unfolded.

A hidden lounge, lavishly decorated with soft lighting and plush seating. And there, at the center, were a group of four men and two women sitting around one table, their laughter cutting through the air like a knife.

In that moment, the reality of their situation crashed down upon them. This was no simple operation. Leo and Rue had been right.

The atmosphere shifted palpably as Kate, Declan, and Sam stepped fully into the lounge, their weapons drawn and faces set in grim determination.

The group of people at the table remained oblivious to the law enforcement that had encroached on their lair. They started to raise their glasses in celebration.

Kate's heart raced as she pointed her weapon at them as Sam and Declan descended on them.

"National Crime Agency! FBI!" Sam and Declan commanded, their voices booming with authority.

The celebrants exchanged confused glances, uncertainty on their faces. One of the women, a striking brunette in a fitted dress, stepped forward, her expression shifting from surprise to defiance. "How did you get in here? What's this about?" She leaned to the side and locked her gaze on Kate. "We are having a party. There's no reason the FBI should be here and you don't have any authority."

"They have authority under my command." Sam introduced himself and flashed his badge. "A private party in an abandoned warehouse?" He let the question linger.

The woman folded her arms across her ample chest. "Is that a crime now?"

Kate stepped closer, scanning the room for any sign of incriminating evidence. "We have warrants to bring you in for questioning and all of your tech regarding suspected financial fraud. This is not a game."

The group's initial shock gave way to nervous laughter, the tension dissipating just slightly. One of the men, a tall figure with dark hair and an easy smile, shrugged. "Financial fraud? You must be mistaken. We're just here to celebrate some recent successes. No one is robbing anyone. As I'm sure you saw on the sign, we are Helix Enterprises. We landed a major shipping contract."

Declan didn't hide the skepticism lacing his tone. "You're throwing a party at night in a hidden room in a rundown warehouse where there are a bunch of laptops just left on a table. Seems a little suspicious."

The brunette glanced back at her companions, eyebrows raised in feigned innocence. "They were probably just forgotten by the previous tenants. This place has been empty for ages."

"What are you doing back here then?" Sam asked, gesturing around the newly refurbished place. "Why keep it hidden?"

"Our boss set it up this way," the tall man explained. "There is fierce competition in the shipping industry. He's worried about corporate espionage." He looked around at the people working with him. "No one has done anything illegal. I assure you. This might seem like a strange set up, but it's all legal."

Declan wasn't buying. "We didn't see any cars out front. The door to get back here was blocked by crates. How do you enter and exit the building?"

The tall man started to walk toward an interior door. "I can show you. We have space in the back of the building."

Declan gestured with his gun for him to back up. "We aren't going anywhere. We have authority to search the entire building. We'll sort that out later."

The man stepped back in line with his friends. "Could you please stop waving that gun at us? As you know this isn't common practice with law enforcement here in London the way it is in the states. We are more civilized here, not gun-obsessed."

Kate felt a surge of frustration. It was too easy for them to play it cool, to brush off their intrusion with nonchalance. "I don't want to listen to any more of your lies. Women who have lost thousands to scammers. Several victims are dead."

The other woman, a blonde with a slight tremor in her voice, took a step toward them, glancing around nervously. "We're not scammers. We're just—" her voice trailed off and she didn't finish what she had started. She stood next to the brunette. "Did you say women are dead?"

"Several women," Kate reiterated. "Six here in London, two in Los Angeles, and one in Paris. You're looking at international crimes."

The blonde stepped back as if she'd been slapped. "I don't know anything about that. That's not why I'm here."

Kate's patience wore thin. "Then why are you here?"

The atmosphere hung heavy, the partygoers glancing at one another, the playful façade cracking under the weight of suspicion. The brunette shifted her stance, attempting to regain control. "What do you want from us? If you don't have any real evidence, you can't be here."

"Evidence?" Declan interjected, his eyes narrowing. "You're all coming with us."

The laughter from moments before faded into the background as the group's confidence waned. Kate gestured for Sam to take position at the entrance, ensuring they wouldn't make a quick escape. "We need to separate you for questioning. You'll each have the chance to tell your side of the story."

The brunette stepped forward defiantly. "You think we're just going to go with you because you flashed some badges? This is ridiculous!"

"It's not a choice," Kate replied, keeping her tone steady. "You're welcome to cooperate, or we can make this more difficult."

The men exchanged glances, uncertainty flickering in their eyes. Finally, the dark-haired man spoke up, his bravado deflating. "All right, fine. We'll go. But you're making a mistake."

Kate felt a mix of relief and unease. They had no solid evidence yet, just a hunch, a lot of circumstantial information and mounting pressure. They rounded the group up, directing them toward the exit.

Once outside, they secured them in the back of a transport van, the ambiance starkly contrasting the earlier camaraderie. The air was heavy with the scent of rain and tension, the streetlights casting a dim glow on their faces.

Kate stood back, watching as Declan and Sam handled the logistics of securing the suspects. The brunette shot her a glare as she was ushered into the van. "You'll regret this, you know."

Kate forced herself to remain calm. As the van drove away, back toward the police station, the woman's words rattled in her mind, a nagging worry that they might be right.

"You all right, Kate?" Declan asked as he reached her side. The rain grew heavier, pelting them in the face. He holstered his gun and pulled the hood up on his jacket to protect himself. He leaned over and tugged up Kate's hood too.

Kate stared off in the direction of the van then turned to look at him. "When I saw those laptops, I knew something wasn't right. They wouldn't take everything else and leave evidence like that behind. I never expected to find women among them."

"They can be scammers too, Kate."

"But to scam other women?" She was struggling to make sense of it.

"We don't know that they weren't scamming men," Declan responded, cracking the case open even wider.

Kate cursed softly. "How far and deep does this go?"

"Hopefully, Ditch can tell us once he starts going through the tech. I think we need to get him on a plane."

Kate agreed. "If you can do that, I'll go back to the station and start interviewing them. I think the blonde might crack. She seemed the most vulnerable." At least that's what Kate was hoping. They needed something to break in the case.

CHAPTER 24

luorescent lights buzzed overhead as Kate sat down at a small table in one of the interrogation rooms. On the opposite side of the table sat the brunette from the warehouse, her arms crossed defiantly, a frown marring her otherwise striking features. Lydia Berman was her name. Kate started with her while the blonde was still being processed by the police.

Lydia folded her arms across her chest, bounced her crossed leg, hitting the edge of the table with each swing. "You think you can scare me into confessing? I've seen tougher interrogators on TV. I'm surprised it's not one of the men in here with me."

Kate leaned forward, folding her hands together. "I'm not here to play games. I want to hear your side. You say you're not involved in anything illegal. Tell me what you were doing at that warehouse."

"We work there." Lydia shrugged, feigning nonchalance. "What you saw today was a celebration of a work accomplishment. You have no proof we were doing anything wrong."

"The FBI employs one of the world's greatest hackers. We will find out what is on every bit of technology in your office," Kate pressed. "We have the reports from women who have lost their life savings to scams just like the ones you're conducting. One of the women hired a tech expert. We know the messages she was receiving came directly from the warehouse. That's what brought us to you. We have all the evidence from the women who died." Kate still wasn't sure how the women's deaths were connected to the romance scams Rue had uncovered.

The woman's demeanor shifted slightly, the bravado faltering. She remained quiet.

Kate felt the flicker of hope ignite. "You can start helping yourself by giving me names. Who else is involved? How many victims and how much money have you raked in?"

The brunette hesitated, her eyes darting to the door as if considering an escape. "There is nothing for me to tell you. Helix Enterprises is in the shipping industry."

The hope Kate felt a few minutes ago faltered. "Tell me about your background then. How did you come to work for Helix."

Lydia scoffed. "I know what you're doing. Getting me to talk about something else and you'll try to trip me up, get me to confess to something I didn't do."

Kate appraised her. She had an icy demeanor and wore her guarded nature around her like a cloak. "If you didn't do anything wrong, then there is no way I can trip you up. You're telling me you work for a shipping company, great – tell me about your work."

Lydia eyed her suspiciously. "I don't have to tell you anything. Besides, I know this is a trick."

"I can't trick you if you didn't do anything wrong." Kate got up from the table, leaving Lydia there. She went to retrieve a file with photos in it. She didn't like having to go this route, but the woman needed a shock to her system. A slap in the face to the reality at hand.

Kate returned, throwing the file folder onto the table. She flipped open the file and shoved one photo after another at Lydia. "Look at them," she commanded. Lydia wouldn't though. She kept her chin up and eyes averted.

Kate came around to the other side of the table behind the woman, putting the photos right in front of them. She jabbed her finger down on an image of Andrea dead in her bed, the bright red line showcasing the trauma that had been done to her. "All of these women were taken for millions of dollars and then murdered in their beds. Is this what you're doing? Is this what you're condoning? Let me tell you scamming people online is one thing, murder is another. If you don't start talking, you're going to go down for all of it."

No matter what Kate said or how much she raised her voice, Lydia refused to lower her head to look at the photos. Kate wasn't having any of it. She put her hand on the back of Lydia's head and forced her to look down. "Look at them!" she screamed. "You want to be involved in this. You can look at the wreckage you caused."

"Get off me!" Lydia shouted and wriggled away from Kate.

Kate stepped back regaining a sense of herself. She rarely put her hands on a subject of the investigation in an interrogation room. She wrung her hands as she tried to get her breath under control. Kate sucked in slow breaths then released them. She licked her lips.

"I need your help, Lydia," Kate said, trying to appeal to the woman's sense of empathy. She tried to come up with a profile on the woman on the fly – anything to help her interrogation. They knew from the quick background check that Lydia was thirty-three from a working class family in Hackney. That was about all the background check and the woman's statement had amounted to so far.

Kate walked around back to her chair, pulled it out, and sat down. She didn't apologize for losing her temper or explain it away. "Where did you go to university?" she asked as she regained her composure.

Lydia shook her head. "I'm done speaking to you."

"That's your right," Kate said not hiding the disappointment in her voice. "One of you is going to flip, Lydia. I was hoping it was you. This is your chance to save yourself. I can help you if you're willing to speak to me. If not, there's nothing I can do."

Lydia flicked her eyes up to meet Kate's. She didn't utter a word.

"Fine." Kate got up and left the room. She paused briefly at the door as if she might have some parting remark to make. Nothing came to mind though. She wasn't going to beg this woman to save herself.

Declan joined her in the hallway from the observation room. "She's tough."

"I don't think I'll break her. What about the men? Is Sam getting anywhere?"

Declan shook his head. "Do you want me to try with her?"

Kate glanced over at the door. "I don't know that you'll have much luck. She didn't ask for a solicitor yet. You might as well take a crack at it."

Declan pointed to a door across the hall and down to the left. "Lucy Barclay is in there waiting for you. If anyone is going to break, I think it's her."

"I don't think she's going to be that hard to break. At least, I hope she's not." Kate got to the door and turned back to him. "Let me know if Sam gets a confession."

Kate nudged open the door and stood there for a moment, arms crossed, assessing the woman seated at the metal table in the center. Lucy Barclay looked out of place in the stark environment, her soft features and polished attire contrasting sharply with the grimness surrounding her. Her skin cast a gray pallor from the cold fluorescent lights that buzzed overhead. A hint of defiance glimmered in her hazel eyes, but fear lurked just beneath the surface.

"Miss Barclay," Kate began, her tone calm but firm, "we have a lot to discuss."

Lucy shifted in her chair, the metal squeaking slightly. "I'm not sure what you think I can tell you. I just… I was in the wrong place at the wrong time."

Kate leaned against the wall, studying her. "I thought you worked there."

Lucy swallowed hard and shook her head, averting her eyes from Kate's. "Wrong place and definitely wrong time."

"I'm not sure I believe that. We both know that the warehouse was a hub for a very sophisticated romance scam operation. We've got several victims who lost substantial amounts of money. As I told you back at the warehouse, it's not just the money. Several women were murdered. That makes this all the more serious. Don't you think?" When Lucy didn't respond, Kate walked over to the table.

Lucy's gaze dropped to her hands, fidgeting with her rings. "I don't know much."

"Why were you there, Lucy?" Kate pressed, her voice remaining steady.

Lucy inhaled sharply, meeting Kate's eyes. "I was helping a friend. It wasn't supposed to be anything serious. I didn't know what they were doing."

"Which friend?" Kate asked, taking a step closer, her interest piqued.

"Lydia, the other woman there today," Lucy said, her voice barely above a whisper. "She said she needed help. I work in marketing. She thought I could help with something."

"How could you help them?" Kate's voice was a mix of disbelief and urgency.

"They…umm…" Her voice trailed off. "Listen, I can't have my name public. I don't think you understand who I am. I thought I was going there to do something harmless. I didn't know anything about scams, dead women, or anything illegal. I swear to you."

Kate studied her carefully, taking in the tremor in Lucy's hands and the sheen of sweat forming on her brow. "What do you mean by harmless?"

"Just helping her with social media profiles and ads. You know, marketing techniques to get more engagement," Lucy confessed, her voice tinged with regret. "It seemed innocent enough. She said it was for a start-up."

"A start-up?" Kate raised an eyebrow. "How many times have you been to that warehouse?"

"Three times." Lucy sighed, rubbing her temples as if trying to alleviate a headache. "It was just brainstorming, but things started getting weird. People would come in and out, and sometimes they'd talk about sending money overseas. I brushed it off. I thought it was just business stuff."

"You thought nothing of it?" Kate challenged, her voice sharp. "You can't be that naïve."

Lucy winced at the accusation. "We were friends. It didn't occur to me that it could be something illegal. I thought they were, you know, a little shady with their business practices, but who isn't?"

"People lose their life savings to these scams, Lucy. This isn't shady, it's criminal," Kate replied, her tone softening slightly. "I need you to be honest with me. The more you tell me, the better chance you have to walk away from this. Who else was involved?"

"I really don't know!" Lucy insisted, frustration rising. "I didn't get anyone's name. I swear the only thing I helped them do was some marketing on social media, how to get better ad engagement. I've never scammed anyone in my life. I don't know anything about murder!" Tears formed in the corners of her eyes and she furiously brushed them away.

Kate wasn't moved by the show of emotion. "Tell me about the ads."

Lucy sniffled. "It was for a dating app. What's so harmful about a dating app? Everyone uses them."

"Why would a tech company for the shipping industry start a dating app?"

"They told me it's a side hustle for a few of the people who work there." Lucy shrugged. "Lydia said it's a way to make some money. I don't know more than that."

Kate leaned her arms on the table. "I don't think Helix Enterprises is in the shipping business at all. I don't think you believe that either, Lucy."

"I don't…" Lucy looked toward the door. "I want to call my father."

"Your father can't help you. I'm the only one who can right now."

"You don't know who my father is, Agent Walsh." Lucy pleaded with Kate with her eyes. "Please, you cannot let anyone know that I'm here."

This was the second time Lucy had made it seem like she was someone known. Kate hadn't run with it the first time, but it seemed important to her. "You're right, Lucy. I don't know who you are or your father for that matter. Enlighten me."

"My father is Lord Bartholomew Barclay. My family is among the aristocracy."

If the young woman had punched Kate in the gut, the blow would have landed easier. "That would make you Lady Lucy Barclay?"

"Lady Lucille Elizabeth Barclay," Lucy corrected her. "The formality isn't necessary though."

Kate knew nothing about the protocol that this might call for. But she knew this young woman had the information she needed. She didn't care if she was the Queen of England herself. Lucy wasn't leaving this room until she told Kate what she knew, and if she didn't, she could find herself in a jail cell. Kate didn't care in the slightest if it caused an international incident.

She lowered her tone and shot straight through the heart of it. "We don't have noble titles in America. I'd say it makes you even more motivated to help me. What was a Lady doing in a warehouse that was being utilized for romance scams? Doesn't seem a fitting place for you. If your father is who you say, I'd guess he'd be horrified."

By the resigned look on her face, Lucy had played her ace and knew now that Kate wasn't going to let her go. Her title hadn't impressed Kate in the slightest. She sighed dramatically. "I didn't know what they were doing at first. Lydia asked me to help her with social media ads and videos and stuff. I have a large social media following on Instagram and TikTok. I'm an influencer and a lot of people follow me. I thought I was helping a friend with a dating app. I didn't know until today the app is used for more than dating."

Now they were getting somewhere. "How else is the app used?"

Lucy gestured with her hand as if Kate already knew the answer. "They would scam people into giving them money. Have fake relationships with them and then get money from them. I'm being honest with you that if I knew that, there is no way I would have helped them."

"How old is the app?"

"A couple of years, but I guess revenue started to slow down."

"Theft slowed down," Kate corrected her with force. "Tell me the name of the app."

"Helix. It's the name of the company." Lucy bit at her lip as her eyes scanned the room before settling on the mirror. "Are other people watching this?"

"No," Kate said, not technically a lie. She didn't believe anyone was in the observation room. "Everyone else is busy. The first person who tells us what we need to know in detail is the one off the hook."

Lucy shuddered, her body shaking. "I swear to you. I don't know much at all. I'll tell you what I know. They were using social media ads to drive traffic, targeting older women and men."

"How much older?"

"Older than forty. All of the profiles on the app are fake, other than the people who sign up for it. I didn't really understand what they were doing. It seemed to be a laugh for them. I didn't know about the money until today and I told Lydia this was the last day I was helping them. I didn't feel right about hurting people like that." She furrowed her brow. "Some people really could get their feelings hurt. I didn't like that and told Lydia today was the last day I was helping her. Then I learned about the money."

Kate asked several more questions. Lucy answered what she knew, giving as much detail as she could. When Kate got to the end of her questions, she had a final one left. "What do you know about Julian Marlowe?"

"I don't know anyone by that name," Lucy said then recognition flickered in her eyes. "The only Julian I know is Julian Barclay."

Kate pulled her phone out and scrolled to a photo. "This man," she instructed Lucy.

She lowered her head to look at the photo. "Yes, Julian Barclay, my cousin."

Kate was rendered speechless.

A noble.

They were after a member of the aristocracy for murder.

CHAPTER 25

Kate's mind raced as she processed Lucy's words. Julian Barclay. A lord. She leaned forward, her eyes locked on Lucy's face, searching for any sign of deception. "Tell me everything you know about Julian," Kate demanded, her voice low and intense.

Lucy shifted uncomfortably in her chair, her earlier bravado completely vanished. "He's my father's cousin. He was disowned by the family some time ago and hasn't been around a lot. I don't know him well."

"Not good enough, Lucy. Your cousin is implicated in multiple murders. Every detail you know about him is important to me and to stopping him."

Lucy's eyes widened, and she paled visibly. "Murders? Julian? That's impossible."

"Is it?" Kate countered. "You admitted to being involved in a scam targeting vulnerable people. You said you don't know him well. How can you be sure that he's not involved? Either you know him well enough to know he's not capable of murder or you don't know him at all. It can't be both."

Lucy's shoulders slumped. "I suppose I don't know him well enough to defend him," she admitted quietly. "Julian's always been different. Charismatic, but cold. As I said, he's technically my father's youngest cousin, so we did spend time together when I was younger. As we got older, we grew up in different social circles despite being family."

Kate nodded, encouraging her to continue. "What can you tell me about his background? His habits, his friends?"

Lucy took a deep breath, seemingly gathering her thoughts. "Julian was always the black sheep of the family. Brilliant. Troubled. He went to Eton, like most of the men in our family. He got into some trouble there. Some scandal involving stolen exam papers, I think. After that, he disappeared for a while. Traveled abroad, or so we were told."

"When did he resurface?" Kate asked.

"Ten or eleven years ago. I don't remember too well. I was young," Lucy replied. "All I remember is he came back to London, all charm and success. He said he'd been in America and made his fortune in tech startups. The family was relieved, thought he'd finally straightened out. He was going back and forth to the states quite a bit for work, he said."

Kate's eyes narrowed. "The family never got specific information about what startups?"

"I honestly don't think people wanted to know. It was easier to believe he'd changed. Most didn't want to ask too many questions. I know my father told me to stay away from him. He never said more than that."

"What about his current lifestyle? Where does he live? Who does he associate with?" Kate knew she was throwing a lot of questions at the young woman. Any other time she might have worried about a witness shutting down. This time Kate needed to press on.

"He has a flat in Mayfair, very posh," Lucy said. "But, as I said, he travels a lot. Always jetting off to exotic locations. As for friends…" She hesitated. "He doesn't seem to have many close ones. Just business associates, really. And women. There are always women around him."

Kate leaned back, processing the information. "Has Julian been involved with Helix Enterprises?"

Lucy shook her head.

"He never mentioned Helix Enterprises to you? Or anything about a dating app?"

"No, never. But…" She trailed off, biting her lip.

"But what?" Kate prodded.

"Well, now that I think about it, he was the one who introduced me to Lydia," Lucy admitted. "He brought her to a family wedding and said she was a friend. He sat her down next to me and we chatted away, quickly becoming friends. She's how I got involved in all this. It doesn't mean that Julian knew what she was doing."

Kate's eyes glinted. This was the connection they needed. "When was this? Did Julian ever come to the warehouse?"

"About six months ago," Lucy replied. "And no, I never saw Julian there."

Kate believed her and believed it was possible Julian had connected her to Lydia intentionally without ever disclosing his involvement with the syndicate. "Have you ever seen Julian get violent with a woman?"

Lucy averted her eyes from Kate. She opened her mouth to speak then snapped her jaw tight.

"Lucy," Kate said her name softly and leaned in. "This is vitally important. I know he's your family and you're worried about your reputation. If you share information with me, I'll do everything in my power to protect you. He's been accused of murdering several women. If Julian is doing this, we have to stop him and you need to help us do that."

Lucy wavered for several moments. Kate thought she might have to get tougher with her. Then the young woman finally relented, her body slumping back in the chair. "When he was at Eton, there was an incident with a young woman and one of his friends. The family never got the full story and there was never an arrest. I know Julian's father paid off the young woman to keep her quiet. There was talk about stripping Julian of his title. That never happened, but it was made clear that he had to get his act together. He didn't leave London on his own. I believe his father sent him away. He cut him off financially, too. His parents are deceased and cut him completely out of the will."

"What about siblings?"

"Julian is an only child. The full estate was left to others in the family."

"The friend. Do you know his name?" Kate asked, hoping for anything that would shed more light on the situation.

"Benjamin. I don't know his full name. I'm not sure I ever did."

"Benjamin Fuller?" Kate asked, her tone so incredulous she couldn't hold back.

"I honestly don't know. I was just a kid when all of this happened. I only heard talk of it through the family. Nothing concrete. Anytime I asked about him, my father told me to stay away from him."

Kate stood up, her mind already racing with the implications of this new information. "Lucy, I need you to write down everything you know about Julian. His addresses, where he goes, the names of any associates you can recall. Everything."

As Lucy began scribbling on a notepad, Kate stepped out of the interrogation room. She needed to share this breakthrough with Declan and Sam immediately.

She found them in the observation room adjacent to where Lydia was being held. Both men looked up as she entered, their expressions a mix of curiosity and concern.

"Kate?" Declan prompted. "You look like you've seen a ghost."

"Not a ghost," Kate said, her voice tight with tension. "A noble."

Sam's eyebrows shot up. "I'm sorry, what?"

"I know why Annabel's didn't want to give you information and looked at you like you should have already known." Kate launched into a summary of her interview with Lucy. As she spoke, she watched their expressions shift from disbelief to grim determination.

"Bloody hell," Sam muttered when she finished. "A member of the aristocracy is involved in murder and fraud? This is going to be a political nightmare."

"We need to slow down a little. It's a good lead, but can we really say for sure?" Declan cautioned.

Kate understood why he didn't want to jump headfirst. She was all in no matter what he said. She knew she had to make her case. "Lucy puts him in the United States around the time of the first murder. She said he's been traveling back and forth from here to the states. He said he got his money in tech startups. It sounds like his parents all but disowned him then cut him out of the will. There were allegations he assaulted a young woman while at Eton. He's probably desperate for money and had the early hallmarks of violence. Not to mention, Lucy identified him from one of the photos. He's our guy, Declan. I'm sure as I'm standing here."

"Right," Sam said, running a hand through his hair. "So what's our next move? We can't exactly go kicking down doors in Mayfair without rock-solid evidence."

"We start with what we have," Kate replied. "Lucy's given us some leads to follow. We need to dig into Julian's background, his finances, his travel records. We need to keep pressing Lydia and the others. Someone will crack. We also need to explore his connection with Benjamin Fuller. The friend Julian got kicked out of Eton with for assaulting the girl and the owner of Helix Enterprises. Lucy connected them."

Declan cursed softly. "I'll get a team on Julian's background check. Sam, can you use your resources to expedite the process? We need to move fast before word gets out."

"On it," Sam agreed. "I'll also reach out to some royal security contacts I have to see what if anything they will tell me about Julian. I can't have the FBI rushing in to interview them. We need to do this quietly."

Kate gestured toward the door. "Did any of the men confess to anything?"

"No," Sam said with frustration. "I couldn't get anything out of them."

Kate turned to Declan. "Lydia?"

"She refused to speak to me."

Kate wanted to get as much information as she could before legal counsel arrived and the whole interrogation was shut down. "Sam, did any of the men ask for a solicitor?"

"No."

"What one of them seemed the weakest to you? The most likely to crack?" Kate didn't have time to go after the hardest right now. She needed to go after the low hanging fruit.

"Gray Tipton. He wavered a few times in what he told me. The rest barely said a word to me," Sam explained. "Gray at least had a conversation. He denied everything. Stuck to the story that they were a tech firm for the shipping industry. I pressed him that a review of their laptops and such would confirm what we suspect. Still, he wouldn't give anything up. I didn't know what you know going in though. You might have more luck."

As Kate entered the interrogation room, Gray Tipton looked up, his eyes wary. He was younger than she'd expected, probably in his late twenties, with disheveled brown hair and a day's worth of stubble on his chin. With so much going on at the warehouse, Kate didn't remember seeing him there. He didn't register for her, not in a memorable way.

"Mr. Tipton," Kate began, settling into the chair across from him.

"I'm FBI Agent Kate Walsh. I understand you've been less than forthcoming with my colleague."

Gray shrugged, affecting nonchalance. "I told him the truth. We're a tech company for the shipping industry and we were celebrating. I don't know what else you want from me."

Kate leaned forward, her voice low and intense. "What I want is for you to stop lying. We know about the scams, the fake profiles, the stolen money. What we don't know is how deep your involvement goes."

She saw a flicker of uncertainty in Gray's eyes before he masked it. "I don't know what you're talking about."

"No?" Kate said, dripping with sarcasm. "That's not the story I'm getting from your colleagues. They were more than forthcoming with information and pointed the finger at you as the one who orchestrated this whole thing. In fact, they said you were the one that had the direct connection to Julian Barclay. The man who before today I knew as Julian Marlowe, who is the prime suspect in the murder of nine women."

Gray's face paled slightly at the mention of Julian's name, but he remained silent.

Kate pressed on undeterred. "You see, Gray, right now you're looking at some serious charges. Fraud, conspiracy, possibly even accessory to murder. If you cooperate, if you tell us what you know about Julian and his operation, maybe we can work something out."

"Murder?" Gray's voice cracked slightly. "I don't know anything about any murders."

Kate raised an eyebrow. "What about Benjamin Fuller? Does that name ring a bell?"

Gray's reaction was subtle, but Kate caught it – a slight widening of the eyes, a quick intake of breath. He knew something. "I don't know who that is," Gray stammered, but his denial lacked conviction.

"Your boss? You don't know your boss at the tech company?" Kate paused for dramatic effect while she watched him closely. "He's the one Helix Enterprises is registered to. How could you not know him?"

"I'm new and didn't meet him during the hiring process," Gray said with a slight break in his voice.

Kate leaned back, her gaze never leaving Gray's face. "Let me paint a picture for you. Julian Barclay and Benjamin Fuller, best of friends at Eton. Both assaulted a girl while there. Now we have multiple dead women and millions in stolen funds. So why don't you tell me what you know about Julian and Benjamin's partnership?"

Gray's composure cracked. He ran a hand through his hair, his eyes darting around the room. "Look, I…" he stumbled over his words. "I just handle the tech side of things, okay? I don't know about any murders or whatever else you think is going on."

"But you do know Julian and Benjamin," Kate pressed. "Don't you, Gray?"

There was a long pause as Gray seemed to wage an internal battle. Finally, he spoke, his voice barely above a whisper. "Julian is the one who recruited me. He told me he had a foolproof way to make money. I thought it was just going to be some harmless online scams, you know? Nothing serious. I needed to pay for university and a place to live. I needed a way to make money."

Kate didn't care about his plights. "Benjamin?"

Gray hesitated again. "They're tight, you know? Always whispering about something or other. Rarely do they speak openly in front of the rest of us."

Kate leaned in. She had him on the ropes and he knew a lot more than he was saying. "What kind of things did they whisper about?"

"I don't know, I swear!" Gray's voice rose in pitch. Kate remained quiet, forcing him to fill the silence. "Look, all I know is that sometimes Julian would come back from a trip all worked up. He and

Benjamin would lock themselves in the office for hours. After that, Julian would always seem calmer. Like whatever was bothering him had been taken care of."

A chill ran down Kate's spine. "These trips Julian took, do you know where he went?"

Gray shook his head. "He never said. Just that he was meeting investors or checking on business interests. But…" he trailed off, his gaze never leaving Kate.

"What?" Kate pressed.

"Sometimes, when he came back, I'd overhear him talking to Benjamin about loose ends. About making sure everything was clean."

Kate's heart raced. This was it – the connection they needed. Before she could press further, the door to the interrogation room burst open.

A man in an expensive suit strode in, his face set in a grim expression. "This interview is over. Mr. Tipton, don't say another word. I'm Arnold Whitaker, Mr. Tipton's solicitor."

Kate stood, frustration coursing through her. "Your client was just about to provide crucial information in an ongoing investigation. Information that could help his case."

Whitaker ignored her. "Let's go," he said pulling Gray up by the arm and out the door.

As Kate left the room, her mind whirled. They were close, so close to cracking this wide open. With solicitors involved, things were about to get a lot more complicated.

Without Ditch confirming the tech, they had nothing to hold them.

CHAPTER 26

Kate found Declan waiting outside the interrogation room, his expression grim. "That was quite a bombshell Gray dropped before the lawyer showed up."

Kate nodded. "He told me enough to make me interested, not enough to seal the deal. We still don't have enough." She looked at the closed interrogation room doors. "Are they all gone?"

"All of the men and Lydia. They left Lucy here on her own."

Kate pulled back in surprise. "They didn't send any representation for her?"

"No," Declan said with a shake of his head. "I even escorted the solicitor to her door, but he said he wasn't here for her."

It was the first time Kate considered Lucy might be telling her the truth. "This case is getting complicated. We still only have circumstantial evidence on Julian. Nothing yet to tie him directly to the murders."

"Agreed." Declan reached out for her but stopped short of pulling her into a hug. They were standing in between the interrogation rooms. Affection of that kind wouldn't be advisable or acceptable. Kate could see he wanted to comfort her and that was enough. "What do you…" Declan didn't finish because Kate's phone buzzed.

"A message from Sam," she said holding up her phone. "Found something big on Julian. Meet me in the tech lab ASAP."

After asking an officer for directions, they found Sam hunched over a computer screen, his face illuminated by its glow.

"What have you got?" Kate asked, moving to stand beside him.

Sam looked up, his eyes wide with a mix of excitement and disbelief. "You're not going to believe this. Now that we have Julian's real identity, we found something strange in his travel records." He pulled up a series of documents on the screen. "Look at these dates. Every time one of our victims was murdered, Julian was in the same city, usually under the guise of a business trip."

Kate's breath caught in her throat. "How did you find this so fast?"

"I didn't. I called one of my contacts who oversees royal security. Julian doesn't have someone on him. He's not important enough for that, but they have been tracking his passport. They knew he was also at times using an alias. They reported it, but nothing was ever done, so they just kept tracking."

Declan leaned in, his eyes scanning the screen. "I don't understand how they knew he was using an alias but still did nothing. Look, Kate, every trip to Los Angeles. Two of them coincide with the murders. We have proof right here that he was there."

"That's still not enough," Kate said turning to Sam. "Did you find his Mayfair address?"

"We found a home registered to him," Sam said, hesitation in his voice.

"What?" Kate knew there was a *but* in there.

"We don't have enough to search his place or bring him in." Sam noted the growing expression of frustration on her face. "Kate, we haven't tied him directly to anything yet. We still need to go through all the tech to confirm that they are running romance scams. We don't have anything. The few vague statements Lucy made aren't enough to do anything in court. Who's to say she won't recant the whole thing? We also have nothing but some video of Julian having a fight with a woman. He couldn't have been the person who attacked Rue. We have literally nothing concrete."

Kate cursed loudly knowing he was right. "Could you send cops over just to see if he's at the house in Mayfair? I want eyes on him. They don't have to approach or speak to him. Just see if he's there."

Before Sam could respond, a young tech analyst burst into the room, her face pale. "Agent Walsh! Lucy Barclay is gone. An officer just sent me in here to tell you."

"What do you mean, gone?" Kate demanded, her heart sinking.

"She asked to use the restroom. The officer didn't stay with her. He was called away," the analyst explained. "When he went to check on her, she was gone. They are searching the building for her. We believe she left down a back staircase and out the back door."

Declan swore under his breath. "She played us."

Kate didn't know if that was true or if she got spooked when the others left. "We don't know that. She could tip off Julian." Kate headed for the door then stopped short. "She might also be in danger. She knows too much. We need to get to her father."

Sam stopped short. "Kate, I don't know if it's a good idea to involve him."

Kate held her hand up to stop him. "I'm forced to agree with you about going after Julian right now. I admit there is a lot more work to be done. I refuse to concede that we can't speak to Lord Barclay. His daughter is implicated in this and now she's gone. He'll also be able to confirm the things Lucy told us about Julian. We have to interview him. We can do it quietly and without fanfare, but it's going to be done."

Sam turned to Declan. "Your thoughts?"

"I agree with Kate." Declan offered him a sobering look. "I'm sorry, but we don't do this aristocracy thing in the states. No one is off limits with an investigation of this kind."

"There are protocols," Sam started to say. "What about your tech guy? How long until he's here?"

"Ditch is on a flight as we speak. The FBI grabbed him from his swanky hotel room in Los Angeles, picked up the tech he was working on there, and brought him to the airport. He's on a private flight." Declan checked his watch. "He should be here late tonight. Once he gets his hands on everything, this will all be a lot clearer."

"He's that good?" Sam asked, not sounding confident.

"He's the best in the world," Declan assured him.

"Don't we want to wait then to talk to Lord Barclay?"

"No," Kate said, not giving him an inch. "If it all goes bad, just blame it on the Americans." She marched toward the door without looking back. She wasn't taking no for an answer.

Kate, Declan, and Sam pulled up to the imposing gates of the Barclay estate. The sprawling Georgian mansion loomed beyond, a testament to centuries of wealth and privilege.

"Remember," Sam said as they approached the intercom, "we need to tread carefully. Lord Barclay has connections that could shut down our investigation if we push too hard."

Declan nodded grimly. "We can't let him stonewall us."

Sam pressed the intercom button.

After a moment, a clipped voice answered, "Yes?"

"This is Agent Sam Harris of the National Crime Agency, along with FBI Agents Kate Walsh and Declan James. We're here to speak with Lord Bartholomew Barclay regarding an urgent matter."

There was a pause, then the gates slowly creaked open. As they drove up the long, winding driveway, Kate couldn't shake the feeling that they were entering another world entirely.

A butler met them at the door, his face an impassive mask. "If you'll follow me, Lord Barclay will see you in his study."

The interior of the house was as opulent as Kate had imagined, with priceless artworks adorning the walls and antique furniture. The butler led them to a large oak door and knocked softly.

"Enter," responded a commanding voice.

Lord Bartholomew Barclay sat behind an enormous desk, his silver hair immaculately styled, his suit perfectly pressed. He didn't stand as they entered, merely regarded them with cool disdain.

"I assume this is about my daughter," he said, his tone clipped. "I'd like an explanation as to why she was detained and interrogated without my knowledge."

Kate stepped forward, meeting his gaze steadily. "Lord Barclay, I'm FBI Special Agent Kate Walsh. Your daughter was picked up during a raid at a warehouse in East London. Were you aware of that?"

The man said nothing.

Kate went on. "We believe the group we raided were conducting romance scams, targeting lonely women, possibly men too, and hustling them for considerable sums of money. The extent of which we are still investigating. Your daughter admitted she was helping them with social media ads, unaware of what they were really doing."

Kate grew bolder and stepped closer to the man "While yes, we're here about Lucy, we are also here about a matter involving your cousin, Julian Barclay."

Lord Barclay's eyes narrowed. "Julian? What has that miscreant done now?"

"Sir," Declan interjected, "we have reason to believe Julian is involved in a series of serious crimes, including fraud and murder."

Lord Barclay scoffed. "Murder? Preposterous. Julian may be a disappointment to the family, but he's no killer."

"We have evidence suggesting otherwise," Kate pressed. "And now, Lucy has gone missing after providing us with crucial information about Julian."

For the first time, a flicker of concern crossed Lord Barclay's face.

"Missing? What do you mean, missing? I spoke to her about twenty minutes ago. She called to tell me the police had detained her for nothing. I was in the process of speaking to my solicitor when you arrived." He pointed a finger at Sam. "I was also calling your boss."

Sam stepped in, his voice calm but firm. "Lucy left the police station without notifying anyone or permission. Given the sensitive nature of the information she shared, we're concerned for her safety. She was found with some dangerous people and has information about their crimes."

"I don't understand any of this." Lord Barclay's composure cracked slightly. He stood, pacing behind his desk. "This is outrageous. You bring my daughter in for questioning without informing me then tell me she left without permission. She didn't tell me anything like that."

"Lord Barclay," Kate said, her voice level, "I understand your frustration. Our priority is finding Lucy and stopping Julian before anyone else gets hurt. We need your help."

He turned to face them, his expression a mix of anger and growing worry. "What exactly do you think Julian has done?"

Kate took a deep breath. "We have evidence linking him to a sophisticated romance scam operation that's stolen millions from vulnerable victims. More disturbingly, we believe he may be connected to the murders of several women across the United States, United Kingdom, and France. Here in London and in Los Angeles, he met women through matchmakers. He exploited them for millions then murdered them. In one case, there was domestic violence caught on video on the lead up to the murder. He's also using an alias – Julian Marlowe. Your daughter identified him from photos we obtained."

Lord Barclay sank back into his chair, the color draining from his face.

Kate pressed on. "Lord Barclay, anything you can tell us about Julian's past, his associates, his recent activities – it could be crucial in finding him and ensuring Lucy's safety."

"I'm calling my daughter." He reached for a cellphone on the desk and typed on the screen. He held the phone to his ear, his face growing more concerned with the passing of time. Barclay left his daughter a message urging her to come to the house immediately. He expressed his concern for her, leaving out that the police were standing in his study. When he was done, he tossed the phone on his desk. "I don't understand. She just called me."

There was a long pause as Barclay seemed to wage an internal battle. Finally, he spoke, his voice heavy. "You asked about Julian. He has always been troubled with a cruel streak. He's manipulative and cunning. One family member described him as a psychopath. I don't know if that's true, but he's *off*. Not normal. There's something broken inside of him."

None of that surprised Kate. "What about what happened at Eton? Lucy told me about a young woman." Kate left it vague on purpose.

Lord Barclay registered surprise. "I didn't realize she knew. There was an incident with a girl, something the family kept quiet. He was expelled for it."

"Was it an assault?" Kate asked, pressing him to continue.

"Yes. Violent. Sexual." He shook his head in disgust. "It was dreadful."

Kate wasn't going to tread lightly. "The family covered it up. Paid off the girl and her family to stay quiet about it. Isn't that exactly what happened?"

Barclay avoided Kate's eyes. "We did," he admitted so quietly she wasn't sure she heard him. "No matter what my uncle tried he wasn't able to curtail Julian's behavior. You have to understand the scandal it would have caused."

Kate didn't feel the least bit sorry for him. Had the family taken appropriate action and let Julian face the natural consequences of his behavior, they might not have nine murdered women on their hands.

Barclay kept making excuses for the family as he watched their faces turn up in disgust. "Please, you have to understand. We tried. My uncle thought cutting him off financially would finally straighten him out. He felt like he was out of options. The whole family felt that way."

"It didn't stop him," Sam prompted.

"No," Barclay admitted. "Instead, Julian left London. We assumed he was off somewhere in Europe – Germany or France finding himself. We hoped having to live on his own would do him some good. Give him a sense of responsibility. Make him grow up. When he returned years later, he seemed changed. Successful, charming. But there was something still *off* about him. I know I keep coming back to that word. I can't define it more. I couldn't put my finger on it. I warned Lucy to keep her distance."

Kate took another step toward him. "Do you know anything about Julian's business dealings now or while he was away?"

Barclay took a breath. "Julian became secretive after Eton. He barely spoke to any of us and didn't tell us anything about his time away or what he was doing upon his return. His answers were vague. You have to understand, none of us wanted anything to do with him. As a result, distance was our best option. We didn't press him."

Declan took a few steps toward him, standing right next to Kate. "What about Benjamin Fuller? Do you recognize that name?"

At the mention of Fuller's name, Barclay's eyes widened slightly and his hand went to his chest. He didn't respond. He got up from the chair and moved quickly to a wet bar in the back of the room.

Kate watched as the man poured himself a shot of whiskey with a shaky hand.

He downed the liquid in one gulp and turned back to them. "If Julian is still associating with Benjamin Fuller, then we have a real problem."

CHAPTER 27

"Explain yourself," Kate demanded, her heart thumping in her chest, matching the panic in Barclay's eyes.

Barclay poured himself another but didn't consume it. He held the glass in front of him, his hand trembling slightly. "Benjamin Fuller and Julian were thick as thieves at Eton. He was the other young man accused of assaulting the girl. My family believes he was the one who got Julian off track. To be fair maybe they are two psychopaths coming together and feeding off each other. Benjamin was institutionalized at one point."

"Mental illness?" Declan asked.

"It was after the assault," Barclay said. "It was his family's response to the unspeakable acts. Maybe that's what we should have done with Julian. I don't know. I also don't know if Benjamin ever received an official diagnosis of anything other than being a terrible human being." Barclay raised the glass to his lips and took a long sip. When he was done, he mused, "We had hoped they'd lost touch, but…" He trailed off, lost in thought.

"But what?" Kate persisted, refusing to take her foot off the gas now.

Barclay lowered his eyes to the floor. "About a year ago, at a family wedding, I overheard Julian on the phone. He was speaking in hushed tones. I distinctly heard him say 'Benji' and something about 'the next round of the game.' I thought nothing of it at the time. Now…" He gestured with his hand as if to say it should have mattered then.

Kate exchanged glances with Declan and Sam.

With urgency in her voice, Kate said, "We believe Julian has been involved with Benjamin Fuller all along. The business your daughter was working for is called Helix Enterprises, owned by a Benjamin Fuller. We believe they were involved in this scam together. It seems Benjamin brought in other people. I assume the thrill of the online scam wasn't enough for Julian and he branched out to meeting these women in person." Kate wasn't sure that's how it went at all. For all she knew, Julian had started it and brought Benjamin in. It was all a theory at this point.

Barclay met her eyes. "While I can't deny that it's a possibility, murder seems such a stretch for me to believe. The fraud and the unscrupulous activity with women makes sense. Murder does not."

Kate understood why he'd think that way. It was often hard for a suspect's family to think a person could do such awful things. "Would you be willing to call him and ask to meet? We haven't been able to get eyes on him."

"He won't see me," Barclay said. "We had a falling out last year after that family wedding. If I reached out to him, he'd immediately suspect me, especially because now Lucy has been dragged into this." It was as if he just remembered his daughter's involvement. "Please believe me, she'd have nothing to do with scamming people. I'm sure it's a misunderstanding."

Kate assured him she believed Lucy didn't know what was happening, even though she wasn't so sure herself. If she accused his daughter now, he might shut down. "Do you know where we can find Benjamin?"

"I have no idea. As I said, we had hoped they lost touch. I didn't know much about him from their time at Eton. I don't know anything about the family either."

"Anyone in your family who would have that information?"

Barclay shook his head. "It was so long ago."

"What about Julian? Where can we find him?" Sam asked, not waiting for a response. He went on, "We know he has a residence in Mayfair. I assume he's not there but we will certainly go there after here. If he's not, do you have any idea where he might have gone? Any properties abroad, favorite destinations?"

Lord Barclay frowned, considering. "The family has a villa in the South of France, near Nice. Also, Julian always spoke fondly of a place in the Cayman Islands, though I'm not sure if he owns property there."

Kate got the address of the place in France. It wouldn't be far from Leo's chateau. The place in the Cayman Islands would take some research as Barclay didn't have the address. "Is there anything else you can tell us?"

Barclay's composure finally crumbled. "Please," he said, his voice breaking slightly, "find my daughter. Whatever Julian's done, Lucy isn't a knowing part of it. She's young and naïve, too trusting for her own good, but she's not...she wouldn't..." He couldn't finish the sentence.

Kate felt a pang of sympathy for the man. Despite his initial arrogance, it was clear he cared deeply for his daughter. "We'll do everything in our power to find Lucy and bring her home safely," she assured him. "Is there anywhere she might be hiding out? Friends? Other family?"

"I can try all of those myself. I'll get further. They might not speak to you if she's hiding from the police. If I find her, I'll let you know."

Kate knew he wasn't going to give up any information to implicate anyone else. "Yes, please do that." She didn't tell him that they'd need to speak to Lucy again. The most important thing now was finding her.

They thanked him for the information and turned to leave. Lord

Barclay called out, "Wait." He moved to a nearby safe, entering a complex code. From it, he withdrew a thick file. "This is everything the family has on Julian – financial records, known associates, properties. I had it compiled years ago when we were trying to keep track of his whereabouts. We've tried to keep it as up-to-date as we are able given his secrecy. I never thought it would come to this."

Kate took the file, nodding gratefully. "Thank you. This could be invaluable."

As they left the study, he stopped them one last time. "Agents," he said, his tone somber, "whatever Julian's done, whatever he's become, he's still family. If he's harmed those women, if he's put Lucy in danger, do what you must to stop him."

The weight of Barclay's words hung heavy in the air as Kate, Declan, and Sam left the mansion. As they climbed back into their car, Kate's mind raced, processing the new information.

Sam started the engine. "Where to now?"

"Julian's house in Mayfair. I realize we don't technically have enough to bring him in. I want to question him. Maybe I can get him to implicate himself." She saw the worried look on Sam's face. "I promise, I'll be gentle."

As they sped away from the Barclay estate, Kate couldn't shake the feeling they were on the verge of breaking this case wide open. With that hope came a chilling realization – the closer they got to Julian, the more dangerous their pursuit. The game, as Julian had called it while on the phone with Benjamin, was far from over. Kate was determined to see it through to the end, all the while mentally preparing for the possibility of two killers working in tandem, or possibly worse, in competition with each other.

The streets of London blurred past as Kate, Declan, and Sam raced towards Julian's Mayfair flat. Kate's mind was in overdrive, piecing together the fragments of information they'd gathered.

Kate recalled Sam's earlier conversation about speaking to the security service. "Sam, what else did you find on Julian's background?"

Navigating the London's streets with ease, Sam responded, "It's a mixed bag. On paper, he's clean as a whistle since his return to London. He has stayed out of the public eye, which is probably why no one recognized him from the photo on the news. Things on the surface look good. Dig a little deeper and things get murky. There are gaps in his history, periods where he seems to vanish off the grid entirely. Much of what Lord Barclay just told us."

"Benjamin Fuller?" Declan asked from the backseat.

"We haven't been able to find much." Sam slowed for a stop light. "Benjamin is much more careful. Very few public records. It's like he's a ghost."

Kate nodded, her suspicions confirmed. "I think they are a team and always have been. Julian's the face, the charming aristocrat. Benjamin's the one who stays in the background, handling the dirty work, the online scam." Kate didn't know anything about Benjamin, so it was hard to create a profile. Even if she found out the name of the place where he'd been institutionalized, they weren't going to share records with her.

"Do you think there is any chance they compete with each other?" Declan asked, touching her shoulder.

"The *game* he referenced on the phone?"

Declan confirmed. "If it's a game, are they in a competition?"

Sam didn't seem to catch on. "Do you mean how much they are stealing from people?"

"I don't think that's all Declan means." Kate turned halfway around and shared a look with him. He knew exactly what she had been thinking. "He's wondering if they set up this team to scam people online and they have both taken it offline. He's wondering, and it occurred to me too, that they might both be killing people."

Sam's grip tightened on the steering wheel. "That's not possible, is it? I searched for every possible connection across Europe and the United States. I didn't find other victims."

"Did you check male victims?" Declan asked.

Air deflated from all of them. "It didn't even occur to me," Sam said after a moment.

The truth was they didn't know anything about Benjamin. They didn't know his sexuality or his preferences. They knew he had possibly assaulted a girl at Eton but nothing more. If he was competing with Julian, they didn't know if he was killing in the same way each time, which was a hallmark of a serial killer. The truth was they knew almost nothing more than they had earlier in the day.

"We're going to have to do a lot more research." Sam pulled the car to the curb in front of the address.

The Mayfair house stood like a sentinel of wealth and secrets, its elegant façade a blend of Georgian and contemporary architecture. Cream-colored stone adorned the exterior, polished to a glimmer. Window boxes overflowed with fall blooms, their colors a stark contrast to the season. A wrought-iron fence brokered the property line from the street, typical of the neighborhood. Kate guessed none of his genteel neighbors would assume a serial killer lurked behind the home's glamorous exterior.

Kate's eyes scanned the property as she stepped out of the vehicle. "This place screams money and influence," she murmured, adjusting her jacket against the crisp London air.

Declan followed suit, his expression a mix of awe and wariness. "If Julian's in there, it's a fortress." He turned back toward the car. Sam was still seated in the driver's seat, his phone now pressed to his ear. He tapped Kate on the shoulder to alert her as she started toward the house.

As she turned back around, Sam ended the call as his brow furrowed with urgency. He called her back to the car. "Julian's not here. He's at the airport in a private jet."

"What?" Declan exclaimed, eyes widening in disbelief.

Sam replied, "We need to go now if we are to have any chance to stop him. I asked my contact to see if he could do anything, but it's unlikely he can ground the plane. We don't have the authority."

With little time to waste, Kate and Declan slid back into the car. "How long does it take to get to the airport?" she asked as she strapped herself in.

"Forty minutes," Sam replied, slamming the gear into drive and turning on the police lights. The tires screeched as he sped off, weaving through the traffic that seemed unusually thick for a Thursday afternoon.

"Can't you send closer officers there?" Declan urged his voice a mix of impatience and fear. "You have to have some pull."

"I can't," Sam said, his knuckles turning white on the steering wheel. "As I said, we have no authority to ground him. The evidence just isn't there yet. I'll never get the authority in time. The best we can do is get there and see if he'll talk to us."

"That's never going to happen." Kate leaned forward, her mind racing. "If he's got Lucy with him—"

"Then we need to get to that plane," Sam interjected. "We need to intercept them before he leaves the country."

The streets of London blurred into a streak of colors as Sam maneuvered through the congested traffic, his eyes fixed on the road ahead. "Hang on!" he shouted as he swerved around a double-decker bus. The vehicle's sudden lurch sent Kate and Declan bracing against the seats.

Declan reached for his phone. "I'll try to get through to the airport security. They must be able to do something to delay them."

The thought of Lucy being in Julian's clutches made her heart race.

"We can't let him escape," she said, her voice steady despite the urgency that gnawed at her gut. She turned back to Declan. "Call! Try anyone and see what you can do!"

Declan frantically tapped at the screen of his cellphone, and when he reached someone, he shouted directions that Kate wasn't sure anyone would follow. His frustration evident.

As they approached the airport, Sam navigated through the main entrance and then cut down a service road to the private hangers. He quickly found a spot to park, the engine still running as they piled out.

An array of luxury jets lined the runway. Kate's heart pounded as she scanned the area, searching for any sign of Julian or Lucy.

"Which plane?" Declan asked, anxiety evident in his voice.

"I don't know," Sam admitted, frustration creeping into his tone. "We need to find someone who can help us."

Suddenly, a shout broke through the din. "Stop right there!" A security officer was sprinting toward them, gesturing for them to halt.

"I'm with the National Crime Agency!" Sam shouted, stepping forward, showing his badge. "We're looking for a suspect who boarded a jet. Julian Barclay. I was informed he was about to take off. We need to know which plane! Now!"

The officer's expression shifted, recognizing the urgency. "That one," he said, pointing toward a sleek black jet that was just beginning to taxi down the runway.

"Come on!" Kate shouted, adrenaline surging. She dashed toward the plane, her heart pounding in sync with their footsteps. They hit the tarmac as the roar of the jet engines grew louder and the plane started its ascent, taking any hope of stopping it with its flight.

Kate tipped her head back, shouting a string of curses at the sky. She got out her frustration then turned to Declan. "We may have lost Julian for now," she said, her voice steely, "but Benjamin Fuller is still out there. I bet he knows exactly where his partner has gone."

CHAPTER 28

Sam wasted no time in rushing back to the security agent. "I need to see the manifest and know where the plane is headed." The man didn't move fast enough for Sam. He snapped, "Move! This is a matter of international security."

He followed the security agent back inside the terminal, leaving Kate and Declan standing outside. Declan noted the frustration on her face. "I know it seems like we keep getting close only for the rug to be ripped out from underneath us. We are getting closer, Kate."

"I know," she said dismissively. "We need eyes on that address in France and to find any property he owns in the Cayman Islands."

"Let me call and get us some help," Declan said reaching for his phone.

Kate reached out and stopped him. "Let's use Leo for this. He has...contacts."

Declan arched an eyebrow. "Don't you think we've gotten a little too comfortable relying on information from those contacts?"

Kate wasn't going to deny the obvious. They both knew Leo had connections that the FBI and its database didn't. If Leo was on the team, they were going to use him. "I'm not questioning how he gets the information. We don't know how many are truly dead between Julian and Benjamin, not to mention the countless scammed from the app. You wanted Leo on the team and I'm going to use what we have available." She knew her tone had come across as snarky and meaner than she had intended. The truth was Kate felt conflicted about using Leo in this way.

The pressure to stop Julian was too great.

Declan found middle ground. "How about you tell him to use both avenues and cross-reference the information?"

"Fine by me," Kate said and stepped away to call Leo. She reached him immediately and provided a brief update about where the case stood and what she needed from him. "Everything you can get me about property connected to Julian Barclay. We've searched for his alias Julian Marlowe and came up short. With this new information, we might get further. The Barclay family is noble. Julian is a lord, so you might want to include that in the search."

"You can't be serious. This guy that you think has done all of this is a nobleman? How can that be?" Leo sounded completely perplexed by it.

Kate felt the weight of his concern and confusion. "It's too much to go into. Let's meet tonight for dinner and I'll update you completely. Declan is meeting Ditch at the airport later. You and I can get together then. Please, as soon as you find anything, let me know." She paused then added, "I know you'll use our database, but if there's any other way you can access the information, please do it. I know we need to discuss your methods. There are many lives at stake right now."

"I'm on it, Kate," was all he said before the call ended.

She knew he meant what he said and she could trust him. Kate raised her eyes to Declan who was staring at her. "Don't give me that look. You're the one who brought him onto the team."

The corners of his lips turned up in a teasing smile. "I'm surprised how quickly the tides have turned. You were always such a stickler for the rules."

"I know," she said with a sigh. "I'm tired of always feeling so behind.

If we have an ace up our sleeve, we should use it. We haven't asked him to do anything illegal or that will jeopardize a case. It's finding background information."

Before Declan could respond, Sam rushed out of the building. "He has Lucy with him. Her name is on the manifest. The people I spoke to said she seemed willing to go. They were chatting amicably and she didn't appear to be in any distress. It's only the two of them. The destination is unknown."

Declan's voice growled with anger, "What do you mean it's unknown? How can it possibly be unknown? Is that even legal? Wouldn't he have to arrange customs?"

Sam held a hand up to stop him. "He isn't doing anything illegal. That much I can tell you. I assume someone here at the airport has the information. It's going to be finding a needle in a haystack."

Kate knew that would take forever. "I'm going to call Lord Barclay and see what he can access. Knowing that Lucy is definitely on that plane should give us some authority."

"She's an adult, Kate," Sam reminded her. "We also had no legal authority to hold her. It wasn't right that she left the way she did, but she wasn't technically in custody. She was free to leave."

Kate blew out a frustrated breath, knowing Sam was right. "I'm calling him regardless." Kate walked back toward the building away from Sam and Declan. She placed the call, got past the gatekeeper who answered the phone, and had him on the line in a few minutes.

"Have you found my daughter?"

"She's on a flight with Julian. His private jet did not report where they were headed. I can't say for sure if she went with him willingly. The airport staff said they were chatting amicably. While that might be true, we don't know if she was doing it because he instructed her to do so. What connections do you have that can help us find that flight?" Kate explained about the legal bind they were in and that they had no reason to hold Lucy or consider her a kidnapped or missing person.

Her explanation was met with silence.

Kate waited a beat then apologized. "I'm not used to having my hands tied like this. If there was anything I could be doing, I'd be doing it. I believed your daughter and I believe her to be in danger. I'm out of my element here in London and don't have the power or contacts I'd normally have in the states. We need your help, Lord Barclay. Your daughter needs your help."

"Understood," he said finally after a painful amount of silence. "I'll be in touch."

Kate walked back to Declan and Sam. "We need to go back to the office and search the database for any unsolved murders with men that might fit these crimes. We can also search other romance scams and see if we get any hits."

With no one in disagreement, Sam drove them back to the police station. They fell into contemplative silence on the way. Once back at the station, Kate lingered outside, telling Sam she'd be there shortly. She wanted some fresh air. Once Sam headed in, she pulled Declan aside.

"I want to find Lydia's address and interview her," Kate said, keeping her voice low.

"She invoked her right to counsel," Declan reminded her.

"I know but things have changed. We know about Julian and Benjamin. Lydia and Lucy were friends. Lydia is the one who got Lucy involved. She might want to protect her. I'll see if she's willing to speak to me. If she invokes counsel or refuses to speak to me and sends me on my way, I'll be gone." Kate saw the doubt in his eyes. "I swear, Declan, I'm not going to do anything to jeopardize the case. Sam is more rigid than I expected and I understand his reasoning. We need a break and I think I can get through to Lydia."

"We do need a break in the case, a big solid break," Declan agreed, glancing back at the building. "Go. I'll cover for you with Sam. Be careful, Kate. We don't know if she's dangerous."

Kate assured him she'd be safe. As he walked back toward the building, Kate used her phone to search for the woman's address. She found a flat for Lydia Berman in Notting Hill.

The scent of freshly brewed coffee hung in the air outside of the flat Kate believed belonged to Lydia. A bakery took up the space on the ground floor. The lights were still on even at this late hour, but the sign read closed at four. Kate checked her watch and it was nearing six. She considered the baker might be working on tomorrow's goods.

Kate rang the buzzer on the outside of the door for the flat on the top floor. She waited as a light drizzle fell down on her. "Yes?" a familiar voice asked from the small metal box.

Kate had no reasonable pretext to get into the building. She had to be honest. "Lydia, it's Agent Kate Walsh. I need to speak to you. It's important."

"Go away," the voice insistently echoed back.

"Please," Kate pleaded, her voice steady but laced with urgency. "Julian has Lucy. They left about an hour ago on a private flight. We don't know where they are headed, and we don't know if she went with him willingly. She disclosed information about him – damaging information about the romance scam operation. I'm here alone. Just me, against the wishes of the National Crime Agency. I'm not here to arrest you. In fact, I can't arrest you. I don't have the authority to do that. I can help get you immunity if you help us."

Kate stood there for several long moments until a buzzing sound rang out and she grabbed for the door before Lydia changed her mind.

Once at the top floor and seated at the woman's round kitchen table, Lydia shifted in her chair, her fingers nervously fidgeting with the hem of her oversized sweater. She was more casually dressed and her posture looser than it had been earlier in the day.

Lydia shook her head. "I don't know where she is, Agent Walsh. I wish I knew. I haven't spoken to her since we were at the warehouse earlier today. I was surprised she didn't leave with us when the solicitor showed up. I grew concerned for her then. I assumed her father came to retrieve her. She hasn't responded to any of my texts and calls."

"You brought her into this mess. You had to know she might have been angry about that," Kate interrupted, leaning forward. Lydia said nothing in response. Kate got the sense that no matter what the woman told her, she wasn't going to implicate herself much.

"Look," Kate started, "I know you and Julian are connected. Lucy told me as much. He's dangerous, and right now, he's taken Lucy on a chartered flight to a destination unknown."

Lydia's face paled. "I don't know anything about his plans."

Kate's voice remained firm but coaxing. "Help me find Lucy. You know Julian. Tell me what you know."

Lydia looked away, her gaze drifting to the window where the bustling street outside continued obliviously. "I can't betray him like that." She licked her lips nervously. "You can't make me betray him."

There was something sad in Lydia's eyes, more than betraying an acquaintance or even a friend. Kate took a swing based on a flicker of intuition. "Were you romantically involved with Julian?"

The question pierced through Lydia's icy demeanor. Tears welled in her eyes, and she blinked them back defiantly. "I don't want to believe he's capable of hurting anyone. He's been a part of my life for years."

"What about Lucy? Is she just collateral damage in your loyalty to Julian?" Kate pressed, her tone softening slightly. "Think about her. What would she want you to do?"

Silence hung between them, thick and charged. Finally, Lydia let out a shuddering breath. "The Julian I met years ago has changed. You have to understand he's not the same man I once knew."

"Are you involved with him?"

"Not anymore," Lydia admitted. "We met at a party years ago. He was charming and funny. He took me on extravagant holidays. He bought me expensive jewelry. Did anything to impress me, and I was more than impressed." She sighed deeply. "I was head over heels in love with him. I'm probably still in love if I were to admit it to myself. We've not been together like that in a long time, four years or more. I stopped counting."

"You remained friends though?" Kate asked, trying to get a sense of the relationship.

Lydia offered a curt nod. "We stayed friends. Having a little bit of Julian in my life was better than having none. He's also not here in London much. He travels extensively."

"Do you know about the other women he's been involved with?"

Lydia averted her eyes, fixing her stare on the counter next to them. "I knew he was involved and there always seemed to be excess around him – cars, watches, designer clothes, high-end travel. I also knew his family cut him off financially. I had questions. He told me he ran an online business but wasn't forthcoming about what that was, until later."

Kate needed to pin down the timeline. "You said you stopped being involved with him four years ago. When did the involvement start?"

"Two years before that. We had two years together. We met at a charity ball and hit it off right away. He pursued me relentlessly until he stopped."

The first murder was ten years ago. He came back to London after that and had killed several women while he was also involved with Lydia. Kate had to walk a fine line. "Did you know he was in Los Angeles?"

"I knew," Lydia said, not being clear.

"Did you know about the murder in Los Angeles or just that he was there? That's two drastically different things."

Lydia wiped a tear from her eye. "I knew about women in Los Angeles. Not murder. I was always faithful to him. I couldn't say the same for Julian. The worst was when he was back here in London and I'd see him with them sometimes. He said they were rich older women who were willing to pay him to sleep with them. He assured me he didn't care about them at all, as if that mattered. He told me he needed a way to make money and he threw it in my face that he was using some of that money on me. He said unless I had a way of making that kind of money, he was going to continue doing what he was doing and I could live with it or leave."

Kate caught the anger that rose up in Lydia's tone. "That sounds like a harsh way to have a relationship with someone. Julian sounds like a man who has little respect for women."

"You think so?" Lydia scoffed. "The only problem is you don't see it until it's too late. He's great at what they call love bombing. That's the word for it now. I didn't know it then. I thought he had fallen in love with me and we were going to spend the rest of our lives together. Then as soon as I was in love with him, he changed."

Kate was seeing a different side to the cold detached woman she'd seen in the interrogation room. "Was he abusive to you? We know he was physically abusive to a woman in Los Angeles."

Lydia shook her head. "Never physically. Probably emotionally and psychologically."

Kate resisted the urge to ask her why she stayed. "How did the relationship end?"

"I have some self-respect, Agent Walsh. He was back here in London and out with a different woman every night. I wasn't a priority. I couldn't take it anymore. His sweet talking was no longer working.

I saw through the charade and once you see through it, there's no going back." Whether Lydia sensed the next question or noted the look on Kate's face, she added, "I know I said I still loved him. The feelings remained even when I could no longer stand to be around him romantically."

"Tell me about the romance scams."

Lydia laughed ironically and rolled her eyes up toward the ceiling. "If you can believe it, Julian said that was my consolation prize. He couldn't be faithful to me, but he could show me how he made money." She lowered her head and locked her gaze on Kate. "I grew up in a poor family with little means. Money was my ticket to a better life."

Kate didn't relate to the feeling because she'd been fortunate to grow up with means. She'd certainly seen how money could take an otherwise rational person and turn them into someone they weren't.

She dropped any judgement from her tone. "Tell me about it."

CHAPTER 29

Lydia got up and got a glass of water. She sipped it as she leaned against the counter looking down at Kate, stalling as if deciding how much to tell her. Finally, after Kate assured her about immunity again, she relented. "Julian introduced me to online romance scams. At first, it was just fun—nothing serious. I enjoyed flirting with men."

"But?" Kate sensed there was more she wasn't saying.

"It was hard toying with people's feelings like that. People got more attached than I realized. The money was good and I was living a better life than I'd ever lived." She shook her head in disgust. "It was hard to hurt people."

"Tell me how it worked."

"An app. We usually target lonely individuals, recently divorced or widowed are the prime targets. Those who never found love are also the most desperate for attention. We create a persona, gain their trust, then ask for money, usually for some emergency. Typically, it's an emergency that allows us to keep talking to them, to keep them on the hook or make them feel bad for us. It works eighty percent of the time, which are fairly good odds."

"The rest of the time? When it didn't work?"

"We bailed," Lydia said as if it were obvious. "If we couldn't get them to say yes to the first amount of money we ask for, then we cut off communication. Block them in burner phones and move on. The threat of that sometimes reeled them back in. We'd manipulate. Say things like 'If you're not even willing to help, how much can you love me?'"

"Did you target men or women?"

"I targeted men. It's all online, so I could have targeted women too. I found men easier. More natural for me."

"Is there a difference in how men and women fall for the scams?"

Lydia nodded. "Men are more visual. They require a lot more photos through the process. They aren't happy with one or two like many women. They don't fall for the scam for as long. They want more access – phone calls, video and to meet in person. You might have one or two chances to get money from them as compared to women who will give over a longer period of time. Usually the first ask with men can be bigger financially than with women. You have to ease women in more."

Kate had a lot she wanted to say, admonish this woman for being so cold and calculating. None of that would help her get information. She remained silent as Lydia started to squirm.

She fidgeted with the glass. "It's cruel I know. I didn't even know I was capable of being that cruel."

"When do you know it's time to move on?"

"Sometimes the person cut us off and other times we've taken people for everything they have and they were tapped out. We discard them and move on to someone fresh. The app is full of lonely people looking for someone to connect with. People are lonely, Agent Walsh, and lonely people are vulnerable to any kind of connection."

Kate swallowed the words she wanted to say. "What were you celebrating today?"

"One of the guys got twenty-five thousand. He convinced a woman in France he was going to be thrown out of his house because he was behind on his mortgage. He's been promising her that if he can save the house, he will be freed up to spend time with her."

Kate's stomach roiled with sickness. This wasn't just cruel it was diabolical. She didn't know how anyone could do this to another human being. She asked Lydia several more questions to better understand the operation at the warehouse. They had all been brought in by Julian. Lydia confirmed that Lucy hadn't been involved in any of the scams, only to help them with marketing the app. As Lucy had told her, she'd only found out that day the real reason behind the app.

"Were you concerned Lucy was going to tell someone?" Kate asked.

Lydia shook her head. "Julian assured me that he'd keep her quiet. He said Lucy was a good kid and that she'd help. That she was looking for some excitement in her life."

That confirmed for Kate what she had suspected. "What about their royal connection? Did you think that might be a problem for this...*operation*."

Lydia shook her head. "They are distant, cousins of cousins. I don't even know the full connection to the royal family to be honest with you. I figured their titles would keep us safer. The last thing they are going to want to do is get caught and cause a scandal. I don't know if you know anything about how this works over here, but the last thing posh people with titles want to do is cause a scandal."

"Is the group we brought in today the full network?"

Lydia pursed her lips and breathed out her nose. "I don't actually know. Julian has said he has people all over the globe, small operations like the one here in London. If that's true, I can't confirm."

"I need specifics," Kate demanded.

"I don't have them. Julian is the head of this but he doesn't share much with the rest of us. Benjamin might know more. He was more the business operations side of things."

"Help me to understand the relationship with Benjamin. His name is on the business Helix Enterprises. That's a big risk for him to take. I know their relationship goes back to Eton. What is it like now?" Kate didn't tell her about the accusation of them assaulting a young woman together.

Lydia turned back to the sink and filled her glass with water. She carried it back over to the table and sat. "He's Julian's right-hand man. They've been working together for years. Sometimes I've wondered if Benjamin is in love with Julian. They have a complicated relationship."

"Is Julian romantically involved with him?"

Lydia released a laugh. "Absolutely not. I'm not saying Julian doesn't flirt with him or even act like it might be a possibility. I think he keeps Benjamin on the same string he kept me on. Julian is straight. Benjamin is being played as much as the rest of us. Why do you think he'd be willing to use his name and tie it to a sham business?"

Kate didn't know but being secretly *or not so secretly* in love with him certainly made sense. "What role does Benjamin play in all of this? Has he been scamming people online too?"

"He has. I don't know to what extent. He seems to mostly be the money guy."

Kate needed to pivot for a moment. "How does the money work when you scam someone? Who is getting paid?"

"We have a range of accounts the money goes into. It's all managed by Benjamin and then we get a cut. I get paid once a month based on how I did that month. This is all information Benjamin tracks." Lydia tucked her hair behind her ears. "It's actually quite a sophisticated network. I don't know how he keeps all of it straight, but he does."

"How much did you make last month?"

Lydia shifted her eyes away from Kate. "Nearly twenty thousand pounds and that was a slow month for me."

The pit in Kate's stomach grew. "How many people are you usually scamming at one time?"

"As many as I can manage. Four to six usually. It's a full-time job." There was nearly pride in Lydia's statement then she saw Kate's anger start to rise. "You asked me and I'm telling you. You said I'd have immunity."

"You will," Kate said, begrudgingly. She shifted the conversation back as she recalled the phone call Lord Barclay overheard between Julian and Benjamin. She referenced it now for Lydia. "Do you know if Benjamin is doing what Julian was doing – meeting women in person and scamming them?"

"I never heard him speak of it. As I said he might be gay. I've never seen him with a woman or speak about one."

"What about men? Could he be doing this with men?"

Lydia offered her a non-committal shrug. "I really don't know. Benjamin isn't like Julian. He's quieter. I'd think he's more of a follower. The only conversations I've had with him are financial and he's an astute financial manager." She sat back and considered what she was saying. "The truth is, I don't know Benjamin all that well. The one thing I've learned doing this is that a good scam artist can be anyone they want their target to believe they are. That can be true for Benjamin as much as it's true for Julian. If you honestly believe Julian is killing these women then that's a side of him I've never seen. He's never laid a hand on me or anyone else I know. Psychologically manipulative, sure. Emotionally abusive, possibly. Never violent that I've seen."

Kate wasn't surprised by that. True psychopaths had a way of curating their personalities to fit the audience. Like an actor on stage, they could play the part that was needed to meet whatever end goal they were trying to meet. "Have you spoken to either Julian or Benjamin since we raided the warehouse today?"

"No. The solicitor didn't have any information either. When I asked him who called him in to get us, he didn't say. I got thinking maybe the warehouse has hidden cameras and someone knew the FBI showed up. Benjamin or Julian. Who knows?"

That would make the most sense to Kate, given Julian seemed immediately on the move. "Where can I find Benjamin now? Is he often at the warehouse with you?" Kate asked one question after another without slowing. What she really wanted to know was where she could find all the financial information but didn't want to ask that directly.

"He's rarely at the warehouse. He works from a home office." Lydia hesitated. "He owns a townhouse in Chelsea. I can give you the address."

"Please do," Kate urged, her heart racing. She didn't want to appear too eager. Kate wanted to rush out of there with the information and call Sam and Declan. She had felt her phone buzzing against her thigh the entire time she was meeting with Lydia and hadn't wanted to break the conversation to answer it. She assumed one of them was trying to reach her.

Lydia scribbled the address down and slid the paper across the table. "I can't believe I'm doing this. If Julian finds out..."

"Let me worry about that," Kate said, her voice steady.

"What about Lucy? Do you think he'd hurt her?"

"I have no idea," Kate said honestly as she stood to leave. "Do you have any idea where Julian might have gone? Anywhere he might have taken you away? A cabin or beach house? Something secluded?"

"No," Lydia said with a trace of sadness in her voice. "We mostly stayed at hotels when we went away. For all the years I've known him, now that you've put me on the spot about it, I'm realizing I knew little about him. I'm sorry I can't be of more help. I do hope Lucy is okay."

"Did she have a close relationship with him?" Kate thought she might know better than Lord Barclay.

"Julian spoke of her more than she spoke about him. He had a real interest and fondness for her. Maybe Lucy didn't want to say anything mean about him to me because she knew we were friends."

Kate got to the door and turned back. "Do you think there was any reason Julian had an interest in Lucy?"

"He said she was a sweet kid. I know he hated her father," Lydia said. "He hated his whole family. Lucy seemed to be the only one he ever spoke nicely about. I hope taking her isn't about revenge."

Kate hoped it too. For the first time she considered Julian taking her might be his bargaining chip. "If he contacts you, please contact me directly." Kate left her a card with all her contact information.

She rushed down the stairs out to the street then pulled her cellphone from her pocket. Kate had missed two calls from Leo and several from Declan. She scrolled to her texts. Leo left a message that he had two potential addresses for Julian – one in Berlin and another in France, not in Nice but in Paris. He also had found information about Benjamin. He asked Kate to call him when she got the chance.

Declan had simply texted her to call him immediately. She punched in his number first. The phone rang a few times and when he answered, Kate rushed the news about Lydia's interview. "She talked to me, Declan. I got her to talk. She confessed everything to me. Julian is the leader and Benjamin is the money man. He's the one in control of the business side of things."

Declan wasn't surprised that she had been successful. "I had to tell Sam, Kate. He asked me several times where you went. I tried to stall him but I didn't want to outright lie."

"I didn't expect you to lie. Is he angry?" Kate wasn't sure she cared.

"Sam was at first. I talked him down. I think knowing you were successful might mitigate his anger. He didn't think you'd get information and assumed you'd just cause trouble."

"I got everything, except where we can find Julian. Leo texted me some options." It occurred to Kate that Declan had been trying to call her for the last two hours. She apologized for monopolizing the conversation. "What did you need?"

"We found some suspicious murders, Kate. Four men in rich areas of town. They were all killed in various ways over the last ten years. It's not as consistent as the murdered women in timing and type of murder though."

"Do you know their sexual orientation?"

"I think heterosexual. It doesn't specify in all the files."

Kate worked double time to figure out what that could mean. She turned and stared back up at Lydia's flat. Could she be a killer? Kate didn't think so, but the one thing consistent about this case was no one was who they seemed. "I think it's something we can explore. I don't see it as a priority right now with everything on our plate."

Declan didn't disagree with that. "Are you coming back?"

Kate had something else in mind. "I want you and Sam to meet me in Notting Hill. Lydia gave me a current address for Benjamin. We need to bring him in."

CHAPTER 30

ate kept an eye on the street names as Sam maneuvered the unmarked car through London's congested streets. He had picked her up in Notting Hill and they were racing toward Benjamin's flat. The sleek buildings of Chelsea loomed ahead. In the backseat, Declan drummed his fingers on the headrest of her passenger seat, his usual stoic demeanor betrayed by a hint of nervous energy. It reflected exactly what she had been feeling.

"You sure this is the place?" Kate asked, glancing at the GPS and out the passenger side at a six-story Georgian-style townhouse, black wrought-iron balconies adorning each floor. The entrance was framed by two Corinthian columns, supporting a decorative pediment above a glossy black door with a polished brass knocker. Perfectly manicured terracotta pots flanked the steps, adding a touch of green. The overall effect was one of understated wealth and taste.

The trio exited the car, their footsteps echoing off the concrete as they approached the door. Kate's hand instinctively brushed her holstered weapon as they approached.

Sam rapped sharply on the door. "Benjamin Fuller? National Crime Agency. Open up."

Silence.

Sam pounded his fist again on the door, louder this time and shouting his name and rank. "Open the door now." He seemed to have been emboldened by the information Kate had provided him.

A muffled crash sounded from within, followed by hurried footsteps. Kate's hand flew to her weapon. Before they could act, the door flew open. A man stood before them, wide-eyed and disheveled. He bore a striking resemblance to the photo of Benjamin Fuller that Sam had pulled from his database. The man's features weren't quite right.

"Who are you?" the man demanded, his gaze darting between the three of them.

Kate stepped forward, badge raised. "FBI. We're looking for Benjamin Fuller."

The man's face crumpled. "Benji? You're here about Benji? I'm his brother, James."

There was something about the tone of his voice that told Kate there was trouble. "Sir, is your brother home?"

"What?" he asked, confusion written in his features. "No one's seen him in weeks. I assumed that's why you're here. To tell me he's dead. The police don't show up unless someone's dead. I don't understand."

Kate exchanged a glance with Sam. This wasn't how she'd expected this to go. "May we come in and ask you some questions?"

James nodded numbly and retreated into the townhouse. Kate crossed the threshold and froze. The place was a disaster. Furniture overturned, papers strewn across the floor, drawers pulled out and emptied.

"What happened here?" Sam muttered behind her.

James put his head in his hands. He didn't respond to the question.

Kate wasn't sure if he didn't hear Sam or was ignoring it. "When was the last time you saw your brother?"

"Three weeks ago," James replied, his eyes red-rimmed. "He called me, rambling about how he'd gotten in too deep and that people were after him. I thought he was drunk, but then I haven't been able to get hold of him since. He missed my daughter's birthday celebration two nights ago. That's when I knew something was really wrong. He'd never miss that no matter what he was doing."

"Was that the first sign something was wrong?"

James shook his head. "Benji's always been secretive. For the past year, he wouldn't let anyone in his home. I thought he was in one of his moods. That's happened in the past. This time, when I got here, he was nowhere to be found. Hasn't answered his mobile. No one has seen him."

Declan walked the perimeter of the room, taking in every detail. "Was the place like this when you arrived?"

James shook his head. "No, that was me. I came looking for clues, anything to explain where Benji had gone. I turned the place upside down looking for anything. I found things." He stopped, swallowing hard.

"Found what?" Kate pressed.

James reached for a stack of papers on the coffee table, handing them to Kate with trembling fingers. "Bank statements. Emails. It looks like Benji was involved in some kind of scam. Posing as other people online, conning people out of money. I can't believe he'd do something like this."

Kate flipped through the documents, her suspicions confirmed. They finally had tangible proof, beyond statements, concrete evidence of the romance scam syndicate. She raised her eyes to James. "You didn't know anything about this?"

"Nothing. I thought he was in the tech business. I never fully understood his work. He has a place in East London, a warehouse. Helix Enterprises. They do something with shipping."

"No," Kate said firmly. "It's a front for romance scams."

James took a step back. "What do you mean romance scams?"

Kate explained to him an abridged version of what they knew. With each new detail, James's face twisted in horror. "Your brother's name is on the business. I was told he's the money guy. We were after Julian Barclay and we were lead to Helix Enterprises. It seems he and your brother have cooked up a nice little business scamming lonely people online."

"How could he do something like this?" James shook his head, not understanding. He turned away from Kate to Sam then to Declan as if searching for one of them to tell him it was all a mistake. "My brother couldn't do something like this."

If James couldn't handle this information, what Kate was about to say would surely shock him. "Maybe you should sit down for the rest of it."

"There's more?" he croaked out. He took a few steps back, dropping to the couch with a thud. "I don't know if I can take much more. What do you mean with Julian Barclay? That isn't a name I've heard in a long time."

"You didn't know they were back in contact?" Sam asked.

"Not since the incident at Eton." James said the words then tried to take it back.

"We already know about that," Kate confided. "We don't know the full details. If you could fill in the gaps, that would help."

"No one knows the whole story. My parents and Julian's kept it quiet. I only heard the hushed whispers of my parents when it happened. The Barclays paid off the girl's parents. The whole thing went away." James rubbed his temples and closed his eyes. "My parents weren't happy with that. They said for Benji to have done something like that there must be something psychologically wrong with him. They sent him away to get help."

"James," Kate said slowly keeping her voice calm and steady, "do you believe that Benjamin needed help? What was he like as a child and during his time at Eton?"

"Was he like one of those psychopaths you see on television and hear about in murder podcasts? Is that what you're asking?" There was no anger in his voice. It was instead a certain kind of resignation. When Kate confirmed, he nodded. "I don't know the official diagnosis. Benji has always been different to the rest of us. Quieter, more of a follower, but angry. Deep seething anger that would come out from time to time."

Kate caught Declan's eyes across the room. She gestured toward the doorway. Declan understood, walking over to Sam and tapping him on the arm. As they left the room, Kate went to James, picked up a stack of papers from the couch cushion and dropped them to the floor. "You said before you thought he might be in one of his moods. What does that mean?"

James took a deep breath, turning his body to face hers. "Benji was a troubled kid. He'd isolate himself for hours and even days at a time. There was a point where he didn't speak for six months. He wouldn't say a word to any of us. He barely spoke at school. My parents took him to someone then. They said he was doing it on purpose – that there wasn't anything medically wrong with him. They tried to get him seen by a psychiatrist but he was too young for a diagnosis. My parents tried everything. Eventually, Benji seemed to grow out of it, but he still remained more secretive than the rest of us. Distant and emotionally cut off. He'd have violent snaps."

"What does that mean?"

James pointed to a thin scar that ran up his jawline. "I was twelve and Benji was ten when he caused this. We were playing outside. Everything was fine one minute then he picked up a jagged rock and attacked me. It wasn't provoked. We weren't fighting or arguing. We weren't even the kind of kids who played too roughly. Our mum saw him through the window and pulled him off me. I ended up with quite a few stitches. Benji never apologized nor gave any explanation for the attack." James sighed, his whole body heaving with it. "Agent

Walsh, he's always been this way. I was telling you the truth that he adores my daughter. I don't let Benji around her alone. He's the only one in my family that I'd never let watch my children. I know that's a terrible thing to say about family."

"It's not if you have reason for it, and it sounds like you have good reason." Delivering news that a family member is deceased is slightly more difficult than having to deliver the blow that a family member is a killer. It's a devastating loss either way. Kate knew she still had to tread lightly even if James had just opened the door. "The romance scams aren't the only reason I'm here. I don't have any proof to this, but there were questions that came up about whether Benjamin could be taking the scams offline and meeting people in person. Julian is a suspect in a series of homicides."

James muttered something under his breath Kate couldn't quite hear. The little bit of color that had come back to his face drained again. "It doesn't surprise me to hear Julian killed someone. He's always been out of control and strange. My brother," he paused, his eyes shifting nervously. "I don't know, Agent Walsh. Even after telling you he has a violent streak, it's hard to believe. Maybe I don't want to think he's capable of it."

"I don't know that he is," Kate confirmed. "Someone overheard Julian and Benjamin talking about 'the game.' We believe it's the romance scam. They could have been talking about how much they are scamming people for and competing that way or they could have been discussing a kill count. We simply don't know. We found some suspicious murders that might be connected. We haven't been able to dig into them yet. The only thing is that they aren't just women who were murdered. There were men." Kate hoped he heard the question in there.

"Men," James repeated once then twice more. "My brother only had one romantic partner that I knew and that was when we were in our twenties. It was a young woman he worked with at a bank. They were together for two years. I don't know of anyone he dated after that. I don't know if he dated men or women. I assume women but can't be sure."

"If Benjamin were gay would he have hid it from you?"

"He'd have no reason to, but Benji was secretive about everything. He clearly had this whole other life we knew nothing about. Anything is possible."

Before she had a chance to respond, Sam's voice cut through the house. "Kate, you need to see this."

She looked up to see Sam walking toward her with a laptop open in his hands. Kate left James on the couch, crossing the room to him. She peered at the screen. A series of menacing emails filled the display.

"You can't hide forever," Sam read aloud. "I trusted you, and you betrayed me. I want my money back or I'm going to kill you. Time to pay up." Sam looked over at James. "Looks like your brother scammed the wrong person."

James let out a choked sob. "What has he done?"

Declan emerged from the hallway, holding up an evidence bag. Inside was a phone, its screen cracked. "Found this wedged behind the radiator. Might give us some leads or indicate where he's gone."

A sharp knock at the door made them all jump. The person entered before any of them could react. Gray took a few steps into the house and stopped short, his eyes widening at the scene in front of him. "I…" he started to say and stopped. He tried to back up but Declan had a hold of his arm before the man could flee.

"What are you doing here?" Declan demanded, still holding onto the man. "I asked, what are you doing here?"

"I came to see Benjamin," Gray said, his words sputtering. "I was going to tell him about our arrest. I'm not going to run. You can let me go. I was surprised to see everyone here. Where is he?"

James launched himself at the man with a speed Kate didn't know he had. He shouted rapid fire questions. "Do you know where my brother is? When was the last time you spoke to him? Benji is missing, has been missing for weeks. You have to help us!"

Gray went completely still. "What do you mean Benjamin is missing?"

Kate put herself between James and Gray. "Let's slow down. I think we are all getting ahead of ourselves here." She turned to Declan, who still had his hand on Gray's arm. "Will you take James into the other room while I speak to Gray alone." When James protested, Kate insisted it was better for everyone. Previously, in the interrogation room, Kate had felt Gray knew more than he was saying. Showing up here only confirmed it.

James finally relented with words of reassurance from Declan. He left the room heading toward the back of the house with Sam leaving out the front door. Kate didn't know if he was calling for backup or to get the appropriate authorization to search the home. Benjamin was officially a missing person and no matter what he might have done, they had evidence that someone was threatening him.

When Kate was alone with Gray, she gestured toward the messy living room. "This was caused by James. Benjamin has been missing for a few weeks according to his family. Do you know otherwise?"

Gray's whole body deflated as he reached for a support behind him to keep him upright. "I thought it was only me he wasn't getting back to. That's why I came over here tonight. I figured he'd want to know about what happened today. He hasn't been answering his phone. I finally got fed up and came over. What do you mean he's missing? Like gone, left?"

"We don't know," Kate said, watching him carefully. There was a hint of something in his eyes. He still knew more than he was saying. "I need to know what you know about Benjamin. I know all about the romance scams. I know what Julian has been doing. I even know that Benjamin scammed the wrong person. Fill in the rest of the gaps now or you're going to need to call that lawyer again."

Kate watched as he wavered. He paced a small path in the living room as he muttered to himself.

"They will kill me," Gray said finally looking over at her.

"We'll protect you. Take you into protective custody tonight," Kate assured him.

Gray stopped, gnawed at his bottom lip. "I think Benjamin is dead and Julian killed him."

CHAPTER 31

Both seated on the couch, Kate leaned forward, her tone steady and controlled. "When was the last time you were in contact with Benjamin?"

Gray shifted uncomfortably, his eyes darting around the room before settling back on Kate. "About three weeks ago. That's the last time any of us were in contact with him."

"Us?" Kate's eyebrow arched. "The people we brought in for questioning today?"

Gray nodded. "That's all of us. I don't know how you did it, but you picked the right time to show up. You got all of us. Julian always said he had other groups similar to us working for him. We never had proof of that. I assume it was a threat to make us work more." He swallowed hard. "Things had taken a turn about five weeks ago. It was all getting out of hand."

"What do you mean?" Kate pressed.

A heavy silence hung in the air for a moment before Gray spoke again, his words tumbling out in a rush. "The scams, they were supposed to be simple. Take some money from lonely people online, you know? Benjamin started changing things."

Kate kept her expression neutral, not wanting to give away her growing interest. "How did he change things?"

Gray drummed his fingers against the fabric of his jeans. "He started wanting us to meet them. The marks, I mean. He'd set up dates and times to meet in person. It's what he had been doing for some time."

"Did you meet them in person?" Kate asked, leaning in slightly.

"We didn't. None of us wanted to do that. It was too much, you know? Not what any of us had signed up for. We said we'd market the app better and reach more people. Start talking to more people at once. We were willing to do that, not meet these people in person. None of us wanted that kind of risk."

Kate believed him. He had a nervous twitchy energy about him that conveyed honesty. "What were you supposed to do when you met them?"

A bitter laugh escaped Gray's lips. "He wanted us to do what he was doing – watch them."

Kate's brow furrowed. "What do you mean watch?"

"He'd hide somewhere nearby, observe as they waited. Watched their faces fall when they realized they'd been stood up." Gray's voice was barely above a whisper now. "He got off on it, their disappointment. Their pain. He got a thrill out of the manipulation. We were in it for the money. Most of us tried not to think about how these people were feeling. We didn't want a front row seat for it. Benjamin confided in me he did more than watch."

A chill ran down Kate's spine, but she kept her voice level. "What else did he do?"

Gray's eyes met hers, filled with a mixture of fear and disgust. "He'd follow them home. Started stalking them. And then—" He broke off, his face contorting.

"Then what, Gray?" Kate's voice was sharp, demanding.

"Murder," Gray choked out. "It led to murder."

The word hung in the air like a thunderclap. Kate felt her heartrate quicken, but years of training kept her outward appearance calm. "How many?"

Gray shook his head. "I don't know for sure. Three, maybe four? He was careful at first, but lately, he was getting reckless."

Kate's mind whirled with the implications. "Do you know anything about the murders? How he did it? When? The names of the victims?"

"No," Gray said rushing his words. "Look, I didn't even know if Benjamin was telling the truth. As I said we have been going for years at a steady pace. We bring in good money, Benjamin usually is hands-off. He's the money guy."

That's what Lydia had told her too. "There came a point where that changed?"

"Yeah, last year Benjamin wanted us to teach him how we scammed people online. I showed him how I do that and he said he wanted to meet a few people. He thought it would be funny to scam men while pretending to be a woman. It's easy enough – anyone can be anyone online. He wanted the big initial payouts like Lydia was getting. I have to play the long game with women. Benjamin wasn't interested in that. He stole sexy photos of women online from websites and social media and used those. He created whole fake personas. He was having fun with it. I don't even think it was about the money for him."

"What was it about?" Kate asked, even though she assumed she already knew.

"Lying. Manipulating. He got off on how easy it was to trick people. He liked the emotional manipulation too – reeling someone into a relationship and then toying with their emotions. He said men were easy, maybe even easier than women. All he had to do was show a photo of a hot mostly naked woman and have minimal conversation and they'd be hooked. He felt powerful." Gray stopped and took a breath. "Maybe powerful for the first time in his life."

Kate needed to get back to the most important part. "How did you come to learn about the murders?"

Gray shook his head. "I need immunity, Agent Walsh. I know I'm in enough trouble for the romance scams. I'm not going down for an accessory to murder. I'll tell you everything I know, which isn't much. If I went to the police, I'd have to tell them everything else. I wasn't going to implicate myself."

Kate had been able to offer immunity to Lydia for the scams. It was entirely another thing when it came to murder. She asked Gray to wait and then went out the front door to find Sam. She found him on the sidewalk with his phone pressed to his ear.

He raised his eyes to her. "We were cleared on entering the home and the initial search. I'm getting the warrants to collect the evidence just in case. I don't want anything to mess up the case. We are in the clear."

Kate didn't waste any time getting to the point. "I need immunity for Gray. He knows about murders committed by Benjamin. He's already shared a good deal of information with me. If we want the rest, he's demanding immunity. I say we give it to him."

"I'd need to speak to one of the Crown prosecutors but in the interest of time, I say we offer it. I'll worry about the politics of it on the backend. With Lord Barclay's daughter missing and potentially in the hands of a killer, they will give me everything I need. Does he know anything about Julian?"

Kate wanted to tell him that Gray thought Julian had killed Benji, but she didn't want to share until she knew for sure. "We haven't gotten there yet." She put her hand on his arm. "Thanks for moving this along so quickly."

"Go do whatever you have to do," Sam assured her, offering her a stiff smile.

Kate went back inside with a renewed determination. "We can get you immunity. Tell me everything you know."

"I want it in writing," Gray said in response.

"We don't have time. I've never gone back on my word," Kate assured him, her tone serious and strong. "The National Crime Agency has assured me you have it. We have more at risk right now than Benjamin being missing. Do you know Julian left the country with Lucy Barclay?"

Gray sucked in a breath. "I didn't know that."

"Let me tell you Lord Barclay will do everything and anything he can to get his daughter back. I'm fairly certain he'd kill his cousin Julian, himself, if that's what it took."

Gray pulled back in surprise. "Where did they go?"

"We don't know. That's part of why we were here to see Benjamin. We were hoping he knew where Julian could be hiding. This is a complex case, Gray, with too many pieces. Far too many suspects and deaths." Kate explained what happened earlier in the day and their meeting with Lord Barclay. "You're dealing with two dangerous men. They have known each other for a long time. They have a history you don't have. Who brought you into the operation?"

"Benjamin. We met through other mutual friends and he knew I was strapped for cash. He told me about Helix Enterprises and how I could make some quick cash. I've only known him for a few years. We weren't even all that close, but he seemed to trust me. I don't know why. He trusted me more than he trusted anyone else though. I never told the others what he told me about the murders. The rest of them knew Julian. I was the only one brought in by Benjamin."

Kate was glad he had circled back to that on his own. "I need to know what he told you and when."

"Okay," Gray said, his voice unsure. "As I said, Benjamin had asked me to show him how to scam people. That was about a year ago. A couple of months after that, maybe two or three, he told me about the murder. He admitted he almost immediately took it offline and asked these men to meet. He explained how he had gotten a thrill watching how disappointed they were. He admitted following them and stalking them for a few weeks. It was like the thrill wore off or something. He went to one guy's house, just showed up at the door, and admitted to scamming him. Benjamin said the guy was completely confused and didn't understand. He demanded his money back. Benjamin used his confusion to enter the man's home. Then he attacked him, stabbing him."

Kate didn't know how the men had been killed. She couldn't confirm. "What else did he tell you?"

"Nothing," Gray said, his hands trembling. "He got out of there and went home. He threw out his bloody clothes and that was the end of it. He didn't tell me the man's name or anything. Benjamin assured me he'd never be caught because he was wearing gloves, no one saw him, and the man was a stranger. There was nothing to connect them. I knew the scam connected them, but I didn't bring that up. I didn't even know for sure Benjamin was telling the truth. He made me promise I wouldn't tell anyone. He said if I did, he'd kill me. I did believe that."

Kate asked a few more questions about the murder. Gray explained Benjamin had said it was his first. He told him about two others right after, but the stories seemed to get more fantastical, which is why Gray thought he might be making it up. "I never heard anything on the news either. I figured cases like that would make the news."

Kate didn't have an answer for that. "Tell me about Julian. What was his role in all of this?"

At the mention of Julian's name, Gray visibly tensed. "Julian was Benjamin's partner, in the scams and everything else. I don't know what he knew about the murders. When Julian was around everyone was tense. Benjamin could be easygoing. Julian never. He had a violent temper. He'd break things in the office and scream at everyone. You did things his way or not at all. We were all afraid of him. He threatened us."

"Physically?"

Gray shook his head. "With exposure. He said he knew information about each of us that he'd leak to the press or the cops. We all knew we were doing something illegal. None of us wanted to be on his bad side. Then Benjamin told me he started getting emails. He thought Julian had leaked something. Their relationship started to get tense."

"Emails?" Kate prompted, her interest piqued, thinking about what she'd seen on the laptop.

Gray nodded. "Threatening ones. From someone Benjamin scammed."

"How long ago was that?"

"The threats started about a month ago."

"Did Julian know?"

"As I said, Benjamin thought it was Julian who leaked the information. When Benjamin confronted him about it, Julian was livid. He acted like he didn't know anything about it. Told Benjamin he had to neutralize the threat."

"Did he?"

"I don't know. As I said, no one has been able to reach him for weeks."

"You said you thought Julian killed him. Why?"

Gray's gaze dropped to his hands. "To protect himself. Benjamin was erratic. If Julian didn't leak the information then Benjamin was a threat to the whole thing. If it wasn't Julian, then it was the man he scammed. Something went south."

Kate's pulse quickened. "Who was it that he scammed?"

"You have to understand I didn't know at first. As I said Benjamin started getting reckless." Gray ran a hand through his hair. "He was taking bigger risks, targeting more high-profile marks. It was like he couldn't help himself."

The tension in the room was palpable as Gray hesitated, clearly wrestling with the weight of what he was about to reveal. Kate let the silence hang between them. She resisted the urge to ask her question again.

Finally, Gray looked up, his expression a mix of fear and resignation. "It was Douglas Hartman."

The name didn't mean anything to Kate, not the way it did for Gray. "Am I supposed to know him?"

Gray's eyebrows arched high. "American. I forgot. He's a Member of Parliament. An outspoken, not well-liked member."

The information hit Kate like a physical blow. She muttered a curse, momentarily breaking her professional demeanor. She quickly composed herself. "Gray," she said, her voice stern, "I need you to understand the gravity of what you've just told me. You're sure about this?"

Gray nodded, his face ashen. "I saw the emails, the threats. Hartman was using a pseudonym, but Benjamin figured out who he really was. That's when he started panicking. He told Julian and all hell broke loose."

Kate stood up abruptly, the couch shoved back against the wall with the sheer force of her movement. She fled the room, back outside in search of Sam. She yelled his name, not caring if he was still on the phone. Kate couldn't see him out there in the darkness. He wasn't where she had left him. "Sam!"

"I'm here, Kate," he said coming out from the shadows of the side yard. "What's going on?"

"Douglas Hartman," she said, rushing toward him. "That's who Benjamin Fuller was scamming and who had been threatening him. Julian told Benjamin to take care of the problem. That was the last Gray heard from him. He was headed there to take care of the problem."

Sam raked a hand down his mouth, letting it linger there covering his reaction. There was horror in his eyes. "This is insane."

Kate couldn't disagree with him. "We have to go there now."

"Let me make some calls," Sam said, walking away from her. "I need to at least alert my supervisor."

Kate wished she could call Spade, but her boss was still missing in action.

CHAPTER 32

Sam white knuckled them through London's congested streets. Kate was getting used to his aggressive driving while she sat in the passenger seat, feeling the weight of the impending confrontation pressed down on her. Even Declan was unusually quiet in the backseat.

As if reading her thoughts, Sam turned to her. "Please remember, we're here to ask questions. We don't have enough evidence to make any accusations yet. This is delicate."

"We're not going to do anything to embarrass you," Declan assured from the back. "How do we address him? Does he have a title like Lord Barclay?"

"No, Hartman doesn't have a title. In Parliament, they are known as Honorable so and so. For our purpose, Mr. Hartman will work initially. We can worry about the formality after that." He turned to look at Kate. "Depending on how it goes."

Kate knew the look on Sam's face. She had worn the same expression when she had to handle delicate political matters back home. No one wanted to have to arrest someone high up in government. All eyes would be on the interview and subsequent arrest.

As they approached their destination, Kate couldn't help but marvel at the homes. Each one seemed to outdo the last in grandeur and opulence. Even among these architectural marvels, Douglas Hartman's residence stood out.

The car came to a stop in front of a sprawling Georgian-style mansion. Its red brick façade, adorned with intricate white trim, exuded an air of elegance. Perfectly manicured hedges lined the driveway, leading up to a grand entrance flanked by towering white columns.

Kate took a deep breath, steeling herself for what lay ahead. As they made their way up the steps, the gravity of the situation settled over them.

Sam raised his hand to knock, but before his knuckles could contact the glossy black door, it swung open. A tall, distinguished-looking man in his late fifties stood and stared back at them. His silver hair was neatly combed back and piercing blue eyes regarded them with a mix of curiosity and barely concealed annoyance.

"Mr. Hartman," Sam said, introducing the three of them.

Before he could go on, Hartman interrupted, his eyebrows rose slightly, a flicker of surprise crossing his features before he quickly masked it with a polite smile. "The FBI? I wasn't aware that American law enforcement had any business here in London. Please, do come in."

He stepped aside, gesturing for them to enter. Kate and Declan exchanged a glance before crossing the threshold into a grand foyer. The interior of the house was as impressive as its exterior, with high ceilings, ornate moldings, and a crystal chandelier that cast prismatic patterns across the marble floor.

"This way, please," Hartman instructed, leading them through an arched doorway into a spacious study. Floor-to-ceiling bookshelves lined the walls, interrupted only by large windows that offered a view of the meticulously landscaped gardens beyond. In the center of the room stood a massive mahogany desk, its surface clear except for a sleek laptop and a crystal decanter filled with amber liquid.

Hartman moved behind the desk, his posture relaxed but his eyes alert. "Now then, what can I do for the FBI?"

Kate took a step forward, her gaze locked on Hartman's face. "Mr. Hartman, we're here to discuss your relationship with Benjamin Fuller."

The change in Hartman's demeanor was subtle but unmistakable. His shoulders tensed ever so slightly, and the corners of his mouth tightened. "Benjamin Fuller? I'm afraid I don't know anyone by that name."

"Are you sure about that, sir?" Sam asked, his voice calm but insistent. "Before you go any further and implicate yourself by lying to me, we have evidence suggesting otherwise."

Kate shifted her eyes slightly toward Sam, impressed but hard-pressed to believe he was being so bold after the warning he had issued them in the car.

Hartman's eyes darted between Kate and Declan, a flicker of uncertainty crossing his face. "I meet a lot of people in my line of work. Perhaps you could refresh my memory?"

Kate pulled out her phone, swiping through it before holding up a photo of a man in his early forties with dark hair and piercing green eyes. Sam had sent it to her earlier. "This is Benjamin Fuller. We have reason to believe you two were in contact recently. We believe he might have been coming over here to confront you."

Hartman leaned forward, squinting at the image. His brow furrowed, and for a moment, Kate thought he might continue to deny knowing Fuller. His shoulders sagged and he let out a heavy sigh. With his tone a mixture of embarrassment and anger, he admitted, "I'm afraid I've been rather foolish where he's concerned."

Kate pocketed her phone, her eyes never leaving Hartman's face. "Can you elaborate on that?"

Hartman moved around the desk, gesturing for the three of them to take a seat on the plush leather furniture. As they sat, he poured himself a glass of whiskey from the decanter. Kate had seen this show before and wondered if all men in London drank when confronted with horrible news.

"It's a rather sordid affair, I'm afraid," he began, taking a sip of his drink. "A few months ago, I decided I'd had enough of the single life. I've tried dating in the past, going through all sorts of proper channels to find someone. I kept meeting the same kind of woman over and over again. Then I heard from a friend about a new app for high-net-worth individuals. It was the kind of thing that offered a bit of fun with liked-minded individuals, or so I thought. I matched with a woman named Sophia. She was beautiful, charming, and seemed genuinely interested in me. We started talking, and before I knew it, I found myself falling for her. The only problem was that it was all through the app and then through texting, which I despise. I was trying to be patient, giving her time to warm up to a phone call."

Kate leaned forward, her elbows resting on her knees. "Sophia wasn't real, was she?"

Hartman shook his head, a bitter smile twisting his lips. "No, she wasn't. It was all a clever ruse orchestrated by Benjamin Fuller. By the time I realized the truth, he had already scammed me out of a considerable sum of money. I thought I was helping the poor woman out of some trouble." He rolled his eyes. "It was all so foolish. I didn't know people scammed people like this, not through that kind of app anyway."

"How much?" Declan asked.

Hartman hesitated, swirling the whiskey in his glass. "Two-hundred thousand pounds," he finally admitted, his voice barely above a whisper. "I demanded we meet in person. As you can guess, she never showed up."

Kate felt a surge of sympathy for the man, despite her suspicions. Romance scams were cruelly effective, but she couldn't let empathy cloud her judgment. There were still too many unanswered questions. "How did you send the money?"

"Wire transfer from my bank to an app. One of those payment apps."

Kate didn't understand. "A bank allowed you to transfer that much money to a payment app?" She couldn't think of all the apps available but she figured they had a limit.

"It was an app I'd never heard of before. I looked it up online and it was legitimate. I can't recall all the details now. I think I've been trying to block it out. I'll get you the information before you go."

With her tone gentle but firm, Kate asked, "When did you figure out you'd been scammed?"

Hartman's grip tightened on his glass, his knuckles turning white. "After I got stood up, I texted her and demanded an explanation. I never received one. I never heard from her again. My son happened to see the photos on my phone. I hadn't deleted them yet. He asked and I told him she was someone I had been texting with. He told me the photos were fake – created with artificial intelligence. I was flabbergasted. I know we are getting more and more advanced with AI. I had no idea that the likeness of someone could be created like that. I admit the photos seemed artistic but this app was for people like me. I assumed she had gone out of her way to have photos professionally done with a bit of flare."

Sam had the same expression of empathy that Kate felt. "What did you do then?"

"My son helped me. He's involved in the tech industry and he was able to figure out through the IP addresses and cellphone searches that it was coming from a man named Benjamin Fuller. For a scammer, he didn't do a lot to hide his identity. I sent him some emails anonymously. I was angry and humiliated. I demanded my money. I knew that he knew who I was. The only reason I created a fake email address was so they'd never be traced back to me if someone else got their hands on them."

Hartman didn't know about the full scope of the Helix Syndicate. "Sir, Benjamin didn't know it was you at first. You're not the only person he scammed."

"It wasn't personal against me?" Hartman said with a shake of his head. "I thought he targeted me, some personal vendetta for something I did in Parliament."

"No," Sam said, giving Hartman a rundown of most of the investigation. "This is much bigger in scope than we could have ever imagined. There were murders of several women here in London and in the states. That led us to matchmakers and when one of them was attacked, it led us directly to this romance scam syndicate. At the heart of it are Lord Julian Barclay and Benjamin Fuller. Fuller was watching you the night you showed up for your date. That's how he figured out your identity."

Hartman set his glass down on the desk with more force than necessary, causing some of the amber liquid to slosh over the rim. "This is…" He stared at them with his mouth open and his eyes wide. "Unbelievable. What can I do to help you?"

Kate and Declan exchanged a loaded glance. Kate asked, "When was the last time you had contact with Benjamin Fuller?"

Hartman frowned, his brow furrowing in concentration. "It must have been three or so weeks ago. Nothing recent. He showed up here, unannounced. Can you believe the audacity?"

Kate felt her pulse quicken. "He came here? To your home? What happened?"

Hartman began to pace behind his desk, his agitation clear. "He was ranting and raving like a madman. Saying he was going to expose me and ruin my career. As if I was the one who had done something wrong! He even threatened to kill me. Now that I know he's killed people I should have taken the threat more seriously."

Sam narrowed his gaze. "How did you respond?"

Hartman stopped pacing, turning to face them with a defiant expression. "I told him to leave, of course. I said if he ever came near me again, I'd have him arrested. I started calling for security."

Kate leaned forward, her eyes boring into Hartman's. "Did he leave?"

"Eventually, yes," Hartman replied, his voice tight.

Kate didn't understand why Benjamin hadn't killed the man. She stood up slowly, her mind racing. Something about Hartman's story didn't quite add up, but she couldn't put her finger on what. "Are you aware Benjamin Fuller is missing? He's been gone for about three weeks, right around the time that he was here."

The color drained from Hartman's face, his eyes widening in shock. "Missing? I had no idea. I assumed after I kicked him out, I'd never get my money back. At that point, all I cared about was protecting my reputation. This has been humiliating for me."

"When exactly did this confrontation take place?" Declan asked, flipping back through his notes.

Hartman ran a hand through his silver hair, his composure cracking. He gave them a date and then fumbled for a time. "I think around eight that evening."

Kate's instincts were screaming at her. If Benjamin had come there to kill him, why did he leave so easily? There was more to this story, she was sure of it. "Are you sure about your statement? Because if you're withholding information about a missing person, that's a very serious matter."

"What exactly are you accusing me of?" he asked, his voice full of indignation.

Sam got up from the chair. "Sir, we need the truth. If there is something more you know, you need to tell us. Murder investigations hinge on uncovering the truth. Not to mention Julian Barclay has taken off with his cousin's daughter Lucy. We believe the young woman is in danger. He's fled the country and Benjamin is missing. We need answers."

Hartman righted himself to his full height, puffing his chest out. "Lord Bartholomew Barclay is involved in this?"

"Tangentially," Kate said. "His daughter Lucy was unwittingly helping the scammers. She thought she was helping to market the dating app without knowing the full scope of what they were doing. We picked her up in the raid. Then she disappeared with Julian. She is in danger."

Hartman turned his back to them, his back rising and falling with each breath. He went to the decanter and poured himself another drink. When he turned back to them this time, he licked his lips nervously. "I wasn't completely truthful. Benjamin pulled a knife on me here in the study. He tried to stab me but I dodged him. I was a bit of a fencer back at Eton. I was quicker on my feet. I got the knife away from him in a struggle and jabbed at him. I didn't stab him…fully."

"What does that mean?" Kate and Sam asked together, the panic rising in their voices.

Declan was already in the process of scanning the room for blood and signs of a covered-up struggle.

"He walked out of here alive," Hartman protested walking toward them. "That man, that scammer lowlife, Benjamin Fuller, walked out of here alive. I kept the knife. It's in my safe. You can have it."

Kate didn't know what to believe. "Was he injured?"

"Yes, but he could still walk. I got him in the side – two sharp jabs. There was a little blood but not much as one would expect."

There was still something more he wasn't saying. Kate could feel it in her bones. "What are you leaving out?"

Hartman took a few beats, knocking back the liquid in his glass in two gulps. He set the glass on the desk, defeat deflating his body. "There was a woman. I didn't realize she was with him. She stayed out there in the hall when Benjamin came in. She must have slipped in the front door behind him or something. I didn't see her until after I had jabbed at him. She came in and gave me a stack of cash and left with him. I didn't get a name."

A rush of faces flashed in Kate's mind. She only had photos for two of them. "Here," she said, shoving her phone toward him. "Is it either of these women?" She had photos of Madame Rue and Lydia.

"No," Hartman said with a shake of his head. He raised his eyes to Kate. "All I know, based on her accent, is that she was American."

CHAPTER 33

An hour later, Kate sat in a dingy wooden booth with poor overhead lighting nursing an ale. Leo had suggested food and a drink before she turned in for the night. Sam had remained at Hartman's, getting the knife that Benjamin had used to try to kill him and bringing in a crime scene team to assess the room for traces of Benjamin's blood. Declan had used their car service to pick up Ditch from the airport. He had encouraged Kate to go back to the hotel and get some sleep.

They wouldn't know much of anything until Ditch could start going through all the tech. There was probably more tech in this case that might hold clues than any case Kate had ever had.

"Do you believe him, Kate?" Leo asked drawing her out of her silence.

Kate flicked her eyes up from her half-eaten burger. "Hartman?"

Leo confirmed, taking a sip of his beer. "Do you think he was telling the truth about Benjamin going there to kill him? Then Hartman turning the tables on him before he fled with a woman?"

Kate didn't see why he'd lie. He'd been honest with them about being scammed. "Sam's people are in the process of searching the whole property. Hartman permitted them. He didn't strike me as the kind of man who'd kill someone and hide their body."

"He might have people for that," Leo countered far too casually. He chuckled when he saw the look of doubt on Kate's face. "You know for an FBI agent, you can be a bit naïve."

Kate pulled back in offense. "I don't think anyone has ever said I was naïve. What do you mean?"

Leo took a long sip of his beer, his gaze never leaving her face. "I've seen things, Kate. The people you think are the most trustworthy have hidden their secrets better than anyone else. The more rich and powerful they are, the more they are hiding. It's just the way the world works. If you are sitting there thinking Douglas Hartman isn't capable of murder, he's already got you fooled. Anyone is capable of murder depending on what they are trying to protect. For some, it's family or their relationship. For others, it's their house and possessions. Still others, it's the reputation they have in the public. All people have a motive for murder if pushed hard enough."

Kate was the profiler, but what Leo said was true. "Even though I agree with you, I don't believe we are going to find Benjamin's body at the house or the grounds."

"There's something else on your mind, Kate," Leo said, his gaze taking in the features of her face. He leaned back and rested his arm across the back of the booth, moving his body into the corner to rest his side and back between the wall and booth. He had a casual confidence about him Kate didn't see in most men.

Kate took a bite of her burger and chewed it slowly. The din of the rest of the pub filtered out. "I don't fully believe Benjamin Fuller is a killer. If he was, he could have easily overpowered Hartman. While Hartman is in good shape, no amount of fancy fencing footwork would have saved him. He would never have been able to wrestle that knife out of Benjamin's hands if he was skilled."

Leo didn't disagree with her. "What do you think this means for the case?"

"I believed Gray when he told me what Benjamin told him. Benjamin was scamming people online. He was skilled enough at it to trick Hartman into giving him a sizable amount of money. I also think he was doing what Gray said – setting up meetings in person and watching how disappointed these men got when no one showed up. He has a sick side to him for sure. He might have been scamming and even stalking them, but I don't think Benjamin is a killer."

"The murders Sam found," Leo asked the lingering question.

"Probably what they were initially classified as, home invasions. Benjamin could have read the details about them and parroted some of it back to Gray. He could have made up the whole thing. If he's clever enough to create photos using AI and whole personas tricking men in the app and through text, he's probably smart enough to fake a murder."

"Motive for lying like that?"

Kate enjoyed Leo's straight-to-the-point questions. "That's the unknown right now. I could guess."

Leo gestured with his hands for her to carry on.

Kate liked having his undivided attention. "Benjamin was the quiet one, the one who was a little different in school and growing up. Julian was the leader and Benjamin was the follower. Maybe he wanted to seem tough for Gray and Julian. Then when the chips are down, he can't go through with it."

Leo flicked his eyes up toward her, his smile broadening. "You're quite good at this, Kate. I like sitting here while you bounce ideas off me. I assume you and Declan have this kind of back and forth regularly."

"We do." Kate considered her words carefully. "Declan and I have different skill sets. We've been partners for so long, we read each other's minds. I've never seen someone so skilled at assessing a scene like Declan. He can spot an anomaly at a hundred yards. He has eagle eyes for that kind of thing. I focus more on the people, particularly the suspects. I can dive deep into their psyche and hopefully see what makes them tick to understand why they are doing what they are doing, understand the profile of the killer, and make it easier to catch them."

"What do you mean profile?"

Kate took a sip of her beer. "Part of the work in identifying a suspect is my profile. It's not a concrete science, but in understanding the kind of crime, the method of murder, information about the victims, and other aspects of the case, I can narrow down features about the suspect. Man versus woman, age, occupation, education level, and so forth. It can help us search for a suspect. Serial crime is very different than say someone who kills a family member or neighbor out of revenge, for instance." She cocked an eyebrow. "I had to create a profile when we were investigating the Curators. Every agency across the globe looked to me to profile the Phantom."

Leo sat back, his mouth dropping open slightly. "I hadn't considered that. Were you right?"

"I knew you were born and raised with some means in Europe, well-educated, sophisticated, probably good-looking, and had a certain kind of charm to mingle among the rich and famous. You had a finesse about you that gave you access to the art world and you could move among people unnoticed. I knew you weren't a smash-and-grab kind of criminal. I had you in your forties, given the length of your thefts. You had to have been in good physical and mental shape to pull off the burglaries. I also knew that you were mostly non-violent. You weren't looking to kill people because even when your back was up against the wall, you didn't choose violence. The Phantom was meticulous in his planning and had to have been able to cultivate trust and loyalty among the people who worked for him. That said a great deal about your character and intelligence." Kate trailed off, thinking of what else she should say. "You have good instincts."

Leo raised his glass to her. "All of that is correct and you still couldn't find me. If I had known you back then, I would have let you catch me much sooner."

Kate laughed. "You had me stumped for a while because I couldn't figure out why what you were stealing never ended up being sold on the black market or to unscrupulous collectors. There was a huge part of your crimes I completely missed."

"The burglaries were so random to an outside onlooker. I can understand why no one thought to connect them. I'm glad I can do the same thing now legally."

"I'm glad too," Kate said, meaning it. She leaned back in the booth, the worn wood creaking behind her. The pub's dim lighting cast long shadows across the table, mirroring the dark circles under her eyes. She stifled a yawn and lifted her pint glass, the amber liquid sloshing inside as she took a long swig. Across from her, Leo nursed his beer while watching her. The tension like static electricity between them – neither going to do anything about it.

Kate was getting used to it being there, pulling them together.

She broke the eye contact, letting her gaze drift to the window, watching raindrops chase each other down the glass. The street beyond was a blur of neon lights and shadowy figures hurrying through the downpour. She blinked, fatigue weighing heavily on her eyelids.

Then she saw him.

A man stood on the sidewalk, his face half-hidden by the upturned collar of his coat. There was something familiar about him. The profile of his face.

Kate's heart raced, adrenaline cutting through the fog of exhaustion. She leaned forward, squinting through the rain-blurred glass. The man turned slightly, and a flash of neon illuminated his full face, not just a profile now.

Benjamin Fuller.

Kate gripped the end of the table and dragged herself out of the booth, her hip bumping the table, rattling their glasses and cutlery as she stood abruptly.

Leo looked up, startled. "Kate? What's wrong?"

Kate didn't hear him, she was already moving, weaving between the tables with a single-minded focus. The pub's chatter faded to a dull roar in her ears as she reached for the door handle.

The blast of cold air hit her like a slap to the face as she stepped onto the rain-slicked pavement. Kate's eyes locked onto Benjamin, who stood frozen in place, his own gaze wide with recognition.

For a heartbeat, they stared at each other, the rain pelting down around them.

Then all at once, Benjamin bolted, spinning on his heel and taking off down the narrow street.

"FBI! Stop!" Kate shouted, her voice hoarse. She launched into a sprint, her shoes splashing through puddles as she gave chase.

Benjamin darted around a corner, his coat billowing behind him. Kate followed, her lungs burning as she pushed herself harder. The streets of London twisted and turned, a labyrinth of brick and stone. Leo's footsteps pounded behind her, his breath coming in ragged gasps.

"Kate!" he called out. "Where are you going? What's going on?"

"Benjamin Fuller!" she yelled over her shoulder, never taking her eyes off their quarry. "We can't lose him!"

They raced through winding alleyways, past startled pedestrians huddled under umbrellas. Benjamin, surprisingly agile, vaulted over a low wall, his desperation lending him speed. Kate gritted her teeth, pushing through the burning in her legs as she followed suit.

Leo, with his longer stride, began to gain ground. As they emerged onto a wider street, he put on a burst of speed. With a flying tackle, he launched himself at Benjamin, wrapping his thick muscular arms around the man's waist, bringing them both crashing to the ground.

Kate skidded to a halt beside them, her chest heaving as she fought to catch her breath. Leo had the man pinned, his face pressed against the wet pavement.

"Benjamin Fuller," Kate panted, rain streaming down her face. "You're under arrest." She had no real authority to arrest him, but she didn't care. She was taking him into custody and not letting him out of her sight.

Benjamin twisted his head, his eyes wild with panic. "Please," he gasped. "You don't understand. I can't."

Kate ignored his pleas, pulling out her handcuffs. "Everyone's looking for you. Your brother, James, has been in a panic looking for you. Did you really think you could just disappear?"

As Leo hauled Benjamin to his feet, the man's shoulders sagged in defeat. "I didn't have a choice," he said, his voice barely audible above the patter of rain. "I couldn't do what Julian wanted. I couldn't kill Douglas Hartman."

Kate froze, her hand on Benjamin's arm. The admission they had been seeking was so easily supplied she didn't think she heard him correctly. "What did you say?"

Benjamin's eyes darted between Kate and Leo, terror etched across his face. "I'm not the one you want," he pleaded. "Julian's the real monster. I got in too deep. When I tried to back out, he threatened my family." He shuddered. "He said he'd kill them if I didn't go through with the murder. He wanted me to kill people too, so I was in as deep as him. I faked it. I faked it all."

Leo's grip on Fuller tightened. "Why should we believe you?"

"Because I can prove it," Fuller insisted, his words tumbling out in a desperate rush. "I have evidence. Recordings, documents, everything you need to bring down the whole operation. I have it hidden so

Julian won't find it. It's everything you need to bring him in. I can't go to the police. Julian will find me. He'll know. You have to protect me."

Kate studied Fuller's face, searching for any sign of deception. Rain trickled down her neck, sending a chill down her spine. "Julian is gone. He left on a flight early today. I saw him leave, but we couldn't stop him in time. If you wanted to run, why are you still in London?"

Benjamin stared up at her, no words of explanation crossing his lips.

"No answer for me?" Kate stared down at the man. "Who is the woman who retrieved you from Hartman's home when you went there?"

Benjamin swallowed hard, recognition that Kate knew far more than she was saying took hold. "She's not working with me. Julian sent her. He's insane. He's going to kill us all."

Leo wasn't buying it either. "If you're that afraid, you run. You don't stick around where Julian can find you."

Benjamin winced his eyes closed. "It doesn't matter where I go, Julian will still find me. There was no point in leaving. Hiding here in London gave me a better shot at living. As soon as I used my passport or credit cards to leave, he'd know."

The rain pelted them harder. They had to get off the street into shelter. As Kate grabbed him by the other arm, she asked, "Do you have any idea where Julian might have gone? He has his cousin, Lucy, with him."

"Take me someplace safe and I'll tell you everywhere he might have gone."

Kate expelled an exhausted breath and let the rain fall on her face.

CHAPTER 34

Kate woke the next morning with the sheets twisted around her bare legs. She groaned as she stretched her arms overhead and arched her back in a deep stretch. "Declan," she called clearing her throat. Kate had no sense of time as the room was still dark with the curtains pulled tight. She didn't know how long she'd been asleep either.

After bringing Benjamin into the police station, the man refused to speak to Kate or Sam, demanding instead a solicitor and an immunity deal. Given the nature of his crimes and what the others accused him of, no one was likely to give him full immunity even if it meant finding Lucy. Sam promised her he'd work with the prosecution to work out some kind of deal all the while telling her there was no way full immunity was even a possibility.

Declan had arrived soon after, explaining Ditch wanted to go to the hotel first to get a few hours of sleep. He was scheduled to start going through all the tech in the morning. Declan knew better than to argue with the temperamental tech whiz.

Kate heaved herself to a sitting position, her eyes slowly adjusting to the darkness. "Declan," she called again then swung her feet to the floor. She tugged her sleep shorts back in place and padded out to the main living area of the hotel room. There she found Declan hunched over his laptop deep in concentration at whatever was on the screen.

Kate made her way over to him, resting her hands on his shoulders and peering at the laptop. It was a map of some sort with a blinking dot indicating a location. "Who are you tracking?"

Declan glanced back at her, finally realizing she was standing there. "We found Julian," he said, pointing at the black flickering dot. Declan explained that Lord Barclay had spoken to a few family members and they pooled their collective memories to identify a few properties where Julian might be, as well as tracking down Julian's private pilot. What they were looking at was the plane's beacon location. "The plane landed in Barcelona and has been sitting there. When I spoke to the airport there, I was told that a man and a woman got off the flight but no one confirmed they got back on or where they went."

"Are we able to get a team to the airport to pick up the pilot?"

"Already done by police there. He doesn't know anything. Julian and Lucy got off the flight. He was told to stay there for two days then return to London. We have little to tie Julian to the murder and with his status, our hands are tied."

Kate didn't need the reminder. All they had was the word of scammers who had flipped to save their own hides. No court was going to rely solely on that evidence. They needed Ditch to find something concrete and they needed Benjamin to flip. Ditch couldn't be rushed and so far Benjamin couldn't be convinced.

Kate sighed as Declan turned and pulled her into him. He gazed up at her with sheepish eyes then lifted the hem of her shirt, trailing wet kisses on her belly. She rested her hands on his shoulders and closed her eyes "What are you doing?" she murmured. "Shouldn't we be focused on work right now?"

"Nothing we can do at the moment. I've been waiting days for even a few minutes alone with you when we aren't either focused on the case or sleeping." Declan gave her belly one last wet sucking kiss then stood to his full height. He tucked her messy hair behind her ears and looked deep into her eyes. "Come on, Katie. We have been running ragged for days. Leo is with Sam this morning and Ditch is hard at work doing his thing. We deserve some downtime, even if it's just an hour before we head into the office."

Kate didn't need any more convincing. She could still feel the heat of his body against hers, the softness of his lips lingering on her skin. She craved him as much as he did her. Kate leaned her head back and raised up on tiptoes, kissing him, returning the same level of passion he had greeted her with. When they broke apart, "Lead the way and I'm yours," she murmured, her voice filled with lust.

Declan didn't need any further encouragement. He slipped his hand into hers and led her straight back into the bedroom. Kate let her mind go blank, fully losing herself in the moment.

Later, when both of them were spent and Kate was still trying to catch her breath, her mind drifted back to the case. She hated that she couldn't allow herself a moment longer to relax. She rolled to her side, curling next to Declan, who lay on his back with his eyes closed. "What do you think about the American?"

"The television show?" Declan asked, absently.

Kate laughed. "The American woman involved in this case. It sounds like there is a third person involved; it's not only Benjamin and Julian." Declan groaned an inaudible response. He was drifting off to sleep, but Kate wasn't going to allow him to do that even for a minute. She nudged his side. "You had your fun now we have to get back to work."

Declan turned his head to face her as his eyelids fluttered open. "You're very bossy," he teased before closing his eyes again. He pulled her close, snuggling into her. "I barely slept last night. You've been tossing and turning and even talking in your sleep."

Kate laser-focused on him, worry crinkling a line in her forehead. "What have I been saying?" she asked, trying to sound casual.

"Just mumbling. Two nights ago it sounded like someone was chasing you. Last night, you were worried I was going to find out something, but you never said what the something was." Declan opened his eyes again. "Do I have *something* to be concerned about?"

"Nothing." Kate couldn't imagine what was roiling around her subconscious. The only thought was that it might have been about Leo. On a rare occasion, after spending time with him, her subconscious played out what she could never have with him in her waking life. She had woken from a handful of dreams dripping with perspiration and her mind betraying her with images of intimacy with Leo that would never happen. "I have no idea what my brain does while I'm asleep. You should probably ignore all of it."

"I do." Declan burrowed into her until his face was firmly pressed between her breasts. He sighed deeply and was soon snoring softly.

Thirty minutes later when Declan woke, he dragged her into the shower and they went about their regular morning routine. After, on the way over to the police station, Kate finally received a text from Ditch. *I found encrypted messages between Julian and Benjamin on one of the laptops. I'm in the process of decrypting them. I assume it's going to be the evidence you need.*

They were so close to the police station that Kate didn't bother responding. She told Declan who smiled over at her in the back of the car and squeezed her hand.

"I told you he'd find something. He's a complete pain but always comes through."

"Are you warming up to him?" Kate asked, thinking of all the past tension between the two, mostly caused by Ditch because he could antagonize Declan like no other.

"He's a necessary evil. I'm working on not taking the bait."

That was all Kate could hope for between the two who had vastly different personalities. Declan's unruffled, get-things-done workstyle conflicted with Ditch's diva ways. The two men would always be at odds. Kate assumed once they met, Leo and Sam might have the same issues with Ditch.

That's why she was so surprised when they got to the police station and found Leo and Ditch sitting side by side at a conference table surrounded by the laptops and phones that had been confiscated at the warehouse.

Declan said he was off to find Sam to inquire if he made any headway getting Benjamin a deal, leaving Kate to deal with the tech. "Text me as soon as we have something actionable."

Kate assured him she would. She stood on the other side of the glass wall watching the two former criminals at work. Ditch instructed Leo how to plug specific data in his hacking software before turning back to the laptop in front of him.

Kate pushed open the door and Leo raised his head from the screen. Ditch remained focused. "I got your text, Ditch. Can you really decrypt the messages?"

Ditch glanced up, his glasses slipping down his nose. "You think I'm sitting here playing with my toys?" He adjusted his focus on the screen, illuminated with lines of code and encrypted messages. "I'm peeling back layers." Ditch resumed typing, fingers flying across the keyboard. "You'd think they'd be smarter," he muttered. "These laptops are a goldmine, full of traces left behind. Just one more code to crack. Ask Leo what else we found and let me work."

Leo smirked and rolled his eyes. It was a sign to Kate that he was merely tolerating Ditch as much as Declan did. "It's a vast syndicate, Kate. Bigger than I think you realize."

"I was able to hack the app completely. We have everything off it, every profile and every chat conversation. It's where it all started," Ditch said without raising his eyes from the laptop.

Kate pulled up a chair next to Leo, wanting more information than she knew Ditch would provide. She'd let him work for now. "What was found?"

Leo pulled the stack of printed pages in front of him. "Benjamin created this app with the help of a friend in tech. The tech guy had no idea that he was creating an app to scam people. Benjamin said as much in an email to Julian. They created a dating app for rich singles forty and older. It works like a regular dating app, except when a man is on the app it will only show him curated profiles of women that are fakes. The same with the women. There is a block in the app that doesn't allow the men and women who join to connect with each other. It will only show them the profiles created by Helix. There is tech inside the app that shows Helix people how long a person stays on a particular profile and which ones they swipe yes to choose. They use that information to decide which fake is going to make contact. Once they match, the scam starts. The Helix staff are grooming the users for a relationship – laying it on thick, backing off, and constantly testing what's working or not. There is never a request for money through the app itself. That comes later once the mark has the Helix staff person's phone number – a more intimate form of communication after trust is built."

"I have all those conversations available too," Ditch said, again not looking up.

"How many users?" Kate asked.

Leo's eyes got wide. "The app was created six years ago and since then there have been more than two-hundred thousand active users, Kate. Now, I'm not saying that's how many people they scammed, but that's how many joined the app to meet someone. I'm sure some bailed once the request for money was made. Others maybe didn't see someone they liked. The Helix staff zeroed in quickly on those who had the most potential. It's hard to tell how many people got scammed. Records of Helix bank accounts show an intake of more than twenty million a year was made almost from the start. This year they will probably rake in close to thirty million if estimates are correct."

"You have bank records too?" Kate asked, not hiding her surprise.

"This isn't a hobby, Katie," Ditch barked, using the nickname only Declan used.

Leo shifted his eyes from Ditch to Kate and gave her a knowing glance. She shook her head. It was best to ignore it. "How many bank accounts?"

Leo responded after waiting for Ditch who didn't utter another word. "Seven. Two here in London and the rest are international. No banks in the United States. Most are offshore accounts. I can see transactions from those accounts to the banks here in London. They were moving money fairly frequently, probably to pay for advertising and the business as well as to pay employees."

"All of this communication is between Julian and Benjamin?" Kate asked and Leo confirmed. "Is there any clear CEO of the operation?"

"Julian seemed hands-off the app, at least in the communication we have. He'd message Benjamin from time to time in email letting him know he needed to push the employees harder and that he was letting them slack too much," Leo explained.

It's what they had told Kate. "Is it fair to say Benjamin was running the Helix app and Julian was doing his own thing?" Leo confirmed and Kate asked another question. "Given the age of the app and the first murder ten years ago, can we assume Julian started first?"

Ditch raised his head then. "Based on what I'm reading, Julian scammed a few people in person then told Benjamin who thought of a safer, more profitable, hands-off way to do it. Some email communication suggested Julian has been scamming women for a long time. There is nothing about the murders that we have found – yet. As I said, I'm working through the encrypted stuff now."

Kate got up from her chair and walked behind the table, leaning over Ditch's shoulder, watching the screen flicker as he navigated through a labyrinth of data. Lines of encrypted text glowed, each waiting to reveal its secrets. She waited to be told to sit down or stop breathing down his neck. He allowed her to watch him work.

The tension grew thick in the room as Ditch worked.

"Bingo!" he yelled finally and they all lurched toward the screen.

CHAPTER 35

A stream of messages filled the laptop screen. Names, dates, and a flurry of digital breadcrumbs spilled forth. Kate's heart raced. "What have you got?"

"Benjamin's text logs," Ditch replied, glancing up with a spark of excitement. "He's a chatterbox. He initiates most of the conversation with Julian, who is never around according to what's being said here. You can read it for yourself. You wouldn't be getting this information if it wasn't for me."

"Yes, Ditch, you're amazing. The god of all hackers," Kate said dryly, knowing this is exactly what he needed to hear. He lived off praise for his skill. Kate leaned over Ditch's shoulder until she was breathing on his neck, trying to read the communication.

Ditch finally shooed her back. "Let me scan this. There's still a few things encrypted. I'll tell you what I'm reading."

"Fine. Fine." Kate stepped back even though it was the last thing she wanted to do. Leo gestured for her to come back over to where he was sitting. She plopped back down in the chair, waiting for Ditch to give her the information.

Ditch clicked the keyboard, his fingers making a dancing staccato sound as he worked. "Looks like Julian's got Benjamin under his thumb. He's reporting to Julian what's happening. There are instances of Julian definitely admonishing him for not bringing in enough money. There's something else – a woman being referenced. Not a mark. I can't tell if she's working with them. She might be cleanup."

"Can we get an ID?" Leo pressed, leaning over Ditch's shoulder.

"Not yet. They just refer to her as the Lady Liberty," Ditch said, chewing on his lip as he scrolled through the messages.

"Are you sure she's an American?" Leo asked. "The Americans got the Statue of Liberty from the French. Montesquieu's doctrine of the separation of powers also influenced American constitutional thought. Liberty was a French concept before it was an American one."

"The 1791 French Constitution borrowed a lot from the American Constitution of 1787," Kate countered, not surprised by Leo's knowledge of history.

Ditch stared over at both of them, an eyebrow arched. "Do we really need a history lesson?"

Leo turned to him. "It matters if we are dealing with a woman from France or the states."

"Fair enough," he said and went back to work. "They call her Lady Liberty throughout their chat. They never name her."

"Douglas Hartman said it was an American woman who came to get Benjamin from his house."

"A lot of people can fake an accent, Kate," Leo reminded her. He had done that very thing numerous times during his criminal days.

Kate resisted the urge to stand back up and hover over him. "What's her role? You must be able to tell from how they are talking about her. What's the context?"

Ditch went back to tapping the keys. He mumbled words as he read. Kate picked up only a few words here or there, not able to make sense of it. "Okay," he finally said, slowly drawing out the word. "It seems like she's been Julian's friend for a long time. He's known her almost as long as he's known Benjamin. They actually have an argument here about who he has known longer and therefore trusts more. Julian firmly said Lady Liberty, much to Benjamin's disgust." Ditch clicked a few more keys then leaned into the laptop so closely his nose was an inch from the screen. He squinted, eyes narrowing. "This is weird."

Kate straightened, instincts flaring. "What is it?"

"There's mention of a city. Not an address, just a city." Ditch's voice was laced with disbelief as he traced a series of messages, revealing a sequence of coordinates embedded in the chatter. "Julian's been sending Benjamin messages about meeting Lady Liberty there. The last message…" he paused as he struck the keys more violently now.

"What does it say?" Kate urged as she leaned forward, her voice rising.

"It's a plan for a meeting, but it's cryptic. Something about the finale if all goes south."

Leo caught her eyes. "It doesn't surprise me he had an exit plan. It seems like he might have left Benjamin here to take the fall."

"He's got Lucy with him," Kate responded, her worry for the young woman growing. She had no idea what to think. Was an exit plan an escape? Suicide? One last homicidal act? She had no idea. "What's the city, Ditch?"

"Marseillan." Ditch turned to them. "Ever heard of it?"

"I have," Leo said before Kate could tell him that she'd not heard of it. "It's in southern France. It's a small fishing village on the Etang de Thau, which is a large lagoon, a sea-lake. It's almost across the sea from Cassis where my chateau is located. About three hours by car. I'm not sure how much by boat." He made a triangle with his fingers. "The point is just north and east from Montpellier. That's the closest biggest city. There's also an airport there. Montpellier Méditerranée Airport. We'd fly into there to get to Marseillan."

Before Kate had a chance to react, Ditch said her name, slowly drawing it out. There was fear in his tone like she'd never heard before.

He pointed at the screen. "You need to see these other messages. I think Lady Liberty might be a total psycho."

It wasn't the first time Ditch had labeled someone a *total psycho*. "Why do you say that?"

Ditch stared at the screen then blew out a sharp breath and sat back. "Come read it for yourself."

Kate complied and once she was leaning over his shoulder, she saw exactly why he was afraid. Julian told Benjamin that Lady Liberty was hard to please. She was egging him on to find his next victim. Julian said she got off on his murders and the sheer power he possessed. He bragged that the sex after each kill was incredible, especially if Lady Liberty was there to witness it herself. He confided in Benjamin that he'd share the details of the murder with her and what it was like to feel the life being choked out of someone as he made love to Lady Liberty. He told Benjamin she had a special cord she liked him to use for the murders.

Kate's stomach turned as she read the details – this was sick, sicker than she could have ever imagined. A curse escaped her lips as she recalled something from Andrea's house. There were three chairs pulled out. Three wine glasses. She was there.

"I wasn't exaggerating," Ditch said. "You think the two of them are going to kill the girl and escape or maybe kill the girl and then themselves? Go out with a bang and leave all the people here to take the fall?"

Kate would like to have said she'd already thought of that, but the truth was she was still trying to process what she was reading. Her thoughts hadn't turned that dark yet. Kate righted herself. "I need to talk to Benjamin right now. I don't care what we have to offer him. We need to know what this plan means and we need to get to Marseillan."

"We don't have an actual address though," Ditch reminded her.

"Hopefully, Benjamin does." Kate gestured toward the stacks of papers on the table and the rest of the tech that Ditch hadn't gone through yet. "Ditch, keep building the case for us, gathering as much digital evidence as possible. Leo, you're coming with me. You're the only one of us who speaks French."

Kate rushed from the room to find Sam. He was the only one who could access Benjamin. She didn't care at this point if he had a solicitor or not. She needed to interview him now. She rushed to the other conference room Sam had been using but found it empty. Then she made a beeline to his office, dodging and weaving in between people as she went.

When she finally found Sam in his office, Kate had to catch her breath. "I have to interview Benjamin and you can't say no."

Sam ran a hand through his dark hair, his head cocked to one side staring at her. *No* was on his lips, but Kate stepped toward him, pleading with him again. "Kate," he said with a firm shake of his head, "you know that violates every protocol we have."

"Lucy's life is at risk, Sam. If I can't get the information I need out of him, we might get her killed. How is that going to look in the papers? The National Crime Agency didn't do everything in their power to protect and find Lady Lucy Barclay."

Sam winced. "That hits a bit below the belt. You know we are doing everything legally that we can. I'm not sure what more I can do. He has a solicitor."

Kate knew that was true. She also knew that sometimes, in cases like this, investigators couldn't be so rigid. "If he refuses to speak to me, he refuses. If he talks, he talks. I'm not going to hurt the man, Sam. You are tying my hands here." Kate's throat constricted and she balled her fists. She told him what Ditch had found. "We have the evidence. What I need from Benjamin doesn't have anything to do with his crimes. It's ancillary information about Julian and this other woman."

Sam screwed up his mouth in contemplation. She could see signs of him breaking and she pushed harder until Sam held up his hand to stop her. "Benjamin is at the local reception prison. We are still figuring out how to charge him for these crimes. We are relying on information Ditch can pull up from the tech. I'll give you the address because given you're FBI and the one who brought Benjamin in, you have a right to know where he's located. I'm out of this after that, Kate. You do what you have to do and I'll get out of your way. If the FBI does something illegal, I'm not going to help you in the process. I cannot lose my job or good standing."

Kate could have leaned in and kissed the man as he told her the prison address. "There will be no blowback on you, I promise." She rushed from the room and ran right into Leo. "I got the address and I'm going there now. You need to go to Declan and prepare our trip to France. When I get back, we need to be wheels up."

Leo assured her everything would be ready for them. "Are you sure you don't want me to go to the prison with you?"

"No," Kate said sharply. She didn't want anyone in the room with her and Benjamin. She didn't have the time or the patience right now to finesse the situation as she normally did, not when a young life was on the line. She didn't want to compromise anyone else.

"Be careful, Kate," Leo said as she turned and rushed out of the building.

Kate barely heard him, her mind was already focused on getting to Benjamin and what she was going to ask him. She'd have to get past the guards first but she hoped with a flash of her badge that wouldn't be an issue. The FBI shield held a lot of weight.

Twenty minutes later, Kate found herself arguing with the guard at the front desk of the prison. He needed more prep time to get Benjamin from his cell and into a conference room. "I don't have time," Kate told him. While they were wasting time arguing he could have been getting her Benjamin. Finally, Kate leaned on the man's desk, bringing her face down to eye level with him. "If you don't get me Benjamin right now and Lord Barclay's daughter is murdered as a result, it's going to be you he comes after. Got it?"

The guard's eyes flicked up to Kate's. "Lord Barclay? His daughter?"

"She's with a serial killer and only Benjamin knows where he might have gone. Do you understand me?"

He shot back in his chair, knocking it over. He stood and shouted instructions to someone behind him to bring Benjamin Fuller to the interrogation room for questioning. He buzzed the door and let Kate through, directing her to the hall with the interrogation rooms. She didn't bother thanking him as she yanked open the door and went on her way. He had cost her valuable time.

Kate paced the small cinderblock room that held nothing more than a metal table and two chairs. The floors were black, littered with scuff marks and gouges from where the chairs were pulled in and pushed back. Kate tugged at the collar of her shirt, the sheer heat inside the tiny room suffocating her.

By the time the door finally opened and Benjamin was shoved inside, Kate was ready to explode. If he was surprised to see her, his expression didn't betray him. "I don't have time for games, Benjamin. I'm not here for you. I'm fairly certain you're being set up to take the fall for all of this. If you're the only one left standing, trust me the Crown is going to make you pay. I can't offer you immunity or anything else, but you can help yourself by telling me where Julian might have gone in Marseillan and what exactly is his exit plan. If you can help me save Lucy Barclay, I'm sure the Crown will consider that in sentencing you."

"Exit plan?" Benjamin asked with a gulp, his Adam's apple bobbing up and down with each swallow. "How do you know about

Marseillan?"

Kate took a few steps toward him, resisting the urge to grab him by the front of his prison shirt and slam him into the wall behind him. She balled her fists. "I told you I have a tech genius who was going through all of your communication. We have enough on you, Benjamin, to keep you locked away for the rest of your life. The only one who might be able to ensure you see the outside of prison walls again in your lifetime is you. I can't promise you anything but you can help us. In turn, I can make a case for you at sentencing. You knew Julian was killing people and did nothing."

Benjamin took a deep breath. "My solicitor thinks he can get me off, clear my name."

Kate shook her head. "He's either arrogant or lying to you or both. You cannot walk back what you've done. The only thing you can do right now is get in my good graces and I will speak for you at sentencing. That's your only move. Do you want to take the rap for Julian, who has committed more serious crimes than you? Help us take him down."

Benjamin turned his head away from Kate. He stared at the cinderblock wall as if it might give him some secret message. He stayed that way for so long Kate nearly shook him out of the trance.

"Benjamin," she said sharply. "I don't have time. Will you help me?"

He turned his head to her. "You think you can really get my sentence reduced?"

Kate sighed. "I can try. If they know you are stalling and Lucy is murdered in the meantime, no one can help you."

Benjamin ran a hand down his stubbled face. "Okay, I'll tell you everything I know."

Kate pulled out one of the metal chairs and gestured toward the other.

Now they were getting down to business.

CHAPTER 36

"Let me start by saying that I've never killed anyone," Benjamin said, wringing his hands.

"I know that. You told me that already," Kate assured him, not wanting to waste time on things she already knew to be true. "That's why I'm here with you right now. If I believed you killed someone, I couldn't and wouldn't help you. Now tell me what I don't know."

"I don't know where Lady Liberty has a house in Marseillan. I know about the city and know she has a house there, but I don't know the address."

Kate blew out a frustrated breath. She believed him. "What did he say about the house?"

"Just that it wasn't on the sea. That it was only a few miles from it and that it was a refuge for him. He'd go there when he needed a break from life."

Kate cocked an eyebrow. "Do you mean he'd hide out there in between murders?"

Benjamin shrugged non-committedly. "I mean exactly what I said. Julian told me he'd go there when he needed a break from life. He was never without a woman he was scamming. I preferred to stay behind the computer."

"Except when you watched them in person."

Benjamin shifted his eyes from her. "Except then. I never approached them. Only watched."

Kate couldn't wrap her mind around enjoying the cruelty of that. She pushed her revulsion aside and kept going. "You said Julian was always scamming a woman. When did he first start that?"

"Back at Eton. We'd meet girls here and there and he'd trick them into thinking that he liked them. He'd see how far he could get them to go sexually or scam them for money. Julian would tell them that his family cut him off and he was broke. He wasn't at the time. The irony is that's eventually what happened, but back then, Julian didn't want for anything. He took money from them or gifts because he liked having control over them like that. Julian never had trouble attracting women. I've also never known him to be serious about one, except Lady Liberty."

Kate stopped him there. "You keep calling her that. What is her real name?"

"I don't know," Benjamin said with his eyes wide. "The first time I met her was when she came to get me from Douglas Hartman's house. She didn't tell me her name. Honestly, for a long time I thought she might be an alter ego of Julian's. Some made up fictional woman that egged him on. I wouldn't have been surprised if it was a multiple personality kind of thing. Then she showed up in the flesh and called herself Lady Liberty."

Kate stopped him again. "Is she French or American? Hartman thought she was an American."

"I can see why he believed that. Her accent was flawless."

"Then she's not an American?"

"No, she's French. She has perfect British and American accents though."

It brought up many more questions. "Where did they meet?"

"During our last year at Eton."

"It goes back that far?" If that were true, Kate knew that they might have developed their psychosis together. It would be that much more ingrained. The bond would be unbreakable.

"It was the only thing Julian ever kept from me. She was going to a nearby boarding school for girls and they met in town one afternoon. Julian came back and told me he was in love. I laughed it off, thinking he must have found his new mark. As I explained, he was well into scamming girls by then. The relationship didn't take that turn though." Benjamin's tone was wistful, nostalgic even. "I tried to get him to tell me more about her, but he refused. He said his relationship with her wouldn't be sullied. Nothing I said would convince him otherwise. I didn't think to try to follow him or anything like that. I didn't want to cross him. He had a temper even then."

"What did he say about her?"

"Just that she was his perfect match. He barely told me or anyone else anything about the relationship. Julian said it was his special secret he was keeping all to himself."

Kate recalled the disgusting messages she had read between him and Julian about Lady Liberty. "That's not entirely true, now is it, Benjamin? Julian did share with you some rather intimate moments between him and the woman, didn't he?"

Benjamin chewed on his lower lip. "I'm not sure what you mean."

"I told you I read all of your communication. This woman was egging Julian to commit these murders. Then he was giving her details after the crimes were committed." Kate stared at him across the table, letting it sink in just how implicated he was in the murders after the fact. "You could have stopped him. You could have gone to the authorities and told them Julian and this woman were committing murders. You kept that information all to yourself to continue the scam."

"I was afraid of Julian. I still am," Benjamin said in a rush of breath.

"I'm only talking to you now because you said he was gone."

"Nothing you're telling me is helpful. I thought you said you could help me." Kate rested her arms on the table and locked her gaze on him. "What's the final exit plan?"

Benjamin raised his eyes to hers. "Julian and Lady Liberty are going to commit a murder together and then disappear. You'll never find them. If by chance you do, they will kill themselves. They honestly believe they will never be caught. Julian never thought the police would be able to connect the murders to each other or back to him. He said his plan was foolproof. I don't even understand how you tracked him."

There was a question in there Kate wasn't going to answer. "Did they say who they were going to kill?"

Benjamin shook his head. "I don't know. It was Lady Liberty's plan. She was much more the planner between the two of them."

Kate cocked her head to the side. "Are you suggesting she planned some of the murders?"

"I don't know for sure. I wouldn't be surprised. Back when we were at Eton, Julian said he enjoyed how diabolical she was. She came up with crazier things than he did. I think they fed off each other. There was even that one time…" He trailed off not finishing his thought as he looked away from Kate.

She paused waiting to see if he would continue. "What is it, Benjamin?"

"I shouldn't say."

Kate took a wild guess. "Julian was accused of assaulting a woman at Eton. You were accused of it as well. Neither of you were brought up on criminal charges for what happened. I'm going to take a shot in the dark here and suggest she was involved."

Before Kate could say anything else, Benjamin pulled back in surprise. "How do you know about Eton?"

Kate shot from the hip, a gut feeling. "We know a lot more than we've told you, Benjamin."

Benjamin rubbed his forehead and closed his eyes. He mumbled a response. "We were at a party. At the beginning of the night, I met a young lady. That's why she remembered me with Julian. I was gone well before the night was over. He showed up in my room the next morning and begged me to say I was with him the whole night. That was before I knew what he did. By the time I realized, I had implicated myself. The young woman said two people had assaulted her. She was so out of it, she had no idea what was going on. I believe Julian drugged her. I never had proof of that though. The last thing she remembered was drinking with Julian and she recalled him assaulting her. Bits and pieces of it anyway. I had said I was with him all night and she remembered me with him. He begged me not to back out. My parents sent me away after that. An institution. Do you have any idea what that's like? I did nothing wrong. I was never right after that."

Kate couldn't imagine what that had been like for him. She didn't want to and she was sure that it was part of his deep-seated need for control and revenge that he had been able to take with the romance scams. "Why stay friends with Julian after that?"

He scoffed. "After what I was accused of he was my only friend. I was a pariah even among my own family."

Kate was getting information that would help her have a better understanding of Julian and the woman but nothing that would solidly help her find them. Time was ticking. "Is there anything else you can think of that would help me find them before it's too late? Do you know anything about her?"

"The only thing identifying about her was Julian told me she went to St. Mary's Academy not far from Eton. That's the first thing he ever said – that he had met a girl from St. Mary's. He never told me her name. I think he might have known right away that the two of them would wreak havoc together."

"What does she look like? You saw her at Hartman's."

Benjamin went on to describe a woman about five-foot-eight, dark hair and eyes. "She's beautiful and cultured. Strong like she lifts weights frequently. The only time I saw her she had a hoodie on with the hood pulled up over her head. I saw her hair briefly when she walked into Hartman's to get me. As soon as we were outside, she pulled it up and that's where it remained as if she were shielding herself."

Kate had a clear image of a woman in her mind. "Madame Rue, the matchmaker. Do you know her?"

"Julian used her services. I've never met the woman."

"She was attacked in her office. Stabbed multiple times because she could identify Julian. Rue suggested to me that it might have been a woman who attacked her. I had trouble believing it at the time. I thought it might have been you. Now, it seems possible it was Lady Liberty."

"Julian told me that she would protect him to the death. He knew that wasn't going to be the case with me." Benjamin sat back in the chair and expelled a breath that it seemed he'd been holding for a while. "He was never going to protect me, was he?"

"No," Kate responded with a shake of her head. "He was never going to protect you. I need to find them."

"My phone, Agent Walsh."

"What about your phone?"

"I snapped a photo of her on the night she came to get me at Hartman's house. She had no idea I took the photo. Go through my phone and you'll find the photo. Take it to St. Mary's and ask for her name. That's what I was going to do but never got the chance."

Kate laid her hands flat on the table. "Was it on you when you were arrested?"

Benjamin nodded. "That other investigator you were with took it from me. You'll need code 7258."

"FBI or National Crime Agency?"

"FBI."

Kate scraped the legs of the chair on the floor as she shot upright. "Is there anything else you think I should know?"

"Julian's not going to let you take him alive."

She thanked him, reassured him she'd speak at his sentencing and bolted from the room.

Before Kate even shut the door behind her she was on the phone to Declan asking for Benjamin's phone. When he told her he had it on him and that Ditch was going to look through it next, Kate told them not to move or do anything.

She couldn't risk anything happening to that photo.

By the time she got back to the police station, Declan, Leo, Sam, and Ditch were in the conference room awaiting her arrival.

"Did you get him to talk, Kate?" Declan asked as she rushed into the room.

"He doesn't know much. I suspect it was this woman who attacked Rue and has been Julian's accomplice all along." She wasn't focused on what they were asking her. All Kate wanted was the phone. She took it from Declan and went straight to the conference table to sit. She punched in the code Benjamin had provided.

Sam stepped toward her. "You believe him?"

"I do," Kate said as she raised her eyes to see doubt crease the features of his face. "He's finally realizing that he's going down for the whole thing if we don't find Julian. He doesn't know the address in France, but he did give me enough information to identify the woman."

Kate didn't have time for their doubts or questioning. She opened the phone and went straight to the photo app. She scrolled through until she found the photo of a lone woman with dark hair and eyes who stared past the camera. It was clear she didn't know the photo was being taken. There was something oddly familiar about her face.

"Leo," Kate said, turning the phone to him. "Who is this woman? We have seen her before."

Leo leaned over the table and stared down at the phone. He blinked and pulled back. "Isn't that Madame Rue's assistant? The woman who came into her office while we were there. She had her hair up, not down like in the photo. In Rue's office, she was wearing glasses with thick round frames that covered most of her face." Kate couldn't recall the woman's name as hard as she tried. Leo didn't know it either.

Kate looked down at the photo again. "You're right. You're absolutely right." Her head snapped up from the photo. "We need to get to Madame Rue."

CHAPTER 37

Rue shifted in the bed uncomfortably, still heavily dosed on pain medication as her injuries healed. "I don't understand what you're saying," she said through slurred speech after Kate explained why they were there. "Let me see the photo."

Kate and Declan had come to the hospital together while Leo and Sam prepared for their departure for France. If they couldn't get the information from Rue, they'd have to travel the hour and a half west to Maidenhead where the school was located. Declan had searched St. Mary's on the way over to the hospital. It was a little further west than Eton to London.

Kate pulled her phone from her pocket and handed it over to Rue, helping the woman hold the phone steady as she stared down at the photo. Rue's eyes narrowed. "That certainly looks like Natalie Hughes. I've never seen her without the glasses she wears and her hair up. She's been working for me for the last six years, so you'd think I'd know the woman. I'd say I'm about ninety-five percent sure this is her."

"Did Natalie work with Julian?"

Rue nodded. "She had a keen eye for matchmaking and found a number of women she thought might match Julian. She sent him on several dates. I was busy with more high-profile clients."

Natalie was in control of choosing his potential victims. It would also leave her in a situation of knowing personal information about

297

Rue's clients, things most matchmakers probably wouldn't share with their suitors – their financial situation, vulnerabilities, hopes and dreams for a relationship. It would allow Julian to be a chameleon and slip right in and be the perfect match. It made them even more vulnerable. Kate didn't express any of that to Rue. She didn't need the ailing woman to feel any guilt or anything that would delay her recovery.

Kate focused on the attack. "You said after you were attacked, you thought it might have been a woman. You know Natalie. Is there any chance it was her?"

Rue's eyes got wide. "It could have been. Natalie had a key. When I called her and told her what had happened, she didn't answer. I haven't been able to reach her since. I thought she was afraid and keeping her distance because of the attack." Rue laid back on the pillow. "Do you think I let in my own attacker? I would have never guessed it. She was my best matchmaker."

Kate didn't want to tell her that psychopaths had a way of fitting in wherever they went. "Do you remember much about her background? Where she went to college?"

Rue's hand went to her chest. "Education has very little to do with matchmaking. You can either read people or you can't...and apparently, I did a horrible job of reading her and the situation."

"Don't be so hard on yourself," Declan said. "People like that will show you what they want you to see."

Kate caught every other word of what Declan was saying to Rue as she focused on the text to Sam with Natalie's information. She needed him to run a background check and real estate search for any property in France.

After hitting send, Kate raised her head. "Rue, we need to find Natalie. We believe she is working with Julian and they might be plotting their next murder. She must have given you an address. Do you remember it?"

Rue provided an address in the Notting Hill area of London. "She was from there, she said. Living in the home she grew up in as a child. She said her parents had left it to her in their will when they passed. The one thing she mentioned was that she was an only child without much family."

Kate ignored the similarities to her backstory. "Did you ever detect an accent?"

"What do you mean?"

"We suspect she might have been French."

"Not that I heard. Where did you hear that?"

"Julian and Benjamin referred to her as Lady Liberty. We believe she was faking an American accent and we were told she could fake a British accent."

Rue sucked in a sharp breath. "Natalie was always making me laugh with her accents. She could mimic just about all of them. We'd have a little downtime in the office and she'd get on a roll doing one accent after another. She was quite good at it. I did sometimes wonder about the money. I wasn't paying her enough to afford the designer clothes and accessories she had. I assumed it was what her parents left her."

"We are going to check the address in Notting Hill. Until then, we will give the guard at the door strict orders that if they see Natalie not to let her in. Do you recall the last time you saw her?"

"The morning you were in my office. After you left, I met with her to tell her about Julian. She took lunch after that and said she had to run a few errands. She called me about an hour later to say she wasn't feeling well and would be working from home. I didn't think anything of it. We were so busy preparing for that night, remember?"

That's how Julian knew the dinner date was a set-up. Kate patted the woman's hand. "Let us worry about all of this. You need to focus on getting better."

After leaving Rue, Declan and Kate headed for the Notting Hill address. She was starting to feel like she was spinning her wheels. She didn't think that going to this address was going to get them anywhere. She assumed Natalie was already in France.

Before they got to the address, a text came through. She read it quickly, disappointment sinking in her stomach. "Sam hasn't been able to find anything on Natalie Hughes. He doesn't think that's her name. I'm going to ask him to go to the Notting Hill address and speak to some of the neighbors while we go to St. Mary's. I have a feeling she was using an alias."

"I'd assume she was using an alias," Declan said agreeing with her.

More than an hour later, they sat in Margaret Winslow's office. She had been the headmistress of St. Mary's for close to forty years. There wasn't a student she didn't remember, so when Kate showed her the photo of Natalie, Margaret knew her right away. Only her name wasn't Natalie Hughes. It was Natalie Bollier.

Margaret had pulled the woman's file. "Her disciplinary file is significant. Her grades were exceptional in some, not others. This is filled with notes from her teachers indicating Natalie was manipulative, combative at times, cunning at others, and a professional liar. Even when caught, Natalie would deny the truth pathologically. She was referred to counseling and even expelled from the school in her final year."

"She didn't graduate?" Kate asked.

"No."

Kate's mouth fell slightly open as if she didn't know how to respond to that. "She was smart though, a good student?"

"When she wanted to be." Margaret glanced down at the file then looked just as quickly back up at them. "Natalie could have been anything she wanted to be, if she put in a little effort to something more than causing destruction. Early on she had grades to advance on to higher learning, university and beyond. Her test scores were off the chart. Natalie was highly intelligent but funneled those skills into manipulation and destruction. She got into fights with other girls. She played terrible pranks on her teachers. She refused to follow any order or direction."

Margaret went on to describe all the ways Natalie had hurt her fellow students and teachers while she was at the school. When she ran out of steam, Margaret summed it up. "We tried every intervention known to man to try to help her and turn her life around. The bottom line is that either Natalie wasn't interested in changing or it wasn't psychologically possible for her to change."

"Did you ever have her evaluated?"

Margaret offered a solemn nod. "Natalie tested high on psychopathy. It might not surprise you to know, Agent Walsh, that she had nearly every marker for being a psychopath, especially the cold, detached demeanor, thrill seeking behavior, pathologically lying and avoidance of blame, unafraid and unaffected by consequences, total disregard of norms and rules. We should have seen it earlier. You don't want to label children though, especially not with something like that. I didn't feel like I had a choice after a while."

"What about her family?" Declan asked, shifting in his chair.

She explained, "Natalie came to school here from a primary boarding school. She was sent away to school very early on. Her parents were killed in a car accident and she was raised by an aunt in London, who couldn't care for the girl. Her father was French and her mother was British. It was the mother's sister who took her in initially. The aunt said that she sent Natalie to boarding school because she didn't know how to control the girl's behavior and thought the structure of a boarding school was what she needed. She went through three of those lower schools before coming here. I thought we were up for the challenge. We have never not been able to turn around a young lady here at St. Mary's."

Kate knew no matter what they did for Natalie, if she was truly a psychopath, that nothing could be done for her. Natalie had to want to choose differently for herself, get into therapy, take the medication prescribed, and work on herself. That was hard for most people, it was near impossible with someone that scored that high on a psychopathy test. While not an official diagnosis, Kate was sure she had the official antisocial personality disorder comingled with other mental health issues. "Was Natalie with her parents during the car accident?"

"No, she was staying with her aunt while her parents were away on holiday." Margaret sighed and shook her head. "It was a sad story. They were in France buying a holiday home for the family when they were killed."

At that, Kate and Declan lurched forward in their chairs. In a rush of breath, Kate asked, "Do you happen to have an address for the home in France? Did Natalie keep it?"

Kate had been so forceful in her question, Margaret's hand fluttered over the file. She stammered, "I'm…I'm not sure."

"Look in the file," Kate demanded pointing at it. If Margaret didn't immediately open it Kate was going to reach for it and look herself. "There is a young woman's life at risk and we believe Natalie and the man she was with are in France. We need to know now if you have that address."

"I…" Margaret stammered again but flipped open the file and scanned one page and then another. "Yes, it's here." She gave Kate and Declan an address in Marseillan.

Kate was already on her feet heading toward the door when Margaret called after her. "We don't have time," she said over her shoulder.

"Please, stop." Margaret waited for Kate to turn around. "After Natalie was kicked out of here, she went back to live with her aunt.

Her aunt died within three months. The police suspected Natalie killed her for the inheritance. It was the aunt who held the purse strings to the whole family estate. With the aunt gone, Natalie could do whatever she wanted. She was of age by then. It was terrible and tragic and the police inquired about her. There wasn't enough evidence for an arrest. She got away with murder."

Nothing surprised Kate at this point. She thanked her for the information and sprinted from the building. They'd be lucky if they got to Lucy in time.

CHAPTER 38

Somewhere over the French countryside after the small, chartered plane had reached cruising altitude, Kate released the grip on the sides of her seat and calmed her mind enough to look to Sam. Since rushing back from St. Mary's and finding Sam and Leo waiting for them at the airport hangar, she hadn't had any chance to ask him what he found at the Notting Hill address.

"Did you find anything?" was the only question she had.

"There was no one home. I spoke briefly with a neighbor who confirmed the address was connected to a woman by the name of Natalie Bollier, but that they didn't know her well. When she's home, which is rare, she never answers her door. When she leaves the house, she wears dark sunglasses all year round, even in the dark dreary weather of London. Most described her as odd."

Kate detailed what they found out at St. Mary's. "She was an extremely troubled young woman who grew up to be an even more troubled adult." Kate went on to explain the psychological testing.

"Bottom line," Declan said as Kate finished, "Natalie is a psychopath and a danger to everyone she encounters."

"Where does that leave Lucy?" Sam asked, explaining that Lord Barclay had continued to try to reach his daughter and Julian without any luck.

Kate didn't want to say aloud what she had been thinking.

Sam watched her carefully. "Say whatever you're thinking, Kate. We need to be prepared for the worst."

Declan reached over and grasped her hand. When Kate still couldn't get out the words, he spoke for her. "Kate thinks she might already be dead."

Leo raised his dark eyebrows. "Is that true, Kate? Do you think Julian would kill his cousin?"

Declan still spoke for her, sensing rightly Kate was still trying to gather her thoughts. "Revenge for pointing the finger at him. Lucy was the one who gave us his real identity."

"I'm more worried about Natalie's behavior," Kate said finally, drawing everyone's attention to her. "I'm not sure Julian would have it in him to kill a family member like that. For all Julian knew, it could have been Benjamin or one of the others working in the warehouse. There were enough people there who knew about him. At first, I thought it might be Julian who might harm her. The more we have uncovered, the more I realize that Julian and even Benjamin by extension have been pawns of Natalie. That's who concerns me the most."

"We have no way of knowing that Natalie is with them or if they are still in France," Sam countered. "They could be anywhere."

Declan didn't disagree with him completely. "You're right. All we know is that we have the proof that Julian is the killer and he had an exit plan. We know they got off the plane in Barcelona but that's all we know. This one address in France seems like our best bet."

Leo offered a counterpoint. "All of the police agencies across the globe have Julian's and Lucy's photos. There is nowhere for them to hide. The information didn't go out until after we considered the France aspect, so it's likely that wherever they are, they aren't on the move. Lucy doesn't have, to our knowledge, any other identification so she must be using her own. If they were on the move, someone somewhere would have seen something by now."

Kate knew that to be true. The only thing that kept tripping her up was the fact that there were no hits on immigration when they crossed into France. She knew with resources like those Julian and Natalie had, there were ways to hide. She couldn't explain it any better to the rest of them, who were still looking at her for confirmation.

Kate agreed with them. "I can't say with certainty that they are in France. We have ruled out everything else though. Lord Barclay hasn't been able to locate any other places where Julian and Lucy might be. We have this address in France. If they aren't there, then we regroup."

"They will be there." Declan squeezed her hand to reassure her.

Kate glanced over at Sam. "Did you speak to the French police and tell them to wait for us?" One of the other concerns she had was the French rushing in before they got there, not fully understanding the delicate situation.

Sam looked over at her, his expression unreadable. "I told them we had an issue with a rogue aristocrat and we needed clearance to address it. I didn't even mention the city. Just that I was coming to France with the FBI and it was delicate. If we need backup, we can call. Otherwise, I figured we'd be better served going alone. Not exactly protocol."

The relief washed over her. "The French haven't exactly been cooperative with us in the past."

"They wouldn't be cooperative now, except I threw in the royal family," Sam explained with a look on his face that told them this better be worth it. "I had to use that. It was the only card we had to play."

They grew quiet for a few moments, all of them probably feeling the same weight Kate felt on her shoulders – they had to save Lucy. Kate didn't know the full scope of the damage of Helix Syndicate, and she wasn't even sure given time that they'd ever fully be able to identify all the victims. All she knew was she'd been involved in many destructive homicide cases in her career and she couldn't think of one that had the scope of this.

"We need to talk strategy for after we land," Declan encouraged, bringing them all out of their heads. They spent the rest of the flight and even some of the drive from Montpellier to Marseillan gearing themselves up for what was to come.

Kate was positive that the pair would not be taken alive. For as much as Julian thought he could smooth talk anyone, he wasn't cut out for prison. That much was abundantly clear to her. She hadn't needed to read the communication between Benjamin and Julian to understand that about the man.

Once on the ground in Marseillan, they pulled off the side of a country road on the way to the address to ensure each of them was armed, vested, and ready to go.

Kate looked at Leo. "Are you sure you're ready for this? There's no shame in staying back. I know this isn't what we hired you to do."

Leo had a steady confidence. "I'm all in, Kate. I said that when Spade made me the offer. You need me to knock down doors, I'm there. You need me as backup, I'm your guy. I'm one of the team. Tell me what you need."

"Okay," Kate said, feeling the true weight of what he was saying. In truth, given Leo's long criminal history, he had probably accepted that the life he led increased his risk of death. He had faced the danger head-on and he was willing to do the same for the FBI.

Declan barked directions to all of them. Once at the home, Kate and he would approach the front while Sam and Leo would take the back of the home, which had a sloping lawn that led directly to the lake. Kate had noted that the lagoon was close to the sea. While they could flee by boat to another part of the land, there would be no sea escape. It at least closed down one avenue.

They were back on the road again in minutes heading directly to their mark. They wound their way through tight roadways and people walking hand in hand in the tiny village. Some were biking, others carried groceries.

None of them knew that monsters might be hiding out among them.

The black car with tinted windows pulled to a stop three houses away from their target. Sam cut the engine and turned to look at Kate in the back. "We should walk from here."

Kate could see the wrought iron gates of Natalie's home about a hundred yards from where he parked. People on the roadway took passing glances at the car but kept moving on. She knew they didn't have long before they'd start to attract attention. That attention would result in local police showing up and that was something they needed to avoid at all costs. Not just for Sam, but it would put their lives at risk. They were about to break all kinds of international law – they had no warrant in France to break into the home. They weren't planning to knock on the front door and be invited in. It was the kind of situation in which everything that could go wrong far outweighed what could go right – yet it was still worth it to potentially save a life.

Declan caught her eye and a lifetime of moments passed between them. Kate allowed herself one last meaningful look then let her training take hold. Her breath evened out, she slowed her heart rate, and she focused only on the mission at hand.

As they approached the home, the Mediterranean sun cast long shadows across the weathered limestone façade of Villa Serenité, its shuttered windows, and flowering ornamental vines masking whatever darkness lurked within. Kate tightened her grip on her weapon, the weight of her FBI vest pressing against her ribcage as she studied the three-story mansion perched above the lagoon. A salt-laden breeze carried the scent of lavender and rosemary from the manicured garden, a deceptively peaceful scene.

Kate exchanged a passing glance with Leo as he followed Sam around to the back of the home. He maintained his steely confidence, looking more the part of an embattled FBI agent every day.

"You ready, Kate?" Declan said at her side.

"Always," she murmured, eyeing the home. The weathered Villa Serenité sign shifted in the breeze. Serenity. That's what the sign meant. The irony of that wasn't lost on her.

They took position on opposite sides of the ornate wooden door. Kate counted down but didn't reach one before Declan's boot connected, the crack of splintering wood shattering the coastal tranquility. Kate surged forward, weapon raised, scanning the marble-floored entryway. Pale stone columns stretched toward a coffered ceiling, and crystal chandeliers threw rainbow prisms across walls adorned with Renaissance art. Everything screamed old money, taste, refinement – everything Natalie Hughes pretended to be and her family probably was before their deaths.

"Clear," Sam called from the back of the home. "Dining room clear," he shouted again, his voice echoing off empty walls.

"Clear," Leo confirmed from the kitchen.

The silence pressed in, broken only by their boots on the herringbone floors. A study off the main hall caught Kate's attention – leatherbound books, a massive mahogany desk, and a half-empty cup of tea, still warm.

"They're here or they were," she said, feeling the mild warmth of the cup.

The grand staircase curved upward, its wrought-iron railings casting serpentine shadows. Kate took point, hyperaware of every creak, every shadow. The second floor opened into a gallery of sorts, walls lined with black and white photographs. Kate stopped at an image of a woman's hand poised at her throat. A deep red line laced behind her fingers, peeking out from the gaps. Something about the image was familiar to Kate. She leaned in, studying it. At once her stomach turned as she recognized the crime scene photo from Andrea's murder reimagined as art.

Natalie or Julian must have taken photos and created macabre artwork.

"You seeing this?" Declan's voice was tight with disgust.

"It's sick," Kate said, swallowing. "We have to press on."

They cleared room after room, a music parlor with a dusty grand piano, guest suites with undisturbed beds, and a conservatory drowning in light. No sign of Natalie, Lucy, or Julian. The wrongness of it all prickled at Kate's neck.

A door at the end of the third-floor corridor stood ajar.

Kate steadied herself, the metal of her weapon slick against her palms as she edged forward. The room beyond was dark, with heavy curtains drawn against the sun. As her eyes adjusted, shapes emerged – a four-poster bed, an antique armoire, and a figure slumped in a velvet wingback chair.

"FBI! Show me your hands!"

No movement.

Declan flanked her as she approached, his breath catching. "Kate."

Julian's unseeing eyes stared past them, his face a mask of surprise frozen in death.

CHAPTER 39

Kate slammed her palm against the wall. "How long has he been dead?"

Declan checked his limbs. "Based on body rigidity a few hours."

Sam appeared in the doorway, his face grim. "Found this in the master suite." He held up a cellphone with a green checkered phone case just like the one Lucy had in the interrogation room. "There's more. Photographs of Lucy and Natalie together. Walks on the beach, lunches, shopping. I think Julian probably took them. Lucy probably thought she was safe with them."

It's exactly what a psychopath did until they showed their true face.

Kate stared out the window at the light shimmering off the lagoon, its beauty now seeming like a mockery. "We have to call this into the French authorities now," she ordered. "I want every law enforcement agency on alert. Borders, trains, airports – everything."

The Mediterranean sun was starting to set. In the distance, church bells began to toll, their mournful sound carrying across the water. Too late for Julian. But maybe, just maybe, not too late for Lucy.

Kate turned to all of them. "Before the local police get here, let's tear this place apart," she ordered, her voice echoing through the villa. "Every drawer, every floorboard. I want to know everywhere Natalie Hughes has been and everywhere she might go."

Julian's body remained like a waxed figure, the metallic tang of blood lingered in the air, mixing with the villa's perfume of old wood. Once they each chose a section of the villa to search, they left the body alone. Kate closed the door behind them, happy to leave the room.

She retreated with Declan back downstairs. He went to the back of the home and Kate focused on the study off the main living room. She rifled through stacks of papers, each movement sharp with barely contained fury. She didn't know how long she searched the room but found nothing.

Declan emerged with frustration etched across his features. "I found a safe behind a wine rack in the kitchen. Just cash and some fake passports."

"Keep looking." Kate yanked open another drawer, sending expensive fountain pens rolling across the polished wood. "Natalie wouldn't leave without a backup plan. She's too methodical."

Declan and Kate kept at it despite finding nothing of value. They worked in tandem from one room to another, growing more frustrated and desperate as the time ticked on.

The light slanted through the windows, casting long shadows across the marble floors. Somewhere above, floorboards creaked under Leo's boots as he searched the upper levels. Sam had taken the garden house and two guest houses closer to the water's edge, though Kate doubted Natalie would leave anything important so exposed.

"Kate! Declan!" Leo's voice crackled through the villa.

Kate and Declan took the stairs two at a time, following the sounds of his voice. From the second floor, they found a door at the opposite end of the hall from where they had found Julian. Attic access. They reached the top of the landing as dust motes danced in the beam of Leo's flashlight.

Kate pulled herself up into the musty space under the rough-hewn beams. Declan ducked his head low unable to stand fully upright in the space.

"Here." Leo gestured to them from across the attic. Kate's eyes adjusted to the darkness to see a stack of photographs scattered across the top of an old steamer trunk. "Look familiar?"

Kate's breath caught. The images showed Natalie and Lucy in various poses before a sprawling chateau, its limestone walls golden in summer light.

"I know this place," Leo said, his voice tight with anticipation, drawing Kate back to the present. "It was abandoned for years. Children used to play among the rubble that was left. Later, some wealthy family purchased it and set about restoring it to its original splendor. It made the news locally. They poured millions into this place."

"Where is it located?" Kate asked as she reached for one image then the next, studying them. She had no idea if Natalie might have gone there. They had no other leads.

"About thirty minutes north, in the hills." Leo looked at her with an unspoken question on his face.

"We need to go there, Kate," Declan said, standing beside her. As she finished looking at one photo, she handed it off to him. His eyes were fixed on the images. "This seems like the perfect place to hide, especially since it's out of the city and away from everything." Declan raised his head to Leo. "How remote is the area?"

"Remote. Woods block nearly all of the property except for the back where there is a small stream. The area there is open but more woods beyond that. The stream is narrow enough to cross, though not without getting wet. I'm not sure how deep it is or how strong the current," Leo explained then added a caveat. "At least, that's how it was the last time I was by there, which is a few years ago."

Declan was already on his phone searching for the property. In less than a minute, he pulled up a property and showed the phone to Leo.

"Is this it?"

Leo leaned in and confirmed with a nod.

"It's still remote then," he explained to Kate.

Kate wasn't sure. They were running from place to place but not getting anywhere.

"We need to go there now." Declan wasn't leaving any room for discussion. He was already calling out to Sam as he made his way back down the attic stairs.

As Kate moved in the same direction, Leo pulled her back. "Don't you think we should call for backup? It's a lot of ground to cover with just the four of us."

Kate didn't even need to think about it, and she didn't have time to explain. "No. You're going to have to trust me on that." She shook free of his grip and headed for the stairs.

"What about Julian's body?" Leo asked as he followed right behind her. His tone was more inquisitive than commanding.

Kate got the sense he was more confused about procedure than anything else. "Sam already called it in. The police will arrive here and we'll already be gone. We need to be gone before they get here or we won't be able to leave and get to this location. It's all timing right now, Leo. You're just going to have to trust us."

"I trust you completely," Leo said as they reached the landing.

The drive through the countryside was tense, vegetation a blur of colors outside their unmarked SUV. Kate's mind raced through scenarios, each worse than the last. If Natalie wanted Lucy dead, she'd have been dead there alongside Julian. It meant Natalie wanted her for something else. There was some reason she was being kept alive.

Kate also had no idea why Natalie might have killed Julian. She could have easily killed Lucy right after she shot Julian. There was something they were missing.

As Sam inched the SUV forward up the dirt road surrounded, as

Leo had told them, by thick woods, the chateau emerged from the landscape like something from a fairy tale, its towers stark against the afternoon sky. No vehicles visible, but the drive showed recent tire tracks. There was more than enough property that the car or SUV Natalie drove could be hidden from view.

There was a considerable amount to be covered. She understood now why Leo had asked about having more backup with them. Kate looked out the window at the chateau as Sam pulled the car to a stop. "Sam, take the east wing. Declan, west. Leo, with me through the main entrance."

"Are we just breaking in?" Sam asked from the driver's seat. He turned his body to look at her in the back. "I can add it to the list of things that are going to get me fired."

"No one is getting fired, Sam. I promise you that," Kate reassured. "Yes, we are just breaking in. We have a missing member of the aristocracy in the company of a psychopath who just killed her partner. This is the only lead we have. I don't think anyone wants us to stand around waiting on proper procedure."

Sam held his hands up in surrender and exited, his shoes crunching on the gravel.

After catching up with Sam, they moved as one unit, weapons ready, footfalls crunching. Kate waited for the shots to come. They were too exposed walking the grounds, but they had few other options. The chateau's massive doors hung open, hinges groaning in the wind. Inside, their footsteps echoed off stone floors and walls. The soft smell of lavender hung in the air.

"Natalie!" Kate called from the front door, hoping for a response. "This is the FBI and National Crime Agency. Come out slowly with your hands up. We have the place surrounded and more law enforcement on their way." Kate paused a beat and was met with silence. She called out again and silence echoed back.

They split off in their assigned directions. Declan and Kate shared a look before he left her and Leo. Kate's frustration mounted as they cleared room after room. Checking in closets and even cupboards, rifling through desk drawers in the study. Nothing. More dead ends. Sam called out "Clear" from the east followed by Declan from the west. If Natalie was here with Lucy, they were well-hidden.

They convened back in the main foyer, ready to give up.

"I don't know where they could be. It doesn't even look like anyone has been here in a while," Declan said.

The gunshot cracked through the air like thunder.

"Outside!" Declan yelled, already moving past Kate back out the front door. Declan and Sam ran to the left and Kate to the right with Leo right behind her. She rounded the corner of the chateau, weapon raised, but found nothing.

Kate stopped unsure of which direction to go when a second shot rang out.

"Toward the stream," Leo called, running in front of Kate to show her the way. Sam and Declan were right behind them.

The dense woods closed in around them as they sprinted, the underbrush crackling beneath their boots. Each breath came in sharp bursts, mingling with the faint echoes of gunfire that had pierced the tranquil air just moments before. Beside her, Leo kept pace, his face set in grim determination while Declan trailed slightly behind, scanning their surroundings with hawk-like vigilance.

Shadows danced between the tree trunks, the fading sunlight creating an eerie mosaic on the forest floor. The air was thick with the scent of damp earth but an unsettling chill threaded through it.

Kate veered left, following Leo, where a narrow path wound deeper into the thicket, each step sending twigs snapping underfoot. With every stride, Kate felt the weight of uncertainty pressing down.

"Do you see anything?" Leo shouted, straining to keep his voice steady.

"Not yet," Declan replied from the back.

"The stream is straight ahead!" Leo picked up his pace, forcing all of them to keep up.

As they broke free of the dense trees Leo stopped in his tracks. Kate stopped right behind him. She worked to make sense of the scene.

Natalie Hughes lay sprawled on the grass, blood blooming across her expensive blouse. Above her, Lucy stood holding the weapon with surprisingly steady hands.

She was unaware of their presence.

"Lucy?" Kate called, lowering her weapon as her mind raced to process the scene before her. "Lucy!" she called out again, this time shaking the girl from her trance. The young woman turned to Kate, wide-eyed. "Put the gun down, slowly. You're safe now."

Only then did the girl's hand begin to shake. She released the gun, letting it fall to the soft ground. Sam and Declan rushed to Natalie's side, checking for a pulse, and shouting instructions about calling for help. Declan leaned over the woman and tried to speak to her. Blood gurgled from the woman's mouth as she took her final breath.

Lucy remained frozen in time. The air was electric between her and Kate.

"Are you okay?" Kate asked, finally taking a few steps toward her. Her blond hair straight to her shoulders looked untouched. Her makeup was still perfect and her clothes were clean. Whatever had happened here, there wasn't a struggle. Kate asked her question again.

Lucy sucked in a sharp breath and water stained her eyes. She dropped down to her knees and sobbed. Kate crouched beside her, rubbing her back. "It's okay. You're safe now."

"Is she dead?" Lucy stammered between sobs.

"She's dead. Natalie can't hurt you anymore." Kate put her hands around Lucy and helped her back to her feet. Lucy wiped the tears from her eyes. Kate gave her a few moments to compose herself. "What happened here? We found Julian and then found photographs of you and Natalie together."

"How did you find us?" Lucy asked not responding to Kate's questions.

Kate explained how they found photos and Leo knew where it was located. "Are you okay? Did they hurt you?"

Lucy took a few deep breaths, her body rising and falling against Kate. "Natalie killed Julian. She wanted to kill me. She was tired of dragging me around with her. Julian tried to protect me."

It didn't make much sense to Kate. "Why are you here? If Natalie wanted you dead, she could have killed you after killing Julian."

Lucy remained quiet. Kate asked her again, only to be met with silence.

Finally, after a moment, softly she said, "I need to tell my father that I'm okay."

"We can call him, but first you have to tell me what happened here."

"Okay," Lucy responded with resignation in her voice. "Let's go inside and I'll tell you everything."

Kate gestured for Leo to follow them while Declan and Sam were busy with the scene.

A feeling nagged at Kate, something she couldn't quite define or explain. She didn't want to do the interview alone. More specifically, she didn't want to be alone with Lucy.

CHAPTER 40

Once seated in the study with the door firmly closed, Kate leaned against the corner of the desk while Lucy sat on a leather sofa and Leo took the chair across from her. Leo watched Kate with an intensity that unnerved her. He knew something was wrong – that she was picking up something she couldn't quite define yet.

Leo knew she was scared and Kate was so rarely scared. She didn't mind that he knew. He'd have her back no matter what went down.

"Why did you leave the police station, Lucy?"

"My father," Lucy said softly. "I didn't know what was going to happen and he was going to be so angry. I was scared. I saw a door to the stairs not far from the bathroom. I was surprised the officer didn't see me, but he wasn't in the hall when I came out. I just ran the first chance I got."

"What happened after you left?"

Lucy sat with her knees together, hands clasped in her lap, staring down at them. "I called Julian. I didn't understand what was happening. I know I wasn't supposed to call him, but you suggested he had murdered women. I couldn't believe that he would do that. Do you know the scandal that could cause for our family?" She turned her head slightly to look up at Kate with her big round eyes. "When I told you I didn't know about the scams, I meant that. I didn't know what

I was getting into. Scamming people is one thing though, murder is another. Not Julian. Even now I don't believe it."

Kate wasn't going to argue with her or make the case that Julian was a killer. "You said you called Julian. Then what happened?"

"He came to pick me up from my apartment. Julian told me we had to leave the country. It was going to be the only way to protect us." Lucy took a deep breath, letting it out slowly. "We were on a flight within an hour. Julian told me we were going to Barcelona and then doubling back to France. He handed me a fake passport and told me that's what I had to use to get into France. That you'd be searching for us and he needed to protect me."

Kate folded her arms over her chest. "At any point did Julian admit to what he'd done?"

Lucy shook her head. "He said he'd been falsely accused and that's why we were running. He said we'd never get a fair shake because of who we are, everyone is looking for you to fall. That it would be in the papers. If we stayed we'd be hunted by the press and the police."

Kate wanted to back up for a moment. "I found photos of you and Natalie in front of this chateau and others. When were they taken?"

Lucy stared past Kate. "I've spent a lot of time with Julian and Natalie. My father didn't know, of course. They all thought Julian was a bad seed. Julian was always good to me and he's known Natalie for a long time. I never had reason to fear either one of them..." Her voice trailed off. "Until today that is," she added with sadness in her voice.

"What happened today?"

Lucy breathed heavily. "I heard them arguing about what they had done and what they were going to do with me. I waited until Julian was alone and I confronted him. He told me what they had done."

"He admitted the murders?"

"Yes, all nine of them. He said he didn't want to kill them, just take their money. Natalie wanted them dead and he'd do anything for her. Do you understand the scandal that would bring on our family? Julian was much too reckless."

Over the next hour, amid a blur of French police, evidence technicians, and preliminary statements coming and going from the residence, Kate listened to Lucy's story.

Once Julian and Lucy met Natalie in France, things grew tense. Julian and Natalie were fighting more than they ever fought. She was pushing Julian to escape from Europe, maybe hide out in Russia or Poland or even South America for a time. She was convinced with Julian gone and Benjamin and the rest taking the fall, law enforcement would stop searching for them.

"The question remained what they were going to do with me," Lucy said. "Then Julian got this idea that they could escape if I went back and told their story."

"What story was that?"

"That the police got it all wrong and he had no choice but to flee. He told me to leave and find my own way back."

"Julian is dead," Kate said evenly, trying to make sense of what Lucy said. "I assume he couldn't convince Natalie of the plan?"

"Natalie didn't want me to leave. She grabbed me as I was heading out the door and put a gun to my head. She told Julian that she was going to kill me." Tears formed in the corners of Lucy's eyes. "He begged her to let me go. Natalie shot him. Then she brought me here. We struggled and I got the gun away from her. That's when I shot her."

Kate watched the young woman, knowing the story didn't add up. Warning bells rang in Kate's mind. The way Lucy's hands never shook. How her story hit all the right emotional notes without ever quite reaching her eyes.

"She tried to kill me, Agent Walsh," Lucy said with no trace of emotion in her tone. "I had no choice but to kill her."

"That isn't what happened, Lucy. We found Julian sitting in a chair. He wasn't struggling before his death. There wasn't a fight. Someone surprised him and shot him before he could even react."

Lucy rose from the sofa. "My father will be waiting for me."

Kate had no evidence to hold the young woman – she was thought to be a victim after all. Kate had told everyone who would listen that Lucy was a victim. Lucy's own statement was that she had killed Natalie in self-defense.

Two people who had wreaked havoc on lonely women were dead. Technically, justice had been done. They had the evidence of that. Still, this wasn't the ending Kate imagined. But no one would allow her to hold Lucy. The evidence wasn't there.

When Leo and Kate reached the doorway, they watched as Lucy asked one of the cops for their phone so she could call her father. That's how it would go. She'd make it back to London to the safety of their home, their titles a shield.

"She's good," Leo murmured, standing beside Kate as they watched a law enforcement officer escort Lucy to one of the waiting vehicles. "Maybe even better than Julian."

Kate shouldn't have been surprised but she was. "You sensed it too?"

Leo leaned against the doorjamb. "She's a young girl, Kate. She just killed someone and she sat there talking to us like it was any other day. No trace of fear or worry or even sadness. She wasn't in shock either. It was like she was dead inside."

They watched as Lucy slipped into the police car, her posture relaxed, almost regal. She caught Kate's eye through the window and smiled – not the traumatized smile of a victim, but something altogether more chilling.

"We need to stop her," Kate said, but even as the words left her mouth, she knew it was too late. Lucy's story was perfect and her performance flawless. No jury would convict her. No evidence would stick.

Kate watched the car disappear down the winding road as Sam and Declan joined them. She lost herself in quiet contemplation as Leo filled them in. Sam had been in disbelief arguing there was no proof to the theory. Kate knew he was right, it was just a theory after all. She had nothing to confirm it, but she truly believed it was Lucy who had turned on Julian and then Natalie.

Kate suspected Lucy might have known the truth all along – she had pointed them in the right direction. It was Julian who had connected Lucy to Lydia. Had he been grooming Lucy? Had she spent so much time with Julian and Natalie that he recognized the same tendency in her?

There was what Kate could prove – Julian had murdered the women and Natalie was present at the scene. It was written in the messages. Lucy confirmed it. Then there was what she believed – Lucy was involved somehow and for some reason had taken matters into her own hands, killing them both. Something Lucy said twice reverberated in Kate's mind.

Do you know the scandal this will cause?

Lucy knew they were caught. She's going home a hero.

"Will you interview her more thoroughly when you get back to London?" Kate asked.

"The French police insist on interviewing her now," Sam said.

Kate knew Lucy would put on a show. She had even fooled her during the initial interview.

Behind them, the chateau stood silent, its windows dark with secrets. Somewhere in the distance, church bells began to toll, marking the end of another day in the French countryside. The wind picked up, carrying the scent of lavender.

Julian and Natalie were dead. Benjamin and the rest would face justice. To the public, the threat had been eliminated. The story had a happy ending. Justice was served. Kate didn't doubt that she'd hear Lucy's name again. Next time it wouldn't be as a victim. It would be a headline.

"Come on," she said finally, turning away from the vista of hills and vineyards. "Let's get out of here."

"Where to, Kate?" Leo asked.

"I have to go right back to London," Sam said, wishing them all well. "I'll be expecting your reports," he said as a parting shot.

"You'll get them," Kate said, leaning slightly against Declan.

"Back to Boston, Katie?" Declan asked, brushing strands of her hair out of her face.

Kate wasn't ready for that. "Leo," she said his name in a sigh. "Can we go to your chateau for a break?"

Kate saw out of the corner of her eye Leo looking to Declan for approval of the plan. Declan offered a nod. Leo agreed. "We could all use a break. I'll call ahead and make sure some dinner is ready for us."

Four Days Later

Kate sat in the kitchen of Leo's chateau finally relaxing. The days before had been a flurry of activity, reports being filed, conversations with Sam about his interview with Lucy, reading the report of her interview with the French police, and watching the press footage of Lucy being brought home safely to London. Lucy had played the part of victim well. Well enough that there were even moments Kate had started to second-guess the feeling she had about the young woman.

Sam still hadn't been swayed. He told Kate that Lucy's story held up. She was an unwitting participant in the whole thing. There had been a struggle for the gun out by the stream. Natalie had marched Lucy out there to kill her. Once Lucy got the gun away, she had no choice but to kill Natalie in self-defense. Lord Barclay and his solicitors had created a shield around the young woman and she was, for now, untouchable.

Kate would have to let it go. That's what she was doing at Leo's – taking a break from all of it. It was good that Declan and Leo were getting to spend some quality time together. They took long runs each morning and bonded in the late afternoons drinking and talking. Dinner with the three of them together had been like old friends on a long-deserved vacation.

At night, Leo retreated to his room. Kate and Declan took long walks through the orchards. They had time to reconnect. Still, they hadn't been able to reach Spade.

It was why that morning when Kate's cellphone rang, she hadn't jumped to answer it. She let it go to voicemail and only reached for it when it immediately rang again. She sipped her coffee with one hand and reached for her phone with the other.

Spade flashed on her screen.

"I'm here, Spade," Kate said as she answered. She explained that Leo and Declan were in town at the market buying fresh fish for their dinner.

"I apologize for my absence. I hear you did exceptionally well on the latest case. You deserved the time off that you've taken. It's time for the three of you to return. There's another case."

There was always another case.

Before Kate could ask, Spade launched in. "You know the podcast host, Trevor Fontaine?"

She'd heard the name but she'd never listened. Kate wasn't the target audience. She was the target of everything Trevor and his ilk stood against – strong, independent women. "I'm aware of him," Kate said dryly.

"He's dead, Kate. Tortured in his Upper West Side apartment. The killers left a calling card. Dyed black lilies. They call themselves The

Midnight Lilies."

"Killers?" Kate asked. She wasn't surprised someone had gotten to him. Trevor's brand of outrage put a target on his back.

Spade confirmed. "They have made significant threats to keep going, targeting these specific kinds of personalities. They are calling it a reckoning." Spade paused to allow her to absorb the information. "The killers are women, Kate. We have kept it out of the press for days now. The report of his death leaked this morning. The press doesn't know about the other threats yet. I need you back before there's a firestorm from the media."

"Oh," Kate said in a rush of breath. "We'll be back tomorrow. Send us the initial file when you can." Spade promised he would and congratulated her on their recent case. She wanted to tell him that Lucy had slipped away, but she had no evidence to back it up. "Thanks," was all she could say.

Kate left her cellphone on the table, carrying her cup of coffee to the doorway. She nudged it open and breathed in the fresh country air. She didn't want to go back to Boston. Kate didn't want to leave France, more specifically, she didn't want to leave the safety and peace of Leo's chateau.

She had known the peace wouldn't last.

Work would always call her home.

About the Author

Stacy M. Jones was born and raised in Troy, New York, and currently lives in Little Rock, Arkansas. She is a full-time writer and holds masters' degrees in journalism and in forensic psychology. She currently has four series available for readers: the completed cozy paranormal Harper & Hattie Magical Mystery Series, the hard-boiled PI Riley Sullivan Mystery Series, the FBI Agent Kate Walsh Thriller Series and the new Conner Fitzgerald Thriller series. To access Stacy's Mystery Readers Club with free novellas, visit StacyMJones.com.

You can connect with me on:

- http://www.stacymjones.com
- https://www.facebook.com/StacyMJonesWriter
- https://www.goodreads.com/StacyMJonesWriter
- https://www.bookbub.com/profile/stacy-m-jones

Subscribe to my newsletter:

✉ http://www.stacymjones.com

Also by Stacy M. Jones

Watch for the next FBI Agent Kate Walsh Thriller in Fall 2025

Access the Free Mystery Readers' Club Starter Library
   PI Riley Sullivan Mystery Series novella "The 1922 Club Murder"
   FBI Agent Kate Walsh Thriller Series novella "The Curators"
   Harper & Hattie Mystery Series novella "Harper's Folly"

Sign up for the starter library along with launch-day pricing and special behind-the-scenes access. Hit subscribe at http://www.stacy mjones.com/

Please leave a review for Helix Syndicate. Reviews help more readers find my books. Thank you!

Other books by Stacy M. Jones by series and order to date

FBI Agent Kate Walsh Thriller Series
   The Curators
   The Founders
   Miami Ripper
   Mad Jack
   The Fuse
   Dead Senate
   Close Killer
   Diamond King
   The Magician

Conner Fitzgerald Thriller Series

Midnight Judge

PI Riley Sullivan Mystery Series
The 1922 Club Murder
Deadly Sins
The Bone Harvest
Missing Time Murders
We Last Saw Jane
Boston Underground
The Night Game
Harbor Cove Murders
The Drowned Boys
What He Saw
Fear City
What Stays Buried

Harper & Hattie Magical Mystery Series
Harper's Folly
Saints & Sinners Ball
Secrets to Tell
Rule of Three
The Forever Curse
The Witches Code
The Sinister Sisters
Scandal Knocks Twice
A Treasure Most Deadly